ONE NIGHT

THE SULLIVANS BOOK 4

LENA HENDRIX

LENA HENDRIX LLC

To anyone who has ever felt like you were fading into the background. You deserve a man who looks at you and says, "For you, I would."

LET'S CONNECT!

When you sign up for my newsletter, you'll stay up to date with new releases, book news, giveaways, and new book recommendations! I promise not to spam you and only email when I have something fun & exciting to share!

Also, When you sign up, you'll also get a FREE copy of Choosing You (a very steamy Chikalu Falls novella)!

Sign up at my website at www.lenahendrix.com

AUTHOR'S NOTE

This book contains contains explicit sex scenes, including sex while pregnant. {I promise, it's super hot.} There are also some scenes that overlap with previous books—I hope you enjoy revisiting some of your favorite scenes and seeing the hidden dynamic you may have missed!

One Night also references the death of a parent (off page/not detailed, but referenced), a mother leaving her children, and a parent with early onset dementia.

This book contains a surprise/accidental pregnancy, including descriptions of pregnancy and pregnancy symptoms. Because the surprise nature of this fictional pregnancy, Sylvie and Duke discuss whether or not she would want to terminate her pregnancy. Ultimately, they decide together and their choice is simply that: *their choice.* Their choice is simply the journey these characters chose to go on and is not a judgement in any way of others' choices.

Finally, Duke is a blueberry farmer in Michigan. As such, he employs seasonal agricultural workers. I would like to extend a very special thank you to Krystal Martinez-

Regan (@lit.chicana) for providing a thorough sensitivity reading of One Night. It remains important to me that the representation of immigrant workers is continually done with care and authenticity.

Now . . . let's get Sylvie knocked up, shall we?

ABOUT THIS BOOK

Duke Sullivan is the oldest brother of my family's hated rival. He also happens to be my *good morning* text and the man I have no right to have a secret crush on. **Duke is strictly forbidden.**

After months of keeping our friendship hidden, the stars align, sparks ignite, and we finally give in to temptation.

Knowing our relationship could never be more than stolen glances and longing looks, we agree to stay secret friends—***until two pink lines change everything.***

With our small town and both our families in an uproar, Duke does the unthinkable.

He packs up my belongings and *moves me into his house*. Despite agreeing to weather the storm together and to try to figure out how to co-parent, living with Duke proves nearly impossible.

Every soft smirk, every brush of his calloused hand against my sensitive skin, makes me want to burst into flames. **It becomes clear, despite the feud, that**

Duke is relentlessly going after what he wants, and I think that might be . . . *me*.

I'm the quiet daughter with the wrong last name, but it's obvious he wants so much more than just ***one night.***

ONE

SYLVIE

"Just don't spit in my coffee, okay?"

I blinked, letting the customer's words settle over me before realizing he did, in fact, ask that I don't *spit in his coffee*. Standing across the counter was Matty, a cousin of the Sullivans and a guy I'd known since I was in kindergarten.

Stunned, I nodded and kept my expression calm before moving to fill his order. The sounds of the bustling bakery flowed over me, and the aroma of hot espresso clung to the air and mixed with the sweet cinnamon-sugar smells coming from the kitchen. Clinking forks and mindless chatter continued around me, and I could feel the tension form a tight ball between my shoulder blades.

It was a Saturday morning, and the Sugar Bowl was known to have the best pastries in town so, of course, we were swamped. It didn't matter that early-October temperatures meant the tourist season was officially over—it was known Outtatowner, Michigan, drew people in year-round.

Just don't spit in my coffee.

My eyes narrowed at his coffee as I shoved down my

irritation at his comment. A small, petty part of me thought I *should* spit in it, just to spite him and the idiotic rivalry. The long-standing feud between the Sullivan family and the Kings was a thing of legends, going back longer than I could remember. Both sides trying to one-up each other with ridiculous pranks. Though Outtatowner was a coastal tourist town, those who were from here, us townies, knew the line was drawn. You were either with us, or with them. No two ways about it.

For years I watched my brothers try to pull one over on the Sullivans, just to have them return it, jab for jab. Until recently it had remained innocuous, though I had noticed my brothers were edgier than ever, and the Sullivan name coming up more and more.

The only two who'd managed to find some peace were Aunt Bug and the Sullivans' aunt Tootie. Even though they didn't like each other, they took it upon themselves to make sure we didn't tear down the town around them when things got heated. For the tourists' sake, we kept outward appearances, but it wasn't unheard of for my brothers to have a throwdown outside the pub on a Saturday night. Hell even the bar's name, the Grudge Holder, was an homage to the tension between our families.

I couldn't care less about the feud. For most of my life, I'd hidden in the background, watching my brothers trip over themselves trying to get back at a Sullivan for one thing or another. But not me.

I am Switzerland.

Switzerland probably wouldn't spit in Matty's coffee, so I pressed the lid on and handed it to him with a tight smile. I had become a pro at sucking air in through my nose and delivering a cool, judgment-free dismissal.

"Spit free." My joke didn't land, and his eyes flicked down to the cup, more wary than ever.

"Great." Matty left, and I didn't miss the slight roll of his eyes. Like everyone else in this town, he didn't bother to see me as anything more than a King.

Behind him the line was stacked up six customers deep, and my eyes scanned to note that our busser wasn't keeping up with clearing tables. Three high-tops had cups and plates stacked on them, with customers weaving around tables to find a clean place to sit.

Hurrying through the next several customers, I dropped any attempt at being friendly. Being perky wasn't worth it when no matter what I did, we'd still be behind, and I would continue to receive narrowed glances just for being a King at the town's most popular breakfast stop.

With a deep breath, I powered through, like I always did.

I can do this.

Huck, the owner of the bakery, had taken his fiancée on a surprise two-week trip, so it was up to me to hold down the fort. I'd worked at the Sugar Bowl for years now—starting as a server and eventually taking on more and more responsibilities until I became an unofficial manager of sorts. He was counting on me. Huck was a great boss, and given the fact he didn't put much weight into the King–Sullivan feud, it meant a decent place to work, away from my father.

"Can you get someone to clear this table?" a customer I didn't recognize called from the back, and my eyes sliced to the busser, who was balancing the already-full tub on his hip. "Yep! One second please."

I ignored the additional grumblings and, with a gentle huff, flicked a strand of hair that had come loose from my ponytail. Trying to keep my cool, I steadied my breathing as the next customer stepped up to the counter.

My eyes tracked upward as I took in the tall man in front of me. Beckett Miller wasn't a townie, but he was damn close. He'd been vacationing in Outtatowner for years and had been best friends with Duke Sullivan since they were teens.

In our small town, the divide between Kings and Sullivans was clear, and Beckett had planted himself squarely in Sullivan territory. More so after agreeing to help renovate Ms. Tootie's farmhouse, and if the rumors were true, he and Kate Sullivan had gone from tearing at each other's throats to tearing at their clothes.

That particular piece of hot gossip had made the rounds at the Bluebird Book Club, since Beckett was actually the moody older brother of Kate's weaselly ex-boyfriend.

Beckett stepped up to the register and I suppressed a small smile. Up close he was handsome, and I was happy for Kate, even though our long-standing family rivalry told me I shouldn't dare be happy for a Sullivan. "Welcome to the Sugar Bowl. What can I get started for you?"

"Do you know Kate Sullivan?"

My eyebrows lifted. "Of course I do."

He pressed his lips together and nodded. "Great. Do you happen to know what her favorite is?" He wagged a finger toward the glass display case overflowing with scones, muffins, and danishes.

A small smile twitched at the corner of my mouth. *Guess the rumors are true.* "Katie likes the cheese danish but usually only lets herself get it once a week."

Beckett grinned. "Perfect. Two cheese danishes for her, whatever her coffee order is, and the blueberry crumb muffin with a black coffee for me, please."

Mentally replaying his order, I nodded and rang him up. Then I turned to Skinny Kenny, who was working the espresso machine, to relay the order. Poor kid was still living up to his nickname—another strange occurrence in this town. He could gain twenty pounds of muscle or fifty pounds of flub and he'd still always be Skinny Kenny. That was just how things worked here. If you were lucky, or invisible like me, you could skate by without a nickname.

Moving to the display case, I loaded up the pastries into a small white bag, quietly adding in an extra petite lemon scone just because, and handed the bag across the counter to Beckett.

Behind me Rebecca, our longest-employed server, came through the swinging double doors from the back with a worried expression painted across her face.

"Sylvie . . . there's an issue with this week's produce order. Huck isn't here, so someone needs to talk with Duke Sullivan. Can you do it?"

Heat flooded my cheeks as I ground my teeth. It was always something. I looked around at the bustling bakery and mentally calculated how bogged down we would get if I wasn't up front helping to get customers through the line. I cast a wary glance behind Beckett at the growing line of customers. "Right now?"

Rebecca grimaced. "He's waiting in the back."

Of course he is.

Resigned, I sighed and wiped my hands on the front of my apron. "I'll be right there." I turned to Beckett to find a strange grin spreading across his face.

I forced a smile and ignored the wobble in my stomach. "Have a good day."

I turned, steeling my back and gathering my breath

before pushing my way through the saloon-style doors to the kitchen.

There was one thing guaranteed to ruin my mood, and he was standing in the kitchen with his hip cocked against the steel counter and his signature scowl furrowing his brows, arms crossed over his huge chest like he owned the place.

Duke freaking Sullivan.

With skin kissed by long hours in the blueberry field and muscles that showed off his life of hard work, he was *all man.* Dark hair that bordered on too long threatened to cover his deep, moody eyes. They were the kind of intense brown that held whispers of secrets—secrets a man like him let few people privy to. The dark irises faded into black pupils and added an edge of mysterious danger to the oldest of Red Sullivan's children.

It didn't matter that he was the kind of hot that made women all over town stupid. He was a Sullivan, and I was a King. Decades ago our families decided they hated each other, and ever since then, we've been taking turns making each other's lives miserable, usually in the form of ridiculous pranks.

Instead of growing up and letting the past die with the ancestors who created it, our families doubled down on the feud. Though it was a nuisance, it did keep life in our small town interesting.

Irritation rolled off Duke's broad shoulders.

But that was the thing about Duke, he *always* looked irritated. It was probably because the Wranglers he wore were too damn tight—not that I'd ever noticed how they molded to his perfectly muscular ass.

Standing in front of him, I planted my hands on my hips. "You need something?"

He scoffed and kicked off the steel counter to face me. "I need you to not mess up my delivery schedule."

My face scrunched. "Me? What did I do?"

Duke released a breath, which spoke volumes to how my mere presence was an annoyance. "Huck's out of town, so I'm assuming it's you who forgot to put his order for the week in?"

My eyes started to widen before I stopped myself and leveled him with a cool stare. Per Huck's request, I had placed the bakery's usual weekly order of blueberries with Sullivan Farms.

Right?

My mind raced back to the past few days, but it was blank.

Shit.

Between staffing issues, a temperamental oven that didn't want to work unless you kicked it twice on the right side, and the early mornings prepping while Huck was gone, I must have totally forgotten to place the order.

Double shit.

My mouth popped open and snapped closed again when Duke raised his hand. "The usual?"

"Um . . . " My mouth went dry with panic.

"Do you want the usual?" He spoke slowly in a way that made me feel even more dense than I must have looked. *Jerk.*

When I continued to stare, he sighed. "Huck does sixteen pounds, unless he's got something special on the menu. Do you need it or not?"

Heat flooded my cheeks. Flustered, I moved past him, completely ignoring the warm, masculine scent that clung to his suntanned skin. In the adjacent office, I flipped through a few pieces of paper until I came to the notes

Huck had left me. One finger scanned down the sheet as I felt Duke's hot glare at my back.

"Yes." I turned to find him staring. His eyes flicked up to mine. "The usual. Please." I added a please to the end only because I'd be royally fucked this week without those berries.

Duke's lips were pressed together in a firm line. "Fine."

He turned to leave, and a sound caught in my throat. "Did you—are you leaving the berries right now?"

"No. Deliveries were done for the day, and for some reason it dawned on me that we didn't make a stop here. I came to check up on it. I'll have to pack and deliver a few boxes this afternoon."

"Oh . . ." I started to chew the inside of my lip before I could stop myself. Duke rearranging his day to help correct my mistake caused a strange and uncomfortable feeling in my chest.

Duke was an asshole.

Cold and grumpy and moody.

A Sullivan.

He wasn't supposed to act all neighborly and go out of his way to help us out.

"Thanks, I . . . I really appreciate it."

A muscle flexed in his jaw, and I tamped down the low flutter in my belly.

"Yep." Duke turned toward the back exit of the kitchen, then stopped.

I stared at the expanse of his muscular back, wondering what had stopped him from leaving.

Filling the uncomfortable silence, I gently cleared my throat. "We close at two. If you can't make it by then, I completely understand. Maybe you could call, and I will be sure to be here so I can prep them and get everything moved to the walk-in?"

He turned, his dark eyes meeting mine and rooting me to the spot. "Call you?"

My throat was hot and tight. There was no reason for my physical reaction to Duke, but it was there all the same. His masculine energy filled the kitchen until the air was thick with it.

"Last time a King got my phone number, I got nothing but crank calls for months," he said.

I stared, stunned. *That was definitely my brother, Royal.*

"Cat facts," he continued, not at all seeing the humor in the ridiculous prank. "I was texted cat facts—*fifteen* times a day. I had to get a new phone number."

I put my hands in the air, stifling the laugh that threatened to escape. "It wasn't me, and I wouldn't do that. I swear. I just want to be sure the kitchen is open when you get here."

A low grunt rumbled in his throat as he looked me over.

When he reached his hand into the pocket of his jeans, I couldn't help but notice how thick and veined his forearms were. Slipping the phone from his pocket, he hesitated before finally unlocking it and handing it to me.

I rolled my eyes and quickly typed my phone number into his phone, texting my own so I would also have his number. When the text alert came through, I slid my phone from my back pocket and saved his number.

I held his phone toward him. Reaching out, his rough fingertips dragged against my palm as he retrieved his phone. Heat spread up my arm and danced across my chest. I snatched my hand back before he could notice.

He looked at the phone, and his frown deepened. "Daryl Hall?"

I held up my phone. "Yep. And you're John Oates."

He eyed me, and tiny prickles danced on the back of my neck. I swallowed. "Well, I can't have *Duke Sullivan* flash across the screen and give my brothers a collective coronary."

Realization dawned over his dark features. "Hall and Oates. Like the eighties pop duo?"

I swirled a finger in the air as a classic, upbeat Hall and Oates song flowed softly from the kitchen speaker. "Thinkin' on my feet here."

With a nod and not another word, Duke sailed out the back exit. The door slammed and I stared after it.

What the hell was that?

A crash at the front of the bakery shook me out of my stupor. "Sylvie! We need some help up here!" Rebecca called.

"Coming!" I lifted my shirt at the collar to drag in some air, wondering why it was suddenly so freaking hot back there.

TWO

DUKE

THE DRIVE to Haven Pines was one I could do in my sleep. The fact my dad's early-onset dementia had gotten unmanageable and required him to live in the memory care wing of a retirement home was a constant lance beneath my ribs.

With my siblings gone in the wind, Aunt Tootie and I did our best to care for him, but with the demands on the farm, it eventually had gotten to be too much. It felt like yesterday that I had spent a long afternoon in the field, only to end my day with a call from the police that Dad had wandered to town, gotten confused, and been picked up. Irate and confused, he'd taken a swing at the officer trying to help him.

I'd failed him.

Tootie couldn't care for her brother on her own, and it wasn't long after that I was forced to admit defeat. Dad was safer at Haven Pines.

Walking through the automatic doors, I was immediately greeted by the nurse at the main desk. "Afternoon, Duke!"

I offered a terse nod and continued around the main

desk toward the wing that housed my father. The memory care ward had a separate nurse's station in front of the locked double doors. It was designed for the residents' safety but bore a striking resemblance to a prison.

The nurse was on the phone but offered me a bright smile and buzzed me in without having to question who I was. As a regular visitor I saw my dad nearly every day. If I couldn't make it, Tootie or one of my siblings would make the trip to Haven Pines to check in on him. On the good days, we'd even take Dad with us for a family dinner or a scoop of his favorite ice cream downtown.

Immediately through the doors, the decor changed from sterile old folks' home to a faux neighborhood. When the wing was built, they had modeled it after downtown Outta-towner. The hospital rooms were set up to look like a neighborhood of houses stacked like dominos, one after the other. Doors to the rooms were made to look like the front doors to actual homes, and the outsides were landscaped with flowers, faux windows, and lampposts.

It was quaint, if you could forget the fact that most residents were so far gone they couldn't remember their own first names. I shook the thought from my head as I approached my dad's room.

In true Red fashion, Dad was dressed and sipping coffee on the makeshift porch outside his room. Despite the fact he no longer needed to, I knew he still woke before the sun. Old farmers were a different breed. Though he was pushing sixty, he still had a full head of hair, combed and styled the same way I'd known it since I was a kid.

His eyes caught my movement, and they locked onto me. There was a flicker of confusion—that half second where he didn't recognize his own son—and it always gutted me. Then, just as quickly as it came, it was gone, and recognition split his face into a smile. Dad had kind blue eyes, and today they were clear.

He stood and shoved a hand in my direction. "Afternoon."

I shook his hand and clamped the other onto his shoulder with affection. "Hey, Dad."

"No work today?"

I huffed a humorless laugh. There was *always* work, but Dad was a priority. "Slow day. New bushes are being planted this week and next. We had a few rows affected by shoestring virus."

Dad's brows pinched down. "Removed the infected bushes and burned them?"

I nodded. "Yes, sir."

"You'll have to watch that spot from now on. Four years at least. How many rows?"

I laughed inwardly. While some memories, like his children or his wife passing, became hazy, the man never forgot a damn thing about blueberries.

"Only two. We're taking care of it."

Dad patted my arm. "I know you are, Son." He gestured to the two chairs on his mock porch. "Have a seat." He lifted his Styrofoam cup. "Unless you want something to drink. Coffee is like tar today, so I wouldn't recommend it." He grimaced into his cup but took another sip.

Shaking my head, I sat next to him, as I had done a thousand times before, and stretched my long legs against the porch railing that butted up to the hallway.

We sat in companionable silence as he offered friendly nods to other residents walking on the "sidewalk" and to the nurses pushing their large computer carts down the hall. I wondered if he ever noticed how much younger he was than anyone else on his block.

When Dad finally broke the silence, my heart sank. "Your brother's got a big game." He shook his head, lost in memories. "Big game."

He wasn't talking about coaching a game at the university. It was a common occurrence for Dad to relive Wyatt's glory days as Outtatowner's *Golden Boy* quarterback—a nickname he fought long and hard to ignore, but in Outtatowner, people were more known by their nicknames, and most hated them.

Except me. I was born August Sullivan—my mom loved that her oldest son was August and she was June. Often we'd be sitting on the porch, watching Dad make slow, winding progress through the rows and rows of blueberry bushes. She would sigh, lay her head on my shoulder, and tell me August was her favorite month. She'd wax poetic about life in our small town and how everything could change with a single decision, if only we were brave enough to make it. She would often sprinkle tiny gems of wisdom I was too young to comprehend.

My chest squeezed at the memory. Mom had always been the brave one.

As a kid with the name Gus, my peers were ruthless. Especially the Kings. JP King once teased me that he was a King, and all I'd ever become was something akin to a *duke*.

Beneath him.

He teased and called me Duke so often most people assumed it was my birth-given name.

The joke was on him because I preferred Duke to Gus any day, especially after Mom died. It was too painful to even recall the way she would ruffle my hair and call me Gus-Gus. Every time my face would screw up and I would swat her hand away, begging for her not to call me that. Now, I'd kill to hear it one last time.

"Think he'll break the record this time?" My dad's eyes were unfocused. He was as lost in thought as I was.

"Hmm?" I asked, pulling my attention back to the present.

"Your brother's got a hell of an arm, but he's not focused. If he's going to break his own record, he needs to *want it*."

I hummed in agreement. Correcting Dad would only agitate him, and I was too drained to tackle it today.

"Wyatt always gives it his all," I conceded.

And he did—Wyatt had gotten to chase his NFL dreams and now, he found his calling as a university coach. He poured his heart and soul into that team, and the only things that came before it were his daughter, Penny, and his woman, Lark, now that he'd fallen for her.

Lee got to fuck around as the town's favorite bachelor— not that I blamed him. He did his time in the service and saw more shit beyond the borders of this town than anyone. Still, he may have come back changed in ways I didn't always understand, but he didn't see his time away in the same way I did.

Freedom.

Even Kate had finally moved home after a brief stint in Montana. I was glad she was back, though I'd be lying if I didn't say my best friend Beckett falling for my little sister had thrown me for a loop. It wasn't that he wasn't a good guy, it was just that I thought there was a code. An understanding. Apparently *Don't fuck my little sister* was supposed to be explicitly stated.

No matter—the house, the farm, and my dog, Ed, were all I needed.

It wasn't hard to see that Kate was undeniably happy, and Beckett seemed to be the reason. I wasn't such an asshole that I'd ever stand in her way of true happiness. She deserved it more than most, and I could eventually learn to get used to the googly eyes those two shot each other across the room.

"Afternoon, Red." The voice from beyond Dad's porch drew our attention. "Time for your medication." MJ King, the youngest King sibling, smiled down at us.

We both stood to greet her, and despite MJ being a King, the manners my father had ingrained in me won out.

I wanted to hate her on principle, but her sunny disposition and the way she cared for my father made that nearly impossible. It didn't matter that Red Sullivan came from the wrong family. MJ was patient and kind despite the unpredictability of his moods. I'd learned to put MJ in a different category of Kings—a category titled *Not a Prick*.

My secret soft spot for members of the King family ended at MJ.

I watched as my dad grumbled, like he always did, and argued about not needing the medication. MJ spoke with patience and smiled sweetly until Red was, quite literally, eating out of the palm of her hand.

Her older sister Sylvie's face flashed through my mind.

Our interaction from earlier had rattled me, and I still couldn't shake the feeling that something odd had occurred in that kitchen. After leaving the Sugar Bowl, I'd headed straight home to the farm. I packed up the boxes of berries and didn't wait to haul them back to town. Sure, I could have taken my time and delivered them when the bakery wasn't quite so busy, but I didn't need any more time alone with Sylvie.

Her presence just *did* something to me.

Maybe it was the way she had let her typically cool, dismissive demeanor slip, or how her light-blonde hair contrasted with the rich honey browns in her eyes. Whatever it was, the last thing I needed to think about was a King woman and how she had somehow gotten under my skin with one conversation about Hall and Oates.

Rather than risk having to call her, I'd dropped the berry order off with zero fanfare and figured she'd find them on the kitchen counter whenever she went back there. I also wasn't sure why I didn't bother to delete her phone number, now that I didn't need it.

Days later I'd caught myself looking at the contact and smiling a bit at myself that it was even in there. Like some forbidden little secret that only I knew about.

Fucking dumbass.

"Good to see you, Duke." MJ smiled at me, and there was a glint of something more in her eyes, like she was trying not to laugh at me.

I nodded and offered her a terse smile. "You too."

"Got a minute?" The slight tip of her head told me she preferred to speak in private, away from my father's ears.

"Yeah." I turned toward my dad, who was already chatting with a neighbor. "I'll see you tomorrow, Dad."

After a quick handshake farewell, I walked alongside MJ as she pushed the cart.

"I wanted to talk to you about a new drug trial I heard about. I think your dad might be perfect for it." She handed me a pamphlet. "Think about it. You never know, right?"

I looked down at the glossy trifold, and my stomach turned in on itself. I'd learned a long time ago that hoping his dementia would improve was a lost cause. I slipped the pamphlet into my back pocket. "I'll look into it."

I had taken one step away when she called over my shoulder. "So you chickened out, huh?"

I turned to look at her over my shoulder. "Excuse me?"

Her lips curled in as though she was holding back a smile. She blinked innocently. "I think she was bummed you didn't call."

My heart plummeted to my stomach.

Sylvie.

Even her name in my head felt like a betrayal to my entire family, but I couldn't deny the uptick in my heartbeat at the way it rolled around in there.

"You know . . . your secret is safe with me." The mischievous grin that split MJ's face was a problem.

My jaw flexed. "There is no secret."

She only smiled and shrugged before she singsonged, "If you say so."

I was another two strides down the hallway when she called over my shoulder: "But if you ever *did* text her, I wouldn't say a word."

STRETCHED OUT ON MY BED, I draped my hand over the side to scratch at the scruff behind Ed's ears. He groaned, like the old man he was, and plopped onto the floor. The old hound dog and I had been through the wringer. He'd earned his name Three-Legged Ed because he was also a dumbass who liked to chase cars.

His grumble matched my mood as MJ's words played in a loop in my head.

She was bummed you didn't call.

Reaching for the nightstand, I grabbed my phone and unlocked it, staring at the contact I had yet to delete.

Daryl Hall.

A small smile cracked at the corners of my mouth. I pulled up a new text thread and typed a message.

ME

Cat Fact 159: Cats can dream.

I hit send and immediately felt foolish texting Sylvie King a random, stupid cat fact. When three tiny bubbles appeared, then disappeared, my heart pounded.

DARYL HALL

Nice try, but I have your number saved, remember?

I swallowed a laugh and typed again.

Cat Fact 160: Cat whiskers are the same width as their bodies.

DARYL HALL

Wait, is that true?

Hell if I know, but now I have random cat facts rolling around in my head. If I have to suffer, so do you.

My eyes darted around my bedroom. Despite knowing I was alone, the mere fact I was texting Sylvie King gave me anxiety. If her brothers knew, they'd be pissed. Hell, if *my* siblings knew, they would be hard-pressed to understand it.

DARYL HALL

OK, give me another one. Fair's fair.

Cat Fact 161: A cat butthole in your face is a gesture of friendship.

As soon as my fingers flew over the send button I wanted to reach through the phone and undo it. I pressed my thumb into my eye socket.

I just texted the word butthole *to Sylvie King.*

> **DARYL HALL**
>
> A little soon for me to be showing you my butthole, don't you think?

More than a little shocked, I stared at her response. The image of her perfectly round ass in the air flashed through my mind, and I stifled a groan.

Almost immediately, a slew of texts came pinging through.

> **DARYL HALL**
>
> Oh my god.
>
> Please don't read that.
>
> It was a joke. A bad one.
>
> I'm going to go crawl into a hole and die now.

I chuckled, feeling her embarrassment expand with every rapid-fire text.

> All good. I laughed.

And pictured you naked.

> **DARYL HALL**
>
> You? Laugh? I didn't know that was possible.

> Stranger things have happened. Just look at us.

My words sank in, and I knew them to be undoubtedly true. I could never be friends with Sylvie, not really. The feud was a tie that bound the entire town together, and a genuine friendship between a Sullivan and a King would cause an uproar. That thought alone caused a ripple of irritation to roll down my back and put me in an even shittier mood.

DARYL HALL

True. I have to go, but this has been. . . interesting. Maybe we could do this again sometime. What do you say, Oates?

> I'll let you know if I remember any more cat facts. 'Night, Hall.

DARYL HALL

Unsubscribe. (good night!)

I smiled. For years our families had been slinging insults at each other. Somewhere along the way, aloof Sylvie King had become *fun*.

I couldn't wait to do it again.

THREE

DUKE

Eight Months Later

It had been an endless loop of unremarkable days melting into one another.

Wake up. Tend the fields. Check on Dad. Watch the sun sink below the tree line. Some nights I let my brothers talk me into grabbing a beer at the Grudge.

I leave when I realize she's not there.

As one day folded into another, only subtle differences changed the endless loop of my life. Earlier in the day, while walking the fields, I found an abandoned duckling. His mother was nowhere to be found, and the pathetic little squeaks were kind of cute. Ed was standing guard as I figured out what I was going to do with the thing.

It was early for most, but I woke up before the sun and was settling in with a cup of coffee and Ed at my feet. I needed to check in with my field manager, Cisco.

Migrant workers were common in Michigan, and without them Sullivan Farms wouldn't have been the operation it was. Cisco acted as a liaison between me and the migrant workers employed at Sullivan Farms. Not all farmers felt the same way, but it was my duty to ensure they were treated with the respect and dignity they deserved. I supplied housing and transportation for the workers, along with state-mandated schooling for any children in their families, while they lived and worked on the farm.

It was a relationship I took seriously.

Already June, there was a lot of work to be done before the U-pick season started in a few weeks, and we needed to be sure the fields were prepped and ready to go. We also needed to be sure that, come July, harvest could go on without a hitch—and one of our blueberry pickers had been acting up again.

The crunch of tires on gravel pulled my attention from my phone.

I recognized Wyatt's car a split second before Three-Legged Ed ran off to circle his car as it meandered down the driveway.

While Ed took off, I didn't bother to leave my chair. I had already put in a long-ass morning, walking the fields and dealing with the duckling, and I could tell it was gearing up to be an insufferable June afternoon. Enjoying my coffee felt like the only fifteen minutes of solace I got in the day.

That, and getting a message from *her*.

My brother exited his car, draping an arm across the open driver's-side door. "Morning," he shouted across the yard.

I lifted my mug in salute.

Wyatt shook his head and slammed his door closed as he walked across the yard and up the steps to my porch. He was dressed in slacks and a Midwest Michigan University–branded polo, which meant he was likely on his way to the campus in St. Fowler, where he worked.

I looked him over. "What do you know?"

"Not much. I've got a wide receiver camp coming up, so I'm going in to make sure everything's ready to go. Thought I'd swing by on my way out of town."

I frowned down into my cup. I loved having my brother back in town, but the years of him being gone and our strained relationship often left me feeling unsure of what to say to him, how to connect.

I tilted my black coffee toward him. "Want a cup?"

"Nah, man, I have to hit the road." Wyatt grinned and my stomach tightened. *He's up to something.* "But I wanted to tell you, we're going out tonight."

I didn't hide my annoyed sigh and eye roll.

Wyatt pointed at me. "I'm serious. You need to get out of that house, off this farm. Live a little bit."

My deep sigh was laced with a grunt as I slowly released my breath. I didn't need my little brother telling me how to live my life, but I also hated to admit that he was partially correct.

I wasn't currently living much of a life at all. Grueling days of prepping the fields, managing the migrant workers, and filling orders and contracts ate up every spare minute of my time.

My phone buzzed, and I glanced down just briefly enough to see the name *Daryl Hall* flash across the screen.

My mouth twitched at the corner. "Okay. Fine."

The only other reason I ever took a few minutes out of my day every morning was the quick *good morning* text and chat with Sylvie. It still boggled my mind how we had somehow slipped into such an easy friendship. She was thoughtful and funny and kind—not at all the aloof ice princess I had thought her to be.

Hell, I think most people saw her that way, and a sick

part of me loved that there was a piece of her reserved only for me.

I quickly flipped my phone upside down, but Wyatt caught the guilty flicker in my eyes before I could suppress it.

"Who's that?" he asked.

I scoffed in dismissal. "No one."

"Bullshit." Wyatt smirked. "We all know you're a terrible liar."

Which is exactly why I can never tell a soul about my friendship with Sylvie King.

Wyatt crossed his arms and looked down at me. I worked to keep my expression calm despite my heart hammering behind my ribs.

"She a tourist?" he asked, lifting one eyebrow.

I only glared at him.

"Oh shit, she's a townie!" Wyatt laughed and clapped his hands.

Annoyed, I stood, swiping my coffee mug off the side table hard enough for it to splash over the rim. I had him beat in height, but only by a half inch or so. Still, I was just petty enough to use it to my advantage. "It's nothing."

He narrowed his eyes, and his mouth hooked into a smirk. "If you say so, man."

When I turned to walk back into my house and dump my cold coffee, mood soured, Wyatt stopped me. "Hey, I'm serious about going out tonight."

With my back to him, I sighed, and my shoulder slumped.

"We miss you." His words brought a fresh ache to my chest. "You're getting out of this house, and we're going out tonight. One beer. That's all I'm asking for."

He wasn't asking for much. Just two brothers spending

time together. Years ago I had wished for that exact thing, but I'd convinced myself that our family was too broken to ever have that. Now he was offering it to me on a silver fucking platter, and I was being a dick about it.

Over my shoulder I nodded.

"Yeah? All right." Laughter laced through his words as he bounded down the stairs back toward his car. "I'll pick you up—that way you can't Houdini on us. Be ready at eight."

I offered my brother a halfhearted salute, knowing I would have to spend the better part of the day thinking of an excuse to bring my own truck so that I could fulfill my one-beer obligation and make my silent exit, like I normally did.

Inside, I dumped the cold coffee and glanced at the clock. Wyatt's impromptu visit had interrupted my morning routine, and I wasn't happy about it.

Hurrying, I picked up my phone and unlocked it.

DARYL HALL

Morning.

Along with her *good morning* text was a picture of Sylvie dressed in tight running gear. With sunglasses perched on her nose, her face scrunched up, and her flashing a peace sign. A riot of oranges, pinks, and deep plum swirled over her shoulder as the summer sun rose behind her.

She was so stunning it stole my breath.

Sylvie didn't often send pictures, but when she did, I saved every single one. I would venture a guess she would stop sending them if she knew they had become my only spank bank material in the last eight months.

I dragged a hand over my face.

Jesus Christ. I am a creep.
I quickly typed back.

> Morning? I've already been up for four
> hours. The day's wasting.

DARYL HALL

> Well, not all of us are built like machines.
> Some of us need our beauty sleep.

> Looks to me like you've been getting plenty
> of that.

My breath caught in my chest, as it always did when our conversations casually morphed into subtle flirting. I lived for it, but part of me worried it was too much, too aggressive. I know Sylvie didn't think of me that way, but she also didn't seem to mind either.

DARYL HALL

> Ha. You're sweet, but a liar. I wish I could
> say I was glistening. But in reality, I'm
> sweating like a pig. Why is it so hot this
> early?

My blood ran hot with thoughts of Sylvie sweating in a different scenario. One with her pinned beneath me as I drove my cock into her. My jaw clenched as I typed out a response.

> Humidity's up. They're calling for rain
> overnight.

I inwardly rolled my eyes at myself. The world's most gorgeous woman was taking time out of her day to text me, and I was talking about the fucking weather.

> What are you up to?

DARYL HALL

Just work, but then I think MJ and I might head up to the Grudge tonight. The band that's playing is supposed to be good. She says we're celebrating.

I perked up at the news that Sylvie would also be at the Grudge tonight.

Guess I would be staying for more than one beer after all.

> Celebrating?

DARYL HALL

The date auction remix happened, so I am no longer paired up with Stumpy Larson. The rest of the dates will be with Charles. Definitely celebrating.

Outtatowner had recently held the annual Matchmaker's Gala. It was a charity ball and an opportunity for the women in town to play matchmaker, pairing off the singles in town through a ridiculous date auction disguised as fun.

Fuck that.

It was no surprise to anyone that I refused to go. I didn't care that it made me look like a prick for not attending a charity auction, even if it was for a good cause.

But I was glad Sylvie wasn't paired with Stumpy Larson anymore, because that guy was a fucking weirdo. Had it not been for her overbearing brothers, I may have been forced to step in myself.

Thankfully it hadn't come to that. Though I wasn't sure Charles Attwater was much better. He was a nice enough guy, I guess. New in town and had opened up some fancy wine bar that the tourists couldn't get enough of, but there was something that just didn't sit right with me. Charles didn't pay any mind to the King–Sullivan feud, and the women of either side of that feud seemed to flock to him.

He had even set his sights on Annie Crane, who'd grown up so close with us she was practically another sister. I thought my brother Lee was going to pop a blood vessel when Charles started giving Annie his attention.

It took me a minute to figure out how to respond to Sylvie. I had no claim over Sylvie King, so it shouldn't have irritated me that she was going out on a date.

I hadn't dated anyone in a long time. She was free to date whomever she wanted, but *fuck*. I wanted to warn her about Charles—tell her that my gut told me getting attached to him was a mistake. A mistake, but also, if she really wanted to go to the Grudge and celebrate, I'd be happy to take her. I could push her around the dance floor to some fun country song while I held her in my arms.

I let out a dry humorless laugh at my stupidity. There wasn't a world in which that could ever happen. I could never betray my family, and her brothers would certainly have a lot to say about it if I crossed that line.

Texting in secret would be all there could ever be between us. Hell, we had never even had a conversation in public, so I couldn't imagine the collective gasp and jaw dropping that would happen if we ever went on an actual date.

It seemed childish yet so inevitable all at once.

> Stumpy is the worst.

DARYL HALL

> You couldn't have come to the auction and made a bid? Way to leave a girl hanging.

My mouth went dry. Had Sylvie *wanted* me to bid on dates with her? What the fuck . . . in our months of texting, Sylvie tended to be playful—that was likely all it was.

> The auction is more Lee's thing.

I banged my head against the wall. It wasn't a lie. I *was* glad that I hadn't been set up on the date auction because *fuck that*. It didn't escape my notice that the thought of being set up with Sylvie, in some alternate universe where that wouldn't cause World War III, was the only appealing part of Outtatowner's archaic date auction. I hadn't been on a date in forever. A random townie hookup held little appeal these days.

Especially when I couldn't seem to stop thinking about a certain forbidden blonde with mysterious caramel eyes.

Sylvie and I would never be anything more than friends —that much I knew for certain. Hell, we couldn't really even be *friends*. Tension between the Kings and Sullivans were at an all-time high. Someone was poking around, asking questions about mineral rights and land ownership, and I had a pretty good idea of who that was.

I didn't fucking like it.

DARYL HALL

> I figured as much . . . I'm sorry. Did I make this weird?

> No. You should have fun and celebrate.

The lies were stacking one on top of the other as they wedged themselves in my chest, burrowed deep, and made a home there. I prayed it was only a matter of time before

Sylvie also saw Charles for the weasel I suspected him to be.

> **DARYL HALL**
>
> Thanks. I'll just be glad when all of this date auction bullshit is over.

I let out a breath, but it was more like a sigh of relief. The hot ball of tension in my chest unfurled at the realization that she wasn't all that happy about the dates she was going on either. I let myself cling to the sliver of hope she wasn't joking about wishing we could have been set up.

> **DARYL HALL**
>
> I gotta run, but talk to you later?

> You bet.

I scrolled back to the picture Sylvie had sent and stared at it for a few heavy moments. A part of me wished I didn't have to hide out in my house, wary that if I went into town, I might accidentally run into her and smile before I could catch myself.

It pissed me off, but it was the way that it had to be. Like everything else in my life, what I wanted didn't matter. I was a Sullivan, bound by duty. Dad, the farm, holding my family together, even the feud. There was no getting past it.

I hated knowing that tonight we would be breathing the same stale bar air and that I couldn't stand close enough to see her head tip back in a laugh and finally hear what it sounded like.

Good morning texts and the occasional flirty banter were all that it would ever be.

And I fucking hated it.

INSIDE THE GRUDGE HOLDER, an invisible divide separated the Sullivans and the Kings. Tourists had no clue, but Kings stuck to the east end of the bar, while Sullivans took up space on the west. While the owner may have named his bar after the infamous feud, he had a zero-tolerance policy about starting shit in his bar. It was an unspoken rule we all stood by.

Usually.

The band was already a few songs into their set, Lee was on the dance floor politely turning down a dance with some woman I didn't recognize, and Wyatt was getting our first round.

I scanned the bar again. I hadn't seen Sylvie, and irritation rolled across my back.

Should have just stayed home.

DARYL HALL

You know a night out is supposed to be
fun, right?

My heart clunked. It was something we had never done before—an invisible line we had yet to cross. Texting in public was risky. I looked around, and for the briefest moment my eyes landed on hers.

My jaw flexed as I controlled the urge to break out into a grin.

DARYL HALL

You look like you're about to murder
someone.

What do you mean? This is my happy face.

Across the bar, I could see her look at her phone and cover her laugh with a cough. Heat radiated across my chest.

Wyatt's shoulder bumped into me. "Dude, you are so fucked."

My eyes flew to his as I slipped my phone back into my pocket and shot him a harsh glare.

He only smirked and nodded toward the phone secured in my pocket. "I know that look. You are so gone for that girl."

At the high-top table, I shrugged him off and leaned on my elbows, letting my bottle rest between my hands. Fresh tension set in between my shoulder blades. Sylvie was hanging around, so my typical one-beer exit strategy evaporated, and I ordered another.

Over time I had learned that Sylvie wasn't the kind of woman who laughed loudly or sucked up the energy in the room. Instead, she was all subtle smiles and assessing eyes. Her loud-ass brothers may have demanded attention, but somehow she had stolen mine.

Once I found her, I didn't let my eyes stay on her longer than a fraction of a second. Especially not after Wyatt was already suspicious of whoever I was texting. Plus, I didn't want to creep her out by staring at her across the bar like some lovesick puppy whose face apparently looked like a murderer's.

From my peripheral, I watched as conversations overlapped around Sylvie. Her long fingers traced a drop of moisture down the outside of her wineglass. Leave it to a King to be the only person in a dive bar drinking white wine.

She contributed to the conversation only a time or two as voices flowed over her, crashing into her like a wave and swallowing her up. I wasn't sure if anyone even acknowledged her comments, and that pissed me right the fuck off. It was as though she was present but not fully included.

Finally, MJ grabbed her hand and pulled her toward the dance floor. I sat back and relaxed a little in the stool. Whenever she danced, I knew I could watch her weave through the crowded dance floor without worrying about getting caught staring.

To any outside onlooker, it would appear like I was just a silent observer as my friends and neighbors enjoyed a night out on the town.

If only they knew.

By my third beer, Wyatt clamped a hand on my shoulder. "It's about your bedtime, isn't it, Cinderella?"

I harrumphed but drained the last of my beer and stood, dropping a nice tip on the table for our server.

The truth was, I could stay all night and watch Sylvie sway and move to the music on the dance floor. Out there she let herself go in a way I'd never seen her do anywhere else.

She was free. And fucking gorgeous. Breathtaking.

It was a sick kind of punishment to watch the one thing you could never have. Drowning in self-loathing, I agreed with Wyatt to call it a night.

Outside, the June air was thick and oppressive. Even the breeze off the lake was stifling. We headed out the front of the Grudge and walked through the alleyway between buildings toward the packed parking lot near the back. Wyatt's car came into view, and I eyed it, wondering if a King had covered the windshield with sticky notes or swapped out the washer fluid with colored liquid, or any other of the mindless pranks they managed to pull.

My boots crunched against the gravel parking lot, and

the sudden hushed voices drew my attention. Leaned against his truck at the far end of the lot was Royal King and his brother Whip. When they saw Wyatt and me, Whip straightened to his full height, while Royal slowly turned to face us.

My fists clenched at my sides. I was already irritated at the way their entire group seemed to ignore Sylvie, and I hated how I could never seem to escape the ridiculous feud. I couldn't even get a fucking beer without it being thrown in my face.

"Just keep walking." Wyatt's low tone let me know he saw them, too, and was well aware of the way they were tracking our movements.

My blood ran hot. In Outtatowner, loyalty was *everything*. My secret friendship with Sylvie would be enough to ignite the tinderbox of our small-town feud, but I couldn't convince myself to stop—not when her messages were the only things dragging me out of bed some days.

It's only a few text messages. No one has to know.

I grunted a response to Wyatt and kept walking. I sure as fuck didn't need her idiot brothers souring my already piss-poor mood. The metal back door of the Grudge swung open, and a clang rang out as it hit the brick wall. Lee shot both arms in the air as he sauntered out of the back exit and across the lot. His eyes were glassy, and his smile widened when he saw Royal and Whip.

Fuck.

"Well, hey, boys! Just came to stretch my legs." Lee shot a thumb over his shoulder and grinned. "Had to turn down your sister in there. Man, she was desperate."

Whip took a step forward. "The fuck did you say?"

I knew that glint in Lee's eyes. He was fucking with

them and itching for a fight. "Lee." I ground out the warning.

My little brother ignored me as he took a step toward the Kings. "Said I had to tell your little sister I couldn't tussle. Broke the poor girl's heart, I think."

"Lee, shut your mouth and get in the car." Wyatt sounded as pissed as I was, but Lee ignored him too.

"Back up, *Bill.*" Lee stared, coming nearly chest to chest with Whip. The man was born William, but everyone in town knew him as Whip. Lee loved to call him Bill, just to get under his skin.

Whip inched closer as Royal hovered nearby. The tension in the air was thick, and it was about to get ugly. Wyatt and I stepped up, flanking Lee.

I glanced at Royal. "He's drunk. We're leaving."

Whip lifted his chin. "Yeah, go home before I lay you out."

The corner of Lee's mouth tipped up. "Nah, man. That's your sister's job."

The sentence wasn't even out of Lee's mouth when I grabbed the back of his shirt with two hands and pulled him backward. Whip's fist swung wide, missing Lee but landing with a crack against my face. The force of it snapped my head back, and Lee tumbled to the ground.

I steadied my legs, hunching until I surged forward, wrapping my arms around Whip's body and slamming him into the side of Royal's truck. A surge of anger coursed through me as I braced for the impact of Whip's fist against my ribs. I gripped the back of his neck and shifted my hips, tossing him to the ground. I glanced quickly enough to see Wyatt in the middle of a shoving match between Royal and Lee. A small bit of blood trickled from Lee's lip.

I was done with these assholes thinking they owned this town—tired of working my ass off for it to mean *nothing*.

Whip was in my face, and I dodged a left hook. Limbs tangled as voices yelled around me. Our fighting began to gather a crowd. As Whip and I wrestled, my knees bit into the gravel. Anger and adrenaline consumed me as I straddled Whip and landed a blow to his side while his forearms covered his face.

Chaos filled the dark parking lot. Onlookers chose sides and yelled, amping up the charged atmosphere. My teeth ground together as Whip bucked his hips, tossing me aside. We rolled, and hands grabbed at me, pulling me and preventing me from charging Whip again. Royal stepped between us, shoving Whip backward. Wyatt's arms clamped over mine, pinning them to my sides as I struggled to break free. I sucked hot breath through my nose, and my heart hammered between my ears. Behind me, Lee bounced on his toes and laughed, wiping away the drop of blood trickling from his lip.

I wrestled my arms free. "I'm fine!"

Royal shoved Whip back a second time and wrenched open the passenger-side door before shoving his brother inside. As he rounded the hood, he pointed at us. "This isn't over."

I spat blood on the ground and stared at him.

You bet your ass this isn't over.

Wyatt pulled at my shirt. "Let's go before someone calls the cops."

My jaw clenched as I scanned the crowd, but I didn't see her. My ribs ached, and I had to tamp down the overwhelming urge to punch something again.

Wyatt dropped Lee off at his apartment and drove me back to the farm in tense silence. I was relieved when he didn't bring up the texts again. Things with the Kings were getting out of hand. Harmless pranks were escalating to physical assaults, and a dark part of me *craved* that release— to take my frustrations out on someone. *Anyone.*

I hated myself for it, but it had felt damn good to temporarily stop stifling my feelings. I checked my phone, and there was a missed text that made my chest ache.

> DARYL HALL
>
> Did you leave? I can't believe you missed it! I finally convinced the band to play a Hall and Oates song!

Bile rose in my throat. She had no idea why I missed the song.

> DARYL HALL
>
> It's funny, Royal made a weird comment tonight. He said he never sees you stay longer than one drink at the Grudge, but I feel like I always see you there! What's with that?

Hot coals lined my throat as I reread it. The text had come through right around the time I was beating the shit out of her older brother.

After Wyatt pulled onto the farm, I climbed out of the car without a word. He left in silence, and when I climbed my porch steps, I dumped my sorry ass into a chair. My phone dinged with a new message, and I closed my eyes and sighed before looking at it.

> DARYL HALL
>
> Everyone is talking about what happened in the parking lot. Are you okay?!

My fingers itched with indecision. I should ignore her—

stop the ridiculous charade of pretending that a Sullivan and a King could ever be friends. Our families would always be rivals. Neither side had any desire to move past the generations of mutual hatred.

I even considered glossing over her comment with a flippant line, when I paused. *Or do I tell her the truth?*

Nerves rattled under my skin, and I swallowed hard.

Fuck it.

> Things got heated. I'm fine. To answer your question, I only ever stay on nights you're there.

FOUR

THE JULY HEAT WAS OPPRESSIVE, and I wiped a small bead of sweat from my hairline. Beyond the quaint downtown area, a side street was alive with the pulsating rhythm of the weekly farmers' market. It was a big moneymaker for the Sugar Bowl, as tourists and townies alike were drawn in by the rich aroma of freshly brewed coffee intermingling with the intoxicating scent of warm cinnamon pastries.

I loved working at the farmers' market, since it was an opportunity to meet and mingle with lots of new faces. To them I wasn't a King but simply a soft smile behind their favorite bakery. It seemed coffee and carbs made everyone's Saturday better.

It was also an opportunity to sneak glances across the market at the Sullivan Farms booth. Duke was in his stall, where he sold blueberries by the pint alongside various jams and jellies, all while looking like his typical grump-ass self and glaring at customers. I stifled a giggle as I packed up an order and handed it across the table.

Two weeks had passed since the scuffle in the parking lot of the Grudge, but tensions were still at an all-time high. After that night, Duke and I hadn't talked about it again, and I tried to ignore the uneasy feeling I got whenever I thought about an *actual* fight between my brother and Duke. I was ashamed to admit that the abrasions on Duke's knuckles were kind of hot, especially since they were the cause of my brother's bruised ribs. Of course, no one was taking any responsibility for what happened. Depending on who you overheard, blame was laid squarely on the shoulders of the offending family. I heard Lee had tossed a martini in Royal's face, or Whip had slapped Wyatt, or Duke had rammed his truck into Royal's in an attempted murder.

Each story was more ridiculous than the last.

I sighed and stared into the bright midmorning sun, hoping the vitamin D would boost my mood. Today was also the sixth and final date of the Outtatowner date auction.

I had come up with a ridiculous excuse that I needed to work the booth for the Sugar Bowl while Huck and Casselyn enjoyed the market. Truth was, Rebecca could have more than handled it.

"Hey, Sylvie!" Stepping forward, Annie Crane held me with her bright smile. Her unruly red curls bounced with the lake breeze as she scanned the table. Annie was a Sullivan by association. She'd been practically adopted by the late June Sullivan as a kid and had fallen into a close friendship with Lee Sullivan—though the fact Lee was staring at her ass told me it was likely the rumors were true and they were finally an item.

Despite the King–Sullivan rivalry, Annie and I were a part of the Bluebird Book Club. The club met weekly, and despite family ties it was a place for the women of Outtatowner to come together in secret to gossip, solve problems, and maybe even just be ourselves.

No doubt, the Bluebird Book Club was my happy place.

"Good morning. What can I get you?"

Her blue eyes danced across the table of pastries. "A couple of coffees." She leaned in to whisper. "Are there any Junkers left?"

The small scraps of homemade biscuit dough discards were rolled in cinnamon sugar, then baked. They were Annie's favorite and a bestseller at the bakery.

From behind the table I pulled a small white bag I had stashed earlier and handed it to Annie. "If you tell Ms. Tiny I sold these to you, I'll deny it."

Annie grinned and moved one finger over her lips in a zipping motion. "I won't say a word." Annie rifled through her oversize purse to pull out cash for the coffee and pastries. Behind her, laughter blended with the hum of our community and the rustling of paper bags. The farmers' market was a patchwork of bustling stalls and smiling faces. A happy bark echoed through the air, and I allowed the sunshine to warm my face while I waited.

After she paid, Annie paused. "No date today?"

I blinked at her, unsure of how to navigate the conversation. While I was relieved to no longer be paired with Stumpy Larson, the last few dates with Charles had been . . . underwhelming. Sure, he was cultured and charming and accommodating, but something was missing.

I was self-aware enough to know I came across as cold, but deep down I had been actually *hopeful* about the date auction. Turns out it was just another pitiful check mark in the disaster that was my dating life. Plus, at one time, Annie and Charles had been on a few dates.

I swallowed. "Um . . . I'm working the stall while Huck

and Cass enjoy the market. He's taking over in about ten minutes, and Charles is meeting me here."

Annie smiled with no hint of jealousy or judgment. "Nice. Have fun!"

Relief washed over me, and I offered a small smile. "Thanks. You too."

I watched her curls sway as she bounced away, and my eyes flicked to Duke, who was standing with his brother Lee at his booth. His gaze immediately fell, and I was interrupted by the next customer. I shook my head, not knowing what was worse—Annie's leftovers or secretly lusting after her surrogate older brother Duke.

He was broad and commanding behind his stall. Women flocked to him for the opportunity to flirt with the broody farmer, I had no doubt. Had I had a different last name, I might have done the same. Instead, I learned to school my features and fade into the background. Unlike my little sister, MJ, who flounced up to my table with sunbeams practically shooting out of her ass.

"Good morning!" she singsonged.

I smiled at my little sister and immediately began making her favorite coffee. MJ propped herself up on a stack of milk crates beside the booth. She scanned the crowd, and her eyes stopped. "How's your secret love affair going?"

My eyes sliced to hers. "Shh! Cut it out."

MJ giggled and swatted the air. "Whatever. You might say you're just friends, but there's no way that man can be friends with a woman." She gestured toward Duke, but I refused to give in to her. "Just look at him."

My face warmed as I shoved the paper cup into her hands. "I regret ever telling you."

She grinned, knowing it was actually true. "It wouldn't

be the worst thing, you know." She lifted a slim, hopeful shoulder.

"Are you kidding?" I struggled to keep my strained voice at a whisper as I smiled and worked my way through another customer's order. "It is the *definition* of the worst thing. What am I supposed to do, ride off into the sunset with Duke Sullivan? Come on. I'd be a pariah. The boys would never speak to me again. They would *kill* him."

MJ chewed her lip and sighed. "It would be weird, but they'd get over it eventually." She shrugged. "Probably."

I shot her a bland look, because even she knew it was a stretch of the imagination to think my brothers wouldn't hold on to a grudge, especially if a Sullivan was involved.

"Did you hear Royal duct-taped a harmonica to the underside of Duke's truck? I guess Duke took it to a mechanic to get it looked at with concerns of a 'whistling noise' when they found it." MJ snorted.

I clenched my jaw to keep from smiling. It was ridiculous to think I was *relieved* that things were going back to normal. The pranks were dumb and childish, but sometimes even I had to admit they were pretty funny. "I bet he was *pissed*."

MJ nodded. "No doubt, but at least things seemed to have settled back to harmless pranks. It's been weird lately, right?"

I nodded. My sister wasn't wrong. The Kings and Sullivans had always fought by way of pranking each other, but after the fight, things seemed to change for the worse. Even my brother JP had been more secretive than usual. I'd caught him in more than one hushed conversation with Dad. Plus, Kate Sullivan was acting a little strange at book club, and there were whispers she had uncovered something during the renovation of Tootie's farmhouse, but no one was really talking about it.

All around it really was *weird*.

Regardless, it all added up to anything between Duke and me being completely unrealistic.

A tiny ripple of sadness washed over me. I looked at MJ. "And what about Dad?"

MJ's smile faltered. When it came to Russell King, no one crossed him and survived it. Even precious little Mint Julep understood that. "Dad's not that bad. With you and him, things are just . . . complicated."

I scoffed. Complicated didn't even begin to describe the relationship between my father and me.

Duke and I weren't even supposed to be *friends*. I gritted my teeth to hold back the sting of tears and continued smiling at patrons who passed the booth.

When it was clear I wasn't going to talk about it anymore, MJ hopped off the crates and wrapped me in a hug. "Gotta run. Lunch tomorrow?"

I nodded, but then she looked over my shoulder and squeezed. "Incoming."

Following her gaze, I watched Charles walk up to the booth, lost in friendly conversation with Huck. His smile was easygoing and bright. I tried to search his face for *something*—any kind of *more than friends* feeling—but came up lacking.

He was just *so clean* and, god, I wanted to get dirty.

A low flutter erupted in my belly as my mind flickered to Duke's wide stance and deep scowl.

I sucked in a breath as Charles approached, and I plastered on a fake smile. Huck took over filling orders for customers, thanking me as I slipped out of my white apron and balled it up behind the table.

"You look lovely." Charles's eyes respectfully moved over me, never dipping too low.

"Thank you."

He held out his elbow. "Ready for the final date?"

A small flicker of relief hummed through me. Perhaps Charles had no intention of asking me out beyond the auction dates—*thank god*—and I wouldn't have to come up with an excuse to let him down gently.

I gave him a tight-lipped nod and slipped my hand into the crook of his elbow. Charles set a steady pace, and together we walked down the rows of the farmers' market. He was an expert at small talk, and though I tried, I couldn't find anything between us.

Not a single spark.

As we made our way up the opposite side, my shoulders stiffened when I realized he was headed straight for the Sullivan Farms booth. My heart stuttered.

As we approached, Duke's eyes zeroed in on Charles and, more specifically, my hand tucked into his elbow. Subtly, I dropped my hand from his arm and shifted the tiniest step away from Charles.

Duke's eyes were dark and penetrating, a stark contrast to the easygoing, friendly smile Charles wore. "Beautiful morning, isn't it?"

Duke's response was akin to a grunt as he held Charles in his stare. My heart wedged into my throat. It was rare I was ever this close to Duke, and my senses were on over-drive. Mixed with the warm, sweet smell of ripe blueberries was the unmistakable, masculine scent of *him*. Tiny hairs on my arms stood on end, and I averted my eyes, looking at the berries, jams, and jellies—literally *anywhere* but the intense face of my secret friend.

When I dared to look up, Duke's eyes flicked to mine

for a fraction of a second before looking out beyond the stall and into the crowd. His jaw was flexed, nostrils flared, shoulders pulled back tight. He was like a warrior, ready for battle. Heat tingled and pooled between my legs at the intensity radiating off him.

Seemingly unfazed, Charles let Duke's cold and dismissive attitude roll off his back. Once we'd finished our loop of the market, I thanked Charles for the small bouquet of flowers he had insisted on, and we parted ways.

On the drive back home, I couldn't get Duke out of my head. The harsh reality settled over me: in a small town, royalty was everything, and I was a King.

FIVE

SYLVIE

THE NEXT MORNING after my shift at work, I pulled into my driveway. For the past few years, I had lived with my aunt Bug in her opulent home. MJ lived there, too, and most days, it was nice to have someone to talk to, and the money I saved on rent was a bonus. I had budgeted and planned to move into my own apartment by spring. Not just move out but *away*. I'd already filled a Pinterest board with ideas—the southern charm of Savannah, Georgia, was calling my name. The only thing holding me back was savings. That I could tackle, and then I'd be gone.

Maybe then I would feel like my life had *finally* started. *Eventually*.

Nestled amid the lush greenery and picturesque surroundings, her home stood as a testament to my family's wealth and opulence. When I scanned the driveway, my heart sank. Instead of MJ's little red sports car, my father's luxury Porsche was taking up her space. I swallowed past the lump that formed in my throat. Reaching into my bag, I sent my sister a quick text.

I thought we were doing lunch today?

MJ

I'm sorry to bail on you. Red had a bad morning, so I decided to stay a little longer. Rain check?

Of course. See you when you get home.

You're the best. Just don't tell Dad, okay?

My heart squeezed, and I immediately thought of Duke. Growing up, Red Sullivan had seemed larger than life. Beloved in our community. He was also my father's rival. However, unlike my father, Red always wore a smile, and no one spoke an ill word of him. No one except my father, of course. As far as I could see, the two men didn't have a reason to be at odds. Dad hated him on principle and, for him, that was enough.

After losing his mother, the last thing Duke needed was to carry the burden of the family business while his father's health declined, but that was exactly what he did. I'd always assumed he *wanted* the burden, but as our unlikely friendship unfolded over the last eight months, I began to see the truth behind it. Duke stepped up to save the family farm, and it may not have ever been what *he* wanted.

I had started to put my car in reverse—I didn't have the energy to deal with my father today—when Aunt Bug stepped onto the front porch and waved.

Fuck.

I pulled off to the side and parked, holding my head high and shoulders back. The scent of blooming flowers filled the air, guiding me toward the immaculate front lawn.

"This is a surprise. I thought you were busy today." Bug opened her arms to me, and I stepped into her embrace. An adult woman living with her aunt may seem pathetic, but really, Bug's house was huge, and she always gave me space. Plus, knowing it was temporary helped me feel like less of a loser.

"MJ and I had lunch plans, but she got tied up at work."

My aunt held me at arm's length. "You look tired."

A humorless laugh escaped me. "Thanks."

Bug was a straight shooter and rarely sugarcoated anything, but deep down I knew she meant well.

My eyes shifted to my father's car, and she sighed. "Be nice."

Slow-building anger simmered beneath my skin. *Be nice? Me? How about he be nice for once?*

I nodded and followed Bug into the house. As I climbed the elegant steps, the smooth texture of the polished wooden handrail was a delightful contrast against my fingers. The grand oak door, adorned with intricate carvings, opened to reveal a pristine interior. Sunlight danced through the floor-to-ceiling windows, casting a golden glow over the tastefully arranged furniture. Every corner exuded a sense of sophistication, with delicate lighting hanging from the high ceilings, and thick drapes cascading gracefully down the windows. It was a far cry from how I would have decorated my own house, but for now, it was home.

As we entered, my father's eyes skated over me, and I offered a small smile. He didn't bother with a greeting, and I could feel my shoulders shrink into myself.

Not even worth a hello.

"Hot out there. Lemonade?" Bug squeezed my shoulder. She hadn't missed my father's cold welcome either.

I shook my head and swallowed. "No, thanks. I have lunch plans with Sloane and Layna. I was just stopping by to see if MJ wanted to join us."

Bug's eyes narrowed, but she let me get away with the tiny lie. "How is Sloane?"

My friend Sloane had recently moved back to Outta-towner after a messy divorce that left her with young twins and an ex-husband who was downright scary. To add insult to injury, she'd moved in with her grandfather and recently survived a house fire. Lee Sullivan had saved her son Ben when the boy panicked and hid in a closet.

"She's rattled but surviving."

A look of pride and affection softened Bug's features. "She's tough, that one."

As my father's only sibling, Aunt Bug had been a part of the King family dynasty for as long as I could remember. Until her retirement, she'd had a hand in nearly every one of the business deals my father and brothers made. She was whip-smart and levelheaded, whereas Dad often ruled with an iron fist. He was known for making quick, ruthless decisions. Bug was the only person he trusted, and it was a miracle she could ever get through to him, but somehow she did.

Uninterested in our polite conversation, my father took a call on his phone. I watched as his face turned red and the vein in his forehead bulged. As a kid, I had wanted to poke it and wondered what would happen if it finally burst. As an adult, I kept as much space between Russell King and me as I could.

"Finally got the Crane girl to leave." Dad interrupted the conversation between my aunt and me with a mocking laugh. An oily trickle of sweat slid down my back.

An unsettling feeling formed in the pit of my stomach. "Annie Crane?"

Annie had a small art studio downtown where she sold gorgeous pottery and adorable knickknacks to tourists.

Rumors flew that the business wasn't doing very well with more inexpensively priced tourist shops popping up around town.

"Out by the end of the month."

Bug stayed quiet but nodded. My eyes searched hers, but she revealed nothing. My father was a ruthless business-man, unafraid to have people hate him if it meant his bottom line increased.

Granddad would be ashamed.

My grandfather Amos King was the kindest, gentlest human I'd ever known. He was a simple man, a farmer who prided himself on working the land and contributing to his community. I tamped down the errant thought that Duke was so much like him—dedicated to his land and his community.

Granddad kept peppermints in his pocket, and I still thought of him every time I smelled even the tiniest hint of peppermint.

I missed him every day.

With Granddad, you didn't have to outperform your siblings. Your best was always enough. I recalled one day in seventh grade I presented my father with my report card. I had been proud of my hard work. All As, save for one B I had earned in a math class I had struggled in. Instead of praising my efforts—the long hours being tutored and staying up late at the kitchen table to study before a test—he looked at it and said, "Could have been an A" as he flipped the paper back at me.

I wished I could say I stopped trying to impress him after that.

I didn't.

The same small little girl who curled in on herself threatened to overtake me. Was it too much to seek approval and affection from your father? If your father was Russell King, it was.

Funnily enough, he adored his other children. JP was the spitting image of Dad and was set to take over the family businesses. He prided himself on finding and buying out struggling businesses to turn a profit, almost as much as Dad did. Whip had a job as a firefighter, which brought honor to the King name. MJ was a nurse and was continuing her education—on Dad's dime. Even Royal's tattoo shop was a source of pride for Dad's entrepreneurial spirit. Abel had his own struggles, but when he opened the brewery, our father saw it as a business opportunity and forgave him all his past sins.

I was the daughter who worked at a bakery and still lived with her aunt.

I also bore an uncanny resemblance to our mother. That alone condemned me to a life of snide remarks and general disdain. Maryann King had survived twenty years married to her husband before she could no longer bear the weight of it all. She packed her bags and left her children with a man who didn't have the capacity to love.

She had chosen her freedom over her husband. Over her children. I hated the small part of me that empathized with her decision.

Heaviness threatened to overtake me. There was no point in reasoning with my father or pleading with him to allow Annie to stay in the space she rented from him. He'd made his decision, and she would suffer the consequences.

"I have to go." I gritted my teeth against how small my voice sounded. The barely whispered words went unacknowledged, and I quietly left my aunt's house feeling smaller than I had in a long time.

As I left, I let my mind wander to thoughts of Duke.

The look on his face when he saw me walking with Charles had been dark and intense. Surely he knew there was nothing between Charles and me.

Right?

I wanted to text him, but he'd been unusually quiet and hadn't responded to my earlier *good morning* text. It was silly to think that one unanswered text meant anything, but I couldn't remember a time since we'd started texting that neither Duke nor I had had something funny or quippy to say to each other in the mornings.

It never failed to start my day off with a smile.

As I drove down a quiet country road, I sucked in a lungful of coastal air before pulling into a parking space that butted up to a sand dune cliff that overlooked Lake Michigan. I got out and leaned against the hood of my car and let the wind whip my hair as I closed my eyes and soaked up the sun. My phone sounded with an incoming text message, and I quickly dug through my purse to look at it. My pulse danced as I opened my messages.

It was from my friend Sloane, asking how my date with Charles had gone.

Meh.

SLOANE
Want to talk about it over coffee?

Make that mimosas and I'm there.

I've got orange juice!

I'll bring the booze.

Settling back into my car, I smiled down at my phone. I might have a shitty dad, but at least I had a few good friends. I was thrilled Sloane had moved back into town and couldn't wait to invite her to the Bluebirds.

On impulse, I tapped back to my most recent texts with Duke. *John Oates.* Every time the name flashed across my screen, the skittering of nerves made me want to giggle.

Giggle.

It was unreal.

I wondered what Duke was up to. It was a Sunday, and while most people were enjoying a day off or maybe watching sports or something, I imagined Duke walking through the rows of blueberry bushes on the farm. Maybe he was even begrudgingly getting ready for a family dinner at Ms. Tootie's house.

Family dinner was something Kings never did, and I wondered what it would be like to be in her warm, stately farmhouse, surrounded by Sullivans.

Totally fucking weird.

Despite the nerves tickling my tummy, I quickly typed out a new message to him.

> Busy day?

I stared down at the phone, waiting to see the three bubbles pop up. It was needy, sure, but I didn't care. Something was off, and I hated that my involvement with the date auction might be the cause.

But what was I supposed to do? It wasn't like Duke and I were dating. Not like we could *ever* date.

When a few minutes went by and there was still no reply, I sighed and tucked my phone back into my bag. Pulling out of the parking space, I headed toward town in search of champagne.

SIX

DUKE

With the month of August just around the corner, the days of dealing with the U-pick blueberry season were nearly coming to a close. The influx of tourists traipsing through the northern fields was winding down. As much as it was a hassle for people to be walking through the bushes, it was undeniable that one of the primary reasons people flocked to Remington County was the opportunity to pick their own berries.

After only a few short weeks, the bushes would be picked clean, and we would shift our focus to preparing the fields for what was predicted to be a grueling Michigan winter. On the remainder of the farm property, berries were being harvested to sell locally. Migrant workers picked alongside industrial farm equipment to ensure our customers received the best product possible. In an ideal world, yields were high and losses low.

As I crossed the path from one field to another, the grim look on Cisco's face as he approached me said I might not be so lucky. We met between two fields, and he held out his hand with a firm line on his lips.

"Boss." He nodded once. I had told him repeatedly to just call me Duke, but for whatever reason he still insisted on the formality.

"How are things looking?" I paused to pluck a ripe berry from a nearby bush and popped it into my mouth. The burst of sweetness washed over my tongue, and I hummed. This field was perfect and ready for harvest. It didn't matter that I preferred the slightly underripe tang of a blueberry at the beginning of this season. The end of July meant the best possible berries we had to offer our customers.

Cisco walked in step beside me. "Everyone's been working hard. Harvest is going well. No issues that anyone has brought to my attention."

I nodded, satisfied that the agricultural laborers I employed were not only getting the job done, but they were content. Cisco updated me on the progress of each field, which contained workers handpicking berries as we walked toward my home and the main entrance to the farm.

Cisco took his job seriously. He had a strong work ethic and was a good manager. He took care of his people, and he had high standards. He was also a no-bullshit kind of man.

I liked that too.

As we got closer to the long path that led to the entrance to Sullivan Farms, the squeal of school bus brakes drew our attention. Beyond the small berm that acted as a wind barrier, the top of a yellow school bus stopped at the entryway and held my attention.

As a part of the Michigan Migrant Education Program, any children of migrant workers were entitled to attend school year-round. The bus, which the farm happily funded, picked the children up every morning and brought them to the local school, where they received an education. Despite the fact that bare minimum was required by law, I prided myself in our approach. We took care of our own here.

Laughter filled the air as a group of children ran up the drive. Various ages—from kids barely out of kindergarten to those pushing high school—raced up the driveway. The littlest ones had eager waves, and I held my hand up in greeting.

Rather than continuing down the path and turning right toward my home, the group went left toward the area of land where I supplied housing for any family that worked on Sullivan Farms. The rows upon rows of double-wide trailers were nothing fancy, but they were clean and safe homes for the people who dedicated their days to harvesting blueberries for me. It was a benefit of working at Sullivan Farms that drew many of the same families season after season. I liked getting to know the families as they lived and grew on my farm.

One little boy, Nicolas, broke from the group and came barreling toward me. His face split into a wide grin, and he waved one arm wildly. Cisco and I laughed as his backpack bounced behind him, nearly half the size of the young boy himself.

His enthusiastic rapid-fire stream of Spanish poked a hole right in my chest. Nico was damn cute.

I crouched to listen as he relayed the events of his day at school. I nodded and responded in Spanish, telling him how happy I was that he had had a good day. I wasn't sure exactly when I had become fluent, but it was important to me to be able to communicate with the people who worked for me. If they were living and working on my farm, it seemed like the bare minimum for me to be able to speak with them freely and in a way that made them more comfortable.

Over time the giggles and chuckles at my misspeaking became less and less frequent until finally I was fluent.

In school, the kids were also learning English, and Nico was excited to share with me a few new words he had learned. "Blueberry. Character. Setting. Mr. Duke."

Mr. Duke.

The way my name rolled off his tongue and the evident pride sparkling in his eyes shifted something inside me. I ruffled his hair and squeezed his shoulders with a grin. *"Perfecto."*

I stood and pointed in the direction of his waiting mother, then waved to her. She smiled and waved back as Nico bounded off in her direction.

Cisco scrubbed a hand behind his neck.

I sighed, sensing he was dodging an uncomfortable conversation. "Just say it already."

"There's another family. Benny's brother-in-law. They're hoping there might be space to work at Sullivan Farms."

I listened despite the tension that crept its way into my jaw.

"He and his wife have three children, but their oldest boy is thirteen. Benny said he's willing to have him work the fields."

I shook my head. "No. Absolutely not." Cisco's expression faltered, and he went to speak before I held up a hand to stop him from interrupting me. "He's a kid. He needs to be in school."

I quickly calculated the mounting cost of adding an additional family to the number of people already housed at Sullivan Farms. It would mean adding an additional trailer.

Transportation. A discussion with the school for the children.

I looked at Cisco. "When were they hoping to start?"

"As soon as possible, *jefe*."

I pressed my lips together and nodded. "We'll figure it out. It will take some time to get another trailer set up, but if they can stay with another family in the meantime, I'll work out the details."

Cisco held out his hand and breathed a sigh of relief. "Thank you, sir."

I shook my head as I gripped his hand. "Just Duke."

He laughed and patted my shoulder. We both knew he wouldn't be calling me Duke anytime soon.

ALONE IN MY LIVING ROOM, I stared down into the deep amber bourbon as I swirled my glass. I pulled my black reading glasses off and pinched the bridge of my nose. Once I realized I had read, and reread, the same page of my book twice, I was giving up.

Ed lifted his head and rested his jowls on my knee, peering up at me with sad hound dog eyes. He let out a small whimper as his butt started to wiggle.

"You want to go check on him, don't you?"

The butt wiggles got faster as Ed let out a small yip of excitement.

I sighed, gripping the sides of my armchair and pushing myself to stand. "Let's get it over with then."

Ed danced in happy circles as I made my way to the front door and out into the open evening air.

To the west the sun was setting over the blueberry fields, silhouetting them with a riot of oranges, hot pinks, and streaks of white. If old farmers' superstitions were to be believed, the colors alone told me tomorrow would be another scorcher.

With Ed at my side, I walked down the steps of my porch, across the wide drive, and toward the red barn in the distance.

As I pushed through the door, two rogue barn cats scattered as I flipped on the light. Happy little quacks greeted me as I approached the makeshift pen. I peered down at the little duckling as Ed sniffed cautiously at the side of the enclosure. The duck was still scrawny, his downy feathers slowly being replaced with coarser adult ones. He looked like a gangly teen deep into the stages of puberty.

I hadn't known what to do with the thing, and it didn't feel right to leave it to fend for itself, so I created a makeshift pen that opened on one side to an enclosed area next to the barn. He wasn't very brave so he rarely ventured more than a few feet past the opening. Every night as I made my final rounds around the farm, the little duck quacked happily at my feet and followed me into the barn, where I closed him in for the night.

Ed had formed some kind of maternal bond with the duck and was constantly checking up on him during the day. It was a cute kind of friendship—one you might see on the farm calendars people loved to buy in the shops downtown.

"Hey, Duck."

He quacked back at my voice. I looked down at Ed, who continued to sniff at the enclosure and whine.

"I told you, he's fine."

I reached toward a shelf to grab a handful of blueberries and plunked them into Duck's water dish. The berries floated on top of the water, and Duck greedily gobbled them up as he flapped his wings in delight.

A smirk pulled at my lips. I slipped my phone from my pocket and impulsively snapped a picture. He was kind of ugly, but pretty damn cute.

With my phone in my hand, I opened the text messages from Sylvie. It had been two weeks since I saw her at the farmers' market. She had been so stunning it was like a punch to the gut. The way her caramel eyes played off the bright blues of the July sky was intoxicating. It had taken every ounce of willpower I had not to get lost in them in the middle of the crowded market.

It also didn't help that she was there with *him*.

Sylvie hadn't made it seem like she was very interested in Charles, but the harsh reality of seeing her hand tucked into the nook of his elbow didn't sit right with me. It was a harsh reality that I had watched each of my siblings find their soulmate, and I was left with nothing. Well, not nothing—an overwhelming knowing that *my someone* was an impossibility. I could only watch from a distance as another man walked with her hand on his arm. Charles didn't see that Sylvie was more than the woman who tried to hide in the background. She was funny and kind and incredible. He had no fucking clue—of that I was confident.

Eventually our conversations went back to the easy camaraderie they had been before, but something inside of me had shifted.

My feelings had gone from affection and secret longing to something deeper.

Hungrier.

Possessive.

I had imagined pulling her body to mine in the middle of the goddamn day at the farmers' market and setting the record straight. Though I had no claim over Sylvie, it didn't make seeing her with another man any easier. She was the worst person I could ever want, but I was consumed by her.

I wasn't mad at her. My feelings were mine alone, and it wasn't her fault that I was having trouble controlling them. To cope with my torturous, frustrated emotions, I threw myself even deeper into work, micromanaging every aspect of the July U-pick berry season until I thought Cisco was going to lose his mind.

As if merely thinking of her conjured her into existence, a new text from Sylvie lit up my screen.

DARYL HALL

> Do you think drinking on the job is a fireable offense?

>> I would think so.

> Damn.

>> Rough day?

> Kind of. Just a thousand tiny annoyances, I guess.

>> Want to talk about it?

> Not really. I'd rather hear about your day. What's going on around the farm?

It had become easy to shoulder the weight of being the sole decision-maker at Sullivan Farms. But there was something about Sylvie that changed me. I *wanted* to let her in. My fingers twitched with hesitation, but I finally decided to share a piece of myself with her I had been holding back.

> Things should be slowing down in the next few weeks, but I also got word that a new family will be working with us.

DARYL HALL

I'm not really sure how all of that works. Is that a good thing?

I considered.

> I think so. It's good for them. Good for the kids. I should be able to help them get enrolled and started in a few of the Head Start classes before the school year officially begins.

Sounds like you like having them around. Who knew that grouchy old Duke Sullivan was really a softie? Don't worry, your secret is safe with me.

I smiled down at my phone, something I caught myself doing more and more and usually only when I was texting her or thinking about her, or getting a glimpse of her walking down the street.

I scrubbed a hand over my face. *Jesus. Wyatt was right. I am so fucked.*

> I'm not a softie. I just think some of our kids are pretty cute.

Our kids?

Shit.

> I mean the kids that live here on the farm. Not like *our* kids.

Immediately an image of a gaggle of children with my

mother's smile and Sylvie's honey-flecked eyes and blonde hair flooded my brain. Maybe they'd love life like my brother Lee or be determined and headstrong like Kate, or have natural leadership ability like Wyatt. Maybe one would even want to follow in my footsteps one day, and I could teach our son or daughter all about what it means to be a responsible farmer and to take care of the people who worked for you.

The sound of an incoming text pulled me from my irrational spiraling thoughts.

> **DARYL HALL**
>
> Have you ever thought about having your own kids?

I stared down at her question before typing back the most honest answer I could muster.

> Kids aren't in the cards for me.

I let out a frustrated breath. I didn't want to think about that and put myself in a shittier mood. Texting with Sylvie always felt good. It was the best part of my day, and I didn't want to ruin that by killing the mood and being mopey on her.

I pulled up the picture of Duck and sent it to her.

> But it looks like I am the proud father of a new duckling.

> Oh my god, he is the cutest. What's his name?

> Duck.

> You named the duck Duck?

Yeah. At first I didn't want to give him a name because I didn't want to get too attached. In case he was sick or something happened to him. He is a wild duck after all. I fully expect him to fly away when he's strong enough.

I hate to break it to you, but I think you might already be attached.

I smirked again.

Yeah, I think you're right.

Trouble was, I didn't know if I was talking about the fuzzy duck in the barn or her. I shook my head. It was finally time I admitted to myself I might be harboring a crush on Sylvie King.

And she was the one woman I could never have.

SEVEN

"CAN I DRIVE THE SIDE-BY-SIDE?" My little niece looked at me with hopeful eyes.

I shrugged and answered "Sure" at the exact moment Wyatt ground out a harsh "No."

Penny looked at her dad with an exaggerated pout, and he lifted his eyebrows, deepening the tiny scowl that had already formed on her cute face.

Not wanting to overstep, I backtracked. "How about this? I'll drive you around in the side-by-side, and we'll even go to the west pasture over some of the bunny hills."

Penny's eyes went wide with excitement. That kid had been born with a thirst for adventure and was turning out to be a bit of an adrenaline junkie. I was certain she was the cause for a few of the gray hairs sprouting at my younger brother's temples.

"Can we go fast?"

Beside me, Wyatt sighed, and I shot Penny a conspiratorial wink. "I've got something to show you in the barn first."

Without waiting for us, Penny took off like a shot,

running toward the barn with Three-Legged Ed at her heels.

Wyatt sighed again. "That kid's going to be the death of me."

I watched the ground as we walked. "Ah, she's all right. She just has an adventurous spirit."

"She's fearless." He shook his head and watched her enter the barn.

I smiled. "Reminds me a lot of Mom."

Wyatt dragged a hand through his hair. "Right? Sometimes the similarities are downright eerie."

We let the painful subject of our mother hang in the air between us. Wyatt looked out onto the fields. "Do you ever get lonely out here all by yourself?" I glanced over at my brother but didn't answer. "Ah, who am I kidding? You've always been solitary. Duke Sullivan needs nothing and no one."

A low grumble was my only response. I wasn't sure if that had always been true or if over time I'd been hardened to become like that. Either way, it was what it was.

As we approached the barn, Penny's small figure filled the doorway. Her arms pressed against the entryway. "Shut the front door!"

Wyatt tipped his head to his daughter, knowing full well it was pure luck a swear hadn't come flying out of her tiny mouth. She moved forward, grabbing one of her dad's hands in both of hers, dragging him through the entrance of the barn. Her eyes danced with excitement.

Joy rippled off her as she pulled her dad forward. "Daddy, you won't believe it. It is the cutest thing I've ever seen!"

I tucked my hands into my pockets and followed the

duo into the barn, where Duck was making an absolute mess of his water.

Wyatt squatted beside Penny. "Hey, you're pretty cute."

Penny looked at me with wide, hopeful eyes. "Can I go inside, Uncle Duke?"

"Yep." I hoisted her under her arms and lifted her over the small fence into the pen. "He seems pretty friendly, but a little scared of the farm equipment."

"Aww . . ." Penny clucked her tongue. She gently stroked his head, and Duck leaned into her. "Look at him. He's so cute. Can we keep him?"

Wyatt laughed and shook his head. "Sorry, Pickle. He doesn't belong to us."

Undeterred, she looked back at the duckling. "Come on. Come on, little duck."

Penny moved through the end of the enclosure toward the opening that led to outside, flapping her wings in hopes Duck would follow her. Sure as shit that cute little bastard started quacking happily and following behind Penny.

Wyatt stood and laughed. "Well, you're gonna have a hard time getting rid of her now."

I rocked back on my heels. "I think she's all right. It's nice having someone around."

Wyatt shot me a sidelong glance. "Oh? Maybe the impenetrable Duke does get a little bit lonely."

I nudged his arm with my elbow. "Shut the fuck up."

Wyatt laughed. "I like this side of you." He leaned against a support beam and looked me over. "You know, it's good to be back. So Penny can have all of this."

I grumbled and looked over my younger brother. "I think Lark is rubbing off on you."

Wyatt laughed and shook his head. "Yeah, I think you're probably right."

"You going to be able to hold down that job of yours, or are they going to be transferring you somewhere else?"

Wyatt crossed his arms. I knew that determined look in his eye. "This season is shaping up to be a good one. I'm not planning on going anywhere."

I liked that. I liked it a lot.

"Kids are back on campus this week, so my schedule gets busier, but with Penny starting school soon, it'll be good to get her into a routine. My kid is smart as hell, but man does she love to stir up trouble."

I laughed as I watched Penny lift Duck in her arms, climb over the outside gate, and hoist herself onto the driver side of my side-by-side. With Duck still nestled in the nook of her arm, she flashed me a wicked grin.

"Yeah." I clamped my hand on Wyatt's shoulder. "Yeah, she does."

I strolled toward the side-by-side and held my arms out for the duckling. After handing Duck off to Wyatt, I scooched Penny over to the passenger side for a joyride.

Once we were out from under her father's watchful eye, I pulled down a row of blueberry bushes and got out. "Scoot over."

Her eyes went wide in disbelief. Out of the back, I pulled out a pint-size helmet and plunked it on her head. Penny gripped the steering wheel in anticipation as I buckled the strap beneath her chin. Her little body was itching to go.

I looked her in the eye. "We'll start off slow and easy."

She nodded. I climbed into the passenger seat and gave her a brief lesson on how to drive the side-by-side.

After making sure she was securely buckled, I settled into the passenger seat. "All right, easy does it. Ease into the gas pedal."

Without warning, the side-by-side lurched forward as Penny let out a tiny battle cry. My own laughter exploded from my chest as I gripped the frame and used my left hand to help her steer down the path. Once she regulated her speed, we cruised and bounced through the fields toward the west pasture. Before coming to the small bumps of sand, Penny looked at me with anxious eyes.

I lifted a shoulder. "Up to you."

The little daredevil gripped the wheel tighter. "Abso-freaking-lutely."

She bounced over the tiny bunny hills with ease, giggling and jostling as we made a loop around to do it again.

Once she finished her third lap, her tiny fist shot in the air. "Hell yeah!" Immediately she looked guilty and bit down on her lower lip. "Don't tell Dad."

I shook my head, a serious expression overtaking my face. "You shouldn't keep secrets from your dad. He's a good guy, and he'll understand. We just had a little fun, and we made sure that you were safe. If he gets upset about it, he can be upset at me, but no secrets. Okay?"

Her lashes lowered before her trusting eyes flashed to mine. "Okay, Uncle Duke. No secrets."

I winked at her. "All right, let's get this rig back home."

As I HAD SUSPECTED, Wyatt wasn't all that pissed—or surprised—that I had let Penny drive the side-by-side. She explained all the safety precautions we had taken, and Wyatt pulled her into a hug and said, "I'm just glad you didn't hide it from me."

A sense of pride washed over me when she beamed her gap-toothed grin at me.

Still riding high from my visit with Penny and Wyatt, my normal farm chores went by without a hitch. When I got a call from Huck asking if I had an extra ten pounds of berries, I knew my day was about to get even better.

Despite his offer to send someone to pick them up, I insisted on delivering the berries myself. I wasn't about to miss an opportunity to sneak a glance at Sylvie. More and more I'd found excuses to stop by the Sugar Bowl. It was playing with fire, and I couldn't seem to care.

I cleaned up and even ran a comb through my hair before pulling on a navy T-shirt, jeans, and boots.

At the back entrance, I typed in the security code to the Sugar Bowl and pulled open the door. I was immediately greeted with the warm smells of pastry and fried doughnuts. My stomach growled, and I realized I hadn't remembered to eat that morning. I adjusted the crate of berries on my hip as I let the steel door click behind me.

Moments later Sylvie walked through the saloon-style doors to the kitchen. "Oh. Hi. I heard the bell and thought I'd see who came in."

Sylvie wore jeans, cropped at the ankle and tight through her hip and thighs. My eyes moved upward, taking in the nip of her waist and the apron tied around it. Her blue Sugar Bowl T-shirt clung to her ribs, giving me the perfect outline of her chest. When I reached her face, I noticed a smattering of tiny freckles that danced across the bridge of her nose.

Her pale blonde hair was piled on top of her head in a messy bun. A few strands had slipped loose, and had I not been holding a crate of berries, it would have been damn hard to resist the urge to tuck one of those strands behind her ear.

Her light-brown eyes were wide as she took me in. I was about to offer her some quippy line or flirty banter but instead settled on telling her how gorgeous she looked.

"You are—" I halted when Huck walked in behind her. Instead of finishing, I cleared my throat and raised the crate slightly. "Anywhere in particular you want me to put these?"

Huck moved around Sylvie—she was still rooted to the spot. "That was quick. Thanks for bringing them by. Over here on the prep table is perfect."

I didn't answer but nodded and moved toward the steel table in the center of the room. Instead of giving her a wide berth, I eased myself between Sylvie and the table, letting my forearm brush against hers.

Her pull was magnetic.

It was the first time we'd ever made contact, and electricity shot through my arm and across my chest. Her skin was warm and soft—exactly how I had imagined it would be.

At the contact, Sylvie cleared her throat and moved away, and I immediately missed the feel of her skin on mine. Her eyes scanned my face, bouncing from left to right before dipping down to my mouth and shooting back up to my eyes again.

I fought and lost against the smirk that tugged at the side of my mouth. My heart thumped harder.

"What do I owe you for the rush delivery?" Huck asked.

My attention never left Sylvie's face, but I raised a hand. "No rush fee. I'll just add the cost of the berries to your tab."

I shook Huck's hand, finally breaking my gaze and turned toward the door.

"Thank you." Sylvie's voice was high and tight.

I turned and looked at her over my shoulder. "See you around." With the heat of her stare still on my back, I walked through the exit, hoping the cool coastal air would help me catch my breath.

EIGHT

It was rare I ever came face-to-face with Duke. Sure, he occasionally made deliveries at the Sugar Bowl, but typically I steered clear of him. I had the worst poker face, and I didn't trust myself not to turn into a puddle of giggling goo around him. When I found myself alone in the kitchen, his muscular body taking up a whole lot of space, it was hard to breathe. I'd imagined what it might be like to finally have a real, in-person conversation now that we'd been texting for so long.

Stuck to the ground, staring at him was *not* how I envisioned it.

Duke was all man. His eyes were so dark—and the area where the irises melted into the blackness of his pupils was a much deeper shade of brown than I'd realized. His hair was thick, and stubble dotted his square jawline. His navy T-shirt stretched across his chest and tapered down to a well-worn pair of jeans. Duke did *rugged* in a way that was impossibly sexy.

It was a miracle I could make it through the rest of the day. My brain was in a fog as I went through the motions and found myself daydreaming about Duke Sullivan. Twice Huck asked me if I was feeling okay, and hot embarrassment stained my cheeks.

After my shift I pushed all thoughts of my impossibly hot, impossibly forbidden friend out of my mind. I was lying in bed that night, wondering what Duke had thought of our bizarre interaction, when the ping of my phone startled me. I knew it was him before I even flipped over my phone.

> **JOHN OATES**
>
> Didn't mean to blindside you at work today.

So he *had* noticed my wide-eyed, mouth-breathing impersonation of a fish.

Awesome.

> It was fine. Just caught off guard a little. It was silly.

> I can wear a bell next time, if that helps.

In my bed, I giggled at the thought of Duke wearing a tiny bell around his neck like a cat.

> Please do. Thanks.

> Yes, ma'am.

I swallowed hard. I liked this side of Duke—a fun and playful side that felt so different from his typically stoic persona. Maybe it was a part of him he reserved just for me. I bit back a smile at the thought that *any* part of Duke was mine.

> Sneak around startling any other strange
> women today?

Duke didn't respond right away. It wasn't uncommon for either of us to be interrupted. More times than I could count I'd had to quickly exit the conversation and hide my phone before someone started asking questions. Usually we just picked up our chat later or the next day, and it never seemed like a big deal.

I jumped when my phone vibrated with an incoming call.

John Oates calling . . .

I stared at the name. My hands trembled as I fumbled to answer.

"Um, hello?" My voice was soft, as if I could get into trouble by talking with him, even though I was alone in my room.

"Hey." Duke's voice was liquid over gravel—warm and low. A tingle ran down my spine. "Figured this is easier. I hope it's okay."

I stared at my bedroom door, wondering how good the insulation was in that house and whether my sister or aunt would be able to hear me. I gently cleared my throat. "Great. Yeah. Totally fine."

Get your shit together, Syl.

He chuckled and I squeezed my eyes closed.

I took a breath. "Where are you right now?" I gritted my teeth. My voice was breathy and definitely sounded a whole lot more like I had asked *What are you wearing right now?*

"Just got back from Haven Pines. Taking a few minutes before I get back to a few chores." I could almost picture him leaning against a fence on his blueberry farm, the warm sun illuminating his rugged features.

"How is your dad?"

He was quiet, as though he wasn't sure exactly how to answer. "Good as he can be, I guess. He's tough. We're getting through."

It was clear Duke held a lot of love and respect for his father—a feeling I wished I could muster for my own. "MJ has always spoken so highly of him."

"Yeah, she's all right." There was humor in his voice, and I warmed at the thought that maybe Duke didn't despise my *entire* family.

"Oh, one of the Kings you can stand?" I teased.

He let out a low grumble, sending butterflies fluttering in my stomach. "Well, she's in the top two at least."

Did that mean—was I his number one?

It was a strange and wonderful thing to feel seen and important—especially by a man who you were expected to hate simply because your family told you to. There would always be old, bad blood between the Kings and Sullivans, and the mutual dislike ran deep.

"How was the rest of your day?"

I smiled, warmth spreading through my cheeks as I rolled to my back and sprawled across the comforter. "After my shift I went for a walk on the beach. Bootsy was selling shell bracelets, so I got one."

"You know that's just trash he finds and resells, right?"

I smiled. "Eh, that's okay. It was pretty trash."

He hummed but didn't offer any judgment or criticism for helping out one of Outtatowner's residents. Bootsy was always around. He was eccentric and needed some extra care, something that the people of Outtatowner were happy to provide. Sometimes I thought it was the one thing everyone in town could actually agree on. On occasion I even saw my father speaking with Bootsy and giving him money. It was one of the only things that made me think my father may still own a heart.

I stared at my ceiling, feeling like a teenager with her first crush. "After that I worked out, had dinner. I'm boring."

"You aren't boring. You're . . . special, Sylvie." He was quiet, and I was too stunned to speak. "Don't let anyone make you think otherwise."

His words touched me deeply, and for a moment I forgot about the animosity between our families. With Duke, I felt seen and appreciated in a way I never had before. It was both exhilarating and terrifying to have someone like him in my life.

Even if he was a secret.

Over the past eight months, with each flirtatious remark exchanged, the tension between us grew, and it felt like we were dancing on the edge of something exotic and dangerous.

Unsure of what to say, I stumbled with a response.

Before I could find one, Duke cut in. "I've got to finish up a few things around here. Can I call you again sometime?"

I toyed with my lip and tried to keep my voice light despite the awareness that prickled along my skin whenever I thought about him. "I'd like that. Maybe text to be sure it's a good time to talk, though . . ."

Duke was quiet on the other end, and a small sliver of panic poked beneath my ribs.

"Of course. Good night, Sylvie."

"'Night, Duke."

I stared at my phone after the call ended and focused on breathing. The giddy zip of excitement danced through my chest, and I held on to the feeling, ignoring the sadness that nestled next to it. Talking with him was a guilty pleasure. If anyone found out, I would have a *lot* of angry people to answer to.

But there was no denying I had a big ol' crush on Duke, and I definitely wasn't supposed to.

NINE

SYLVIE

THE MORNING SUN glowed behind the treetops as I hefted a garbage bag and pushed through the metal back door of the Sugar Bowl. The air was cool, and a bright moon still hung in the inky sky, casting an eerie glow over the quiet streets. Clutching the heavy bag, I navigated my way toward the dumpster tucked behind the coffee shop, hidden in the predawn shadows. The scent of coffee already clung to my skin, a nagging reminder of the long day ahead of me.

Just as I reached the dumpster, a rustling sound nearby sent my heart racing. It could have been a raccoon, or maybe just a gust of wind, but my imagination got the best of me. The hairs on the back of my neck stood on end as I listened.

Please be a raccoon and not a serial killer. I do not have time for this today.

The soft rustling sounded again as a rat with its disgusting ropelike tail scurried across my shoe. I dropped the trash, and a scream tore from my throat, echoing into the alley.

My heart pounded like a drum, and my body shivered

with a disgusted rattle as I shook my hands and stomped my feet. My mind screamed *run*, but I was rooted in place.

From the depths of the darkness, a deep voice called out, low and concerned. "Sylvie."

I knew that voice.

Duke.

Within moments his tall, muscular frame loomed over me, and the intensity in his dark eyes caught my breath. *Where the hell did he come from?*

"Sylvie!" His voice was rough, urgent, and his hands reached out to my shoulders to steady me. "Are you all right?"

"I—yeah," I stammered, still trembling from the adrenaline rush as I looked around. "There was a rat." I shivered again. "Oh god, I hate those things!"

Duke didn't let go of me, his grip on my upper arms surprisingly gentle.

"I'm being ridiculous," I muttered to myself, trying to calm my racing heart as his wide palms began to smooth over my shoulders.

"You are not ridiculous," he murmured. Duke's gaze locked onto mine, his breath warm against my skin. His voice was filled with intensity, and his eyes moved over my face, pausing on my lips. The dim light of the moon illuminated the hard angles of his jaw, making him look even more irresistible.

I couldn't tear my gaze away from him, the charged tension between us palpable. I could feel his breath on my skin, warm and inviting. My body responded, betraying me in a way I hadn't expected as I melted into him.

I tried to compose myself, to shake off the fear that still clung to me like a stubborn shadow. But then, without warning, he closed the distance between us, his lips crashing against mine in a searing kiss. It was fierce and passionate. Heat unfurled in my belly. Our bodies pressed together, and I could feel the undeniable desire that coursed through him.

My spine turned to liquid as his tongue teased my lips and I opened for him, sighing into the kiss. His arms banded around me, holding me upright as his mouth moved over mine. His tongue was warm and commanding, giving as much as he took. I stretched to my tiptoes and wound my arms around his neck. Duke's palms flattened against my back, pressing my chest into his. His heart hammered against me.

The kiss was fierce, *hungry*—as if all the longing and desire we had suppressed for so long had finally found release. My hands tangled in his hair, pulling him closer, and his arms wrapped around me, holding me tight against his powerful chest.

My legs tangled with his as heat built between my thighs. One hand slid through my hair and my head tipped back, allowing him access to every part of me.

"Duke . . ." I barely recognized the breathlessness of my own voice. Then the metal clank of a door had us jumping apart.

Duke pulled away, his chest heaving, just as the back door to the Sugar Bowl opened. Huck filled the doorway, concern knitting his brows downward. "You okay, Syl? I thought I heard something."

I swallowed hard. "There was a rat. I screamed." I clamped down a nervous chuckle.

Huck's eyes flicked between Duke and me.

"I heard it too," Duke finally said. "Everything seems to be fine now." He cleared his throat. "I've got your delivery. I'll head in."

Without looking at me, Duke stomped toward the delivery truck. Huck stood by the door, holding it open. His lips were flat as he looked between us again.

Fuck. Did Huck suspect anything? Did he see us?

I flicked a strand of hair from my eyes and reached down for the trash bag. With a grunt, I tossed it into the dumpster and smoothed my sweating palms down my apron.

Holding my head high, I willed my pulse to calm the fuck down as I walked through the door, praying I could forget all about the most incredible kiss I'd ever experienced.

TEN

DUKE

I WAS FUCKED.

Honestly, there was no other way to describe how I was feeling about Sylvie King. I had known it even before I kissed her, but feeling her in my arms, the way her body went pliant and wrapped around mine, I was a goner.

Over the past two weeks, early-morning texts had turned into stolen moments of laughter over the phone. As our conversations continued, playful banter morphed into a genuine exchange of thoughts and feelings.

More than once, I almost broke down and told her the truth. Twice I'd had the text message typed and ready to send, but chickened out.

I wish I could have you. I wish you were mine. In reality, I have wanted you for years and I hate that I can't have you. I thought that taking care of my dad and giving up every-thing was the hardest thing that I have ever had to do, but the truth is that wanting you is by far the single hardest thing I have ever had to do.

Instead, I pretended like the world didn't stop every

time she texted or called. The more we talked, the more I realized how much we had in common despite our families' differences. We laughed, we shared stories, and in those secret moments, the world outside faded away, leaving just Sylvie and me.

But even as the connection between us grew, there was an unspoken understanding that we couldn't let it go any further. The consequences of our secret friendship being discovered would be too great. So we danced on the edge, savoring the forbidden thrill of our late-night conversations, all the while ignoring the fact that this delicate balance couldn't last forever.

By mid-August, the realization that Sylvie could never be anything other than a secret had pissed me right the fuck off. I was a fool to think one stolen kiss would ever be enough.

As a distraction, I had roped Lee into helping me mend a few wobbly fences, but even he got tired of my piss-poor attitude. I barked orders at him and ignored his suggestions. Grueling farmwork was something I understood. Something I was good at. Something I could control.

I used a mallet to drive the fence post deeper into the soil as Lee held the base steady. The rhythmic pounding sent angry vibrations up my arm, and I swung harder.

"Seriously, dude. Who pissed in your Cheerios?"

My jaw clenched and I ignored the jab.

"Grab the next one. Hurry up."

Lee was fit but breathless from my unrelenting pace. He lifted his shirt to wipe the sweat from his face, and I glared at him.

I pointed with the mallet. "I said grab it. Let's go."

My little brother shook his head at me. "You know

what?" Lee pulled his gloves off one at a time before tossing them at my feet. "Fix it yourself, asshole."

He stomped away in angry strides, but I didn't stop him. The heavy mallet hung limply at my side as the August cicadas buzzed in the humid air.

Shit.

I knew Lee was giving up part of his weekend to help me out, and he was right—I *was* being an asshole.

Frustrated with myself, I worked solo for another punishing hour, pushing myself and letting the unrelenting self-loathing thoughts wash over me. When I finally reached the last post that needed mending, I hung my arms across the fence in defeat.

Looking out onto my fields, I reminded myself why I was doing this. Carrying on the family farm *meant* something. No one else was going to do it, and nobody loved it like I did. I couldn't expect them to see what I saw or feel what I felt when I walked the rows each morning.

I glanced at the afternoon sun, wrung out.

Tension still radiated through me, and I knew I needed a break, to put some distance between work and myself before I lost my mind or damaged any more of my remaining relationships.

Once I'd decided what I wanted to do, the overwhelming urge to ask Sylvie to come along nagged me. My fingers itched with hesitation, but I typed out a quick message.

> Cat fact 215: Cats bring you dead animals because they think you're a crappy cat who can't survive on your own.

It was another ridiculous code Sylvie had come up with.

Cat facts became our way of asking if it was a good time to talk on the phone. When my phone vibrated with the incoming call, I immediately answered.

"Hey." She sounded breathless, and desire surged straight through me.

"Are you busy today?" I had to get the question out before I lost my nerve.

"Um . . . no?" She was panting.

"Are you okay?"

Her laughter rang out over the line. "Yes, sorry. I hustled outside and got myself all winded."

A small laugh escaped my nose. She was damn cute.

I flexed my hand to release my nerves. "Can you meet me at Van Buren State Park? There's something I want to show you."

Silence hung in the air. I could practically hear her thinking over the phone. We had never intentionally met. It felt like taking a leap from an airplane without a parachute.

"Now?"

I looked at my watch. "Thinking so."

"Um, yeah. Sure."

My heartbeat ticked higher. "Perfect. Bring a swimsuit."

I hung up the phone before she could ask too many questions, and I climbed into my side-by-side. I tore through the fields toward my house.

Today was going to change everything.

VAN BUREN STATE Park was a secluded, hidden gem on the shores of Lake Michigan. Not attached to any of the local tourist towns, the park's beach was a quiet reprieve during the bustling tourist season.

Standing with my back to the water, I waited.

Then, through a clearing in the trees, I watched her walk down the gravel path from the parking lot and come into view.

With her hand shielding her eyes from the afternoon sun, she scanned the beachfront. My heart rolled in my chest, and my gut clenched.

She was stunning.

The mid-August sun bounced off her blonde hair, creating a halo and framing her face. Though they were in shadow, I knew her warm caramel eyes were sharp and assessing as she looked down the sandy beach.

When those eyes landed on me, her face split into a grin, and I had to swallow. Sylvie's hand moved into a tentative wave, and I lifted my own in greeting. I watched her as she slipped off her flip-flops and held them in one hand to navigate through the sand. Her long legs were bare, and I traveled the length of them, stopping at a small pair of bike shorts. A loose-fitting tank top only hinted at the bikini top she wore beneath it.

My gut clenched in anticipation of seeing Sylvie in nothing but a bathing suit.

She stopped in front of me, tipping her face up to meet my eyes. "Hi."

She sounded as nervous as I felt.

"Hey." We stood for a fraction of a second, staring at each other. I fought the urge to touch her—reach over and pull her into a hug. I stuffed my hands in my pockets instead.

Finally her eyes flicked down to the paddleboard at my feet and whipped back up in my direction. "Seriously?"

I suppressed a smile. "Have you ever tried it?"

I watched the muscles work in her neck as she swallowed and shook her head.

"If you want to give it a try, I'll help you. It's a lot of fun and a great workout."

Sylvie exhaled as she scanned the beach. I knew she was being careful, looking around to see if there was anyone who might rat us out for meeting. Being a weekday, only a small handful of families dotted the secluded beach. Massive sand dunes hid the water from the trees behind them, creating a quiet alcove.

Her eyes moved over the families and small groups of people enjoying the quiet beach. "I don't recognize anyone here."

"I know. Isn't it great?" I flashed her a mischievous grin.

She looked around; then a smile bloomed on her face. "It is pretty nice."

I gestured toward my board. "What do you say? Want to give it a try?"

She nodded, and I could see the giddiness building in her expression. I loved that she was excited to try this with me—that I could show her a small piece of myself that I kept hidden from almost everyone else.

As I reached behind to grab my collar and pull my T-shirt off, her eyes tracked down my chest and abs. I fought the urge to beat my chest like a caveman at her approval. Sylvie slowly peeled her shorts down her long legs and gathered the hem of her tank top in her hands.

I cleared my throat and pretended to organize the board and paddle. I lifted the small waterproof backpack out of the sand. "You can throw those in here if you'd like."

Carefully, Sylvie folded her clothes and stuffed them in my bag. Beneath that oversize tank top Sylvie wore a sporty blue bikini that was nearly the same shade as the water. My gaze snagged at the base of her neck, where her heartbeat hammered through the thin skin there. Her delicate collar-bone was irresistibly sexy—something I was sure I had never thought about any other woman before.

It was damn difficult to maintain respectable eye contact when the woman I had been fantasizing about for weeks was standing in front of me wearing nothing but a bikini. I cleared my throat, stuffing my T-shirt into the bag with her clothing.

I gestured toward my board. "This one should be big enough to hold us both, but we can also get you standing up on your own." She smiled as I closed up the dry bag. "It'll be fun, I promise."

I reached down and scooped up the life jacket I had picked up for her.

Her eyes flicked between the vest and me. "You brought me a life jacket?"

I shrugged. "It was no big deal."

It was actually a pretty big fucking deal because after I got a narrow-eyed look from the curious checkout clerk, I'd had to lie to the old woman's face and tell her it was for my sister.

Sylvie slipped it on, and I helped her adjust the straps so that it fit her properly. I patted her side, letting my pinkie graze the sliver of bare skin at her waist. "Perfect fit."

She hummed in agreement and fiddled with the straps again as I slipped on my own vest and tossed the cross-body dry bag around my shoulder.

Sylvie pulled on the small whistle attached to her vest by a stretchy cord. "A whistle?"

"Well, I can't go losing you out there."

She lifted one sculpted eyebrow. "Well, I'm not planning to go far from you, so hopefully I won't need to use it."

I'm not planning to go far from you.

I liked that.

I liked that too much.

She followed as I waded into the crisp Lake Michigan waters. After we got past the first few rocky feet of the shoreline, the lake bottom transformed into soft sand. My toes curled into it.

Once we were knee-deep, I stopped and positioned the paddleboard between us. From the end of the paddleboard, I ran my hand down the rope leash until I got to the ankle strap. "This is what keeps the board close to you if you fall off." I tapped my fingers on the top of the paddleboard. "Prop your leg up here."

Her eyes held mine, but she did exactly as she was told. I watched as water ran in rivulets down her calf and pooled beneath her feet.

Jesus Christ, it's just an ankle.

I steadied my breathing as I opened the ankle strap and wound it around her, securing it in place. I flipped the rope end over the board, and Sylvie slipped her leg back into the water.

Her eyes looked a bit worried. "Is it hard?"

As a fucking rock.

I tipped my head to the side in a shrug. "It's not easy, but I'm here to help you. I'll hold it steady while you work your way onto the top."

I held the board by the edges and guided it so that the center point of the board was in front of her. "You're going to want to keep your hands on the side of the board to stabilize it, but I'll help hold it steady. Work your way onto the board so you're kneeling."

A determined line formed between Sylvie's eyebrows as she nodded once. As I steadied the board, she did exactly as

I'd instructed her. Her right hand came between mine, and her left gripped on the opposite side. Carefully she maneuvered herself onto the board until she was kneeling.

She let out a satisfied huff.

"That was perfect. Now keep your hands on the sides and slowly move one foot at a time. You're not going to just pop up right away. You're gonna start by keeping your knees bent—almost in a squat—until you feel steady."

"Like this?" Sylvie slowly raised one knee as I struggled to keep respectful eye contact. The muscles in her legs worked as she wobbled, and she let out a small squeak.

"Don't worry. I've got you."

She released a shaky breath as she attempted to move her other leg until she was in a squat.

Keeping my voice calm, I continued my instructions. "Now when you're ready, slowly stand up."

Sylvie started to rise, and as she released her hands, she began to wobble. Instinctively, one hand shot out, gripping Sylvie's leg around the lower part of her calf. Her smooth skin was like a brand on my palm as my thumb stroked her. "I've got you, you're all right. Slow and steady."

"Okay." She nodded. "Okay."

When she rose to her full height, I looked up at her and saw the sun shining down on her pretty face.

"I did it." Her words came out in a whoosh of breath. "Holy shit, I did it!" She shot both fists up in the air. Her unexpected movement jolted the board, and though I tried to steady it, her feet did a little tiptoe dance until she toppled over my shoulder.

"Fuck." I grumbled and reached into the water to haul her up by the vest. I expected her to be annoyed that she had gotten soaked and frustrated that she fell, but when her laughter rang out across the water, happiness danced under my skin.

As I gripped the sides of her vest, her hands found my shoulders. "That was incredible. Can I go again?"

I stared into her golden eyes and grinned.

ELEVEN

It took a few more tries to get my balance and be steady on my feet, but I did it. It didn't matter how many times I wobbled or forgot all the small adjustments Duke had instructed me on—he never got frustrated or annoyed when I didn't get it right.

Instead, he smiled up at me and let me try again until I was satisfied. Finally, after I was steady, I was able to paddle a few circles as Duke followed me into slightly deeper water and called out encouragement. After the last time I stumbled and hit the water, I climbed back on the board and sat, letting my legs hang and watching the waves lap over my knees.

Duke slid in next to me, holding the board steady in the waist-deep water. Droplets clung to his thick dark hair, dripping onto his sculpted shoulders. They burned a path down his chest and back, and I fought the urge to drag my tongue up that line just to see what the crisp lake water tasted like on his skin. I had convinced myself that the kiss behind the Sugar Bowl was some kind of fever dream. I desperately wanted him to do it again, but so far he'd kept an annoyingly respectful distance.

I pointed to a small sandy tree-lined clump of land in the distance. "What's that place over there?"

Duke followed my gaze, but I couldn't stop thinking about the proximity of his bicep to my leg. I carefully widened my knee and touched it to the outside of his arm. When he didn't move away from my touch, I relaxed into the warmth of his skin on mine.

"Want to go check it out?"

I nodded as excitement danced through me. "Let's do it."

"All right, hold still."

I gripped the edge of the board with one hand to balance myself and watched as Duke effortlessly pulled himself onto the paddleboard. He widened his stance, his corded leg muscles on full display, and held out one hand to me. I gently placed my hand in his and let out a small yelp when he hauled me up to standing. My free hand clamped around his waist. I stared down at the cut lines of his abs— that little V that apparently made all women, including me, stupid.

Duke cleared his throat, and when my eyes whipped to his, a sexy smirk tugged at the corner of his mouth. He reached for the paddle in my opposite hand, and I released it.

Duke centered himself and glanced over his shoulder at me. "Just try to keep steady, and I'll get us over there."

I rested my hands on his hips. "Is this okay?" I whispered.

He grunted in response. "Yeah. It's okay, Sylvie."

Heat pooled between my legs as I inched closer, resting my front against his back. I hated that our life jackets kept me from capturing his warmth. I was playing with fire, but the seclusion of the beach and the freedom of the lake made me not care.

Duke's muscles rippled as he paddled us through the water toward the small island. Despite seeing the beach in the distance, it felt like we were miles away from civilization —miles away from a life that told us that being here together was so wrong.

Beneath us, the crystal waters of Lake Michigan revealed rocky formations below the surface as fish swam around and scattered as he moved us through the water.

When we got close enough, he turned his head to me again. "All right, hop down. We can walk from here."

Gently hopping off the board, I let myself sink below the surface before my vest popped me up, and I wiped the water from my eyes. Duke continued watching me. Heat rose in my cheeks, and I lowered my lashes. I followed him, and when we reached the beach, it was softer and sandier than the main coastline. Long lake grass dotted the area and led to small groupings of trees around the island.

I took in its seclusion. "Think anyone else is here?"

He shrugged. "I doubt it. The only way to get to it is by boat or board, and I didn't see anyone else around."

It was an island oasis all to ourselves. Excitement danced through me as I walked with Duke toward the beach. Once we were there, Duke dropped the paddleboard and paddle, along with his vest and bag, near the edge of the tree line. I unclipped my life jacket and stripped it from my body, letting the cool breeze ice my skin.

"Are you cold?" For the briefest moment, Duke's eyes flicked down to my hard nipples, and I didn't have the audacity to tell him that I was burning up, and that it was standing so close to him that had turned them into needy little pebbles.

I shook my head and he looked away. As we walked, exploring the small island, I couldn't help but inch closer to Duke. His kiss proved he felt something for me—there was definitely something more than casual friendship going on between us—but indecision and nerves kept my hands at their sides.

Finally, Duke's wide, rough palm smoothed down the inside of my arm from elbow to wrist before he clasped my hand in his and gently squeezed.

He towered over me and looked down at our joined hands. "Is this okay?"

I swallowed hard as I was internally *screaming*. "Yeah, it's okay."

I smiled up at him. He had no idea just how okay it was.

Together we walked hand in hand, exploring the small, secluded island. With Duke there weren't awkward silences, simply quiet stretches where I let my mind wander and imagine *what if*.

I leaned into him, and he gripped my hand harder. With him I felt alive. Free.

I felt like *me*.

Putting a little distance between us as we walked along the beach, I kicked up some water, splashing him. His fierce scowl forced a bubble of laughter to escape me. His jaw flexed before he growled.

Laughing, I released his hand and took off running. His footsteps pounded behind me, and I didn't make it five steps before his arm banded around my waist and I was hoisted in the air.

I released unbridled laughter. Duke tossed me over his shoulder, throwing me into a fit of giggles. He stomped and splashed in the water, soaking us both. His playful laughter mixed with mine, and I couldn't recall a sweeter sound.

I slid down his front as he placed my feet in the water. When my eyes met his, they were dark and intense. "Are you dating Charles Attwater?"

My cheeks flushed. His hand held mine as I shook my head. "After the auction date remix, we pretty quickly realized there was no magic. No spark. So we parted as friends—"

Before I could even finish, Duke's hands were on my face, and his mouth was on mine. A soft, surprised squeak escaped me, and he used it to deepen the kiss. I melted into him, pressing my chest against him as he held my body up. One hand wrapped around my waist, pulling me into his chest.

It wasn't a dream—Duke Sullivan is kissing the fuck out of me.

The kiss went against everything I'd ever been taught to do, and I didn't care. Everyone and everything dissolved around me in fizzy bubbles.

Duke's throaty grunt sent sparks of electricity through me, igniting my need. I went slick for him as his mouth moved across mine. His kiss was warm and deep and *mine* as his tongue moved against my own. My hands roamed over the hard planes of his body. Time and physical labor had hardened every part of him, and my hands explored his muscles.

My nipples scraped against his hard chest as heat spread through me. Waves lapped around our legs. At my hip Duke was rock hard.

And huge.

A fresh wave of need moved through me as I imagined

everything I wanted him to do to me with that monster of a cock.

With his hands still gripping the sides of my neck, he stopped the kiss and stared down at me. "I know this is unexpected. Do you want me to stop?"

I shook my head, breathless. "Hell no."

It was all the permission Duke needed. He bent his knees, wrapping his hands around the backs of my thighs and hauling me against him. My legs straddled his waist, and his hands moved over my ass, pressing me into him. I tilted my hips, grinding my aching clit against any part of him I could.

Duke's powerful legs carried us out of the water, and he lowered me to the sand at the edge of the tree line, where it met the soft beach. He laid me down on the paddleboard beside our discarded bag and vests. When he looked down at me, his eyes revealed one thing.

Possession.

And I wanted to be possessed by him—owned in the best way possible. He took my mouth again as his hands skated over my breasts. When he broke the kiss, I was a panting, needy mess.

"Take those tits out and let me see them."

I had never imagined Duke being so bold and filthy with me. I loved it.

Emboldened, I leaned back, slowly pulling my bikini top apart and showing him my breasts.

I loved the flare of heat in his eyes when he finally looked at them. His body covered mine, pushing me into the board. His thick cock pressed into me, and I wound my legs around him, digging my heels into him and begging for more. His hand tangled in my hair as he took the kiss deeper.

He pinched one nipple and ground his hips into me, and I moaned into him. I slid my hands over the expanse of his back, skating over the muscles and sinew. He was broad and powerful. The soft hair on his chest teased my sensitive skin, and I wanted to feel all of him—to explore his body as he kissed and licked and sucked.

"Duke," I panted.

He broke the kiss to stare down at me.

"Please," I pleaded, and my hands moved to the band of his swim trunks. Hunger flashed in his eyes. I shook my head. "I know this is reckless, but I want you. I need you." My palm moved over his hard length through his trunks, and he bit back a moan. "Right now."

On his face, desire and need were at war with the consequences of my begging.

"Just this once," I added before he could shoot me down. "And we won't tell anyone."

His dark eyes stared down at me as he sat back on his heels and looked at me, splayed out and begging for him. "When I'm done with you, you'll be lucky if they didn't hear you screaming my name."

He took my mouth again in a dark and possessive kiss. Duke moved off me, and I immediately pulled my top all the way off and shimmied out of my blue bikini bottoms. Duke moved quickly to remove his trunks, and when I got the perfect view of his dick, my core clenched in anticipation.

It was long and thick and veined. I wanted to feel my tongue drag down its length, but he reached into his bag and pulled out a condom. The fact that he'd brought a condom —that he wanted this as badly as I did—turned me on even more.

I watched in awe as his skilled hands made quick work of unrolling it down his length.

"Spread your legs. Show me where you want this cock."

Leaning back on my elbows, I ignored the bite of sand beneath me as I let my knees drop open. Duke sucked in a breath as he stared at my pussy. On his knees, he inched closer to me. I dragged my fingertips down his chest and watched as his abs flexed at my touch.

"I want to take my time with you. Touch you and taste you—savor every drop."

I shook my head. "I don't want you to go slow. I need you. Right now."

His jaw flexed. "If you need it rough and dirty, I can give that to you. I swear I can give you everything you'll ever need."

My head tipped back as Duke dragged the head of his cock through my pussy. I was achy and wet. He circled my clit with the tip and my hips tilted upward, begging for him to fill me.

I didn't want hearts and flowers and promises. I wanted *him*.

Duke's hand moved across my chest, slid down my belly, and stopped between my legs.

His thumb pressed against my clit as he stroked his dick with the other hand. "I've been dreaming about your tight, wet cunt for weeks. Every night I come with my dick in my hands and your name on my lips."

The image of Duke touching himself while thinking of me was too much. I arched into him, tilting my hips and guiding his cock toward my entrance.

"Take it. Please," I begged.

One hand gripped my hip and squeezed while he guided his cock lower. Slowly, he pressed forward, stretching my pussy open until the head was just inside. He was thick and long, and I hissed at the way he stretched me open.

Without waiting for me to adjust, he gave me more.

His head tilted back, and I stared at the muscular column of his neck as he filled me. A throaty moan rattled out of him. *"Fuck."*

My pussy squeezed around him as he shifted his hips, and I reveled in the drag and pull of his cock sliding through me. I whimpered as Duke fucked me on the beach, hidden only by the towering trees above us.

He covered my body with his, leaning forward to kiss me. His heat, his scent, had me spiraling. When he pinched my nipple, pleasure bordered on pain, and I cried out. "Yes! More."

He ground his hips into me. My hands moved over his chest as the muscles rippled with every thrust. It had been so long since I'd been with anyone, and it had *never* been like that. Desire and need were intertwined, and all I could think was *more. More. MORE.*

I needed more—of him. Us. *This.*

Pleasure zipped down my spine, and I knew I was close. "Shit. Duke. Yes." My words were nearly incoherent, and I prayed he knew what I meant.

He stared down at me, the intense furrow in his brow only making me hotter for him as he pounded into me. He reached down to grip my thigh and pull it against his hip. The deeper angle was all it took, and my pussy clamped around him, my orgasm tearing through me. I clenched and released as he continued to stroke in and out of me with long, deep thrusts.

A growl formed in his throat, and then his hips jerked forward and stilled. The base of his cock teased my clit as he throbbed inside me. We moaned in unison, and he shuddered.

Covering my body, he slumped over me, bracing his weight on his elbows and looking down at me. His cock still nestled inside me, we stared at each other. Only inches from each other, I searched his eyes. Without a word, his mouth was soft and sweet on mine. He shifted his arms, tucking them under me and holding me to his broad chest.

His body was heavy in the best way.

Duke lifted his head, and the fierce expression he'd worn earlier had shifted into something different. Softer.

Contentment, maybe?

He ran his nose down mine with a tenderness I'd never experienced. Duke kissed me again before slowly lifting off me. Immediately I missed the heat and weight of him. His hand grazed down my body as though he was memorizing every dip and curve. I sighed and closed my eyes, watching the sunlight dance behind my eyelids as the trees swayed overhead. I reveled in its heat as it warmed my skin, wishing I could pause this moment and keep it forever.

When I opened my eyes, Duke was staring down at me, but the content look he'd worn only moments before was replaced by something . . . sadder.

"Let's get you cleaned up."

I nodded and pushed myself to a sitting position. Sand was fucking *everywhere*. I gathered my bikini, shaking it out as Duke took care of the condom. He slipped on his trunks and walked toward the water, giving me the opportunity to dress in private.

A sinking feeling tugged at my belly, and my chest ached. The thought of having to go back to talking with him only in secret was unbearable. I watched him look out onto the waters of Lake Michigan and wondered if he was having the same inner crisis, or if maybe this was something else entirely for him. Maybe it wasn't as life-altering for Duke as it felt for me.

After redressing, I stepped up beside him, looking out onto the lake as the late-afternoon sun hung heavily in the distance. The vast emptiness of the unending water mirrored my insides.

Duke's hand briefly found the center of my back, but he dropped it just as quickly. "We should get you back."

I nodded. My throat was tight, and though I desperately wanted to beg him for answers, to figure out what we were supposed to do next, I let the silence stretch between us.

Just this once. And we won't tell anyone.

Stupid.

Stupid.

Stupid.

Why had I said that?

I wished I could take the words back, but I also knew, deep down, that we couldn't tell anyone. No one would understand. But it also hurt a little that Duke hadn't disagreed with me.

A thousand scenarios played out in my mind, and none of them ended without one of us being broken.

After we gathered the board and bag, the trip back to the main beach was quiet. I stood behind him as he paddled and leaned into him, closing my eyes and wishing things could be different.

My only comfort was his warm hand covering mine. I pinched my eyes closed.

What had I done?

TWELVE

JUST THIS ONCE. *And we won't tell anyone.*

Sylvie's breathy words, whispered on the beach just before she turned my world upside down, replayed on an endless loop.

When she said them, I was stunned. Angered.

I was a fucking idiot.

I should have told her that wouldn't work for me, but instead I panicked. I knew in my gut I would take Sylvie in any way she would allow, even if that meant secret texts and whispered conversations.

But I didn't have to like it.

My silence may have made me complicit, but I wasn't giving up. Not on her and not on us—whatever *us* was.

After our secret date on the beach, Sylvie consumed my thoughts more than ever.

Fall was stirring in the August air. Berry picking had slowed, and the workers shifted their focus to weeding between rows and preparing for the inevitable dip in temperature. The chaos on the farm was nothing compared to the thick swell of emotions residing in my chest.

There has to be a way.

Russell King was a ruthless businessman and a prick, but he was still Sylvie's father. There was no getting around that. Plus, her overzealous brothers were a separate issue. There would be no tears shed by me if they ceased to exist. But I knew falling back into the pattern of pining for Sylvie from a distance wouldn't work.

I simply couldn't do it.

"Can I help you find something?" Bug King looked up at me as I wandered aimlessly through the stacks of the Outtatowner public library. Her lips were pursed and her arms crossed as though it caused her physical pain having to assist a Sullivan.

"I'm looking for . . ." Bug's eyebrow raised and my hand dropped. "You know what? No. I don't need help."

She swiveled on her heel and stomped away from me. I still didn't trust her, or any of the Kings apart from Sylvie. There was a reason behind the Sullivan–King feud and why it had persisted for so long.

When Kate uncovered the speakeasy hidden in the basement of Tootie's farmhouse, someone was sneaking around the property, and it sure as fuck wasn't us. Add in the tire tracks I'd found near the west pasture *and* the inquiries into mineral rights on Sullivan land, and it was all too much.

I wanted answers.

Annie had pored over old news articles and public records to help us. In her search, she'd uncovered that the Kings and Sullivans had once been allies—friends and neighbors. Something had gone sideways, and I was willing to bet a King was behind it.

When I came upon a younger librarian, I cleared my throat to get her attention. She glanced up at me, pushing her glasses up her nose. "Any chance you can point me in the direction of town records?"

She dropped a pen on her desk and motioned for me to follow. "This way."

The musty smell of old books filled my nostrils, and we rounded a corner toward a staircase that led to the basement.

"Almost everything is kept digitally—that makes it easier to search." She glanced back. "What are you looking for?"

I shrugged. "I'm not exactly sure."

She sighed. "Well, that will make it more difficult, but things are arranged by periodical type and by date." She gestured to two computers at the center of the space and swept her arm toward bookshelves along the back wall. "Anything not yet converted to digital will be on those shelves. Nothing here can be checked out, but copies can be printed or photocopied. Ten cents per page."

I nodded and thanked the woman before she disappeared upstairs. The air down there was stale, and the room itself gave off serious murder vibes. I checked my phone.

No service. Awesome.

I knew from Annie's research that the Sullivans and Kings had been close—which lined up with a photo Kate had found in the speakeasy of three people—Philo Sullivan, Helen Sinclair, and James King. It may also explain why there was a bootleg bottle of booze labeled King Liquor down there.

After further digging, Annie uncovered that the three families—likely the grandparents of the threesome, if my math was accurate—had intentionally purchased adjacent parcels of land through the Homestead Act of 1862. It seemed like their families shared a close friendship. Years later, Philo and Helen married. After that, the timeline got fuzzy.

Something that tore the families apart.

It was a long shot, but maybe if I could understand what happened, I could find a way toward peace between our families and make whatever was developing between Sylvie and me work.

I started with the bookshelves, but despite the librarian's claims it was organized, all I found was a fucking mess. Binders were arranged in haphazard rows with no apparent order. Birth certificates, property deeds, and newspaper clippings were shoved into the binders. Pages were falling out, some were stuck together, and a sense of overwhelm settled over me.

I had hoped something—*anything*—would give me something to go on, but there was nothing.

Frustrated and tired, I sat on the old office chair in front of one of the computers. I tapped the keyboard a few times, and it crawled to life. The electric whirs and thunks coming from inside the ancient computer weren't encouraging, but eventually it blinked to life.

I spent a few minutes entering the names from the photograph into the computer with varying degrees of success. Mostly it was information Annie had already uncovered or a whole lot of nothing.

My eyes snagged on one name I hadn't recognized. The document was an obituary that listed Helen Sinclair as a surviving sibling to a man named Thomas "Slick" Sinclair. I printed the obituary before heading home.

I planned to share the information with my family later and see if they remembered seeing the name. For some reason it stuck with me, and I couldn't shake the feeling that there was something more there.

My shoulders were tense as I stepped out into the afternoon sunlight. I closed my eyes and craned my neck, hoping to ease the tension that balled between my shoulder blades. It was more than just the cramped basement that created the ache.

I scanned down Main Street before I pulled out my phone.

> Cat Fact 217: Aoshima is a Japanese island where cats outnumber humans six to one.

I needed to speak with her—to hear her voice and know that things between us were going to be okay. I hated the fact that I was so consumed by her. People looked to me for answers. I was the man who could fix problems and get results, but with her, I was helpless.

DARYL HALL

I'm sorry.

My molars ground together.

No problem.

Can I call you tonight?

Whenever you're free.

I spent the next several hours trying everything I could to stop thinking about Sylvie King. It was fucking hopeless. When the phone rang, I fumbled it trying to answer.

"Hello?" I coughed, trying to cover the tightness that crept into my voice.

"Hi." Sylvie was quiet, her greeting barely above a whispered hush.

"Everything okay?"

"Yeah, it's just hard to get some privacy around here."

I grunted a response. Despite being adults, we were sneaking around like a couple of teenagers.

I knew the reality was I would take her in any version of this life I could have her. She was unusually quiet, and the heaviness of the day before hung between us.

She knew what she wanted. She had made so much clear when she was sure to reiterate that sex between us was a one-time thing.

"So yesterday was . . ." A whoosh of breath came over the phone.

"Yeah." I wasn't exactly sure how to finish that statement.

Amazing.

Confusing.

Life-altering.

Complicated.

I pressed my fingers into my eyes to relieve the pressure. "I was a little bummed not to hear from you this morning."

Her soft laughter was like balm to my soul. "Well, I didn't hear from you either."

I smiled at her sass. She wasn't wrong. "I stared at my phone for a while, but in the end decided to give you space. Every time my phone pinged, I was hoping it was you."

Sylvie laughed again. "God, we are so dumb, aren't we?"

I grimaced but suppressed another laugh. "Yeah, I guess you're right about that."

"I like you, Duke." The way her soft voice rolled over my name—the way she sounded almost afraid to admit those words out loud—hit me square in the chest.

"I like you too. A whole lot more than I probably

should." I exhaled and dragged a hand through my hair as I leaned forward in my seat, resting my elbows on my knees. Beside me, Ed was curled up and sleeping. Duck was nestled beside him with his little bill resting on Ed's front leg.

I chuckled to myself at the scene. "I should have called you this morning. That's on me. I don't want you to ever question how I feel about you."

"I like sharing my day with you. I like getting a glimpse of what 'mean old Duke Sullivan' does in his spare time."

"I'm not that mean."

Sylvie laughed again, and the sound helped me relax a little. She could call me mean all she wanted if that meant she would keep on laughing.

I could tell by the timidness of her voice she was nervous. Vulnerable. "I just don't want to lose this, you know."

"I'm not going anywhere," I reassured her. Truer words had never crossed my lips. Sure, any relationship starting on shaky footing was never off to a good start. Our families hated each other, and the entire town supported a feud that was built to keep us apart, but it was the truth that I would take Sylvie in any form she would have me. Maybe secret texts and whispered phone conversations were enough for her. If it meant I got to hear that laugh and learn about the mundane details of her day, then so be it.

I would learn for that to be enough.

It would have to be. I didn't want Sylvie to feel sadness, especially where I was concerned.

I looked down at Duck and Ed and shifted gears. "Turns out Three-Legged Ed adopted this duckling. Looks like he's sticking around."

Sylvie clicked her tongue and cooed into the phone.

"That is the sweetest thing I've ever heard. I knew you were a big softie."

I chuckled and shook my head. "I'm not a softie. This is all Ed's doing."

Sylvie laughed. "If you say so." Something clattered behind her, and she whispered into the phone, "Shit, I have to go."

I wanted to ask her what was wrong and make sure she was okay, but I didn't get the chance.

"I'll talk to you tomorrow. Good night, Duke."

The call disconnected before I had the chance to wish her a good night. I flipped my phone onto the cushion of the chair next to me and looked out onto Sullivan Farms. I had known better than to get involved with a King, but no part of me felt like anything involving Sylvie was a mistake.

I had no clue how we were going to work this out, but it didn't matter. The day was coming when I was going to claim Sylvie as mine, if she would have me. My whole life had been a series of setting my wants and needs to the side to take care of everyone else.

If I could survive a lifetime of that, I would survive this. If she didn't want me, I would learn to patch the gaping, Sylvie-size hole in my chest for the sake of her happiness.

THIRTEEN

"Hey, do you have a tampon?" Rebecca whispered over my shoulder during a lull in customers at the Sugar Bowl. "I just got a lovely surprise visit, and there's nothing in the employee bathroom."

I shook my head. "There should be some in there. I always restock when I get mine . . ." My brain paused. I had just restocked the bathroom for the female employees. *Hadn't I?* It seemed like my period was the only one around here like clockwork, and it was easier to keep it stocked than to have to cover the servers' tables when they had to run to the store mid-shift.

"It's empty. I just looked. Can you cover me while I run across the street to the general store?"

"Of course." My voice was hollow as I tried to think back to when I last had *my* period. I thought and thought but came up . . . blank.

What. The. Fuck.

After rushing the next customer and getting a well-deserved dirty look, I excused myself to the back kitchen. Huck was arranging his famous s'mores puff pastry mini tarts for Outtatowner's upcoming annual Fireside Flannel Festival.

I hustled to the corner and pulled out my phone to look at the calendar app and counted. Then recounted. And counted again.

No, no, no, no, no.

When my brain couldn't wrap itself around the simple task of counting dates, I moved to the kitchen calendar Huck had hung on the wall. I flipped forward, then back. I was still coming up with the same gut-wrenching timeline.

"You okay?" Huck asked behind me as he waved a small butane torch over the tops of the tarts to slightly toast them.

My voice wouldn't work. I managed a jerky nod and flipped the pages again. There was no way. *No freaking way.*

I wanted to scream. To run. I wanted to melt into a puddle or hide behind a rock and never come out.

My boss came up beside me as I stared at the calendar. "If you're not feeling well, we can cover here."

I swallowed. "No. I'm fine. Rebecca stepped out but she'll be back. I'm fine."

I was very much *not fine*.

Hastily, I typed out a text to MJ, begging her to meet me at the house after her nursing shift was done.

MJ

I'm going to Fireside tonight! Aren't you coming?

I paled. Everyone in town looked forward to Outtatowner's annual welcoming of autumn. Tourists enjoyed tents with snacks, crafters, and food, plus beer and wine tastings. As the evening wore on, the beach was dotted with bonfires and music.

It was one of my favorite nights of the year.

Sorry, I forgot. Yeah, I'll be there.

Forgot? Are you okay?

I ignored her text and slipped my phone into my pocket. I had to be overreacting. There were a thousand reasons my period could be late.

I GOT through the rest of my shift at the Sugar Bowl like a dead-eyed robot. My head was swimming with possibilities, and I did everything I could to remain calm. I needed to be sure. I needed facts. I needed a clear sign that I was overreacting and definitely *not* pregnant with Duke Sullivan's baby.

It had been a month since our secret island date. We had agreed to keep our friendship hidden and hadn't met in secret again since that day on the beach.

I scanned the roadway before crossing and hustling toward the general store. The street around me was already buzzing with excited energy. Storefronts were capitalizing on the Fireside Flannel Festival by offering discounts, hanging plaid banners, and setting up small tables on the sidewalks to catch passersby. Chalkboard signs pointing people toward the waterfront were strewn throughout the town, and far in the distance I could see tents and commotion as the festival got underway.

The general store owner, some distant King cousin, greeted me as I wove through the aisles of the store. Customers were already decked out in flannel for the festival. Their happy, carefree smiles were a stark contrast to the sinking feeling in my gut.

I was always careful. I had *never* had unprotected sex.

We used a condom, for fuck's sake!

I was officially spiraling.

I rounded the corner to the feminine care aisle but came up short when I nearly crashed into a hard wall of a man. My brother Royal's hard features split into a goofy grin when he realized it was me. "Jesus, Syl. Where's the fire?"

I looked into my brother's eyes.

Oh god, what would he say if he knew I thought I was pregnant with a Sullivan's baby? Would he even try to understand?

Of all my brothers, Royal was the softest. His hard tattooed exterior was in opposition to the sensitive soul he worked to keep hidden. He was also the brother that loved to poke and dig at the Sullivans. He was a big reason the pranks and rivalry had continued for so long. He was happy to retaliate any chance he got.

"Hey, what are you doing?" I tried to sound casual and calm but failed miserably.

Royal's eyes narrowed at me. "What are *you* doing?"

Covering my own ass, I reached around him and grabbed the first box of tampons my hand touched, and I held them up to him. "I needed these. Why? You want to buy them for me?"

Unfazed, Royal chuckled. "Why would buying tampons bother me? I've been buying them for you since we were teenagers."

Damn it. My stupid progressive brother and his stupid progressive ideas about gender equality.

"Why are you even in this aisle?"

Amusement played over his face as he held up the small

box of condoms with a smirk.

I rolled my eyes. "Gross." I shooed him away with my fingers as nerves buzzed through me. "Go away. I have other things to look for, and it's none of your business."

He chuckled again and shook his head. "Will I see you tonight? MJ said you two were coming up to the festival."

I nodded and swallowed hard. I had no idea how much or how little my life was about to shift in the next ten to fifteen minutes.

Royal smiled, and affection for my older brother rolled through me. "I'll buy you a beer when you get down there. See you tonight."

My brother turned and headed toward the register. Still holding the box of tampons, I scanned the array of pregnancy tests. I had never needed to use one, so I had no idea what to get. In my indecision, Ms. Tiny entered the same aisle. Heat prickled at my hairline, and I moved to scan a different section.

I definitely should have gone to the drug store outside of town, where everyone minded their own fucking business. When I thought she wasn't looking, I grabbed the first pregnancy test box I could and held it behind the box of tampons. As I moved past Ms. Tiny, I gave her a nod and hurried toward the register.

The store was busy, but thank god for self-checkout. I hid the boxes in the crook of my arm as I waited in line. My hand tapped against the outside of my thigh as I mentally berated the slow customers in front of me. Nausea swirled in my stomach.

Oh my god, is that a symptom?

I blew a slow, steady breath through my lips. When it was my turn, I quickly scanned my items and prayed I would actually need the tampons in a day or two.

By the time I had gotten back to my house, my stomach ache hadn't gotten any better. Thankfully, MJ was still working, and Bug was at the library. The cold, large house was eerily quiet.

As I ran up the stairs and locked myself into the bathroom, I tossed the bag and box of tampons into the sink and sat on the toilet seat, holding the box with the pregnancy test.

I tore it open and pulled out the pamphlet. I was pretty sure it was idiotproof—that you just peed on the stick—but I read and reread the instructions twice just to be sure. Before I took the test, I pressed my hand against my lower belly and breathed in deep. Beside the gnawing pit in my stomach, the early pregnancy symptoms I had googled earlier weren't there. I wasn't dizzy, my boobs felt fine, and other than a late period and worry rattling through me, there were no other obvious signs that I could be pregnant. I was exhausted, but I didn't *think* that was new.

I closed my eyes and tried to feel something. My mind flashed to a fictional scenario of my belly plumping, rounded with pregnancy. I saw Duke smiling down at me as he rubbed my swollen belly. My mind flashed forward to a child with his smile and my eyes, riding gleefully on top of his broad shoulders. A low hum buzzed through me as my eyes flew open.

Oh fuck. Do I want to be pregnant?

I exhaled and opened my eyes.

That was a fantasy world, a world in which the King–Sullivan rivalry didn't exist. A time and place where I felt free to make my own decisions about my life without judgments from everyone around me. It was also a giant leap, assuming Duke would want anything to do with this baby.

Deep down, I knew he was a good man, and I hoped he would stand by any decision I made.

But what if I didn't even know what decision to make?

Steeling my nerves, I lifted the toilet seat and followed the instructions to take the pregnancy test. I set the test face down on the sink and set up a timer on my phone. My foot tapped as my brain flooded with possibilities—some funny, some scary, some downright confusing.

I jolted when the timer went off.

After a quick inhale, I flipped the test over, and my heart stopped.

Two pink lines.

WHEN THE FOURTH text from MJ asking me where I was rolled in, I knew I couldn't hide any longer before she sent out a search party. Not knowing what else to do, I did my hair and makeup and slipped on a flannel shirt to ward off the mid-September chill—and because it was the Fireside Flannel Festival, after all. A flannel shirt was practically required.

> Heading over now.

MJ

> The boys are setting up the bonfire and Abel is working the beer tent. Meet me there and we can convince him to let us drink for free.

> Okay.

I didn't need to tell my sister over text that there would definitely be no drinking for me tonight.

When I rolled into town, I opted to park in the back parking lot of the Sugar Bowl rather than fight the traffic for a spot near the beach. Music floated above the din of the festival and the crashing waves as the crowd grew thicker with people enjoying the evening.

I moved through the crowd until I reached the edge of the beach. To the right, there were tents with snacks, crafters, food, and beer and wine tastings dotting the small parking lot. Up ahead, a long pier jutted into Lake Michigan, with a lighthouse at the end.

Down the long stretch of sandy beach, dotted along the shore, were stacks of wood, waiting for night to fall. All along the beach would be bonfires and music. Somewhere down there, I knew my brothers were busy setting up an epic bonfire.

I continually scanned the crowd for Duke. It was rare that the grumpy farmer came out, but usually his siblings could goad him into attending bigger town events. The likelihood Duke would be at the festival was high, and I had no idea what I would do or say if I saw him.

As soon as I entered the beer tent, I searched for MJ. When I caught her eye, she grinned widely and waved her arm above the crowd. I wove through the line, offering apologies and *excuse me*s as I moved forward.

When I finally made it to my sister, she thrust a plastic cup full of cold beer in my hand and called over my shoulder. "Thanks, Abe. You're the best!"

She raised her cup in salute as our oldest brother only grunted a response and turned his back to continue slinging drinks for impatient patrons.

"Can I talk to you?" I called over the chatter of the music.

MJ took a healthy gulp of her beer. "Yeah," she shouted

and continued to scan the crowd.

I shook my head. "Not here. I need somewhere a little quieter."

MJ eyed me carefully, then motioned her head to the side of the beer tent. As she went to exit the flap behind the table, Abel gave her a curious look.

"Girl talk," MJ shouted and waved a hand in dismissal as she disappeared behind the flap.

I followed her outside of the tent.

Before she could even turn, the words bubbled out of me. "I think I might be pregnant." I covered my mouth, horrified I'd just blurted it out.

Her eyes went wide. "Oh my god. *What? How?*"

I pinned her with a *seriously?* glare.

MJ shook her head. "I mean, I know *how*, but with who? Are you sure?"

"I'm sure." Tears burned behind my eyelids.

MJ frowned. "When was your period?"

I shrugged. "August 6?"

"How late are you?"

I grimaced. "Two weeks . . . ish?"

Her eyes went wide. My sister knew that between the two of us, I was the regular one. "Shit."

I swallowed hard. "I also took a test. I'm definitely pregnant."

Realization suddenly dawned on her, and her hand went to her mouth. "Oh my god . . . Is it Duke? Please tell me it's Duke."

Heat rose in my cheeks, and I nodded, unable to say the words out loud.

"Holy fuck, Sylvie."

"I know." A pathetic whimper tumbled out of me as I bounced on my heels. "I *know*." My palms were sweaty and panic was settling in. "Trust me, getting knocked up by Duke Sullivan was definitely *not* on my bingo card. Shit!"

Her steady hand found my shoulder, and I took a breath. "Does he know?"

I quickly shook my head. "I haven't told anybody. Just you."

MJ quickly discarded her beer in a large trash can and grabbed mine from my hand before tossing it in after hers. "Okay." She nodded resolutely. "Okay. We've got this. We can do this." I could see her wheels turning as she mentally considered the bombshell I'd just dropped. "I mean, I kind of know Duke. Sure, he's got the whole grumpy, reclusive-farmer thing going on, and he *is* a Sullivan—which is a major hiccup . . . but he's a decent guy. He cares a lot for his dad, and I think there's a good guy lurking somewhere in there." Her lips formed a determined line. "This will be okay."

I nodded, letting her words wash over me, giving me a tiny sense of comfort.

MJ blew out a breath as her eyes went wide and her cheeks puffed out with a dramatic exhale. "Dad and the boys are going to be a different story." Her gaze locked with mine. "What in the hell are you gonna do?"

Tears burned in my eyes. "I don't know."

Her shoulders straightened. "It's fine. This is fine. Everything is fine."

My little sister grabbed my hand and started dragging me around to the front of the tent. "We don't have to do this right now. We can have a girls' night in until we figure out what we're going to do."

We.

A tiny spark of hope bloomed inside me that I may not be so alone in this after all. I swallowed hard and nodded.

Going home and taking a pause before figuring out how to tell Duke might be exactly what I needed. I leaned on MJ and allowed her to weave me through the crowd toward the main roadway.

When my toes hit the sand, I looked out onto the beach dotted with bonfires sparking to life as the sun sank below the watery horizon. My eyes skated over Royal, who was finishing up a fire with JP and a few of his other friends and our cousins. He tipped his chin in greeting, but my eyes kept moving.

My gaze moved a few bonfires down, and I froze. Silhouetted by the setting sun, Duke's broad shoulders and tense stance were unmistakable. His mouth was tipped down into a scowl as he looked at the fire, and his hands were stuffed into his pockets.

A flutter rippled through me at how strong and powerful and masculine he was.

Against every internal warning blaring between my ears, against every thought, I moved forward on pure instinct, dropping MJ's arm and leaving her in my wake. My breaths were ragged as I crossed the sand, not pausing to acknowledge the group of Kings staring at me as I sailed right past them.

I caught Duke's attention, and he stiffened for a fraction of a second before I slammed into him. My arms wrapped around his middle as I burst into harsh sobs. Audible gasps and murmurs rippled through the crowd as both Kings and Sullivans gaped at us.

Duke's body was hard and rigid as a fresh sob racked out of me.

Then, ever so slowly, his hands lifted from his pockets, and his arms wrapped around me and squeezed.

"Okay. All right."

FOURTEEN

So . . . this is happening.

Sylvie was gorgeous. And her hair smelled nice. Those were the first two thoughts that popped into my head, until I realized she was crying. *Hard.*

My arms wrapped around her and I held her to me. "Okay. All right."

Glancing around, I saw that a sea of faces were in various states of shock, awe, and anger. JP and Royal King looked like they were each about to pop a blood vessel, and Royal even had a small shovel in his hand from digging at the bonfire.

Next to me, Wyatt stared wide eyed as Lee murmured *dude.*

I gripped Sylvie's shoulders and held her out to look at her.

Her caramel eyes were rimmed in red, and her lip quivered. "I need to talk to you."

Protectiveness coursed through me, and I pressed my lips into a flat line before nodding. Wyatt stepped forward, and I shot him a hard glare. "Not now."

Turning from the crowd, I pulled Sylvie under my arm and ushered her away from the gaping mouths of onlookers. On the walk to my truck, Sylvie's cries muted to quiet sniffles. I helped her into the passenger side and rounded the hood.

Once inside I started my truck and paused. "So, where to?"

Sylvie stared straight ahead. Her knees were locked together, and her hands ran up and down her thighs. "Just . . . away. Somewhere we can talk?"

Nerves rippled through me, but I threw the truck into drive.

Within a few silent minutes, I pulled into my driveway. Sylvie looked around, and I pulled the door open as she started to get out. As far as I knew, she'd never been to Sullivan Farms. Part of me hoped she liked it, though it was a shit view in the darkness.

Ed barked from the window, and Sylvie followed me onto the porch. I let Ed out, and he sniffed us both before trotting off toward the barn. I gestured toward the old hound dog. "Gotta go check on his kid."

A scoff burst from her, and my brows cinched together. Silently we walked up the porch steps. "Do you want to sit out here, or is it too cold?"

Sylvie swallowed and sank into a large cushioned chair. I took the one next to her, resting my elbows on my knees and studying her face.

She still hadn't looked at me.

"What's going on, Hall, I—"

"I'm pregnant."

I studied her face. *Pregnant?*

Sylvie shook her head. "I'm sorry. I—"

"You're pregnant." I was testing the words, seeing how they felt when I said them aloud. "It's mine."

In the dark I couldn't make out the tones of amber in her eyes, but they radiated sadness. Fear. "Yes," she whispered.

I reached for her hand. "Okay."

Her eyes bounced between mine. "Okay?"

I swallowed past the dry lump lodged in my throat. "It's going to be okay." I had no fucking clue what I was talking about, but it seemed like she needed comfort, and that was something I could give to her.

Fresh tears filled her eyes as her chin wobbled. A dark, sinking feeling pooled in my gut at the realization that maybe Sylvie didn't want to keep the baby. In a matter of seconds, my entire world had been upended. Sylvie looked at me with uncertainty and a vulnerability I had never seen before.

I chose my words carefully. I didn't want to spook her, but I also knew that this would be a conversation that would haunt me for the rest of my life if I fucked it up. "How long have you known?"

She sighed and wiped her nose on the sleeve of her flannel. "A few hours? Something came up at work, and I realized I didn't remember the last time I had my period, which is *really* unusual for me."

I nodded. My sister, Kate, was really private with all that stuff, but I could imagine a woman would know her own body.

"Maybe I should have waited to tell you. Until I went to the doctor to confirm, but—"

"No." She blinked up at me as I shook my head. "No, I'm glad you came and found me."

She breathed out a watery laugh. "I didn't really *find*

you so much as I saw you, and your baby grabbed the steering wheel."

My baby.

That was when I realized that I'd done the worst thing I could have done. I got the daughter of my family's rival pregnant . . . and I wasn't even sorry about it.

I took a deep breath, terrified of the next words I had to say to her. "I know I have no right to ask—that it's too much, and I want you to know that I will respect your choice, but . . . would you consider having it?" She stared at me in stunned silence as I continued, "If you're not interested in being a mother, I can respect that, but I would want it."

Her eyes grew wider. "You would want the baby even if I didn't?"

"Of course." There was no hesitation. I could deal with the fallout, but no matter what, I'd take care of my kid, love it like my parents had loved us.

I watched the delicate muscles in her neck move with a swallow. "I want to keep the baby."

I sagged in relief. "Okay."

Sylvie's back went straight as her eyes bounced across the boards under her feet. "I don't have expectations. We used a condom, and it either broke or you have supersperm or something, but it happened." I chuckled at her attempt to lighten the intensity of the conversation.

I nodded, trying to reassure her. "It happens, I guess. We can handle this."

Sylvie lowered her gaze. "Thank you for not questioning me. If you want a DNA test or something, I wouldn't be mad."

I gritted my teeth, annoyed she would assume I would question her. I *knew* her. We'd spent the better part of a year becoming friends, and I knew in my bones she wouldn't lie about this. That baby was mine. Instead, I gripped her hand. "We'll figure this out."

She let out a shaky breath before wiping her puffy eyes. "Can you take me home?"

I fought the urge to point her in the direction of my farmhouse and instead walked her to my truck and brought her where she'd asked to go.

THE MIDDAY SUN slanted across my table, casting a warm, intimate glow as my family gathered for dinner. The clinking of utensils against plates was accompanied by an undercurrent of tension, as if the very air held its breath, waiting for the unspoken to be revealed. After Sylvie had outed our friendship at Fireside, facing them all at once seemed like my best option.

I shifted uncomfortably in my seat, my gaze darting to my cramped dining room as we barely fit around the table. I thought back to how upset and scared she had been. Even now, nearly a day later, the remnants of her presence lingered—a faint trace of her perfume and the ghost of her surprised smile when I told her I wanted her to keep the baby. The memory of her tearful confession still played in my mind, a constant loop that refused to fade.

"Duke, pass the beans?" Aunt Tootie's voice cut through the quiet, and I hastily obliged, my hands betraying the unease I felt.

"You've been quiet." Wyatt's voice was laden with concern, his brows furrowed as he watched me closely. "What the hell is going on, man?"

My niece, Penny, stifled a chuckle at her dad's choice of words, but he silenced her with a look.

I took a deep breath, grappling with the turmoil roiling in my gut. I knew everyone was talking about the scene Sylvie and I had made the night before. "Yeah, there's . . . something."

Lee leaned forward, his piercing eyes fixed on me. "Don't keep us in suspense, man. Spill it."

A nervous glance around the table confirmed that the whole family was watching, their expressions a mix of curiosity and apprehension. Lark's and Annie's wistful eyebrows crept up their foreheads. Wyatt crossed his arms and leaned back in his chair.

"It's Sylvie," I finally admitted, my voice quiet but sure as it cut through the razor-sharp air.

Tootie's eyes widened, and she exchanged a knowing look with Lark. Wyatt's fork paused midway to his mouth, and he exchanged a swift glance with Lee before fixing his gaze on me. "What about her?"

My heart pounded, and I met their collective gaze, the weight of their attention almost suffocating. "We've been friends for a while."

Wyatt's brows pinched down. "Friends?"

My jaw clenched, pissed that I felt the need to explain my relationship because they couldn't understand. "Yeah. Texting and talking over the phone."

A shit-eating grin spread across Lee's face. He'd been poking at me about Sylvie for a while, so I was certain he was patting himself on the back, the schmuck.

I released a breath. "She's pregnant."

The revelation landed with a thud, the silence that followed palpable. Gasps and wide eyes met my words, and I could almost hear the gears turning in their minds.

"Pregnant? Sylvie King, is pregnant?" Lark's voice was

laced with disbelief, her fingers brushing over her collarbone.

Annie's hand slipped into Lee's, her lips forming an O of surprise. "Oh, wow."

Tootie let out a breath, her expression a mix of concern and resignation. "So it's yours then?"

I nodded, my throat tight. "Last night, at the Fireside Flannel Festival, she had just found out and couldn't keep it in anymore."

The tension in the room thickened, the weight of our history with the King family and my own family's legacy bearing down on us.

"The Kings knew something was up." Lee's voice was a low rumble, his jaw clenching. "Lots of angry questions after you left." He gestured toward his jaw and at a small bruise I hadn't bothered to notice.

My eyes narrowed. "What happened?"

Lee rolled his eyes playfully. He liked getting into scuffles with the Kings, so a hit to the jaw was no big deal to him. "Royal and JP got their panties in a twist. Demanding answers we didn't have." He shrugged. "A little shoving match is all."

Beside him, Annie shook her head and frowned. Inside, my heart sank. My brothers had cleaned up my mess, defended me, without even knowing why.

Lee's eyes softened, his grip on Annie's hand steady. "Duke, this kind of changes everything."

The truth hung heavy in the air—Sylvie's pregnancy was a complication we couldn't ignore, a reminder of the ties that bound us together and the consequences that could follow.

Tootie's gaze held mine, concern etched into her

features. "Have you thought about yourself, Duke? What do you want?"

I glanced at my family, my heart torn between loyalty to them and the growing affection I felt for Sylvie. "I want to be there for her. For them."

Wyatt's stern facade wavered, his eyes softening as he exhaled heavily. "We're with you, Duke. No matter what comes next."

Around the table, nods and reassuring smiles followed suit, a silent pledge of unity in the face of uncertainty.

"Do you think they know?" Lark asked.

A nod was all I could manage, the turmoil within me mirrored by the unease around the table. "MJ knows for sure. My guess would be they all do by now."

I hadn't heard from Sylvie this morning, and I hated it. My text wishing her good morning and checking in to see if she was okay had gone unanswered.

Annie grimaced. "She wasn't at the Sugar Bowl this morning, but there was *lots* of chatter." She shook her head. "Everyone was talking about it. Rumors are that Russell King lost his mind." She held up both hands. "You know how small-town rumors are—I'd take it with a grain of salt, but people were saying that he was *unhinged*—breaking things and generally being an asshole."

Beside her, my niece laughed, and Wyatt scolded her with another scowl.

My back stiffened. My chair scraped against the wood floor as I stood.

"Duke. Relax." My aunt's calm voice did little to soothe me. "We all know Russell is a hothead, but he wouldn't do anything to harm his daughter. We're all just a little shocked right now."

I moved to the sink and planted my hands on the edge,

letting my head hang before sighing and pushing off it. "Yeah, I know."

Still, my gut told me something was off. I needed to talk with her. To make sure she was okay.

"Come finish dinner." Tootie's hand found my back, and I let her guide me back to the cramped dinner table.

Penny managed to commandeer the conversation, and I'd never loved that kid more. Still, I couldn't think of anything besides Sylvie and how the hell we were going to figure this out.

Sylvie King is having my baby.

The singular truth in that statement was my only comfort. That, and knowing I would protect her with my life.

FIFTEEN

> Just a reminder that the appointment is at two.

JOHN OATES

> I'll be there.

I STARED AT THE TEXT, wondering if I should finally update Duke's name in my phone. Deciding against it, I slipped it into my apron, closed my eyes, and willed the fresh wave of nausea away.

The first week of October passed in a blur as autumn descended on Outtatowner. Beach visitors were slowly replaced by meandering drivers hunting for the signs of fall foliage, apple orchards, and pumpkin patches.

While Huck refused to serve pumpkin-spiced *anything*, I had convinced him to market toward the cozy fall vibes that drew new customers to the bakery. I was even impressed with the "Fall Leaves & Coffee Please" sign I had hand painted on the A-frame chalkboard on the sidewalk out front.

From what the four online pregnancy calculators told

me, I was about nine weeks pregnant, and *fuck* the exhaustion was real. So was the morning sickness that seemed to pop up out of nowhere, especially if I got too hungry. My boobs were doing this weird tingly thing, and mood swings? Hello, Satan, good to see you again today.

My father was speaking to me only in flared nostrils and shitty comments. My three brothers had spent the last few weeks taking turns pretending the entire situation didn't exist. Aunt Bug could hardly look at me without guilt-tripping me and expressing her shock and disappointment. *As if I didn't know.*

All the while, MJ was my rock.

Well, MJ and *him.*

Duke and I still texted and talked daily, but with the turmoil in my life, I kept my distance. He allowed me the space to navigate the minefield that was my dysfunctional family. I hated living in that house. Savannah was looking more and more like a faraway dream, but I saved a little more with every paycheck. I ignored the dread that washed through me when I thought about how I was going to tell Duke I planned to leave. That I *needed* to leave. Instead of dealing with it, I shoved the thoughts into a compartment labeled *Future Sylvie's Problems* and did what I could to make it through each day. I couldn't walk three feet without sidelong glances and hearing whispers behind my back.

I was about to become a single mother whose baby daddy was from my family's most hated rival. I had been selfish, and the worst part was I'd done it with unbridled *joy.* Consequences be damned.

High-five. Solid choice, Syl.

Sighing, I looked down at my phone. The text exchanges between us were the only bright spots in my gloomy, nausea-filled day. When morning shift finally ended, I pulled into the driveway of my aunt's house. The sound of a vehicle turning in behind me caught my attention. My heart hammered against my ribs after I saw Duke's truck pulling down the long driveway.

Once he parked, Duke got out and stood by the driver's door. "Thought maybe I could drive you."

I brushed a stray piece of hair from my face. "Oh . . . okay, thanks." I glanced down at my Sugar Bowl shirt and flour-dusted shorts. "I just need to change and I'll be ready."

Duke stuffed his hands in his pockets and nodded. I hurried up the steps and through the front door, leaving him standing by his truck.

I came up short when I found my aunt pulling her purse onto her shoulder. "Better hurry up. Don't want to be late."

I paused, glancing only a second over my shoulder. "Um, actually, Duke is here. He's planning to take me to the appointment."

Aunt Bug's eyebrows crept up her forehead. "Oh, I didn't realize." She set her purse onto the counter. She looked at the clock. "It's getting late."

I set aside my worried feelings and ran up the stairs to my bedroom. I tossed my work clothes in the hamper before pulling out a fresh shirt and shorts. Even now, my button-up pants were starting to feel tight. The pregnancy forums I'd been scrolling through said it was likely bloating, and as I looked at my belly in the mirror, it was hard to deny. My stomach hadn't really changed, but I did look like I was about two burritos deep into Chula's all-you-can-eat burrito bar. The linen shorts I chose had just enough stretch to accommodate my growing burrito baby.

When I walked back downstairs, Bug was nowhere to be found, and my stomach rolled. Back in the afternoon sunlight, Bug was standing in front of Duke, hands planted on her wide hips. His hands hung at his sides, and he looked down at my aunt. His face was unreadable as she wagged a finger at him. He only nodded.

I quickened my steps. When I approached, all I heard was Duke's low grumble of, "I understand."

"Ready!" I said brightly, attempting to mask the flutter of worry in my stomach.

Without another word, Duke walked to my side of his truck and opened the door for me.

Bug lifted an eyebrow. "Good luck, and call me later."

"I will!" I tracked his movements as Duke closed my door and walked to the driver's side before sliding into the truck. He shifted to reverse. "Survive the Inquisition?"

The corner of his mouth twitched. "Something like that."

The drive to the obstetrician's office was only about fifteen minutes toward a larger town in the area. I hadn't been this close to Duke since I had told him I was pregnant, and I was filled with the buzz of nerves. My heel tapped a jerky rhythm as he drove toward the doctor's office.

"Nervous?"

I ran my hands down my legs. "A little."

"Me too."

I pressed my hand into my stomach as it rolled. Duke glanced at me, and I chuckled softly. "I've been a little nauseous."

Duke leaned across the cab of the truck and opened the glove box. He fished something out and held his fist in front of me. "Here."

I held out my hand, and when he opened his, a small peppermint plopped down onto my palm. I stared down at it.

"Peppermint is supposed to help with nausea. Ginger is better, I guess, but it's something."

I blinked at him before staring down at the peppermint candy. *How the hell did he know that?*

Once we arrived at the doctor's office, the receptionist checked me in. The office was quiet, and within minutes we were called back to the room. Before entering, the nurse handed me a small plastic cup to leave a urine sample and instructions on where to place it when I was finished. I blushed and excused myself to the bathroom while Duke stood outside of it.

Once I finished, she led us to the room. A boxy ultrasound machine was tucked in the corner, and a long table with stirrups at the end stared back at me. The reality of our situation slammed into me.

"Here's your robe. The opening should be in front. Dr. Hokum likes to perform all first baby appointments, so she'll be here in a few minutes. You can sit at the end of the table while you wait."

I thanked the nurse and looked at Duke as I held my robe. His huge frame took up half the space in the small room. He shifted on his feet. "I'll give you a minute."

Before I could respond, he slipped out of the room. I quickly undressed and folded my clothes, stashing my underwear between the layers of clothing and setting it in a small pile next to the chair. I cracked open the door and let Duke know I was decent.

Perched on the edge of the table, I watched Duke sit in the chair. His shoulders were far too wide for the cramped seat, and tension rolled off him in waves. A soft knock came moments before the door cracked open again.

Dr. Hokum was a soft-spoken woman who appeared to be in her late fifties. Her calm, confident presence did little to settle my nerves. She asked a few questions regarding my last period and any symptoms I was experiencing. She assured me the nausea and tender boobs were signs the pregnancy was progressing normally. The doctor instructed me to lie back as she prepared for the ultrasound.

"This early, we will do an internal ultrasound. It helps us get a better idea of how far along the baby's development is and get you a few pictures." She smiled as she arranged the implements, one of which looked like a slim robotic dildo. Heat flooded my cheeks. I had no idea why I was feeling shy—I'd already seen Duke's perfect dick, after all— but the whole situation felt beyond bizarre.

Dr. Hokum shook a bottle of lube, and as she squeezed, the bottle let out a loud, wet farting noise. "Oh!" She laughed. "Well, that was a silly sound!"

A fizzy, bubbling giggle erupted from me as I caught Duke's eye. A playful glint softened his typically hard features as we both struggled to maintain control of our laughter. Finally, his cough-covered scoff sent me over the edge into a full-blown fit of giggles. Tension dissolved, and I sighed into the table. Duke stood, stepping forward, and placed a hand on my shoulder.

I glanced up at him, offering a small smile.

His dark eyes held mind. "It's going to be okay."

I pressed my lips together. "I know."

Dr. Hokum inserted the wand, and the image on the screen flared to life. A little gummy bear–shaped blob appeared before us, and I heard Duke's sharp intake of breath. His hand tightened on my shoulder as we stared in wonder at the tiny life growing inside me. Dr. Hokum narrated her clicks and measurements while she typed into the large computer. Duke's eyes stayed focused on the screen, as if he was memorizing every word the doctor uttered.

The pressure of the probe was sharp as the doctor pressed onto my belly and moved it around. "The timeline looks good based on your last menses. Intercourse would have been approximately seven weeks ago? Give or take?"

I could feel the heat flare in my cheeks as Dr. Hokum looked at me for confirmation. "Yes." My voice was rusty and tight.

The doctor nodded. "Perfect. You're about nine weeks along. Baby seems to be getting along just fine in there."

Duke released a breath. *Had he been nervous too?*

Dr. Hokum looked between us. "Would you like to hear the heartbeat?"

I nodded, and with the click of a button, a reverberating *whoosh* filled the small room. As she moved the probe again, the jarring whoosh was replaced by a steady *ba-dum.*

Ba-dum. Ba-dum. Ba-dum. Tears pricked at my eyes. "It's fast."

Dr. Hokum smiled as Duke's grip tightened on my shoulder. "The baby's heartbeat is about 160 beats per minute. Totally normal."

I sneaked a glance at Duke. He was wide eyed and staring at the screen. Dr. Hokum reached up and traced a circle around the fuzzy black-and-white image. "There they are. That little flicker here is the heart."

"Wow." I stared at the tiny flicker as it blinked.

A baby.

My baby.

Our baby.

I was terrified, but seeing the baby's heartbeat, something shifted. There was a human *growing inside me*. I had to protect that precious little human. A tear slipped down my cheek as stress and overwhelm rolled over me.

Dr. Hokum clicked a few more buttons on the computer, and a trail of black-and-white images streamed out of the printer. She removed the probe, covered my bottom, and helped me clean up. Lowering the stirrups, I set my feet down and sat up.

"The baby is healthy and thriving. As long as your symptoms are manageable, you won't need to come back for another four weeks. The important things to remember are to eat a variety of healthy, pregnancy-safe foods, take your prenatal vitamins, and try to maintain low stress levels."

A light scoff escaped me before I could stop it.

Dr. Hokum's gaze flicked between Duke and me. "If you experience any significant changes in symptoms—extreme nausea, bleeding, that kind of thing—just call the office." Dr. Hokum gently squeezed my knee before excusing herself to allow me to redress.

Duke waited for me in the hallway, and when I exited the room, he was staring down at the ultrasound photos. My heart rolled painfully in my chest.

On the drive back to my aunt's house, I studied the photograph and wondered if there had ever been a time when such a reckless decision had ever made me happier. There was still a lot to figure out, but for the first time, I felt like maybe I wouldn't have to figure all that out alone.

As Duke's truck pulled down the driveway, the warm, fuzzy feeling from the doctor's office evaporated.

My father's Porsche was parked in front of the house, and knots formed in my stomach. I carefully unclipped the seat belt and shifted toward the door. "Thanks for taking me."

I needed to get inside as quickly as possible, before my father confronted Duke and made a scene.

Duke's hand reached out and brushed my arm, stopping me from exiting. "Are you okay?"

I focused on not glancing toward the car or the house. "Yep. Thanks again." The hollow cheeriness infused in my voice was a lie, but I needed Duke to leave. *Now*.

Without looking back, I closed the truck door and hurried up the porch steps. The heavy door betrayed me, groaning when I opened it.

"Sylvie." My father's voice bounced off the high ceilings and echoed down the hallway.

Steeling my nerves, I lifted my chin and walked toward the living room. My fingers curled around the waxy paper of the ultrasound photos.

In the living room, Russell King was dressed in dark slacks, an expensive navy polo, and shiny dress shoes. Not a hair out of place, he looked like a man who ruled his kingdom.

Because he did.

I stood, shoulders back and chin high as I waited, just as I had been taught.

He looked me over once before returning to pace across the living room. His eyes had a way of moving over me but never really seeing *me*. I knew he saw my mother when he looked at me. How could he not? We could have easily passed as sisters. I'd given up on trying to prove how different from her I was a long time ago. It didn't matter what I did— he would always look at me and see *her* staring back at him.

"I spoke with Bug this morning. She's informed me you're planning to keep this baby?"

I swallowed and prayed my voice didn't break. "I am."

He stopped and turned to me as though he was still surprised to hear that I would keep a baby that was half-Sullivan. My dad never had a poker face, and the subtle disgust smeared across his features was glaring.

Hot, sweaty prickles tingled at my hairline as he stared at me.

With a curt nod, he continued pacing. "Well, then. We'll just be sure he knows he's a King. Raise him right."

Tell him. Tell him you're moving to Savannah and never coming back.

"Yes, sir."

I hated how small and insignificant he made me feel. I hated that I couldn't speak up against him, even now.

He sighed in relief and scrubbed a hand over his clean-shaven face, letting loose an audible sigh. My father rocked back on his heels. "And don't you worry, I'll take care of the Sullivan boy."

I would have laughed at anyone calling Duke a boy until my father's words sank in. "Take care of him? What would—"

My father raised a hand, cutting me off. "That baby is a King. He will be raised as a King by Kings. That's the end of the discussion."

"Duke has every right to be involved with this baby." I scoffed in disbelief that I even had to utter these words. I pressed my hand to my belly. "As the mother of this child, I get to choose."

"You gave up your right to choose when you spread your legs for a Sullivan." His angry words slapped me across the face. "I will *not* have another woman walk into my house and disrespect me." We both knew exactly who he was talking about as his loud, angry words filled the living room.

Tears welled and my lip began to tremble as hurt and fury rattled through me.

"Don't you dare," he spit. "Don't you dare cry and act like you're the victim." He pointed toward the stairwell. "You go upstairs, you fix that face, and hold your head up high. You're a King and you will damn well act like it!"

"Sylvie." The heat and anger in Duke's voice had my head whipping around to see him storming through the doorway of my family home.

My father stammered. "Who the hell do you think you are barging in here like this? You've done enough."

Duke's dark eyes pinned my father in place. "I'm the only one here who gives a shit about your daughter. That's what I'm doing here." Tension filled the air as Duke clenched and unclenched his fists. "Now, I would hate to disrespect a man in his family home, but that's the mother of my child you're speaking to. If you can't speak to her with respect, then you speak to me."

My father's head reared back, aghast that anyone, let alone a Sullivan, would dare speak to him that way. My eyes widened. *No one* spoke to Russell King that way. Duke stepped up next to me, his hand landing gently at my lower back. My father's eyes flicked down to his arm, then back up to me.

"Get out."

I stepped forward to argue with him, to plead with him, maybe defuse the situation. When I realized he was speaking to me, my open mouth clamped shut.

As I sucked in a deep, shaky breath through my nose, Duke's voice lowered to a grumbly whisper. "Come on, let's go."

I squared my shoulders and swallowed back the vomit that threatened to come up.

I turned, stubbornness and hurt driving my feet forward when my father's words stopped me. "I always knew you were just like her."

A whore. A black mark on the King name.

He didn't have to say those words aloud, because I had heard him speak about my mother enough times to know exactly how he felt about her and how he had always, apparently, felt about me.

I turned to look at my father's cold, hard face, ice running through my veins. "Maybe I am like her, but there's a common denominator in these situations. The only person we are running from is you."

I made it all the way down the porch steps, across the lawn, and to Duke's truck before bursting into tears.

Once inside, Duke threw the truck in reverse and peeled out of the driveway. I had no idea where he was headed. All I knew was that the life I had always known was made of tinder, and in a single moment, I flipped a match and ignited it before my eyes.

⁓

DUKE'S TRUCK was pointed toward a quiet, dune-lined cliff. In the distance, waves pounded against the shoreline as tall beach grasses swayed in the October breeze. My tears had dried, and apart from mild nausea, I was numb. I wrapped my arms to hug my middle.

"What do you want to do?"

I was stunned and only managed a blink as I sneaked a glance in Duke's direction. I scoffed and patted my sticky cheeks. "No one's ever asked me that."

"Well, I'm asking you." The hard grit in his voice was undeniably sexy.

I swallowed hard. "I'm moving. To Savannah. Well, I *was* moving. I had plans to move. I have to get out of here."

Duke stilled except for his hands as they clenched the truck's steering wheel. "When?"

"The plan was spring, but . . ." I gestured to my belly. "Plans kind of changed."

"Does it have to be Georgia?"

My brows pulled down in the center. "Um . . . no. I—I don't think so."

His lips pressed into a thin line, and his head jerked. "Will you stay? Once the baby comes, we can figure the rest out, but you heard the doctor. Additional stress isn't good for either one of you, and it sounds like nothing but stress in that house. If you stay with me—even for a few months after you give birth—I can have some time with the baby before you leave."

The tortured look on his face was unbearable. The plan had *always* been to leave. To get out. *Finally* be free.

But now leaving would mean taking Duke's child from him. Could I do that? Even if staying meant losing a part of myself?

He studied my face as I struggled to find the right words. "Look. I know what it's like to want to leave and can't. All I'm asking for is time—to help you while you figure it out. I'm not asking for forever."

I'm not asking for forever.

His words shouldn't have stung. It wasn't like either of us ever planned to get pregnant and a baby bound us together forever. Plus, it was undeniable that it would be nice to have his help once the baby arrived if the minimal sleep that the baby books proclaimed was actually true. Savannah would always be there.

I inhaled and set my shoulders. "Okay, but maybe there should be some rules."

He nodded. "Like?"

"I'm paying rent."

Duke's head made the tiniest shake. "No, you're not."

"But I—"

He softened his look. "You said it yourself; you're saving money. I don't need the rent, and you're doing *all* the work by carrying the baby. A safe place to live is the least I can do. I insist."

The strong finality of his words sent a ripple of heat through me. I swallowed thickly and nodded.

"It's settled then. I've got you while you're pregnant, and once the baby comes, we'll figure the rest out. Anything else?"

"I'd like my family to be able to come over and see me. I know my father is a difficult man, but the rest of my family . . ." I trailed off. In reality my brothers could be difficult too. I needed to rein them in if this was ever going to work.

His jaw twitched as if he knew my brothers would be a pain in his ass. "It will be your home too. You can spend time with anyone you want to." He looked at me. "But they will respect you. That's nonnegotiable."

"Of course." I nodded, hoping it was true. With a deep breath, I sank into the leather seat. "So we're really doing this?"

He looked out onto the violent waves. "Looks like it." The quiet stretched between us. I let his masculine scent wash over me, and the warmth from his body settled my nerves.

Finally, his deep voice broke through the silence. "You know you can do this, right?" I looked at him, questioning. "You're stronger than you think. You don't need anybody. But what I'm telling you is you don't have to do it alone."

Duke was a man who took responsibility seriously, that much I knew. Whether my affection for him was a product of having his baby or something else, I wasn't entirely sure. But I did know one thing: with Duke I felt safe.

For now, that would have to be enough.

SEVENTEEN

DUKE

I HAD NEVER LIVED with a woman. Hell, I was still a kid myself when I hung my dreams in the back closet to take over the family farm. Stepped up. Be steady and stable while I watched my family crumble in front of me.

I had been helpless against it.

After pouring myself into the work, living on the main parcel in the old farmhouse was what had made the most sense. Over time, I took care in updating it and making it comfortable. It was rustic and masculine. No frills.

I looked around the living room with its tall, wood-beamed ceilings and no-nonsense decor.

I should have bought a fucking candle or something.

With MJ's help, Sylvie had planned to pack a few of her belongings into her car and meet me back at the farm that evening. I was uneasy having her return to her aunt's house, worried her father would be ready for round two. Sylvie assured me she was fine and that her sister's presence would help soften her father.

I still didn't like it.

After I left her, I checked in with Cisco and got to work

moving things around the house to make Sylvie more comfortable.

She had texted me forty minutes ago saying she would be by in about fifteen minutes. I checked my watch and glanced at the clock on the fireplace mantel. Since then I had paced by the front window, ignoring the rapidly cooling coffee in my hands. Ed whined at my feet, unsure about my anxious mood. I looked around the farmhouse. It was clean, but simple. Nothing like the austere home Sylvie shared with her family.

The front door opened to a small vestibule for boots and coats. Years ago I had taken a sledgehammer to a wall in the old parlor, opening it up to the living room. A downstairs bedroom had been converted to my office, and the kitchen was at the back of the house with a large window that over-looked the blueberry fields in the distance. The real appeal of the house was the porch. The wide, covered expanse was where I ate many of my meals, but I mostly just sat and enjoyed the quiet, rolling landscape.

Rather than stare out the window, waiting for her arrival, I tracked outside. I sucked in the fall air and took in the view. The sun hung low in the sky as fall's early golds deepened to amber, casting a glow to the trees that bordered my fields. The bushes themselves had already begun taking on the burgundy hue of autumn. The kaleidoscope of color rippled down through the rows and would carry over into the next month or so. The unmistakable scent of fall—pine, wood burning, and drying leaves walked with me as I headed to the barn to check on Duck. Ed happily trotted behind me, eager to check on his youngling.

Once Ed was satisfied that Duck was safe in the barn, he turned his attention to the crunch of tires on gravel. With a deep bark, he loped out of the barn and across the driveway. My chest squeezed as Sylvie's car pulled down the path. Ed came dangerously close to the tires as he made tight loops around the moving car.

That dog will never learn.

A small ball of tension unfurled when Sylvie stepped from her car. She no longer looked stricken—her golden eyes were bright in the late-afternoon sun, and her blonde hair was piled on top of her head.

She rested one arm on the open car door and smiled shyly. "Hey, roomie."

A small laugh pushed out of my nose. I lifted my cup. "Squatter."

She pinned me with an annoyed glare, but the corners of her mouth tipped up. Stress and tension eased out of my shoulders. I hated seeing Sylvie cry, and the relief that she was in a better mood lifted my own. I walked toward her car, looking into the back seat, and was surprised to see she hadn't brought much with her.

Maybe she's already changed her mind.

She looked behind her to where I stared at her small suitcases. "I only brought the basics. Unfortunately not much still fits comfortably." She shrugged and ran a hand down her barely there belly, and a hot poker prodded my chest.

When she went to pull the bags from the car, I stopped her. "I got it."

I led the way into the house, depositing her bags by the front door.

"Duke . . . wow."

I shifted in my boots. "I know it's not much, but—"

"It's perfect." Her hand briefly touched my arm before she snatched it back and clasped it with the other. "Can I get a tour?"

I tucked my hands in my pockets. I didn't trust myself not to lean into her and sneak a brush of my hand across her back. The open-concept first floor was brief, and I led her up the wide stairs to the second floor.

I opened the primary bedroom door and gestured for her to enter. "This can be your room. You can decorate it however you like, but for now it's got the basics."

Sylvie's eyes scanned the room, taking in the large king-size bed, walk-in closet, and attached bathroom. She frowned. "This seems like the main bedroom."

I nodded. "It is."

"Shouldn't that be your room?"

"It was, but I moved out. I wanted you to have the attached bathroom. Plus, it's closest to the small bedroom, which I figured might work well for a nursery. Right now it's just storage."

Her eyes went wide as she looked at me. "Oh . . ."

I cleared my throat. "If you don't like it"—I gestured down the hallway—"there are two other bedrooms. You can take your pick."

"This is perfect, but can I see the others?"

"Of course." I nodded and walked down the hallway. Across the hall was the small bedroom. It was empty except for a bed and small dresser. I'd used it as a spare room in case a friend or one of my siblings ever needed a place to crash for the night.

A wistful look came over Sylvie's features as she looked at the room. Her hand moved to her belly. It was as though she could see it transformed into a nursery for our baby. Emotion was hot and thick in my throat. Babies and nurseries and living with Sylvie were all so new. I still didn't know exactly how it would all work out, but having a safe place for them to live was my top priority.

Farther down the hall, I pointed out the other room I had claimed as my own.

Sylvie's fingertips pressed into her lips. "Oh, Duke." A small laugh escaped behind her fingers. "That bed is way too small."

The bed was shoved into a corner and, with my frame, would likely be comically small, but I didn't care. "It'll be fine."

In the tight confines of the doorway, I wanted to touch her—hold her to me and assure her things would be okay. She smelled so fucking good, and for weeks I had imagined exploring her body, dragging soft moans from her as I found all kinds of new ways to make her come. I was undeniably attracted to her.

Knowing my child was growing inside her only made me want her *more*. That fact alone only made me hate myself. Since our date on the beach, Sylvie hadn't let on that she was interested in anything more than friendship. Given our family situation, dating would have been hard enough, and adding a baby to the mix was downright reckless.

I knew I needed to be careful with her.

I shifted out of the doorway, needing space. "I'll bring your bags up and let you get settled."

Before I could leave, she held me in place with a gentle hand on my forearm. "Thank you for this. I know it's not easy, but if it means anything at all . . ." Her soft eyes looked at me, and my heart rolled. "I think you're going to make a great dad."

My jaw clenched to keep my emotions in check. "Sylvie, I liked you before this happened. You are funny and sweet and full of fire. I am willing to take you in any form you're willing to give me. You have my word that I will be the best father to our kid." I cleared my throat as tightness set in. "Let's get you moved in."

Without looking back, I hurried to move her into my home and, with any luck, out of my heart before she broke it for good.

EIGHTEEN

SYLVIE

I GROANED and stretched as the last hazy images of my dream floated away. The soft glow of the morning sun filtered through the sheer curtains, casting a golden halo upon Duke's room.

My room.

I still couldn't believe he had moved himself out of the primary bedroom to give it to me.

I rolled to my back and stared at the walls, painted in a serene shade of sky blue. Their cool color seemed to hold whispered promises of peace and calm. I gently placed my socked feet on the timeworn wooden floor. It creaked softly under my cautious steps, as if sharing in the secrets of this haven as I made my way to the bathroom. Mornings had become rough, nausea bubbling only seconds after waking if I didn't manage to scarf down a few crackers. I swallowed hard and sucked in a breath through my nose. A faint scent of freshly fallen leaves lingered in the air, mixed with Duke's woody, masculine smell—a reminder of the man who once claimed this space as his own.

The bed, draped in fluffy white linens, stood as a silent

sentinel against one wall. Its broad expanse was inviting, as if urging me to lie back down, unload my burdens, and find solace. I could sleep in that bed all damn day if I wasn't careful. I imagined the worn quilt draped across the high-back chair, tucked in the corner, had seen quiet nights spent cocooned in dreams and whispered confidences. I couldn't help but wonder how many other women had been lucky enough to see Duke's bedroom. My gut told me not many—he seemed like the type of man who kept a space like this for only himself. A reprieve.

As I made my way to the bathroom, I traced my fingers along the rough-hewn edges of the wooden furniture, and a shiver of vulnerability coursed through me. Duke, with his gruff exterior and calloused hands, had carved out a haven that spoke of hidden tenderness.

My heart swelled with a mixture of awe and trepidation, a storm of emotions I dared not voice aloud. With every glance, every touch, I found myself craving him.

I am willing to take you in any form you're willing to give me. You have my word that I will be the best father to our kid.

Maybe it was pregnancy hormones like the internet suggested, but whatever it was, I couldn't get him out of my head. I was learning that Duke was fiercely protective of those in his circle. People looked to him for answers, and he felt it was his job to produce results. He shouldered the pressure of caring for his father, his family, the farm, and its workers. He was up before the sun and put in more work before lunch than anyone I knew.

When Duke said he would step up and be a good father for our child, I wholeheartedly believed him.

Morning sickness finally reared its head, and once I was emptied out, I washed my face and got ready for my day. Thankfully, I had stuffed a few crackers in the bedside table, and the carbs were enough to get me down the stairs without throwing up again. I had learned that if I could make it to breakfast, my stomach could settle enough to trudge through the day with only mild, lingering nausea.

The air held a chill, so I stuffed my arms into the fur-lined flannel I loved. When I put my hands into the pockets, paper crinkled against my fingertips. I pulled out a sticky note, along with a few sour candies, specifically labeled for pregnancy-related morning sickness. I popped one in and read the note, written in Duke's hasty scrawl:

DARYL,
    TEA IS READY TO BREW IF YOU'RE UP FOR IT.
THERE ARE MORE SOUR CANDIES IN THE CUPBOARD
IF THEY WORK.

~OATES

I snickered at his use of our ridiculous nicknames. Had I known they would become a *thing*, I probably would have chosen better ones. Something sexier or less masculine when he thinks of me.

I glanced at the countertop to see a mug and tea bag waiting for me, along with my bottle of prenatal vitamins. My fingertips dragged across the cool surface of the quartz countertop. On the stovetop, a teakettle had already been filled and was waiting for me to heat it up. The sour candies settled my bubbling tummy as I waited. When it was ready, I let the tea warm my belly. Somehow it just tasted better because Duke had thought to get it ready for me. In the two weeks I had been living here, I'd learned Duke often left before sunrise but found subtle, tiny ways to think of me or put my needs first.

It was the first time since finding out I was pregnant I allowed myself to believe things might actually work out in the end. Duke seemed determined to co-parent with me and be an active partner throughout my pregnancy. With a smile, I pulled out my phone.

> How did you know about the candies?

JOHN OATES

> I have Google.

I smiled down at his gruff, no-nonsense response. He might not think it was a big deal, but having someone anticipate your needs was new and something I could *definitely* get used to. I knew Duke was likely somewhere on the farm, but my slow waking meant I was already running behind for work.

Once I made the drive to town, the Sugar Bowl was just opening. A few older patrons were milling around the front entrance as Huck unlocked it and welcomed them inside. The aroma of fresh coffee was enticing, but I'd learned that while it smelled amazing, it was harsh on my stomach and would make a reappearance just as quickly. I was also trying to be mindful of caffeine, since my doctor said no more than one or two cups per day.

Plastering on a cheery smile, I tied my apron over my Sugar Bowl shirt and jeans before making my way into the main dining area. As my first trimester was coming to a close, my burrito baby had subtly transformed into a tiny pregnancy bump. I only hoped my morning sickness would ease up as I entered my second trimester. The baby book I had been reading said it was possible.

Promises. Promises.

Soft conversations filtered over the sounds of the ding of the register and gurgling whistle of the espresso machine. I wiped down open tables, checked on diners, and offered friendly smiles to those who passed by the large front window.

". . . kicked her out. Told her no Sullivan baby was living under a roof he paid for."

I stopped in my tracks as the conversation behind me continued. My ears pricked, and heat flooded my chest.

"With all their family fighting? The pranks? That kid is going to be messed up, for sure."

"The child will have to pick a side, that's all I know . . ."

The not-so-hushed whispers of the gossiping women grated on my nerves. I couldn't help but to imagine their shocked faces as I screamed the answers to all the whispers I'd caught happening behind my back over the past few weeks.

Yes! I am eleven weeks pregnant with Duke Sullivan's baby! YES, THAT MEANS WE HAD SEX! Of course it was amazing. Yes, I am living with him. No, we aren't still fucking. Yes, I wish we were!

Oh, shit.

I hadn't allowed my mind to wander in that particular direction. I knew my pregnancy hormones were the reason I couldn't seem to keep much food down, but I was also blaming them for the wild dreams I had been having of Duke.

Hot, naked, *intense* dreams.

Trouble was, I knew the reality of Duke's gigantic, beautiful dick was even *better* than the dreams.

Frustrated, I turned on my heels and hit the ladies with the sweetest smile I could muster. My glance flickered to their long-empty coffee cups. "All finished, or should I give you a few more minutes to talk about people and pretend they can't hear?" Their stunned eyes widened. "No?" I swiped the coffee cups in one motion. "Have the day that you deserve!"

Huck stared at me as I sailed past him and into the kitchen. I dumped the cups into the sink with a clatter and braced my hands against the counter. Behind me, I heard the familiar squeak of the saloon doors.

I turned to my boss and held up my hands. "I know. I'm sorry. I lost my cool."

Huck shook his head and gestured toward the dining room. "As far as I'm concerned, you did nothing wrong. I let them know if they can't speak kindly to my staff, they can find a new coffee shop."

Huck crossed his arms and looked at me with kindness, not pity. Tears welled in my eyes, and I launched myself forward, wrapping him in a hug. His crossed arms stayed wedged between us as I struggled to get my arms all the way around his broad frame.

When I released him, he looked at me with pinched brows. "You good?"

A laugh slipped out. *Who the hell knows how I am?* "Yeah, I'm good."

By the time my shift was over, my feet were throbbing and my back ached. It had become my nightly ritual to slip into a hot bath, and tonight it couldn't come soon enough.

My body couldn't decide if it wanted to be sick or railed into next week.

Probably both.

Through Duke I had learned that the farm was 325 acres, 125 of which were the rows and rows of blueberry fields. The farm kept him busy, and he often worked long hours—he walked the fields, repaired equipment. It also appeared as though he had a close relationship with his workers. He treated them with kindness and respect, and they welcomed my presence on the farm with warm smiles and friendly waves.

In the afternoons, I liked to get a little exercise by walking in the fields. Duke let me know that while technically it was his property, he considered the section dedicated to the homes for the migrant workers their personal space. He maintained the homes when needed but for the most part allowed them to live in peace and privacy without their boss overlooking their every move.

Apart from MJ, none of my family had come to visit me on the farm. Some days it was like our own bubble of privacy and an oasis from the sidelong glances and whispers that followed me everywhere I went in town.

After work, Sloane had asked me to hang out for a while. She was taking her twins to the local park, and I used it as an opportunity to get some fresh air and shake off the annoyance from the gossipers earlier in the day. Duke had also texted me, letting me know there was an issue with a piece of farm equipment, so he likely wouldn't be around for dinner.

Sloane and I picked up something for us and the kids, and I was reminded of how nice it was to have a friend to talk to. She was still reeling from the house fire that took everything from her, but thankfully—and to everyone's shock—my brother Abel had agreed to give her a job at the brewery. My oldest brother could come across as callous and harsh, and he had his own darker past, but buried somewhere deep in there was a good man. It was there in the way he stepped up for my friend without hesitation.

By the time I got back to Duke's house—I still couldn't think of it as our home—the sun was sinking behind the tree line. I had gotten used to the way Three-Legged Ed would bark and circle my car, but it still nearly gave me a heart attack every time. When I opened the car door, I was greeted with heavy barks and sloppy dog kisses.

I bent over and squished Ed's face between my hands and leaned down to whisper, "You're so stupid." He lolled his tongue and looked at me with affection. I laughed. "You are cute, though."

In the direction of the barn I could hear movement and clanking but couldn't see Duke. "Where's your daddy? Huh? Where's Dad?" Ed let out a loud, yippy bark. "Go on! Go find him." I gestured toward the barn, but Ed took only a few steps before turning back and barking at me, as if to ask, *Well, are you coming?*

The house was dark, so I straightened my purse on my shoulder, grabbed the paper bag from my car, and followed Ed toward the large barn. Muttering and a string of curses got louder as we approached. I pulled my sweater tighter around my middle to ward off the late-October chill.

As we neared the barn, Ed left my side to trot over and check on Duck, who I was sure was tucked away somewhere inside the barn. The huge, boxy blueberry-picking machine was parked outside the barn's large opening. It was clunky and silver with smooth sides. The top held a platform edged with a blue metal railing. On one end was a single seat and a panel of controls for a driver.

Duke had once explained that the machine was tall enough to drive over the rows of blueberries. Inside, soft rubber bristles would shake the bushes hard enough to drop berries onto trays, but gentle enough not to damage the plants themselves. He still preferred to handpick the berries on Sullivan Farms, but often used the machines toward the end of the season if there was a threat of frost.

Now that berry picking season was officially over, I tipped my head, wondering if this was just some kind of routine maintenance.

"You piece of shit!" Duke's irritated voice echoed across the farm as a loud clatter closely followed. I watched as Duke slid himself out from underneath the large machine. His back was pressed against a rolling board that allowed him to move freely under the blueberry picker.

He sat up, and my mouth went dry. The arms of his T-shirt had been cut off, giving me a clear view of his toned shoulders and biceps, despite the autumn weather. Duke hunched over, resting his elbows on his knees, and a V of sweat clung to his back. I took in his scowl and backward baseball hat as heat bloomed between my legs. My clit throbbed, and I had to bite back the moan that almost escaped me.

Thoughts of having sex with Duke, of feeling his large hard body on top of me, consumed me. Seeing him dressed in jeans and a cutoff shirt with that backward hat did not just make him hot—it made him *irresistible.* I wanted to straddle him, to feel his hands on my hips as I ground into him.

What would he do if I begged him to ease this ache that neither my fingers nor a vibrator could seem to make go away?

Duke and I had had conversations about how being around each other was helpful, that we would continue to get to know each other before the baby was born. In theory, it made sense, but in reality, it was pure torture. I'm sure

Duke thought I was quiet and liked my space, but the truth was I mostly kept to my room because I couldn't get enough of him. Just being in the same room as him was enough to throw my sex drive into overdrive.

I will definitely be coming to the thought of him in that fucking hat tonight.

My movements caught his eye, and he looked over. "Hey."

I kept my smile tight in an effort to keep my tongue from hanging out at the sight of him. I lifted up the small brown paper bag. "Not sure if you already ate, but I grabbed the pulled-pork platter from Momma Faye's Barbecue. The fries are probably soggy." I shrugged. "But it's better than nothing."

His dark eyes roamed over me, and flames danced beneath my skin. "You didn't have to do that."

I smiled at him and turned toward the house, then stopped and looked over my shoulder with a smile. "I know. 'Night, Duke."

I closed my eyes and breathed as I took the familiar steps toward the farmhouse. I could feel his eyes pinned to my back. "Good night, Sylvie."

Once inside, I set his dinner on the counter and went straight upstairs to plop down on the bed with a sigh. I toed off my shoes and stared at the ceiling, letting the image of sweaty, muscular Duke run in a loop in my mind. My hand skated over my sensitive nipples and moved lower, teasing over the fabric of my pants and between my legs. I had tried, *really tried*, to think of anyone else when my hormones got this out of control, but it was no use. Hot models, porn on my phone, *nothing* could even get me close to relief. Nothing except for Duke, that is.

Replaying our beach date again in my mind, or imagining new scenarios, like one in which I was pressed against the counter, ass up while he devoured me from behind, was enough to have me orgasming in minutes flat. I imagined his rough, calloused hands tweaking my nipples while his mouth burned a delicious path across my skin.

Deep pressure built between my legs as my clit throbbed. I slipped my hand beneath the waistband of my pants and down to my aching clit. I knew my fingers were a poor substitute for him, but I was desperate. Downstairs I heard the click of the front door and the familiar clack of Ed's nails on the hardwood. He was close, under the same roof, and I could practically smell his cologne waft up the stairs. I bet tonight he smelled like his cologne mixed with a delicious hint of sweat.

My panting breaths were desperate and heavy as I heard his footfalls ascending the stairs. In my mind, Duke growled as he devoured my pussy. Rolling to my stomach, I buried my face in a pillow as thoughts of him drove me closer and closer to relief. I had an image of Duke tucked away—him sitting in the living room by the fire with black glasses as he read a book.

Oh god. Why was Duke in glasses so fucking hot?

My orgasm rolled over me in rich, delicious waves, and as I pictured Duke wearing those glasses while he filled me, I lay on my side with my hands still tucked in my underwear, attempting to catch my breath. The faint sound of a shower down the hallway had me groaning all over again as I imagined Duke sudsy and naked.

I pouted and groaned.

Still unsatisfied, even my body knew nothing could ever replace the real thing.

NINETEEN

DUKE

"Happy Thanksgiving, Uncle Duke!"

My niece, Penny, leaped off the porch stairs of High-field House. My brother Lee and his now-girlfriend Annie had moved in and were in the process of turning it into a beautiful home. Across the driveway, Sand Dune Art Barn was closed up, but tucked inside were the beginnings of Annie's dream art studio. Together they planned to turn it into a gathering place for our community and tourists.

"You brought Duck!" Penny sailed past me toward the truck.

I shrugged. "Ed won't go anywhere without him."

"Ed won't, huh?" My brother looked at me with a smirk and shook my hand. "Happy Thanksgiving." He looked over my shoulder. "Hey, Dad."

Our father closed the passenger-side door behind him and wrapped Penny in a hug. "Hi, Son." Dad looked down at Penny. "Let's get that duck unloaded. What do you say, kiddo?"

Together, Dad and Penny removed Duck from the back seat and set him on the ground. We laughed as he waddled next to Ed and followed the dog out into the yard. I looked across the wide lawn to the fields in the distance. A crushed limestone path was part of a thirty-four-mile former railway that had been converted to a path for walkers, bikers, and horses. In a roundabout way, it also connected Highfield House to Sullivan Farms.

One by one the leaves had fallen in quiet surrender. In the meadow, wild grasses paled, and the honey-and-amber shades reminded me of the gold and umber of Sylvie's eyes. I was pleased to see that at this end of the property winter mulch insulated the base of the bushes. We'd done good work, and the berry bushes could rest as winter quickly approached.

Fragments of unease rolled through me. Earlier in the week, while inspecting the mulching, I once again found unfamiliar tracks in the frosty grass. Cisco couldn't account for them, and it rattled me. The slim parcel of land bordered an area that was owned by the town and was used as an open-space groundwater recharge area.

Vehicles never frequented the strip of land. Hell, maybe it was bored teenagers looking for a place to get into trouble. Still, I didn't like the idea of someone inching closer to Sullivan Farms, especially with Sylvie now living there.

"You coming or do you plan to freeze to death?" My father's voice shook me from the dark thoughts that had started to creep in.

"Yep." I retrieved the pie I had picked up from the Sugar Bowl and headed into the house.

The crisp autumn air clung to me as I stepped through the threshold of Lee and Annie's home, where the savory scent of roasted turkey and simmering gravy enveloped the room. The clinking of silverware against the dishes echoed against the warm, wooden walls, and the flickering candlelight cast a soft, amber glow over the gathered family.

Penny led Dad through the house toward the living room. His once-sharp eyes were slightly distant and cloudy, but I prayed for a good day. I couldn't help but feel a pang of sadness as I caught his vacant stare.

Lark and Penny's laughter erupted from the corner, where they were entertaining Aunt Tootie with tales of schoolyard adventures. Annie's familiar smile greeted me as she bustled about, her apron dusted with flour. She and Lee exchanged a playful look when she walked by, and he pinched her ass. Her curls bounced as she laughed and swatted him away.

My chest was tight. Sylvie's absence was a void that gnawed at my chest. I closed my eyes briefly, imagining her laughter mingling with the others' as her delicate fingers caressed the baby bump that had just started to form.

I wished she were here, sharing in this imperfect yet beautiful gathering. It wasn't all that long ago I had given up on my family ever feeling whole again. Now I was wrapped up in a King, and it threatened to unravel the whole thing all over again.

I knew Sylvie was already across town, surrounded by her opulent world, likely indulging in a luxurious Thanksgiving that stood in stark contrast to the simplicity of our own.

Maybe next year.

I silently chastised myself as I took a seat amid the laughter and chatter. By next year Sylvie and our baby would be in Savannah.

Tootie placed a gentle hand on my shoulder. "How are you holding up?" Her kind eyes spoke volumes.

I frowned. "Everything is fine."

She patted my shoulder but didn't press the issue. My family gathered around Annie and Lee's table. We bumped elbows and shifted dishes as we passed the food around, filling our plates.

With a roll stuffed in her mouth, Penny leaned forward. "Are you getting married?"

"Pickle . . ." My brother flicked his head and her eyes cast downward.

"No." I lifted a shoulder to my brother, letting him know it was fine that my niece had questions. I knew they *all* had questions.

Penny shrugged. "That makes sense. Daddy says parents don't have to be married. My friend Peter's parents aren't married either." Her eyes brightened as she remembered more. "Oh! And Eloise from school has two moms. She says families should be what your soul needs."

I smiled at how progressive and inclusive my niece was. "That's a smart way to look at it."

Wyatt took the opening as an opportunity. "Are you planning to have a joint parenting agreement?"

I shifted in my seat as I felt my family's questions linger in the air. "We haven't really talked about anything legally binding or formal."

He shook his head, frowning. "You should. There needs to be something in place to protect your rights—anything so she can't keep the baby from you or just up and move. You'd never see your kid again."

I thought about Sylvie moving to Savannah. *Was it selfish to get on my knees and beg her to reconsider?*

I had planned to broach the subject with her again. *Sometime soon.* I couldn't let my fears or miscommunication get in the way of being with my kid. "I would never keep her from something that was important to her. We agreed that I would help her during the pregnancy and for a few months once the baby was here. After that, we'll reassess and make a plan."

"What about her family? Does she come from good people?" Dad's question hung in the air. I had yet to fully inform him that the woman I was having a baby with was a King. I wasn't sure how he'd take it, and I was a coward.

"It's fine."

Lark, Tootie, and Annie held me with wide eyes at the harsh finality of my tone. Wyatt shook his head but didn't argue with me. The only solidarity I found came from across the table, where Lee pressed his lips together and nodded.

Tension simmered across the room until Lee spoke up. "Hey, Rat . . ." My niece grinned across the table at her favorite uncle's silly nickname for her. "Pass those potatoes."

I spent the rest of the afternoon sulking in the background. I wondered if Sylvie was enjoying her day. If she would have been here had things been different in this town. I wondered if my child would ever get to experience a Sullivan Thanksgiving.

DAD GOT TIRED, and I used it as an excuse to bring him back to Haven Pines and head home early. The inky November sky stretched over the farm as I pulled down the driveway. Activity and happy voices could be heard from the section of land where my staff were still celebrating their own Thanksgivings. As I pulled down the drive, I spotted Sylvie's car, and I parked in my spot next to it. I let Ed out and plopped Duck onto the ground. Together they meandered toward the barn, where I was sure Ed would tuck him in for the night before trudging back toward the house. Their nightly routine was like clockwork.

I stretched my back and looked at my home. It was dark, and I wondered if Sylvie had already gone to bed or if I would be lucky enough to find her curled up on the couch with a book. Sometimes she'd venture out of her room, and we would spend a few hours reading by the fire or watching some mindless television.

As I walked up the steps, I brushed a hand over the colorful mums she'd potted and placed on each step. I liked the way they looked and would be sure to tell her so tomorrow.

I let a sharp whistle for Ed ring out. When he loped around the far side of the barn, I waited so he could follow me into the house. Tuckered out by the excitement of a family gathering at Highfield House, he made a circle around his dog bed, groaned once, and plopped down in the center.

The house was quiet, but a small light glowed in the kitchen. I carefully tucked away the to-go containers that Tootie had loaded me down with and pulled a small piece of paper out of a drawer and wrote Sylvie a quick note.

DARYL,

TOOTIE INSISTED YOU HAVE THE LEFTOVERS IN THE FRIDGE. SHE SAID YOU NEEDED EXTRAS BECAUSE YOU WERE EATING FOR TWO. APPARENTLY SHE THINKS OUR BABY IS THE SIZE OF ORSON WELLES AND NOT AN AVOCADO.

~OATES

I paused and frowned down at my note.

I hoped she knew I was trying to be funny and not that I thought she looked like an oversize actor from before our time.

I carefully arranged the note next to my favorite coffee mug and a tea bag. I filled the kettle and set it on the stove so it would be ready for her if she wanted tea in the morning.

The Sugar Bowl would be closed the day after Thanksgiving, but work on the farm didn't stop for post-holiday relaxing. I was itching to get to the bottom of whoever had been scouting our land.

I paused, listening again. My ears pricked, but I heard only the quiet creaking of an old farmhouse. I rolled my shoulders and scrubbed a hand across the back of my neck and squeezed, hoping to release the knot of tension that had formed there. Sylvie and I may have been living together, but we were existing apart, a fact that gnawed a hole in my gut.

I unlaced my boots and set them by the back door before climbing the stairs. I sure as fuck wasn't looking forward to another night cramped in that too-small bed, but I took comfort in knowing Sylvie had no complaints about taking the primary bedroom.

Her nausea had seemed to ease up a bit, but she had informed me with a laugh that it had been replaced with the near-constant urge to use the bathroom. It may have been a small gesture, but giving up my bedroom had been the right call. It was the least I could do.

The stairs creaked under my weight as I climbed to the second floor. The old farmhouse walls were thin, and I could hear the faint hum of a fan and the rustle of bedsheets.

I paused in front of her door, indecision gnawing at me. I lifted my fist, prepared to gently knock and wish her *Happy Thanksgiving* and a good night.

An unfamiliar noise stopped me. I paused mid-knock, hearing a throaty moan as it floated through the door. A knot formed in my throat as blood surged to my cock. My dick twitched to life when I realized the hum had come from Sylvie.

I listened again. *Not* the hum of a fan . . . *vibrations.*

Blood pounded between my ears as my cock thickened. An irrational surge of jealousy coursed through me.

Was she in there with someone?

"Oh Duke . . ."

My dick was rock hard, and I palmed it through my jeans. Hearing my name as breathless whispers on Sylvie's lips was too much. I leaned closer to make out the muffled words.

"More, Duke. Yes. Oh my god. *Yes.*"

Holy fuck.

Unless Sylvie was behind the door with someone who shared my name, she was most definitely touching herself and thinking of *me.*

My hand paused above the door handle. I wanted to barge in and give her the real thing, but her needy little hum stopped me. If she actually wanted me to touch her, she would have said something—would have somehow told me that she wanted me like she had that day on the beach.

But *fuck,* if she wanted to get off on thoughts of me, I was fine with that too.

Instead of opening the door, I quickly undid my belt, unbuttoned my jeans, and pulled the zipper down. In one quick movement, I freed my aching cock and gave it a tight tug. I leaned one hand on the doorframe, bracing my weight, and the wood creaked beneath my palm. I stopped to listen.

"Yes, Duke, please keep going."

"Oh, hell yeah," I whispered.

I managed to keep my moan low. Sylvie's vibrator hummed in the background as I spit on my palm and began to stroke. My dick pulsed, protesting against not feeling the real thing. I wanted to be buried in her hot, tight cunt—to hear those desperate moans as I matched her stroke for stroke.

When her moans became muffled, I imagined she had her face buried in a pillow.

My pillow.

"Duke . . ." Sylvie's muffled cry of my name while she touched herself was my undoing.

My fingertips brushed against the wood door as my palm flattened against it.

"Sylvie." I sounded angrier than I'd intended.

Her sharp intake of breath made me pause.

"Don't stop," I commanded, stroking my cock as I closed my eyes and imagined being in the room with her.

Her voice was tight with tension but confident. "I'm not."

I wrestled to maintain control as I stroked. My abs flexed as I pumped into my fist.

"Are you still there?" she whispered.

"Yes," I ground out, hating the distance between us.

"Are you . . . touching yourself?"

"Hell yes."

"I'm close . . . please don't stop. I'm sorry. I just need . . ."

I was hurtling closer to the edge, so I reached back to my

collar, whipping off my shirt as I spoke to her through the door. "Don't be sorry. I need this too."

Her moan, no longer stifled, rattled through the darkness. I couldn't breathe. The air clung to my lungs in thick drags. My jaw flexed, and a knot formed at the base of my spine. A jolt of heat ran down my cock every time my thumb grazed the head. I closed my eyes and imagined Sylvie laid bare before me.

"Duke."

My name on her lips drove me harder. I clenched my teeth, and I was consumed by her, drowning in her.

Sylvie cried out, then released the air from her lungs in a breathless, satisfied huff. I grunted through a few final tugs before biting back a moan and following right behind her. I tipped my hips, angling my cock so cum gathered on my lower abs.

My breaths were as ragged as hers had been. Small black spots filled my vision, and my knees wobbled.

"Thank you." She suddenly sounded shy and uncertain.

Spent, I leaned my forehead against the door.

I need to tell her. Tell her I want her and that existing side by side is killing me.

"Good night, Duke."

I straightened and swallowed down my confession. "Good night, Sylvie."

As the sheets rustled from behind the door, I gathered myself, tucking my cock back into my jeans and heading down the hall to the second bathroom.

I quietly closed the door and flipped the switch. Harsh, blinding light made me squint. I bit back an oath and looked at myself in the mirror.

What a piece of shit.

I had just come alongside Sylvie, listened to her while

she pleasured herself while thinking of me. Maybe it had been wrong, but holy fuck was it hot.

A part of me had hoped that whatever tension had been building between us would finally dissolve. Maybe then she wouldn't consume every corner of my mind. I took one last look at my reflection before shaking my head and flicking off the light.

Fucking idiot.

Somehow Sylvie had burrowed her way into the very heart I had been careful to keep hardened. Knowing she craved me as much as I craved her made it only worse. I hated myself for pretending she wanted me the way I wanted her—all consuming. Desperate and hungry for more.

If Sylvie were anyone else, I probably would have laid my feelings bare already, but she had plans to leave, escape this town, and never look back. It was a dream I couldn't imagine stealing from her. I had never been given a choice, and I wouldn't take that from her.

But one thing I knew for certain, when she and our kid left, Sylvie would be taking the last remnants of my soul with her.

TWENTY

I slept like the dead.

You would think that getting caught by a man while calling out his name and then finishing while he stroked himself behind the bedroom door would have you lying awake contemplating your life's decisions for hours, but *nope*. After I had cleaned myself up, I snuggled back into Duke's bed and had the best night of sleep I'd had in months.

If the harsh light streaming through the window was any indication, I'd even slept in too.

Don't stop.

The memory of Duke's strained, gravelly voice as we both touched ourselves rattled through me. I grabbed a pillow and pressed it into my face as I screamed and kicked my feet. Just thinking about it had my blood pumping and my body gearing up for round two.

Oh my god. How was I ever going to face him?

Was I supposed to walk right up to him and extend my hand and come up with something to say? *Oh. Why yes, hello. Good morning, sir. You did in fact catch me mastur-*

bating and crying out your name when I thought I was home alone. And instead of being mortified, you joined in and came right alongside me. Have a good day.

I swung my legs off the bed and stood, then walked to the window. I peeked out from the curtain and, if I leaned far enough to the right, could just barely make out the corner of the barn. A large door to the barn was open, and I sat back on my heels with a sigh.

Does that man ever not work?

Relieved I would have at least a few minutes to gather myself, I scrubbed both hands over my face.

An image of last night flashed through my mind. How tight and desperate Duke's voice was. How the hard edge of his whisper was what had sent me hurtling over the edge.

I took my time getting ready for the day, even dabbing on a little bit of makeup now that my underlying color wasn't a permanent shade of pukey green.

At seventeen weeks, I was no longer in regular pants. But I couldn't deny it—the stretchy waistband of maternity pants was pretty damn comfortable. A flowy top still hid my bump, but lately I'd given up on hiding. Now that it was more than just a burrito baby, I thought the bump looked pretty cute on my frame.

Maybe this is what the internet meant by the second-trimester glow.

I tiptoed down the creaky stairs. In fact, it was those stairs that helped me notice Duke had come home last night. I'd heard his heavy footfalls on the old wood, and when I saw his shadow stop at my door and didn't leave, I knew he was there.

I could have stopped or been quiet, but I didn't. I *couldn't.*

The farmhouse kitchen was quiet, and I smiled as soon

as I saw the coffee mug and tea along with a note from Duke. It had become an unspoken morning ritual that I looked forward to every day.

I turned on the stove, and while the teakettle heated up, I opened the fridge to peek at the leftovers Duke had brought me. Four Styrofoam to-go containers were stacked to the height of the fridge shelf. Inside was a plethora of roasted turkey, mashed potatoes and gravy, sweet potatoes, green beans, and *two* different kinds of stuffing. In the last container I hit the jackpot: pie.

So. Much. Pie.

Deciding pie for breakfast wasn't all that different from stuffing my face with Huck's pastries, I grabbed a fork and took a huge bite of cold apple pie directly from the container.

I was not proud.

"Mmm," I hummed in delight. Sometimes cold leftover pie straight from the fridge was almost as good as an orgasm.

Almost.

The kettle whistled, and I poured the hot water into the *Sullivan Farms* mug and began to steep the tea. I took one last sneaky bite of pie before holding the warm cup between my hands.

From the window I could see the late-November weather was having an identity crisis. The grass glittered with frost as the harsh morning sun slanted across the lawn. Last week's snow had already thawed, but I was no fool.

Knowing the air would be crisp as I took my tea on the porch, I pulled on my winter coat, plopped a knit hat over my bed head, and slipped on a pair of fingerless gloves.

I frowned down at my winter boots. Bending over to lace them up had started to become a little uncomfortable, and I only wanted to be out for a few minutes to soak up some vitamin D while I sipped on my morning tea.

If I was lucky, I could hide behind the mug and sneak a glance at Duke as he worked on the farm. With a resolute nod, I slipped my feet into a pair of Duke's old worn work boots.

His huge heavy boots were clunky as I charged out the door and onto the porch. I had slowly started decorating it for fall and was pleased when Duke didn't seem to mind the subtle, feminine changes to his *very* bachelor-like home.

The sturdy mums were still holding up, but the stocks of dried corn had seen better days. With yesterday's Thanksgiving obligations over, I was taking that as my sign to start decorating for Christmas.

I wondered how Duke felt about Christmas lights. Did he prefer colored ones or white? I laughed. The grumpy farmer probably enjoyed a no-frills, no-lights Christmas.

Well, not this year, Oates.

I stood on the top step, looking out onto Sullivan Farms, one hand shielding my eyes from the bright morning sun. My heart clunked when I saw him. From his heavy boots to the way his thick thighs tested the limits of his denim to the thick canvas jacket he wore unzipped despite the wintry chill, Duke Sullivan was all man.

His strides ate up the distance between us as I lifted my hand in a shy wave.

He was coming after me, and fast.

I attempted a friendly smile. "Morning, I—"

In three strides he was up the porch steps, and his mouth crashed to mine. One hand gripped the mug while the other balanced myself on his rock-hard bicep. Even under his clothes and winter layers, he was hard and demanding.

My bones went liquid. His teeth teased my lip, and as I gasped, his tongue swept over mine. I gripped him harder, leaning into the kiss. I wanted more—more of him, more of this, more of everything.

He was panting as he broke the kiss and pressed his forehead to mine. "Good morning."

His deep voice sent shivers down my back. "I'll say."

A bubbling erupted just below my belly button. I pulled back, my eyes wide. Duke's eyebrows cinched down the middle as my hand flew to my lower belly.

"I think . . ." I felt around, hoping to experience the fizzy sensation again. "I think the baby just moved."

His eyes flew to my stomach and back to my eyes. His hand flexed as he tentatively reached out. "Can I?"

I swallowed hard but nodded.

Duke's wide palm covered nearly the entirety of my lower belly, and I covered my hand with his. "I'm not sure. It's not the first time I felt something like that, but this was . . . more." I lifted my shoulders. "Different. The books I'm reading say it will probably be a few more weeks before anyone else can feel it too."

"That's okay." His voice was barely above a whisper, awe laced through his words.

I let the warmth of his hand seep into me and prayed to feel it again. I didn't have the heart to tell him that I wasn't really sure if it was the baby or a bubble of gas. I sagged into him, trying to keep my tea from spilling over the rim, and Duke's arms wrapped around me.

"You shouldn't stay out here too long. It's too chilly this morning."

I moved the open zipper on his coat up and down. "What about you?"

"Don't worry about me." Duke released me, and I smiled up at that beautiful man. "Did you eat?"

My smile turned shy. "I had pie for breakfast."

He laughed, and it cracked in his throat like it was rusty from neglect. I fell in love with the rich, warm sound.

"That tracks." He winked as his chuckle faded away. His hand moved from my shoulder down to my elbow before capturing my wrist. "Have dinner with me. I have work to get through today, but I would love to have dinner with you tonight."

Giddiness danced through me, but I shrugged. "It's a date."

I had turned to walk back inside to escape the cold that had started to creep in when he landed a swift smack to my ass. I yelped and whipped my head around to catch his playful grin.

I watched Duke as he walked with long strides across the lawn and back to the barn. The bubbles in my stomach fizzled again, and I pressed a shaky hand to my belly. "I know, baby. I know."

JOHN OATES

Finishing up here. I'd still like to take you out. Can you be ready by six?

For our date, I chose a soft knitted dress in a delicate cream. The sweater dress was roomy enough to accommodate my belly, and the belt accentuated my growing bump. The dress was short, hitting just above my knees, and I paired it with tall leather boots with a flat heel. It was comfy, but also cute. Nervous for our date, I even took extra time to dab on a little makeup and curl my hair into soft waves.

I walked down the stairs and rounded the corner to the kitchen to find Duke standing, his hand clamped on the back of a chair, and I paused. Still in boots and jeans, he had swapped his typical T-shirt for a knitted navy pullover sweater. The two tortoiseshell buttons were undone, giving me the tiniest peek at his collarbone. The sweater stretched across his muscular chest and clung to his biceps. His denim was clean, and he wore a brown leather belt.

My mouth went dry at the sight of him.

Duke took me in and sighed, rubbing his hands together as though he felt just as nervous as I did. "You're stunning, Sylvie."

I smiled and my eyes fell to the floor. "You clean up pretty good yourself."

He helped me into my coat, and as we walked toward his truck, he opened the car door for me, making sure I was tucked inside before he closed the door. I tracked his graceful movements as he rounded the hood and then climbed in.

"I thought we could go to Rivale . . . unless you had a taste for something different."

Rivale Familiare was one of the remaining restaurants in town that hadn't chosen a King or Sullivan side, despite the name. It was both a good and a bad thing. It meant there was an equal chance of running into either one of our family members, but they did have the best garlic bread in town, and my stomach grumbled at the thought. "It's perfect."

The drive to Rivale was pleasant, if not a bit quiet. I had been living in Duke's house for weeks, but a date with him in public felt like a huge step.

A chuckle escaped me as I placed my hand on my belly and laughed at the ridiculousness of that thought.

"What's funny?"

I shook my head. "Nothing. Just thinking about how I feel nervous about this date when, well . . ." I gestured toward my belly.

He chuckled and his face scrunched. "Yeah, it is a little bit *putting the cart before the horse*, isn't it?" He ran a hand across his denim-clad thigh. "I'm sorry about that."

Feeling brave, I reached for his hand. "I'm not."

I swallowed hard and my throat closed tighter. He moved his hand, placing it on top of mine and holding it in place.

Rivale was busy for a Friday night, and with it being outside of the main tourist season, the eyeballs tracking our entrance were all townies'. Mouths hung open. People leaned over to whisper and pretend they weren't pointing. In town, everyone knew a Sullivan had knocked up a King, but there we were parading my little baby bump in front of everyone. We were prime gossip fodder.

Duke's gentle hand at my lower back was my only comfort, and I allowed him to guide me as he followed the hostess to our seats. He pulled out my chair, and as I scooted it forward, I could practically hear the collective swoon coming from behind me.

Duke was the perfect gentleman, allowing me to order first and listening attentively as I told him about my quiet day with a long, hot bath and a steamy book.

Big mistake, by the way. I couldn't stop picturing Duke as the grumpy main character who was presently railing his nanny into next week. *Correction: railing imaginary* me *into next week.*

"I was just so tired after such a busy day yesterday, you know?"

Duke hummed in agreement but didn't look at me. "How was it? Your Thanksgiving."

I sighed and blew a raspberry through my lips. "Oh, you know. Typical King family gathering."

His eyes swept up to mine.

"Oh." I chuckled. "I . . . I guess you don't know, really. Well, long story short, my father didn't bother to show up. JP had his nose in his phone the entire time, working on some business deal." I rolled my eyes as I air-quoted *business deal*. JP always took himself way too seriously, and I hated to admit it, but he was turning out just like my father. "Abel was there, which was nice, but he's so quiet. He's hard to get a read on. MJ didn't have work, so I loved that. She was able to be there with us. And Royal was . . ." I laughed. "Well, he's Royal."

Duke's jaw clenched at the mention of my brothers, but he didn't interrupt me.

"Royal was going on and on about someone listing the tattoo shop's address for a local furry meetup." I gave Duke a pointed stare. "You wouldn't know anything about that, would you?"

I didn't miss the tiny hitch in the corner of his mouth before he shook his head. "Nope."

My eyebrow lifted. "Mm-hmm."

He raised both palms. "I promise I had nothing to do with it, but I can't say for sure when it comes to Lee. He loves that shit."

I laughed and smoothed my napkin across my lap. "I swear, if you really think about it, it's amazing how alike you all are."

My shoulders fell as the reality of our situation hung in

the air. Our families weren't alike, not even close. In fact, they *hated* each other, and here we were going to bring a baby into the center of that negative dynamic. My eyes started to fill.

Duke reached over and placed his hand on top of mine. "Hey."

I let out a shaky breath. "I know, I just wish there was some way for everyone to get along. They don't even have to like each other, but just something a little softer than *hate* would be nice, you know?"

Duke's features were hard. I didn't know all the details, but I knew the origins of the King–Sullivan feud went back generations. I only knew the stories from the Kings' side. Lies. Secrets. Backhanded business deals. Constant one-upping. Lines drawn in the sand as alliances were made.

I could only imagine what the Sullivan side of that story told.

I looked at Duke. "How are we ever going to make this work?"

He frowned and looked at our hands. "I think the trick is to find two pieces that connect—that way we'll have a place to start."

"What do you mean?"

He looked at me with hopeful eyes and shrugged. "Maybe MJ. It's possible she can be our puzzle piece. We start building there, and the rest will fall into place."

I mulled over his words. MJ had a soft spot for Duke, and everyone in my family had a soft spot for her. She also kept my secret friendship with Duke quiet. Maybe she *could* be the piece that helped bridge the gap between our families.

"You really think it could work?"

His dark eyes held mine. "Despite everyone in this town

—in the entire world—it really is just us. Why are we letting them decide when we get to be happy?"

When he put it like that, so confidently, it seemed so simple.

For the first time, I held on to something new.

Hope.

TWENTY-ONE

DUKE

DARYL HALL

Cat Fact 27: Your cat marks you by rubbing against you to combine their scent with yours and claim you as your property.

Did you steal my sweatshirt again?

Sure did.

THE WEATHERED BARK of the blueberry bushes was silver and gray. Mornings were eerily silent. Fresh snow had fallen, blanketing the fields in deep powder. The farm needed that harsh reset. The dormancy only prepared them for the next season as their red canes contrasted against the crisp winter sky. With the fields winterized and equipment put away, it offered the chance to check the books, comparing previous years' profits and losses.

Sullivan Farms had made it through another successful year.

I leaned back in my chair, tossing my glasses on the desk and pressing a thumb into my eye socket. I needed to get out of the house—off the farm—and clear my head. I glanced at the clock and realized it was as good a time as any to see what Dad was up to, so I grabbed my keys and headed toward the edge of town.

They could never hide the distinct smell of antiseptic, no matter how much air freshener was pumped into Haven Pines. My boots beat down on a familiar path toward the memory care wing of the retirement home. I gave my customary nods and terse greetings to the familiar-faced nurses.

Dad's clinical trial was well underway, and while there were still rough days, slowly, the good days had begun to outweigh the bad. It was our first glimmer of hope that we wouldn't lose him entirely—at least not as rapidly as we had once thought.

When I was buzzed into the memory care wing, I noticed Dad's porch light outside his room was off. It meant either he wasn't up for visitors, or he was out and about on the grounds.

I raised my fist to knock, hoping it was the latter.

"Morning, Duke," MJ singsonged, and I turned to face her. She was dressed in hot-pink scrubs as she pushed a large computer cart down the hallway toward me.

"Hey, MJ." I nodded. "You seen Red?"

Her face twisted in shock. "Who? Oh my god, we lost one again, didn't we?"

I gave her a bored look, and she fizzled into a fit of giggles. She leaned on the cart as she laughed. I did always have a tiny soft spot for MJ—not that I'd ever admit that to anyone.

"I don't know, Duke, that joke never gets old." With an exaggerated sigh she rested her chin in her hand. "He tagged along with Fred, our maintenance man. They're over in the new Haven Pines neighborhood. Slapping up some paint, I think."

I nodded. "Good. That's good for him."

Physical labor always seemed to make my dad feel better. Clear out some of the cobwebs in his mind.

MJ gestured toward the radio on her hip. "Want me to call Fred for you?"

I shook my head. "Nah, I don't want to throw him if he's having a good day."

"He's having a great day." She smiled. "I'm hopeful about this clinical trial. It seems to be working well."

I wanted to hope, I did, but I also knew the reality of Dad's diagnosis.

"So . . ." MJ began clicking the keyboard of her computer, but her eyes flicked to me. "I hear you need a spy on the inside."

She waggled her eyebrows in my direction, and I rolled my eyes at her. "I see you've talked to Sylvie."

She straightened and beamed at me. "Of course I did. She's my only sister. And look, I know you're doing this for her, so I love you for that. If you need me to butter up the brutes in my family, I'll do my best."

"I'd settle for them not making things harder for Sylvie."

She winked playfully as she pointed at me. "I knew there was a big old softie in there."

"I am not soft," I gritted out.

She straightened and shimmied her shoulders. "Oh really?"

I sighed and started to walk. "Goodbye, MJ."

Her cackling laugh echoed in the hallway, and she giggled again when she was shushed by a resident. Making an alliance with another King was probably a huge fucking mistake, but I would do it for Sylvie.

❧

WITH PAPERWORK DONE and not much to do in the field, I settled into a recliner with an old paperback. I needed anything to distract myself from the fact that Sylvie had let it slip that she was heading upstairs for a warm soak in my bathtub.

I fought the mental image of the tops of her breasts peeking out above the waterline, surrounded by luscious bubbles.

Goddamn, pregnancy had made her tits round and full, and I wanted to touch them. Taste them.

I had set my intentions to date Sylvie, help us get to know each other and actually see if we might be able to figure this co-parenting thing out. Maybe Savannah would hold less of an appeal if she knew she wouldn't have to do this alone—that there would be somebody here who cared about her and would do anything in his power to take care of the both of them.

I was surprised when Sylvie trudged down the stairs and into the living room in loose pajamas and a pout.

I looked up from my book as her shoulders slumped. "I got hot. Then I felt all sweaty and couldn't relax. I'm just . . ." She raised her hands and dropped them, letting them slap petulantly on the outsides of her thighs. "Uncomfortable."

I pulled my glasses down my nose and set them on top of the book on the side table. She was adorable and perfect, and I hated that there wasn't anything I could do to make her feel better when so many changes were going on in her own body.

"I've got an idea." I stood and moved toward the couch and gestured at it with my hand. "Sit tight."

She surveyed me with pursed lips but plopped herself in the corner of the couch with a huff. I stifled a chuckle and ran upstairs to grab some lotion out of my bathroom.

When I returned, I moved to the opposite end of the couch and patted my lap. "Give me your foot."

I dropped a small blob of lotion in my palm and rubbed my hands together before gliding them over her foot. My thumbs dug into her arch, and her head fell back with a groan. The throaty primal sound had me shifting in my seat.

"What are you doing?"

I suppressed a smile. "I'm showing you what it means to be cared for by a man like me."

Before she could respond, I pressed my thumbs into her foot. "There?" I asked as my thumbs dug into a pressure point on the bottom of her arch.

Her hands gripped the sides of the couch. "Oh my god, yes."

I loved pulling those breathy moans from her. I only wished it was because I was sliding inside her and not from a simple foot rub.

Don't be the dick who pretends a foot rub isn't a ploy to get into her pants.

Do. Not. Do. It.

I worked the lotion into her skin, taking my time to rub both feet before moving up to her calf muscles. She shifted her legs, and I was rewarded with a tempting flash of her bare pussy beneath her flimsy pajama shorts.

Fuck.

My jaw flexed as I clenched my teeth together and focused on her face and helping Sylvie relax. "I just want you to feel good. Your body is putting in a lot of work."

My hands moved above her calf and over her knee. "I'm

just so . . ." She paused and my eyes met hers. "Horny," she whispered.

I swallowed hard as my slick palms moved higher on her leg, and I shifted. "I can help you with that." I squeezed the smooth, firm muscles of her thighs. "If you need me to."

Sylvie's breaths turned to shallow gasps. Beneath her pajama top, her nipples were hard pebbles poking through the thin fabric. She squirmed again. My long fingers moved closer to the hem of those tiny little shorts, but no higher. Not without her permission.

"Is that what you want, baby? Do you need to come?"

"Holy shit, Duke." Her eyes fluttered closed as she leaned her head back against the armrest of the couch. Her hips tilted upward. "Yes." She swallowed hard and whispered, "Please make me come."

I held on tightly to the last remaining thread of control as I licked my lips and sank to my knees. I shifted her hips, careful to be gentle, but rough enough to move her exactly where I wanted her. My eyes roamed over her beautiful, changing body as my fingertips skated across the outside fabric of her pajamas.

My fingers hooked into the waistband of the shorts, and I dragged them with a torturous slowness down her smooth thighs. Her fingers fumbled with the buttons of her top as I carefully lifted her legs and tossed the shorts aside.

I trailed a path of kisses up her thigh before stopping to pull in a deep breath through my nose. "*Fuck,* you smell good." She was trembling and needy before I had even touched her. "I'm going to ravage you until your entire body is relaxed. My fingers, my tongue, my cock . . ." I palmed my dick through my sweatpants. "Whatever you need to come, I will give it to you."

"Yes," she breathed. "Yes to all of it."

I smirked and lowered my head, using my fingers to spread her open for me before putting my mouth on her. I had had dreams of what Sylvie would taste like. Nothing compared to the real thing—hot and wet. I devoured her like a starving man, using every mewl and sigh to learn exactly what she liked.

I palmed the back of one thigh, pushing her leg up and deepening the angle. She cried out, and her pussy clenched around my tongue, her hips bucking. I teased her clit with the opposite thumb, letting my fingers splay across her swollen belly.

My rock-hard cock throbbed. One of her hands threaded into my hair and tugged. I grunted into her and enjoyed the sting and tug of her hand in my hair. I strummed her clit, and she exploded around me. I greedily devoured her cum as she dissolved into her orgasm. I slipped a finger inside of her, enjoying the drag and pull of her pussy as the tiny muscles quaked around my finger.

"Yes." Her eyes were still closed, and her cheeks were flushed as I pumped my finger into her tight little cunt.

"More," she groaned.

I smirked. *That's my greedy little thing.*

"Yeah?" I asked as I palmed my cock again. "Not quite done, are you? I think you'll have enough when I remind you how that pussy stretches around my cock."

A blush crept across her chest as I bent to suck the hard, rosy bud of her nipple into my mouth. As my tongue grazed over her nipple, I hooked my fingers inside her until I found the spot that had her clenching around them again.

"Jesus fuck, you're sexy," I ground out.

I pulled my fingers from inside her and licked them clean as her eyes danced with desire. With one hand I reached behind my neck and pulled my shirt off by the collar. The eager approval in her eyes sent primal pride racing through me. Reaching into my sweatpants, I freed my cock. I angled the head toward her pussy and dragged it through her wetness.

"I can get a condom," I ground out as I teased her entrance with the tip.

"No." She gasped. "Fuck no. I want to feel all of you."

"Bare?" The thought of nothing between us as I impaled her on my cock was too much.

A smirk tugged at her lips as she squirmed. "Can't get me pregnant twice."

I cradled her hips in my hands as I looked down at her beautiful form. "You have to tell me—if the angle is not right or something doesn't feel good—I want you to tell me."

"I will, just . . . please. *Please*."

Her pussy was so fucking tight as I slid my bare cock inside her. We groaned in unison.

As I buried myself to the hilt, I paused my fingertips, making indents in the soft flesh of her hips as I stilled. "You have no idea how difficult it is not to fuck you hard right now."

Her hand gripped the back of my neck and squeezed. "Do it. I don't want soft right now. I want you to fuck me. Fuck me like you can't get enough of me."

Her words were all the permission I needed. I placed one palm at the center of her chest, pinning her down to the couch as I pistoned my hips forward and railed into her over and over. My cock pumped into her tight heat. My balls screamed at me, begging to keep fucking until I came.

I wanted her to come. I wanted to feel Sylvie dissolve under my hands with my cock buried inside her. With long silky strokes I pounded into her. I plucked at her nipples and rolled them between my fingers the way I had seen her do to herself earlier. Her jerking hips met me stroke for stroke.

She pulled her knees toward her chest, deepening the angle as I towered over her and hammered into her tight, wet pussy. The bite of the hard floor beneath my knees was no match for my desire to drag another orgasm from her.

I focused on the delicate features of her face until her honey-flecked eyes met mine. I was lost in them, in her, as I fucked her over and over.

"Mine." The word slipped from my lips as I fucked her. "You're mine."

Her grip tightened on the back of my neck, and she didn't break eye contact. "Yes. Yes, I'm yours."

I shifted my weight, grinding my pubic bone against her clit as my cock pushed deeper inside her. Her eyes glazed, and the tight rhythmic pulses of her pussy squeezed my cock as she came. Her orgasm dripped down the base of my cock to my balls.

So fucking hot and all mine.

My dick pulsed as I emptied myself into her. I braced my arms on either side of her, keeping my weight on the couch and off her. Our panting breaths mingled in the space between us.

Reluctantly I sat back on my heels, dragging my cock from her. She sat propped up on her elbows, biting her lower lip as she watched my cum seep out of her.

I tipped up an eyebrow as I reached forward, catching my release as it slid down her thigh and moved upward. "You like that."

I ran my cum-coated fingers through her pussy, and her breath hitched. "You feel so good. *I* feel so good." She collapsed back against the couch with a contented sigh.

I kissed her knee and sat back with a laugh. "Glad I could be of service."

"Oh, you serviced." She laughed. "Five stars. Ten out of ten. Highly recommended."

She was so goddamn cute, and I was scared to death. I was falling in love with the mother of my child, and I had absolutely no clue what to do about it.

TWENTY-TWO

DUKE

THE FIT of her body shouldn't have felt so perfect as I curled around her. After recovering from the best sex that couch had ever seen, I led her upstairs, drew her a fresh bubble bath, and tried to help her relax.

I sat behind her in the tub, rubbing her tense shoulders as she hummed and leaned against me. I let my lips brush against the wet curve where her neck met her shoulder as she lazily told me about her day. When the bubbles dissipated and the water finally cooled, we had gone for round two in the bedroom. She was insatiable, and I craved her like a starved man.

I was an ambitious, eager student when it came to learning what Sylvie liked in the bedroom. When we were finished, her pliant body molded to mine.

Sylvie let out a satisfied hum as she snuggled closer, pushing her ass into me. "The baby is moving again."

My hand moved across her belly, and I nuzzled my nose into her hair. I wanted to memorize every tiny detail about the woman in my arms—the way her hair smelled like cinnamon and sunshine, the way her laughter built from a shy chuckle to a full-on belly laugh when something really got her going, the curve of her hip and the swell of her belly.

I needed every detail committed to memory.

Sylvie's voice filled the darkened room. "Did you always want to be a farmer?"

A humorless laugh puffed out of me. "No."

I could practically hear her mind turning and the thoughtful frown tug the corner of her lips. "That surprises me. You seem to love it—the way you walk the fields every day, how you treat the people you work with with such kindness and compassion. I can see how much the farm means to you. I guess I just thought that was something that came naturally, since your dad ran the farm before you."

I was quiet, then offered her the simple truth. "I learned to love it."

Her patient silence and the gentle stroke of her hand on my forearm gave me courage to open myself up to her. "When Mom died, it was tough—on everyone. Kate and Lee were so young. Wyatt was wrapped up in football and girls. Mom was the glue. She was a special woman." I didn't bother to hide the hitch in my voice. Even after all these years, it hurt like hell to talk about her.

"You loved her." Sylvie softly sighed.

I nodded. "Still love her, but life moved on. Dad did what he could to manage without her. Aunt Tootie stepped in and helped where she could." My eyes stung and my chest ached, but I kept going. "When Dad got sick, things really changed."

"I can't even imagine what that must be like. MJ has made comments that he's very sweet, but sometimes he has bad days . . ."

Sylvie was curious and I didn't blame her. "He does. It all happened so subtly, you know? Little slips here and there. He'd call Kate by our mother's name or forget the day of the week. Dad's always been upbeat, but he'd be moody and sullen. It started affecting the farm. Bills went unpaid, people were quitting or refusing to work for him because of his erratic mood swings. It was rough." I sighed. "I realized there was no one else to take over the responsibilities. It was completely up to me."

She was quiet. I stroked her arm and let myself find comfort in her soothing calmness.

Sylvie pulled in a deep breath and held it for a fraction of a second. "It was so different when my mother left. I woke up one morning and she was just . . . gone. No note, no tearful hug goodbye. She just left us."

I pictured young Sylvie, alone and confused when she realized her mother wasn't coming back. "Jesus."

A watery laugh spilled out of her, and I banded my arms around her. "The sad part? I was *envious*." Her voice quieted to barely above a whisper. "No one else knows that."

I gently kissed her bare shoulder and considered her confession. "Thank you for trusting me."

"The strangest part of all of this? My whole life, I've been invisible. I was never special enough to warrant my father's attention, and my own mother left without even saying goodbye. I used to be relieved that I was invisible, but now I'm all anyone's talking about."

My hand moved to the smooth curve of her hip. "I'm sorry about that."

Sylvie had never been invisible, at least not to me. There was always *something* about her that wouldn't allow me to look away. Even her ridiculous asshole brothers should be able to see that.

Sylvie lifted a shoulder. "It's okay. Hopefully soon someone will come along and stir up some better gossip." She sighed and turned the conversation back on me. "So if you weren't destined to be a farmer, what did young Duke aspire to be?"

I chuckled, half laughing at the dreams of a kid who had no clue who he was supposed to be. "I was gonna leave this town behind in a cloud of rodeo dust."

"A bull rider?"

"Nah. I was always built too big for that. Though I was a damn good bulldogger."

Her back pressed into me in a nudge. "What is that?"

"The technical term is *steer wrestling*."

Laughter and disbelief danced in her voice. "Steer. Wrestling?"

I chuckled along with her. "Yep. Steer gets a head start, then you chase him down, slide down the side of your horse, and wrestle him to the ground. You grab him by the horns and bring him down."

"That sounds kind of mean."

I laughed. "I suppose it is. Though the rodeo takes damn good care of the animals. In fact, back when I won a pretty big title, I bought that steer and retired him here to the farm. He lived out the rest of his life in an unused pasture."

Sylvie rolled toward me, but I kept my arms around her. "See. I told you you were a softie."

I scoffed. "Whatever. I'm a badass."

Her hand smoothed down my face. "You can be that too." She studied me. "Did you ever get hurt?"

I looked into her light-brown eyes. I was lost in her,

whispering old secrets in the dark. "A time or two. Nothing serious. The whole thing only lasts a few seconds at most."

"I wish I could have seen you do it. I bet you looked hot."

I smirked and ran my nose down the side of hers before pecking a soft kiss to her lips. "Some girls thought so."

Her eyebrows lifted as she pulled back to look me in the eye. "When was the last time you had a girlfriend?"

"Actual girlfriend?" I frowned, thinking back as far as I could. "Well, probably not since Nicole. A few years ago."

"Did you break her heart?"

I scoffed. "More like the other way around. She broke up with me, and though she tried to be nice, it was pretty much the *it's not me, it's you* speech."

"Ouch." Sylvie's giggle squeezed my heart.

I chuckled and snuggled closer. "It was a blow to my ego, but better in the long run."

Sylvie's eyes searched mine. In the darkness, it was hard to read her expression.

How do I tell this woman that no one who ever came before her could measure up? That no one ever would?

A SOFT KNOCK from the door had me turning from my workstation. Sylvie stood in the doorway of the shed with a shy smile and her hands clasped together at her chest. "This looks interesting."

I was only glad she found me out here and not working on the secret project I had started in the main barn.

I wiped my hands on the dish towel and tossed it on the counter in front of me. "Come on in."

Her smile widened, and she stepped over the threshold

and allowed the door to close behind her, casting out the harsh winter wind. Her puffy winter coat enveloped her, nearly camouflaging her growing bump. Her blonde hair tumbled from beneath her knit cap. Her legs were covered in tight black leggings, and her small feet were tucked into a pair of my old boots.

I smiled to myself, not minding in the least that she often threw on a pair of my boots.

"I didn't realize this place was out here." Sylvie ran a finger along the stainless-steel industrial kitchen countertop. "I saw the light on and came exploring."

"I had this shed converted a few years back so I could get a commercial kitchen license." I tipped my head toward the pots on the large, professional-grade range. "I can make things to sell at the farmers' market and use up some of the end-of-season berries we freeze." I shrugged. "Plus it gives me something to do."

Sylvie grinned. "How very domestic of you, Mr. Sullivan."

I returned her smile, stepped forward, and grabbed the belt loop of her pants to pull her toward me. She hummed with pleasure as I pulled her close to me.

"You look beautiful." I ran my hands around her sides to her lower back before resting them on her ass. The pink flush on her cheeks deepened as she leaned into me.

Her hands rested on my biceps. "It smells incredible in here. What are you making?"

"I finished up some blueberry-lime jam. That's Annie's favorite and a big seller at the farmers' market. I plan to make two new flavors. Small batches of a blueberry bourbon and a blueberry lavender." I shrugged, feeling a bit shy to let someone else in and see this hidden part of me. "Figured I'd try something different."

Her caramel doe eyes blinked up at me. "Do I get to be your taste tester?"

I tapped the tip of her upturned nose with my knuckle. "Only if you're good," I teased, "then maybe I'll lick it off you and get my own taste."

She preened and arched into my embrace. "Tempting, but you might change your mind after I tell you who's here."

I frowned at her, and she pulled her lower lip between her teeth. Sylvie scrunched up her face as though she was nervous to tell me about our visitor. It wasn't often people entered into our little bubble, and I preferred it that way.

"It's Royal. We were just having a visit, but he said he wanted to talk with you before he headed out."

I straightened. Royal was a pain in the ass—a big one when it came to the Kings. He was cocky and liked to stir up trouble. In a lot of ways he reminded me a bit of my brother Lee. I grumbled but looked down at her wide, hopeful eyes. I had meant it when I said I would do whatever I could to make things work between her and me, so that included her pain-in-the-ass brothers, apparently.

I looked at the timer on the countertop. "These jars have a few more minutes of processing, and then I've got to clean up." I glanced at the clock. "If he'll still be here in thirty minutes, we can have ourselves a chat."

Her nerves dissolved before my eyes—*as if I could ever tell that woman no.*

"Thank you." Sylvie stretched up on her tiptoes and stroked a hand down my stubble before popping a kiss to my lips.

I wanted to lengthen that kiss to pull her against me and feel her body against mine in that small kitchen. Instead, she turned and flounced out the door. She'd breezed in here and left me with nothing but irritation and a raging hard-on.

True to my word, I made my way back to the main house in just under a half hour. I stomped up the back steps, shaking off as much of the freshly fallen snow from my boots as I could. Michigan winters were known to be fickle, and after a stretch of mild weather, we had been hit with freezing temperatures and six inches of snow and ice a few days after Thanksgiving.

The house was cozy and smelled like Sylvie's tea mixed with freshly brewed coffee. I shrugged out of my heavy coat and hung it on the hook next to Sylvie's. I slipped off my boots and arranged them neatly next to the other size twelves she always stole.

When I rounded the kitchen entrance that led to the living room, irritation crawled up my back. Sprawled out on my couch with his boots on my fucking coffee table was Royal King. Sylvie stood, and she quickly hit the back of her hand against her brother's shoulder.

He stood. "Sullivan."

I took three steps forward and did one of the many things my father drilled into us as teens, and held out my hand. "Royal."

Shoulders squared, he stared at it for a beat. Then two.

This motherfucker . . .

From my peripheral, I could see the panic on Sylvie's face as her eyes flicked from my extended hand to him. After what felt like an eternity, his hand clamped onto mine. His grip was firm but not aggressively so.

After the quick shake, I released his hand and crossed my arms. "Sylvie said you wanted to talk." I gestured toward him. "So talk."

He had the balls to smirk at me before tucking his tattooed hands into his pockets. "Goddamn I don't like you."

"Royal—" Sylvie hissed.

He lifted a hand to silence his sister, and my hand clenched into a fist, but Royal's voice softened. "I may not like you, but I love my sisters, and they seem to think I've got you all wrong. Am I happy about this? Fuck no. But Sylvie is the best judge of character I know, and she says you're a good guy, so . . ." He held out both his palms. "I guess that means you're a good guy."

"That's it?" My eyes searched his, looking for a hint of bullshit.

Royal smirked. He may have shocked me with his blanket acceptance of my relationship with Sylvie, but he was still a cocky asshole. "You're the guy until Sylvie says you aren't. Then I'll learn to like the next asshole. She's my sister. It's as simple as that."

My jaw clenched at the mere thought of this nonexistent next someone. I needed to get my irrational jealousy under control and focus on what Royal was offering. "So is this a truce or something?"

Royal's barking laugh filled the living room. "Fuck no. All it means is that we aren't going to beat your ass if we see you in town. I'll get my brothers on board, and I'd appreciate it if you would do the same."

Fair enough. I nodded.

Royal turned to his sister. "All right, Syl, I'm out of here."

He leaned down and pulled Sylvie in for a quick side hug, then reached his hand out to me. I shook it with a nod. Sylvie followed behind as she walked her brother toward the front door.

"Oh, and hey, Duke?" Royal turned with a shit-eating grin on his face. "I noticed there was a shopping cart on the frozen pond out there. Might want to check it out." He shrugged, feigning innocence. "Or don't. Just thought you should know about it."

I sighed and shook my head as Sylvie stifled a giggle and herded her brother out the door.

Jesus fucking Christ.

TWENTY-THREE

SYLVIE

I SAILED right past the wooden sign reading *Closed for the Bluebirds* posted outside of Bluebird Books. The women of Outtatowner were milling around, gathering snacks and drinks before sinking into the mismatched couches, chairs, and ottoman seats scattered haphazardly at the back of the bookstore. The atmosphere was cozy and intimate, with soft candlelight casting dancing shadows and a soothing melody playing from a speaker in the background. It felt like stepping into a chic, private club, where secrets and stories were shared beneath the watchful gaze of tattered book spines.

As I settled into a comfy love seat, MJ shot me a mischievous grin. "Did Duke get that shopping cart off the pond?" Her eyes twinkled with amusement, and I couldn't help but chuckle. The memory wasn't without its sting, though. The shopping cart prank had been a thorn in Duke's side until his men had managed to rescue it from the half-frozen pond. It was entertaining for the town, sure, but Duke had been less than thrilled.

"Eventually," I replied, a wry smile tugging at my lips. "The pond wasn't frozen enough to hold the weight of a person, so retrieving it was a pain in the ass. Finally, one of his men lassoed the cart, and they pulled it off the ice. It made for some great afternoon entertainment."

MJ laughed, and the conversation shifted naturally to the ongoing pranks between the Kings and Sullivans. Kate Sullivan sat nearby, and she leaned in. Her voice remained low but cut through the air. "We've got a bigger problem than shopping carts." Her tone was laden with both concern and frustration. "Someone's been poking around, looking into mineral rights on the farm."

My heart skipped a beat. Duke hadn't mentioned anything about that to me. The unease bubbled beneath my smile, invisible to the others.

"In the Sullivan speakeasy," Kate continued, "we found a bottle labeled *King Liquor*. And there've been trespassers on both Tootie's property and a few of the pastures."

From across the room, Bug King chimed in. "Can't prove it was a King and not just some curious lookie-loo trying to get a taste of the drama."

Kate's response was a begrudging agreement. "Fair enough."

Amid the chatter, Annie Crane's voice rose like a song-bird, full of hope. "The Kings and Sullivans used to be friends, you know. Connected in ways that seem to have been forgotten. I did some research that proved, without a doubt, they were friends. I just can't figure out what happened, you know?" She looked around the room. "Does anyone know what happened?" Her eyes scanned the faces in the room. Her question lingered like a shadow over all of us. "Old stories, rumors? Anything?"

Mabel, a long-standing presence in town, cleared her throat and spoke up. The wrinkles on her face seemed to hold the weight of decades of secrets. "I may recall something." As she began to speak, her voice took on a hushed and conspiratorial tone, drawing us all in like moths to a flame.

"I remember an old rumor," she began, her words brushing against the air like a gentle whisper. The flickering candlelight cast dancing shadows on her features, giving her an almost mystical air. "Three families shared adjacent land. Kings, Sullivans, and Sinclairs were as close as kin. Two families merged, but things started to fall apart."

I leaned in, captivated by the anticipation that hung in the room. Mabel's voice wove a tale of love and business gone awry, of a romance that had blossomed in our small town. "It was very dramatic, from what I can recall. My parents talked about the friendship between Helen, James, and Philo. Thick as thieves. When Prohibition hit, the trio started bootlegging."

"That explains the liquor bottle with the King name we found." Kate shrugged as pieces began fitting into place.

A sigh escaped Mabel's lips, a wistful breath carrying the weight of a lifetime's worth of memories. "It was highly illegal, but they made a go of it—making liquor and selling it across state lines. The business took a toll on the friendship. My father always talked about how misunderstandings have a way of taking root," Mabel mused, her voice tinged with sadness. "A stolen glance, a whispered word misheard, and suddenly their friendship was rewritten by the hands of fate."

I could almost feel the ache in her words, the ache of a town that had once been united, now torn apart by the very friendship it had nurtured. "Helen and Philo were married and expecting their first child. They wanted out of the bootlegging business," Mabel continued. "The Kings and Sullivans were like two ships passing in the night, their sails once billowing with shared dreams, now caught in the winds of rivalry, pride, and greed."

The room seemed to hold its breath, the very air heavy with the weight of history and Mabel's knack for story-telling. "It's said that Philo and Helen never stopped loving each other, but they turned their back on their friends." Mabel's gaze locked onto mine as if she could see the turmoil within me. "Love alone can't mend the bridges we burn, nor can it heal the wounds that time has etched."

As Mabel's voice fell silent, the room seemed to exhale, the spell of her story gradually lifting. I sat back, lost in thought, the echoes of her tale reverberating through my mind. The love story of Helen and Philo and the aching loss of such deep friendships stood as a haunting reminder of what could be lost to misunderstandings and pride—a reminder that the choices we make can shape not only our own destinies but the destinies of generations to come.

I couldn't help but feel like Duke and I were simply players in a larger drama, a tale of love and rivalry that had been unfolding for generations in our town. As I looked around the cozy enclave of Bluebird Books, at the flickering candles and the faces filled with curiosity and empathy, I knew that the story of Outtatowner was far from over, and that maybe—just maybe—the love I had for my baby could one day mend the fractures that had divided us for far too long.

Tensions between the Kings and Sullivans were indeed at an all-time high, and I was right in the thick of it. The life growing within me was a testament to the bond between Duke and me, yet it also tied me to a feud that seemed as old as time itself. The uncertainty gnawed at me, thoughts of what it might mean for the future tugging at the corners of my mind.

As the conversation flowed on, I found myself lost in thought. The mingling scents of old books, sweet pastries, and the faint hint of the lake breeze wrapped around me like a comforting blanket.

As the evening wound down, my eyes flicked to Bug and Tootie as they approached me, their eyes filled with determination. Bug sat next to me and placed her hand on my knee. "You focus on taking care of yourself." She tapped the tip of my nose gently. "And we'll take care of the rest."

With an unsure nod, I watched as they walked in opposite directions, each step a testament to the unspoken support that surrounded me. In a town where rivalries ran deep, I couldn't help but wonder if love and unity could eventually triumph over old grudges and secrets buried in the sands of time.

Duke Sullivan wanted to *date* me.

Publicly.

Since our outing at Rivale, being seen together in town was a regular occurrence, but Duke had left me another kitchen note asking me to a date night *in*. Excitement danced under my skin as I took my time with an *everything* shower to prepare. At just past eighteen weeks pregnant, hiding my belly was no longer an option, and I was enjoying the softly rounded way it jutted out.

For tonight's date, I had chosen a wrap dress that highlighted my belly. Whenever I did, Duke couldn't seem to keep his hands off me, and I didn't mind that at all. Plus, it had been too damn cold to wear any of the cute maternity dresses I'd bought, so an at-home date night was perfect.

I stared out of my bedroom window, the soft glow of

Christmas lights illuminating the snow-covered rows of blueberry bushes. It was early December, and Duke had managed to surprise me yet again. Not just with his rugged charm and those intense brown eyes, but with his knack for reading my mind. I never would have guessed that mentioning Christmas lights in passing would lead to him decorating the entire house and porch with them.

I couldn't resist Duke's magnetic pull, and despite the gossip swirling behind our backs, with him I felt *safe*.

I jumped at the soft knock on the door, and when I pulled it open, I was met with the sight of him in a well-fitted shirt that seemed to have been designed solely to showcase his broad shoulders and strong arms. My gaze flicked to his lips—a dangerous move, because I could lose myself in his kisses for hours.

"Hey," he said, that lopsided grin appearing. "All set?"

I nodded, looping my arm through his as he offered me his elbow. As I stepped into the hallway, the cozy ambiance enveloped me. A soft playlist of romantic tunes flowed up the stairs, and when we reached the bottom step, my fingers lifted to hide my soft gasp. The room was adorned with twinkling lights and candles. Duke had gone all out, and the gesture made my heart flutter.

"You did all this?" My heart swelled with a mix of surprise and affection.

Duke scratched his head, looking adorably sheepish. "Yeah, I thought we could use a change of scenery. Come on."

He had cooked a simple dinner of rosemary-garlic steaks, roasted sweet potatoes, and a side salad. Knowing my growing list of *weird pregnancy cravings*, he'd also arranged a charcuterie board with olives, cold spaghetti, and frozen grapes.

Hard swoon.

After eating, we settled onto the plush couch, our conversation flowing effortlessly as if we'd been doing this for years. Stories, anecdotes, and laughter filled the room, and it was easy to forget the world outside, a world that buzzed with talk of us—*the forbidden couple.*

"So, wait," I said, my eyes wide with disbelief. "You actually tried to convince Kate that there were chocolate milk rivers in the town park?"

Duke chuckled, his dark eyes crinkling at the corners. "Yeah, well, she was annoying me that day, and I figured a wild story like that would keep her busy for a few hours."

I burst into laughter, imagining a young Duke spinning an elaborate yarn to captivate his sister's imagination. "And did she believe you?"

His grin turned mischievous. "She did, until she went to the park with a straw and a cup."

Laughter bubbled up from deep within me, and I couldn't help but picture his little sister's disappointed face as she realized there were no chocolate milk rivers to be found. It was in moments like these that I saw a different side of Duke—the carefree teenager who had a knack for stirring up trouble in the most creative ways.

As the evening wore on, we continued to swap stories, each one drawing us closer together. Whether it was my embarrassing attempt at baking a cake that ended up resembling a lopsided sandcastle or Duke's adventure of getting stuck in a tree during a poorly planned tree house construction, our laughter filled the room. The weight of our families' feud seemed to fade into the background as we discovered more and more common ground.

We talked and laughed, and I found myself feeling more comfortable with Duke than I'd ever felt with anyone else. It was as if, for those fleeting hours, it was just the two of us against the world, our connection growing stronger with every exchanged tale and every shared chuckle. And in the midst of all the drama and whispered rumors, I realized that this laughter, this genuine connection, was the real magic that had the power to bridge even the widest divides.

I just couldn't shake the rumors that came to light at the book club. Beneath the laughter, a current of tension lingered in my shoulders. The rumor, whispered by the ever-eager gossip mill, about a connection between our families. We'd once *loved* each other, and a greediness that ran in my blood had torn it all apart. Our families' rivalry was tangled enough, and now this?

I found myself nervously fiddling with the hem of my dress, the rumors I'd heard at the book club weighing heavily on my mind. Gossip traveled faster than wildfire in this town, and I felt a strange responsibility to bring it up.

I took a deep breath, trying to gather my courage. "Did you know that our families were bootleggers?"

Duke frowned. "I had heard something along those lines, but we never got a lot of details. Why?"

I shook my head. "It was something that came up at book club. I guess that's part of the reason our families are at odds. Hurt feelings and bad business." I scoffed. "Kind of strange, huh? That we didn't even know that."

He shrugged. "I stopped worrying about what's weird in this town a long time ago."

I laughed, agreeing. I shared with him everything that Ms. Mabel had divulged with the Bluebirds—how our families loved each other as close friends, bootlegging, the Sullivans wanting out to start a family, the Kings' fury and wrath. Not all the pieces clicked into place quite yet, but it was a start. When I was finished, I sighed. "I guess I just don't understand how two families who once cared for each other can hold on to hate for so long. I just know there's more to it."

He considered, his lips pressing into a flat line. "I agree. I would think there was more to the story, but . . ." Duke leaned closer. "I've been more focused on figuring out why you've been avoiding mentioning something that's clearly bothering you. You never have to hide yourself from me, Sylvie."

His words caught me off guard, and I flushed with embarrassment. "I guess I just thought it might be some silly rumor. I didn't want to make a big deal out of it."

Duke reached over, his hand finding mine and giving it a reassuring squeeze. "Come here."

His hand at the small of my back, Duke led me in a slow, swaying rhythm. The scent of dinner still lingered, mixing with the aroma of his cologne.

With a mischievous glint in his eyes, Duke pulled me a little closer, and our feet moved in a slow, comfortable rhythm. "You know, I've had this fantasy," he confessed, his voice low and intimate.

"Oh?" I raised a playful eyebrow.

"Yeah." He grinned. "It involves dancing with a beautiful woman in my kitchen."

I couldn't help but chuckle, feeling butterflies in my stomach as the baby fluttered. "And does this fantasy woman have a name?"

He dipped his head, his breath warm against my ear. "Sylvie," he whispered, his lips brushing my skin.

My heart raced, and the tension between us grew palpable. The music swirled around us, filling the space between heartbeats, and before I knew it, Duke's full lips were pressed to my forehead in a sweet, lingering kiss. It was a gesture that spoke volumes—of his tenderness, his longing, and the unspoken promise of what lay between us.

In that intimate moment, surrounded by the soft glow of twinkle lights and the warmth of Duke's embrace, all the drama and gossip seemed distant and insignificant. It was just me and Duke, for however long I could keep him.

TWENTY-FOUR

DUKE

AMID THE FROSTY bite of a December morning, the twang of country music mingled with the excited chatter of the crowd as the indoor arena came to life. I stood at the edge, watching Sylvie's wide eyes take in the scene. It was like watching a child see Christmas lights for the first time, her cheeks flushed with a mix of awe and curiosity.

Damn, I'd missed this place.

The rodeo had always been my sanctuary, a place where I felt alive and free, before responsibilities clamped down on me.

"You all right there?" I drawled, nudging her with my elbow.

She blinked, her gaze turning to me, and a shy smile curved her lips. "Yes, just . . . it's so much bigger than I imagined."

I smirked, wrapping an arm around her shoulders, pulling her closer to my side. "Yeah, well, everything about this place is big—the dreams, the winnings, the bulls, the hearts."

Her eyes sparkled, and I hoped she understood, not just

about the rodeo but maybe about us too. I slipped my hand into my pocket, fingers curling around the cool metal of the belt buckle I'd won years ago. I'd held on to it, like a piece of my old self, never imagining I would one day give it to a King.

"Close your eyes," I murmured, holding the buckle in my fist in front of her.

She raised an eyebrow, a playful challenge dancing in her eyes. "Why? Planning to blindfold me and steal me away?"

I chuckled, shaking my head. "As tempting as that sounds, just humor me."

Her lashes fluttered closed, and I carefully placed the buckle in her upturned palm.

When she opened her eyes, her fingers brushed over the intricate design of the prize. "Duke, this is—I can't take it."

I shrugged, the corners of my lips tugging up. "Consider it a loan. Something to remember this day by. Can't be a cowgirl without a proper buckle." I tapped the tip of her nose with my knuckle as she beamed at me.

A vise tightened around my chest.

As the rodeo events began, I scanned the chute, my eyes landing on a few of the folks I still knew on the circuit. I leaned in. "Come on. There are a few people I'd like you to meet."

At the edge of the arena, there was Tom, the bull rider who'd broken his leg at least three times and still wouldn't quit, and Jess, the barrel racer with a hearty laugh that could light up the darkest sky. Security tried to keep us from getting too close when Tom spotted me. I raised a hand in greeting, and a grin split his face.

"Well fuck me sideways!" he shouted over the crowd and sauntered toward us.

I gritted my teeth as Sylvie covered her laugh. I held out my hand. "Tom."

He shook my hand eagerly and nodded to the guard. "Come on back."

I gently placed my hand on Sylvie's back, guiding her toward the area where the real action was. We stopped at the edge overlooking the preparations for the show.

"Didn't think I'd see you for a minute," Tom boomed, slapping me on the back with enough force to make my teeth rattle. He looked at Sylvie. "Or with company."

I smirked, wrapping an arm around Sylvie's waist and pulling her close. "Tom, meet Sylvie King. Sylvie, this is Tom. He's the guy who's determined to make every bone in his body a different shade of broken."

Tom grinned, his eyes crinkling at the corners. "Easier than it looks these days." He extended a dusty hand. "Nice to meet you."

Sylvie blushed, offering a shy smile, and took his hand. "Thanks. It's nice to meet you too."

As we chatted and laughed, Tom caught me up on all the drama that came with life on the rodeo. Soon Jess joined our little circle, her horse-scented leather jacket announcing her arrival before she even spoke. "Duke, you old dog! You never told us you were coming, let alone bringing a plus-one today."

I rolled my eyes, shaking my head at her exaggerated wink. "Jess, this is Sylvie. Sylvie, meet Jess. She's the fastest thing on four legs, other than her horse, of course."

Jess chuckled, giving Sylvie a friendly nod. "Pleasure to meet you, Sylvie. Duke here might be a grump, but he's family."

Sylvie's laughter mingled with theirs, and a swell of warmth filled my chest. It wasn't exactly uncomfortable just . . . unfamiliar. These people, these moments—they were the fabric of my past, woven into the present I was building with Sylvie. As we all continued to chat, I noticed the occasional glance down at Sylvie's midsection. It was subtle, but I knew these people well enough to recognize their curiosity.

As if on cue, Jess nudged me with her elbow and gave me a sly grin. "Duke, is there something you're not telling us? Our shy friend here seems to be hiding a secret under that coat."

I shot her a look that was half annoyance, half gratitude for her not beating around the bush. "No secret."

My chest swelled with a mix of pride and protectiveness. She was mine, and I was hers, whether our hometown liked it or not. When the time came to put it all out there, I felt a wave of uncertainty.

I wasn't good with words, especially in front of a crowd, but damn if I wasn't going to try. "Sylvie's my—" *Friend? Girlfriend? Fuck buddy? Roommate? Jesus Christ, man . . .* "Sylvie's my girl."

My girl. I let the words roll around in my head for a second. *Hell yeah.*

That was the only label that seemed to feel right. I wrapped my arm around Sylvie's waist. She curled into me, a hint of a blush staining her cheeks. Maybe it was a bit possessive, but I saw the way she liked it.

Hell, I liked it too.

"Well I'll be damned." Jess beamed at Sylvie. "You did the unthinkable. Saddled old Duke Sullivan."

Conversation flowed around as competitors began situating for their events, and Sylvie tipped her face to me. "Your girl, huh?" Teasing laughter laced through her words.

I leaned in, my voice low enough for only her to hear. "You're mine, Sylvie King. Get used to it."

With an arm around her shoulders, I took in the action. I had to push down my feelings of loss and sadness. A lifetime ago I had thought I'd be at the top of the winner's podium.

A lucky couple of times, I was.

When she started to look restless and a bit tired from standing, I guided Sylvie to our seats.

Without taking her eyes off the arena, she leaned in. "I thought rodeos were a summer thing."

"Regular season typically wraps in October, but there's a lot of money to be won before the summertime grind starts." I shrugged. "Rodeo world really doesn't have an offseason. A good winter run can set up your whole year." I pointed to the men and women fixing their leathers and getting pep talks from their teams. "Guys are coming out hungry—hammer cocked and ready to go." Winters had once provided rocket fuel for some of my best seasons. They created momentum and confidence. "The number of rodeos in the winter months is lower, but the few events that do happen tend to have bigger payouts."

The camaraderie was tangible, the air buzzing with energy and anticipation.

When I looked over, her soft brown eyes were looking at me, studying my face. "You miss it."

My knee-jerk reaction was to deny it. To stuff down the feelings I didn't allow myself to feel. Instead, I offered a jerky nod and the truth. "Sometimes."

Sylvie laced her arm through mine and rested her head on my shoulder as the events began. A surge of gratitude for these people who'd once been my rivals and teammates washed through me. Life in the rodeo was a long time ago, and despite the bumps and turns, it brought me here.

She was mine, despite the obstacles our families placed in front of us, and in this world where strength and grit were revered, I knew Sylvie was tougher than any bull I'd ever faced.

TWENTY-FIVE

SYLVIE

JOHN OATES

Did you know that at twenty weeks the
baby is the size of a troll doll?

> Including the hair or no? Oh god . . . what if
> it looks like a troll on the screen? I'm
> cackling.

With a belly button gemstone? Upgrade!
Guess we'll find out. See you in a few.

A WEEK after Duke took me to the rodeo, I was smiling
down at my phone before walking into Dr. Hokum's office.
Despite his grumbling for not driving me—a few issues at
the farm forced Duke to meet me at the office—things were
finally looking up. I had managed to make it to the sweet
spot of pregnancy that the internet told me about, where I
was less nauseated and more energetic than I had been in
months.

The mid-December wind whipped at my cheeks. The
sky sagged with thick, dark clouds that threatened even
more snow.

At least we're having a white Christmas.

I sighed and smoothed a hand over my belly. The weeks felt like they were flying by, yet were impossibly slow at the same time. Work at the Sugar Bowl was busy as we served our usual customers in addition to taking on holiday orders. Huck often relegated me to sitting on my ass and packing boxes of pastries, tarts, and pies. I would grumble at him, but some days it felt good to keep my feet up.

Nightly foot rubs from Duke helped significantly. I was no longer hiding out in his bedroom, but rather spending the evenings sprawled across him while he read a book or we watched a movie in the living room. Duke had all but moved back into the primary bedroom, and I swear, his mere presence threw my libido into overdrive.

The quiet moments were my favorite. The moments where Duke looked at me and his eyes softened after stomping in from checking the fields or working on what-ever project he was keeping a secret in the barn. Oh yeah, I totally know he's up to something, but I let him think I was clueless. The first few times I had asked him about it, he blushed—yes, *blushed*—got flustered and changed the subject. Knowing each of us has had our fair share of dramatic changes these last four months, I figured I could cut the guy some slack.

After checking in with the receptionist, I hung up my coat and waited to be called.

A few minutes later, Duke burst through the door and beelined toward me. His brows pinched down and his face was hard. "I'm so sorry I'm late."

Right on cue, the tiny baby inside me started what felt like a gold medal gymnastics routine. Whenever Duke was around, it was as if the baby could sense Duke's mere pres-ence—a neon arrow flashing *Hey you! Pick me! Over here!*

Duke's hand moved over my belly, and my heart did a tiny twist. Duke still hadn't felt the baby move, but it didn't stop us both from being hopeful.

I smiled up at him. "You're right on time."

He huffed and slid into the too-small chair next to me. He leaned in. "You look beautiful."

I let my eyes wander over him, shamelessly breathing in his earthy, masculine scent. "You look tired."

A smile quirked at the corner of his mouth. "Thanks."

"Ms. King?" A nurse rounded the corner as we both stood, then followed the young nurse, who had a kind face.

I inched closer to Duke. "Are you nervous?"

His hand found my lower back as we walked down the hall toward the room. "Not even a little."

I chewed my bottom lip. Sometime last week I had fallen down a doom-scroll rabbit hole about the twenty-week ultrasound. Sure, everyone heralded it as the *big one*, the one where you could find out if you were having a boy or a girl. But it was also the one where you found out if the baby's development was on track and whether all their parts and pieces were formed correctly. I couldn't help but worry.

After the nurse weighed me—Duke had the decency to look away after I gave him a death stare—she handed me the robe and quietly excused herself. I undressed and slipped on the floral robe. Instead of looking away, his eyes ate up every inch of me, from tits to toes. His dark eyes smoldered as he watched me. A small part of me wondered if he found me *more* attractive now that my belly was rounded with his baby. I reminded myself to tease him about having a breeding kink when we got home. That would guarantee a growl and send tingles straight to my clit.

Duke stood like a sentry while my legs swung from the

end of the table. "I think I am a little nervous," I finally admitted.

His eyes intensified as he looked at me. "About what?"

My fingers twisted. "I don't know. A lot? Do you want to find out what we're having? I'm not sure. And how do we find out? Does the doctor just blurt it out and that's it? That seems so . . . abrupt. Plus, the internet said this ultrasound is a *big deal*. It's the one they might be able to detect something that doesn't look typical. What if something's wrong? I think I had deli meat before I even knew I was pregnant, and did you know that it could be crawling with listeria?" My voice rose with every statement.

Duke's thick, rough palm glided over my exposed knee as he hovered over me. "Hey." His hand stroked up and down my thigh. "Everything is going to be fine. I have watched you be careful and take your vitamins and even stop using nail polish because of that one article you read."

I looked down at my sad, bare toenails.

"You're doing great, Mama." He kissed the top of my head, and my center ignited. "Besides, there's nothing wrong with our kid. If something *is* atypical"—he shrugged—"doesn't matter. We'll love them either way. It's you and me."

His stern reassurance wasn't only a turn-on, it was all it took to tumble me head over heels in love with him. I blinked up at Duke. I wanted to be brave—to grab his face and plant a kiss on those full lips and *finally* admit what I'd been saying in my head for a while now.

I love you.

I loved Duke so much it manifested as a physical pinch in my chest if I thought about it too long. I had opened my mouth to finally let the words slide out when two gentle knocks sounded, followed by Dr. Hokum's dark hair poking through the door.

Duke's deep-brown eyes flicked up to her, and I straightened in my seat. After a few cursory questions, Dr. Hokum arranged the large computer cart and monitor so she could perform the ultrasound while allowing us to view the baby.

Duke hunched over in a stool with his elbows planted on his knees, his deep eyes studying the monitor. The probe slid across the cool gel on my belly as Dr. Hokum chose different angles to check measurements and make notes. She briefly talked through each part of our baby—spine, organs, blood flow. It was truly fascinating.

The bridge of my nose burned as I looked onto the perfect silhouette of the growing baby inside me. He or she was no longer a gummy bear blob, but a perfect tiny person. I could see the outline of the baby's button nose, and a laugh spilled from me when the somersaults they were doing made it tricky for Dr. Hokum to get a few measurements.

"Feisty one in there." Dr. Hokum chuckled and slid the probe to try a different angle.

I glanced at Duke, whose eyes never left the monitor. His expression was hard and difficult to read, but his eyes flicked across the screen, soaking up every detail.

"Have you decided if you would like to know the sex of the baby today?"

My mouth popped open as my mind whirred. "Um . . . I . . ." My eyes flicked to Duke, who looked at me expectantly. We hadn't talked about it, and I was kicking myself for not being brave enough to bring it up earlier.

He studied my face and then turned to the doctor. "We're still undecided but would like the option." He looked around the small room. "Could I borrow a piece of paper?"

Dr. Hokum regarded the hulk of a man taking up a whole lot of space in the small exam room, and she smiled before swiveling her stool toward the counter. From a drawer, she pulled out a pad of paper and a pen and handed it to Duke. He quickly scrawled something on the paper and handed it back to her.

She looked down and smiled. "Not a problem." When she repositioned herself, she adjusted the monitor. "If you look away, I will do some final measurements, and we'll be all done here."

I turned my head away from the monitor, and Duke moved to the opposite side of the exam table. He crouched next to me so that we were eye level, but he couldn't see the screen.

"What did you write?" I asked.

A smile teased his lips. "You'll see." His large hand tucked a stray piece of hair behind my ear. "Just try to relax."

It took only a moment for Dr. Hokum to click off the monitor and begin wiping the gel off my belly before fixing the robe to cover me. "All set. The baby is growing right on track. All of the physical traits we look for appear to be developing typically." Her smile bloomed. "No concerns."

I exhaled, deeply comforted by her words. She folded the small piece of paper into fourths and handed it to Duke. He took it and stuffed it into the pocket of his flannel shirt.

"I sent a few of the pictures to the front desk, so you can pick them up there." Dr. Hokum's kind smile was reassuring as she pumped a bit of antibacterial foam onto her hands and rubbed it in. "Have a lovely Christmas, and we will see you next month. Good luck."

Duke helped me to sit up, and I redressed quickly. Together we walked to the front desk, where I made my next appointment, and the receptionist handed me our sonogram pictures. I looked down, tracing the outline of our baby's nose. I peered up at Duke.

"What?" he asked as I paused in the vestibule.

I grinned. "Nothing. Just trying to figure out if the baby has your nose or mine."

Duke bit back a smile as a muscle in his jaw worked. He fussed with my coat, drawing it over my shoulders and pulling it around my belly. My hair was tangled in the soft scarf I'd thrown on, and Duke's rough hands scooped behind my neck to free it.

Duke reached to grab his coat off the hook, and I was entranced by such a simple, innocuous gesture. He was all smooth movements and confident strides.

I placed my hand over his pec. "No peeking without me."

Duke leaned down to drop a kiss on my cheek. "I wouldn't dare."

Gripping onto his arm, I let Duke walk me to my car and bundle me inside. He insisted I follow him straight home, because the roads were looking slicker than they had before the appointment. Truth was, I was relieved to have a little space from him after such an emotional ultrasound. I couldn't trust myself not to fall at his feet and finally admit how hopelessly in love with him I was.

But I couldn't do that. Not yet.

Things between Duke and me were going well, but once the baby was born, there was no more living inside our quiet little bubble. Sooner or later I was going to have to decide whether I could give up on my dream of leaving my hometown and starting over in Savannah, when every day that passed made it harder and harder to remember why I'd ever wanted to leave.

TWENTY-SIX

DUKE

METAL SCRAPED AGAINST CERAMIC, and it was the only sound that filled the dining room. I sneaked a glance to my right and noticed Sylvie's warm eyes were downcast to her plate. She shifted in her seat and pushed the untouched food around in circles. She looked as though she was a half second from bolting to the door and escaping into the wintry mix of freezing temperatures and whipping December wind.

I felt about the same.

Despite the fact that it felt like my soul was being sucked through my eyeballs on Christmas Eve, I was only here for Sylvie. Doing it for her.

She was twenty-one weeks pregnant and had a glow about her that seemed to light up every corner of my house. As the days passed, I realized that this feeling—this warmth and poking tenderness beneath my ribs—was so much more than just friendship or impending fatherhood. Every night I curled around her and wished things could have been different. That instead of a Sullivan and a King, we could have just been two people who collided and were tumbling into this adventure together.

But those ridiculous thoughts were locked up—stashed away like precious treasures I wouldn't show the world. No one around here would understand it anyway.

Thanksgiving apart had been miserable, and based on the number of new holiday decorations that seemed to show up at the house every day, I had a sneaking suspicion that Christmas was important to Sylvie.

Memories of Mom flooded my brain—she had always loved Christmas too. Even in the lean years, she took pride in picking out the perfect gift for everyone. I realized now that my parents likely went without in order to make those Christmas mornings so memorable.

So I could suck it up and suffer through a Christmas Eve dinner with Sylvie's brothers scowling at me from around *my* table if it meant it brought her happiness.

Christmas sucks.

At least, it had before Sylvie crashed into my life and upended it. Winter had settled over the farm like a cozy blanket, the air tinged with the scent of pine and the frosty bite of the night air. All but Cisco and a few of his family members had moved on to other farms in the South, and I wouldn't see their familiar faces until spring. That was, if they chose to come back at all.

A flash of little Nico's face went through my mind, and I wondered if I'd see his gap-toothed smile come thaw, if he'd be grown or changed or even remember me.

Abel cleared his throat from across the table, and my eyes whipped to his. He didn't look up as he settled his napkin back into his lap. A chair groaned under Royal's weight as Ed let out a contented sigh from the living room.

The tension was palpable.

My instincts screamed that these people were worlds apart from my own family. As I glanced around the table, I caught JP's scowl and his eyes flicking between me and his little sister. I stifled a laugh and placed my hand on her thigh, just to piss him off a little.

I caught Sylvie's eye, and she gave me a wobbly, forced smile.

She looked past her brothers. "Dad?"

JP leaned back and shook his head. "Work."

Her brows pinched together. "On Christmas?"

"You don't take over the world by taking a day off." Royal jumped in, while Abel only offered a grunt.

I might like that guy.

I didn't miss the way Sylvie's face fell slightly at the realization that her own father had chosen work over his family. I suspected it wasn't the first time.

Bug's voice cut through the awkwardness, acting as a diversion as she smiled at her niece. "Dinner is lovely, Sylvie."

The words were simple, but they were like a lifeline, momentarily drawing attention away from the charged atmosphere. Sylvie's aunt had the uncanny ability to defuse tension with a single sentence, and I sent her a small, grateful nod.

As I surveyed the room, taking in Abel's perpetual scowl and the wary looks exchanged between siblings, I couldn't help but think that maybe Sullivans and Kings had more in common than we'd ever give them credit for. Protecting what was theirs seemed to be a universal trait, even if it was born out of a centuries-old rivalry.

Abel's scowl deepened, and I couldn't help but chuckle inwardly. He was like a bulldog guarding its territory, perpetually on edge. I caught his eye and lifted a brow in silent acknowledgment, a truce of sorts passing between us. Perhaps, deep down, he was just as tired of the animosity as I was.

The charged glances exchanged across the table were like a silent conversation in itself. JP's stern expression, Royal's half-amused, half-concerned grin, and even Three-Legged Ed's grumbling from the living room—it was like a symphony of family dynamics playing out before me. I had to hand it to them—they were loyal to a fault, even if that loyalty came with a side of tension.

My eyes drifted down to the Jell-O mold Bug had provided. It came straight from a round, pistachio-green mold that was older than I was, and she had plopped it on a white platter with a wet slurping sound. The deep red Jell-O was now actively melting on the table, and whatever the hell was floating in it looked like straight-up barf. Royal had scooped a portion onto his plate and was cautiously poking it while Sylvie's fork scraped across the loose Jell-O, picking out whatever the hell was inside it.

Feeling a strange burst of bravery, I cleared my throat and shifted in my seat, capturing the attention of the room. All eyes turned to me, and I flashed a grin that I hoped looked more charming than nervous. "Well, since we're all here staring at each other like a cow looking at a new gate, how about we call a truce? Just for the night."

The room fell into a stunned silence, the weight of generations of hostility hanging in the air. And then Bug's laughter bubbled forth, a sound so contagious that even Abel cracked a smile. Sylvie's eyes sparkled, and she reached for my hand under the table, giving it a reassuring squeeze.

Royal smirked and raised his glass, his dark tattoos

seeping out onto the backs of his hands. "To truces, no matter how temporary."

"To truces," the chorus rang out, glasses clinking in a collective toast that felt like a small victory against the tide of history.

Sylvie's aunt beamed at me, her eyes twinkling with mischief. "You know, Duke, there were probably other ways to break the cycle than setting your sights on our Sylvie."

I chuckled, feeling a warmth spread through me that had nothing to do with the roaring fire in the fireplace.

I glanced down at the weeping Jell-O in front of me. "Well, Bug, if breaking cycles involves surviving your cooking, then I think I'm up for the challenge."

I took a hearty scoop of Jell-O and shoved it in my mouth.

Huh. Not half-bad . . .

Wide eyes stared at me as laughter erupted around the table, the tension of the evening dissipating like mist in the morning sun.

As the tension dissolved, the Kings shared stories, teased one another, and engaged in a lively debate about the merits of holiday desserts while I sat back and quietly watched it unfold. I realized that maybe—just maybe—this Christmas Eve had the potential to be the turning point we never saw coming.

In the midst of the banter and laughter, I stole glances at Sylvie. Her eyes held a depth of emotion that mirrored my own, a silent acknowledgment that we were in this together, no matter the odds. As the evening wore on, I found myself falling even harder for her, my heart inexplicably tied to the woman who had turned my world upside down.

Once everyone left, we stood side by side in the kitchen. Sylvie refused to sit after the dinner, so I propped her on the counter, and she kept me company while I rinsed and stacked dishes into the dishwasher.

"Thank you for tonight." She glanced over at me. "Having my family over, I mean. We could've just done something separate."

I shook my head and dumped the silverware into the basket in the dishwasher.

She smiled, her hand resting on her belly as if the baby could hear her. "I know my family can be . . . difficult. But it means a lot to me that you were willing to do this."

I gave her a half smile, my heart thudding a bit too loudly. "Well, I guess it's a good thing Bug has a sense of humor, huh?"

Sylvie snorted and fell into a full belly laugh, a melodious sound that made everything seem a little brighter. "I couldn't believe it." She laughed again and let it fall into a sigh. "That Jell-O has been haunting us for *years*. It's so . . . odd."

I had returned to the dishes with a smile when Sylvie gripped my arm. "Oh!"

My concerned eyes searched her face as she leaned forward and ran her hand down my arm, capturing my hand and pressing my palm into her belly. I searched her features to try to figure out what was wrong.

Then I felt it.

Tap-tap-tap.

My eyes flew to hers and back down again. "Was that— Is that the baby?"

Her hand squeezed my wrist, then shifted my palm to another area of her belly. "Did you feel it? The baby always goes wild around you."

My fingers spread wider, my hand encapsulating a large portion of her belly as I searched again.

Come on, kid. Just one more time . . .

I waited, not daring to take my eyes off Sylvie.

Tap-tap-tap.

My breath exited my lungs, and my knees shook. I looked up at Sylvie, stunned into silence.

Her hand found my cheek. "Merry Christmas, Duke."

I stepped between her knees, pressing my forehead to hers and weaving my fingers through her silken hair. I sucked a breath in through my nose, selfishly taking a hit of her scent and letting it soak into me.

I stood, looking into her honey-flecked eyes before reaching into my back pocket and pulling out my wallet. She looked down, confusion shifting to awareness as she recognized the small slip of paper from Dr. Hokum's office.

"You've been carrying it around this whole time?"

I nodded. "I didn't look, I swear. I was just too nervous to lose it."

I handed her the paper and she held it, turning the small square over in her hands. "Do you want to know? I think I want to know." She shrugged. "To be prepared."

"I want what you want." The words were pure gravel as they squeezed past the lump in my throat.

"Okay." Sylvie's whisper was barely audible as she looked me in the eyes and unfolded the paper.

TWENTY-SEVEN

SYLVIE

Boy.

My eyes danced over the words *You're having a ____.* Right there, in Dr. Hokum's efficient handwriting, the word *boy* finished the sentence Duke had scrawled on a piece of paper at the appointment.

Duke read the words upside down as I held the paper between us. A thousand-pound weight settled on my chest as I soaked in the words.

Our baby is a boy.

When I glanced up, Duke's strong features were pinched in concentration as though he was also processing the reality of our situation. I took in his dark eyes, sharp features, strong nose, and sharp jawline.

"I hope he is just like you."

Duke blinked and looked up at me. "No." He swallowed hard as he looked over my features, swiping a rogue hair from my temple. "I hope he will be just like *you*. I pray he has your laugh, the kind that carries into the next room and radiates warmth. I hope he won't lose hope for his dreams and he'll let his imagination grow wild. I hope he is as strong as you and that his emotions will run deep. I hope he is exactly like you and loving him will be the easiest thing I have ever done."

Loving him will be the easiest thing I have ever done.

Tears welled in my eyes as I buried my face into Duke's chest. The stress and worry that Duke might not be able to love the baby because it was half-King has gnawed at me for months. But here he was, laying it all on the table and promising me that our child would be loved—that he hoped the baby would be like *me*.

Words eluded me, so I banded my arms around his strong neck and held on for my life.

Days later, I still caught myself smiling when I remembered Duke and I were having a baby boy. I'd already started a list in my phone of names that I liked, and as the list grew longer, I couldn't help but wonder what I wanted to do about the baby's last name.

Would he be a King or a Sullivan?

The original agreement between Duke and me had been that he would help me during the pregnancy and the first few months of the baby's life, but we had yet to discuss what would happen beyond that. If I was really going through with moving to Savannah, a deeply maternal part of me wanted to make sure that my baby shared my last name. I also couldn't even imagine the shitstorm waiting for me if my family found out I didn't give him the King last name . . . but when I imagined the crushed look that would inevitably cross Duke's face if I told him I didn't plan to name the baby Sullivan, my breath caught. There was a painful pinch in my chest every time.

Standing in the doorway to the spare room, which would serve as the nursery, I sighed. According to the internet, I was nesting, because after my shift at the Sugar Bowl, I had the intense urge to wipe down all the walls of the nursery. That morphed into cleaning the baseboards and washing the windows. I should have felt tired, but I had an inexplicable burst of energy and satisfaction.

From behind me, the floor creaked, and Duke enveloped me in an embrace, burying his nose into my neck. "Smells good."

I let the wet rag plop onto the floor as I held on to the thick forearm that banded around my midsection. I loved the way his hand splayed low across my pregnant belly. Even on days when I felt bloated and fat, Duke never failed to make me feel precious and beautiful.

I breathed in, soaking in the buzzy warmth of his embrace. "I got on a cleaning kick today." I leaned back into him.

"I was talking about you." He grumbled in my ear, and tingles raced from my scalp to my toes.

Those second-trimester hormones were no joke. I let my fingertip trace a vein in his forearm as my eyes wandered over the nursery room. It still needed furniture and a coat of paint, but I had been having fun dreaming of possibilities and pinning all kinds of bougie nursery images to a Pinterest board.

"I'd like to paint in here, but I don't think that I am supposed to."

Duke's embrace tightened slightly as his body curled around mine. "Leave it to me. I can take care of everything."

I angled my head to try to look back at him. "You're not thinking, like, deer heads and plaid, are you?"

A deep hearty chuckle rumbled from Duke, vibrating

my back and filling me with warmth. "What's wrong with deer heads? They're masculine. Cool."

"Oh god, never mind. I'll risk it with the fumes."

I was rewarded with another laugh tumbling from Duke as he swayed me slightly. "I promise I will make this room perfect for you and little Coot."

My face twisted. "Coot?"

I felt his shoulders shrug behind me. "Just trying out options. Grenade?"

"Hard pass."

"What about Athol? It's a strong Irish name."

A giggle crashed out of me. "We are not naming the baby *Athol*. It sounds like a bully with a lisp. Are you even Irish?"

"Probably." Duke laughed with another shrug. "Somewhere down the line."

My palms rested on the back of his hands while he rubbed my belly, and my laugh quieted.

"We've got some time. We'll figure it out. But I promise —" Duke dropped a tender kiss in the spot where the base of my neck met my shoulder. "If you trust me, I'll make this room perfect."

If you trust me.

The deep rumble of his voice played on a loop in my head before I finally whispered, "I trust you."

A happy hum sounded from behind me as Duke moved his hands from my belly down my back to cup my ass. "Good, now that we've got that settled, get ready." His hand landed with a *thwack* on my butt. "I'm taking you out."

I spun, facing him with big round eyes. "A date? Dinner?"

God, it was absurd how obsessed with food I had become.

A smirk tugged at the corner of his lips. "A date." He ran the tip of his nose down mine. "But it will also include food. I'm no fool."

I beamed up at him.

"Can you be ready in thirty?"

Excitement danced through me as the baby kicked in delighted agreement. "If it includes something fried, I can be ready in twenty."

Duke's hand smoothed down my cheek before landing softly on my neck as he plopped a kiss on my lips. "You got yourself a deal."

The Fried Fisherman's Feast sat in my delightfully full tummy as Duke held open the large wooden door to the Grudge. Only days after Christmas, it still had the rustic charm of a honky-tonk dressed up for the holidays. Garland swag adorned the stage. The mirror behind the bar held a large wreath, but if you looked closely, there were little skeletons matching the Grudge's logo in Santa hats.

My eyes flicked to the east and west sides of the bar. It was common knowledge that when townies entered the Grudge Holder, you picked a side. I froze with the assumption that Duke would obviously pick the west side, nestling comfortably in a slew of Sullivans and their allies. On the King side, cousins and family friends eyed us, their drinks paused midway to their mouths as they gaped.

The scene unfolded in a matter of seconds. Duke paused for only a fraction of that time before heading straight toward an open high-top table near the center of the room. Relief washed over me as Duke slid out the high-back chair and helped me into it.

"You good?" His eyes searched my face.

"Yep!" I chirped a little too loudly and grabbed the plastic menu to do something with my trembling hands. Duke folded his large frame into the seat across from me and leaned back, looking completely at ease in the tense surroundings, like a king in his throne.

A small laugh shotgunned out of me. The irony of that thought was not lost on me. Duke's chin tipped in my direction in silent question. Instead of answering, I dropped my eyes to the menu and started scanning.

"Is Brutus ready for a snack?"

I shot him a bored look with steady eyes. "Hard. Pass."

He chuckled as I settled against the back of the stool and absently rubbed my bump. "I think he's still content with the fifty pounds of popcorn shrimp I just housed."

His eyes flicked down, then back up as a waitress stepped up to our table. "Hey, folks, what can I get started for you tonight?" Nerves buzzed off her as her smile faltered and her eyes flicked between us.

He nodded for me to go ahead, and I ordered. "A strawberry lemonade with a splash of Sprite, please."

His lips pursed before his attention drew back to the waitress. "I'll have the same and a basket of fried pickles."

She nodded and scooped up our menus before hurrying away.

Duke winked at me. "Just in case."

Butterflies erupted in my belly at the same time as the baby kicked. Clearly, fried food was this kid's love language.

It was early on a Thursday night, which meant a live band hadn't set up yet, but music pumped from the jukebox. My fingers tapped the rhythm to the old nineties country song as I watched couples two-step on the dance floor. I watched as Annie and Duke's brother Lee danced circles around everyone in town. They had for years, but it was only recently they finally stopped denying the magnetic pull toward each other.

My eyes flicked to Duke, and I wondered if maybe we were doing the same thing—letting our names and family history define whatever this was between us when there was no denying there was an invisible string attaching me to him. A string I couldn't imagine ever being broken.

Duke's large hand captured mine, mid-beat. He slid from his chair and stood next to mine, pulling me to stand. He tipped his head toward the dance floor. "Come on."

I looked up at him as his one arm circled my waist and the other held my hand in the proper dancing position. I had to tip my chin to look him in the eye. "I love to dance."

It was a general statement as much as it was a warning to this stoic man whom I'd seen time and time again in the Grudge but never once out on the dance floor.

He smirked down at me, and a tug pulled low in my belly. "I know."

Without another word, Duke led me into a flawless two-step. With my hand securely in his and his other pressed to my back, he pushed and pulled me in a way that made our dancing fluid, like we had been coupled together for years. Exhilaration zipped through me.

As the song faded, I gripped his forearms and looked up at him. Laughter bubbled in my chest as my eyes danced across his handsome features. "Duke Sullivan, you have been lying to me! I have seen you at this bar for years, and not one time have I seen you set foot on this dance floor."

He swayed with me in his arms as the song changed to a moody ballad. "Just because I don't dance doesn't mean I *can't* dance."

"You are full of secrets."

He pulled me closer to whisper in my ear. "You want to know another secret?"

Desire raced through me. "Yes."

"I never danced before, because I could never dance with you." Then, as if he hadn't just shattered my world, Duke continued to hold me close to his chest.

This man.

How had I gone so long and not seen the pure, unfiltered sexiness of Duke Sullivan? It was raw and pure and powerful. I was inexplicably drawn to him. Every part of me, heart and soul, craved that man. I swayed with him, lost in him.

When the music switched back to an upbeat tempo, my eyes pleaded. "One more dance?"

His broody eyes drew downward as he considered my question. "You're not too tired?"

A mischievous smirk danced across my features. "Worried you're going to hurt your back, old man?" I teased.

His eyes grew nearly black in the dim lighting of the bar as he leaned down and let his deep voice caress the shell of my ear. "It's not me I'm worried about, sweetheart. Your back's gonna be hurting later too."

I sucked in a breath as I looked up at him, biting my lower lip to keep from grinning. I was going for coy but fairly certain I looked like a feral cat in heat, ready to pounce on him and make him make good on his delicious promise.

～

WE HAD ONLY MADE it through another two songs before we were tumbling through the front door, a tangle of limbs and sloppy kisses and groans. Duke always knew exactly how much pressure to apply to exactly which body parts to light me on fire and get me humming. His mouth sucked at the pulse point at the base of my neck, as I groaned with my back pressed flat against the door.

"Please," I pleaded.

Duke braced his hands against the wood behind me, his fingers curled tight into a fist. "I'm so hard for you right now." As proof he ground his hard cock against my hip as I arched into him. "I don't want to hurt you, but I can't . . ."

His voice trailed off in a breathless groan as I palmed his length through his jeans. "You won't," I assured him. A fact I knew in the depths of my soul—Duke would never physically hurt me, but I didn't want it gentle. "I need you—" I swallowed hard, willing myself to be brave and ask for exactly what I needed. I knew if I only asked, he would give it to me. "Rough."

He leaned back, searing me with those dark eyes as though he was confirming he had heard me correctly—that I wanted him just as badly as he wanted me. I set my shoulders and lifted my chin, proving to him and myself that I could take whatever he could give me, that I craved the wild abandon.

He drew away from me with a growl. Duke bent low to support my legs as he hoisted me against him. He left ample room for my belly as he swiveled and stomped up the stairs to our bedroom. Instead of depositing me on the bed and fucking me senseless like I thought he would, Duke gently set me on my feet, turning my shoulders so I faced the long wardrobe mirror in the corner.

I watched Duke's reflection as he stood inches behind me. He started at my neck, sweeping my blonde hair to one side as his fingers found the zipper of my dress. My mouth sagged open as he lowered the zipper, achingly slow. When he reached my lower back, his fingertips brushed the sensitive skin there, and a shiver danced through me. He smoothed his palms over my shoulders, allowing the top of the dress to expose my chest.

My boobs had gotten huge during pregnancy, and I enjoyed the way his hungry eyes roamed over the sheer bra. My nipples stiffened to aching points. His hands continued to work the dress over my swollen belly until it broke free and pooled at my feet. I had moved to pull down the warm knit leggings I had worn to ward off the chill, when his hand stopped me.

"Let me." Duke dropped to one knee and gently peeled the fabric down my thighs.

I used his shoulder for stability as I stepped from the leggings, letting my fingertips dance across the short crop of hairs behind his head.

His eyes flicked from the bare spot between my legs to my face. "No panties?"

I jerked my head to the side. "They're starting to dig and get uncomfortable."

I watched as his large palms smoothed up my leg, sliding into my gap. With one drag, he moved through my slit with the side of his index finger, stopping to press his thumb into my clit. My knees threatened to buckle, and my eyes wanted to roll to the back of my head, but I couldn't stop staring at us in the mirror. Duke on his knees, worshiping my body as I watched, was a beautiful sight.

He removed his hand, sucking his index finger into his mouth and moaning around it. "Always so fucking sweet."

I drew in a sharp inhale at his devious words. He looked up at me, noticing my eyes hadn't left the mirror as I watched the scene unfold in front of me.

He glanced over his shoulder and smirked. "You like to watch, sweetheart?"

His hand went back to rubbing my pussy, and my hips started to move of their own volition.

"Say it," he demanded as he slipped one finger inside of me, and I moaned. "You want to watch me fuck you hard."

"Yes. I want it."

"Good girl. I'm going to let you watch while I fill you and bring you to the edge before letting you come." I watched as Duke slipped a second finger inside me, using his thumb to tease my clit and draw me closer and closer to the orgasm my body begged for.

My head tipped back, but my eyes remained locked on the mirror. Duke's fingers pumped in and out of me. It was crass, vulgar, and utterly delicious.

"I want—" I could hardly get the words out between pants. "I want to come on your cock."

His dark chuckle tightened the coil at my core as he nipped at my neck. "Don't worry. You will."

Every nerve ending on my body was on fire as I watched him coax the orgasm from me. With an open mouth and one hand gripping his hair, I came around his thick fingers. Only when the final shudders racked out of me, Duke stood, ripping off his shirt and removing his belt and pants.

I continued to watch as he stripped his black boxer briefs down his thick muscular thighs and clamped a fist around his massive, hard cock.

"Come here." Still stroking himself, he grabbed my hand and guided me toward the edge of the bed. From the corner, he turned me away from him before sitting on the edge. I could still see him in the mirror, his erection jutting up from between those strong thighs. With my hips in his hands, he guided me a step backward before dragging the head of his cock through my pussy.

I called out his name, but he didn't stop his slow, torturous assault. I lowered an inch, worried my knees might buckle under the intense pleasure.

"That's it, sweetheart." His grip tightened on my hips. "Sit down on my cock and let me finally feel your sweet, tight cunt."

I never imagined such filthy words being so freaking hot. But I wanted *more*. I wanted him.

"Relax," he urged as my thighs trembled, attempting to hold the majority of my weight off him. "Sink all the way down. I want to feel you grind against me."

I sighed in relief as I allowed the remainder of my weight to fall onto his lap. He was impossibly deep as he stretched me. "Yes, yes . . ." I panted a rhythm as my hips began to move.

Duke used his hands to set the pace. He moved my hips as he grunted behind me. His mouth clamped down on my neck, his teeth a delirious scrape against the sensitive skin.

"Watch," he demanded.

My eyes flew to the mirror in the corner. Duke's intense brown irises met mine as he pounded into me with my legs spread wide around the outside of his thighs. I could see his dick disappear inside me. It was the most erotic and beautiful thing I had ever seen.

"Goddamn, you are so fucking perfect. I want you to see how we fit. How we were made for each other."

My senses were on overload. Sweat slicked my skin. My clit ached for release. My eyes gobbled up the delicious sight of Duke pumping into me. His thick muscular arms bearing our weight as I rode him.

"More, Duke. I need more."

In one swift move, he lifted both of us as he stood and gently swiveled me around, never separating us. His movements were gentle but sure.

"Knees on the bed," he demanded as his long arm reached forward, yanking a pillow down for my head and chest to rest on.

I scrambled to my knees. That same hand reached into my hair, pulling my face to the side. "Don't stop watching."

In the mirror, I took us in. My knees on the bed, ass in the air, my chest on the mattress with my belly hovering safely above the bed as Duke pulled his long cock out of me. It glistened with my arousal, and we both moaned. With an achingly slow drag, I watched Duke enter me. Over and over he pumped into me as his body coiled tight behind me.

I had never imagined sex could be so naughty and exhilarating. But with Duke, it was *everything*. I knew Duke would give me everything he could. Anything I asked, which gave me the bravery to request exactly what I wanted.

"Slap my ass," I panted. "Don't be gentle."

In the mirror, his dark eyes flared before his hand reared back and a crack of hand on flesh filled the bedroom. His rough palm immediately massaged away the sting. A fresh surge of wetness coated his cock.

"Fuck yes." He groaned as he continued to pump inside me. "Again?"

A jerky nod was all I could muster. His hands and cock brought me to the edge of my climax.

Crack.

"Yes!"

Another rub. His short nails dragged down the curve of my ass.

Crack.

Intense pleasure mixed with pain and forced an orgasm to tear through me. After a few pumps of his hips, Duke was tumbling right behind me. His cock jerked and swelled inside me as he emptied his release deep.

My arms shook as warmth seeped down my inner thighs after Duke slipped out of me. Carefully he collected me in his arms, holding my bodyweight, as I was too weak to stand. When I was nestled on my side on the bed, his large body collapsed behind me, gently tugging me into a close embrace.

"Holy shit." His breath was hot as he panted behind me.

"Thank you," I said softly. "That was . . . incredible." My voice hitched. I was just as breathless as he was.

His hands moved over the curve of my ass, where no doubt there would be a bright-red mark. A devious part of me couldn't wait to see if it stayed until tomorrow as a reminder of the most intense orgasm I had ever experienced.

Duke shifted, propping himself up on his hip, and bent in half to lean over and place a gentle kiss on my butt. "Was it too much?" he murmured, concern laced through his voice.

I hummed with a smile. "It was the exact right amount."

I didn't have the bravery to tell him I knew that the time we had together would never be enough.

TWENTY-EIGHT

DUKE

THE BITTER CLUTCH of a Michigan winter in mid-February was undeniable. Despite the angry wind, the lonely sounds of a mourning dove broke the quiet in the field. After months of silence, I realized how much I missed the call of birds on my daily walks. I stood still, feet firmly planted on the frozen ground, and listened.

The low angle of the late-afternoon winter sun cast long, ominous shadows onto the pristine snow. The crunch of my boots through the snow drowned out the bird as I trudged toward the farmhouse. In another month we'd be pruning the bushes as they emerged from their dormancy, and for the first time since overseeing the farm, I wasn't ready. Every day that hurtled me toward spring was one less day with the woman I loved.

The woman who still planned to leave.

Anger—at myself for being a coward and not laying my battered heart at her feet—simmered next to the chill that tore through me.

There had to be a way.

My hand brushed over the letter I had stuffed in my

pocket. My thoughts were as turbulent as the waves crashing against the shoreline, refusing to be quieted despite the chill. I clenched and unclenched my fists, torn between my loyalty to my family and the love I held for Sylvie and the life growing inside her.

Rumors of inquiries regarding mineral rights on Sullivan land had added an ominous edge to the already tense atmosphere in our town. My mind raced as I sorted through the implications for my family. Months ago I had asked Joss Keller, my friend and local attorney, to look into whoever was poking around when he'd finally sent the letter. Add to it the mysterious tire tracks that continued to show up on Sullivan land, and I was on edge.

The mere idea that someone was eyeing *my* land for minerals was infuriating. JP King's reputation for ambitious business acquisitions didn't help me shake the feeling that the Kings were behind this, stoking the flames of the feud that had divided our families for generations.

So much for temporary truces.

I knew Sylvie belonged on their side, but despite the animosity between our families, I had fallen in love with her. My heart tightened with every thought of her, and yet I hadn't found the courage to tell her the depth of my feelings. To tell her how madly in love with her I was, to beg her to give up her dream and *stay*.

I couldn't escape knowing that she would say yes. One ask and she'd likely give it all up. *For me.* But I couldn't bear knowing I would do to her what had been done to me. So I bit back the words and let my actions speak for me.

I couldn't fight the nagging feeling that if I could only figure out where the feud had started, why it had persisted for so long, Sylvie and I might have a fighting chance to put the feud to rest. If we could find a way to repair the relationship between our families, the fighting, sidelong glances, and murmurs through town could stop. We could exist without the scrutiny of a town divided.

It still wasn't easy, even with the whole town knowing Sylvie was living with me. Only a few days ago someone in town had actually stopped me and tried to set me up with her niece or something. *A nice girl from a* good *family*.

The fucking *audacity*.

As the sun dipped below the horizon, my resolve hardened. I had to confront this situation head-on, not only for my family but for the woman I loved and for the son we would soon welcome into the world. It was up to me to bridge the gap between the Sullivans and Kings, if only to secure a better future for our child.

Trouble was, I needed help.

WHISPERS HAD FLOATED through town for *years* that the Bluebird Book Club was far more than an opportunity for the women in town to talk about books—they discussed, planned events, *schemed*.

My hand hovered over the door handle, and I hoped that was true, and I wasn't about to crash an invite-only, no-men-allowed book club meeting.

Guess I'm about to find out.

I'd stopped by Haven Pines and begged MJ for a favor. I needed her to find any excuse for Sylvie to miss their book club. She smiled and told me not to worry. Instead, a prickle of dread danced up my spine as I entered the bookstore.

The smell of old books mingled with freshly brewed coffee. Quiet chatter floated above the bookshelves as I walked through the stacks toward the quiet conversation. A few wide eyes glanced up at me as a collective hush rippled over the women gathered in the back of Bluebird Books.

"Duke." Aunt Tootie stepped forward, placing her coffee cup on a makeshift bar before stepping up to me.

"Aunt Tootie." I looked past her and nodded at the group of women. "Ladies."

I recognized nearly everyone—those with allegiance to the Kings, Sullivans, a few of my cousins. They sat together in small clusters, sunken back into cozy chairs or plush rounded ottomans. Soft lamps added a warm glow and created a cozy space for them to sit together.

I straightened my shoulders and lifted my chin. Asking for help was so far out of my comfort zone I didn't even know where to begin.

"There's a rumor going around that the Bluebirds can make the impossible happen." I cleared my throat. "I'm in a tight spot, and I could use a miracle."

Soft whispers rippled through the group of women, and my aunt Tootie's eyes softened.

Bug King's hard, assessing eyes flicked down my front and then back up again before she turned to my aunt. "Took him long enough."

Tootie scoffed and swatted her hand in Bug's direction. "You knock it off. He's here now. That's all that matters."

My aunt smiled at me before lacing her arms through mine and patting my hand. "We had been wondering when you were going to show up."

A few women moved to offer me a seat, and I thanked them with a terse nod and lowered myself onto a too-small ottoman. I let my elbows rest on my knees as I clasped my hands and wondered where to begin.

Bug wasn't the only woman with her arms crossed and a skeptical look on her face as I began. "The Kings and Sullivans have been at odds for as long as I can remember. I've had my hand in my fair share of pranks." I scoffed as a litany of childish pranks flipped through my memory. "It's practically a defining characteristic of this town." A few polite chuckles and nods spurred me to continue.

I thought of Sylvie and her quiet nature, her soft heart and kind eyes. I frowned down at my hands. "Things are different now."

"Different?" Bug pressed.

I looked directly into her eyes. "Yes, ma'am."

"Why Sylvie?" *Goddamn that woman is a hard nut to crack.*

I clenched my jaw and offered her the only truth I could. "I fell in love with her. I knew I shouldn't. Tried damn hard not to, but . . ." The collective sigh that floated through the room had me crossing my arms. "She's it for me."

My eyes flicked up to Bug, who looked down her nose and whose cool expression gave nothing away.

"We still have a long road ahead of us." I looked around at the gathered group. "Sylvie can't do her job at the Sugar Bowl without whispers behind her back." I looked directly at Ms. Tiny, who was an egregious offender and known gossip. "She's pregnant, not deaf." Ms. Tiny pursed her lips. "And Martha." I looked directly at Martha Kensington's wide eyes. "I didn't much appreciate you trying to set me up with your niece. I am not single. I am very much off the market." Martha blushed and looked away. "Now I'm not naive enough to think that my feelings for Sylvie will change an entire town's opinion, but I could use some help spreading the word that this feud no longer involves Sylvie and me. We'll have no part in pranks or backhanded comments or outright lies." I stood to hammer home my point. "If anyone has something to say, they can say it to me. And if they know what's good for them, they'll keep Sylvie's name out of their mouths, or they'll deal with me."

Lark looked as though she were about to burst into tears, and I willed my eyes to move over the rest of the crowd. "Can I count on the Bluebirds?"

I looked around expectantly waiting for anyone to speak up, hoping that speaking my truth was enough to garner even the smallest shred of support from the people I knew ran this town.

"Oh shit." My sister, Kate, shot to her feet, staring down at her phone with deep lines creasing her forehead.

Okay . . . not exactly the outpouring of support I was expecting from my sister.

Her panicked eyes whipped to mine. "We have to go."

I took a step toward her. "What is it?"

"Trouble."

"What?" Panic coursed through me as I thought about Sylvie.

Kate swiped a frustrated hand through the air. "No." She shook her head. "I don't know. But something's going down at King Tattoo. It's bad. Wyatt texted me that there's a crowd—a fight or something."

A frustrated growl tore through my throat as I turned and stomped toward the front of the bookstore.

"Wait!" Aunt Tootie called out, but I ignored her, and Kate hustled next to me, typing out a text on her phone while Lark shoved Kate's coat into her arms and slipped on her own.

"What's going on?" I didn't need Kate to answer, because as soon as we exited Bluebird Books, shouts rang out from the direction of Royal's tattoo shop. A small crowd had gathered in a semicircle—a sure sign of a fight as a tangle of bodies in the center pushed, shoved, and shouted in each other's faces.

I recognized my little cousin Matty in the middle of the fray. He was being held back by Wyatt as he pointed and screamed something at Royal King, who looked like he was about to explode. Spit bubbled at the corner of Matty's mouth as he spewed obscenities in Royal's direction.

Adrenaline coursed through me as I shouldered my way through the growing crowd. Through the chaos, it looked as though a shoving match had broken out between Kings and Sullivans. While Matty screamed at Royal, Royal simply looked on, irate as he began rolling up his shirtsleeves, exposing the intricate designs of tattoos that covered him from his knuckles up.

Matty was a fucking idiot. Royal could lay him out flat with one punch if he wanted to, but he was young and a hothead.

"Hey!" My deep voice rumbled above the crowd. "The hell is going on?"

"Why don't you ask your shithead family?" Royal tipped his chin in my cousin's direction, which incited a fresh slew of colorful language from Matty.

I turned toward my idiot cousin. "Shut it."

His nostrils flared, but his jaw clamped shut. The crowd pulsed behind us, disappointed to not see Matty and Royal tussle.

I held my arms out to my sides, palms up in hopes of proving to Royal I wasn't looking to fight. "What's going on?"

Anger rolled off Royal. "Matty and his friends thought it would be fucking hilarious to soap the storefront."

I glanced over Royal's shoulder, and sure enough

someone had taken a bar of soap to the storefront window, obscuring the meticulous paint job.

I looked back to Royal and scoffed. "Come on. It's a harmless prank. You can't say we haven't each done stupid shit." I gestured toward Matty. "He was dumb enough to get caught. That's on us."

Royal pointed at my chest. "Get more creative, more stealthy, or grow the fuck up."

I clenched my jaw as I stared at him, but nodded. He was right. The prank was pretty dumb and childish, and not all that creative—would definitely be a disappointment in Lee's eyes, that was for damn sure.

Sensing the situation was defused, I turned my back to Royal, even though the crowd still egged their respective sides on, hoping for more of an argument. I stomped toward Matty, whose eyes were still wild.

I had put my hand against his chest to move him back a few steps when he sidestepped me, leaning down to pick something up off the planter box near the edge of the sidewalk. "How's this for creative, asshole?"

Time slowed.

From the corner of my eye I didn't register the brick in Matty's hand until it was too late. I could only turn and stare as his arm reared back. The brick sailed in the air over Royal's shoulder and nearly grazed his ear. He flinched and ducked before it had the chance to land squarely against his temple.

Instead, the brick crashed directly into the King Tattoo storefront window. Glass shattered. Screaming rang out.

"The fuck!" Fury coursed through Royal's voice as he charged forward, tackling Matty.

Wyatt and I had moved to pull him off our idiot cousin when I heard a scream. "Oh my god!"

My heart stopped. I knew that voice, though I had never heard it laced with such panic.

Sylvie.

Chunks of jagged glass spread across the sidewalk. Many of the storefronts downtown were relics in themselves and hadn't been updated with anti-shatter glass.

The brick had created a hole in the window and bounced across the tattoo shop floor. A huge spider web pattern inched its way across the remaining glass.

Sylvie and MJ were crouched on the sidewalk beneath the window. I hadn't even realized she was there but assumed the way news travels in this town, she and MJ had decided to come by when they heard something was happening.

MJ held Sylvie as Sylvie clutched her arm, from beneath her fingertips, her face pale and eyes wide.

"Oh shit, Sylvie," MJ cried, alarmed.

My feet couldn't get me there fast enough as I watched MJ rip off her heavy coat and immediately go into nurse mode. Sylvie had been wearing a thin jacket. It was the only one that still fit her, and she'd refused to let me buy her a new one. She called it *pointless* since she wouldn't get much use out of it after the pregnancy. When she fell, a sliver of glass had torn through the thin fabric and into her forearm.

MJ's hand clamped above where Sylvie was bleeding.

I crowded her space. "How bad is it?"

"I don't know. Bad enough. We ducked to get out of the way of the brick and Sylvie slipped." I didn't miss the fleeting flash of panic in MJ's eyes before she tamped it down and got to work, wrapping the belt from her own coat around the upper part of Sylvie's forearm.

Sylvie sank down on her heels, holding her arm out as

though she didn't want to get any of her own blood on her belly.

I had pulled up my phone to call 911 when Kate's hand stopped me. "I already called. They're on their way."

Howling buzzed in my ears as I looked on, helpless. Royal moved to his sister's side while Kate, Lark, and Wyatt worked to disperse the crowd. In our small town, it was only a matter of minutes before the EMTs arrived, my brother included.

Lee spared only a quick glance to the storefront window before taking over and rushing to Sylvie's side. I sagged in relief that he immediately went to help her instead of holding her last name against her.

Unable to help, I did the one thing I knew I could do. I turned to my cousin and hauled him off his ass by his collar. "Stand the fuck up."

"Duke, I'm sorry. I didn't mean to— I didn't think that—"

"Yeah, no shit, you didn't think." I pulled him closer to the window so he could see what he had done and also see that people had gotten hurt.

Not just people, my person.

"Come on, man, let me go. It was just a joke."

"This isn't a fucking joke." I was unhinged, rage clawing at my throat.

Royal stepped up beside me. "She's okay, not as bad as it looked. Lee's getting her wrapped up."

I kept staring down at my cousin but spoke to Royal. "Call the sheriff."

"The cops? Are you kidding me?" Matty whined. "You know Amy King will have my ass if she has the opportunity to arrest me. Come on, man." He pleaded to Royal. "You're not gonna press charges, are you? It was an accident."

I tightened my grip around his collar and hauled him against me. "I don't give a shit if he's pressing charges about the window. *I'm* pressing charges. Assault. I don't give a fuck if you're a Sullivan or not."

That was it. The line. The moment where I *knew*.

Nothing and no one mattered more than her. I would choose Sylvie over all others, even a Sullivan.

Royal clamped a hand on my shoulder. "She's asking for you." My head whipped in his direction. "I'll make sure he hangs around until Amy gets here. Go."

I looked over his face and, with a nod, released Matty and walked to where my brother was putting the final touches on a bandage wrap on Sylvie's forearm. Someone had draped a wool blanket over her shoulders, but she still shivered against the frigid February air.

Lee looked at her with a kindness I realized he reserved for all his patients. He was damn good at his job and loved what he did. Pride filled my chest for my little brother.

When Sylvie's gaze lifted to mine, the tears that gathered on her lower lashes tipped over and streamed down her cheeks.

I brushed one away with my thumb as I crouched in front of her. "About gave me a heart attack, woman."

Her gentle laugh was the balm my heart needed. "I don't know what happened. I think the glass was already on the ground when I stumbled and just caught it at the right angle."

"It's not deep, just a superficial cut that got her in the right spot," Lee assured me. "Sometimes those bleed like the devil." Lee gave a charming smile and winked at Sylvie. My brother turned to me. "I'd still like her to go in, though. Get checked out and make sure everything's all good with the baby, since she took a tumble." He focused his attention back on Sylvie. "Are you sore anywhere? Any cramping? Tender spots?" His hold on her elbow was gentle, and she shook her head. "Do you think you can stand?"

She nodded and allowed MJ and Lee to lift her to her feet. I stepped forward, and she melted into me. "What were you doing here?"

I held her in my arms and swayed slowly. "I should ask you the same thing."

"Sloane texted that there was some drama going down at Royal's shop." She gestured with her head. "We were just over at the café having a slice of pie."

"Playing hooky from the Bluebirds?" I asked, trying to help her think about anything other than my reckless cousin and what had gone down tonight.

"How do you know about that?"

I stifled a smirk, not wanting her to know about my scheming with MJ or my secret meeting with the Bluebirds. Not yet at least. "Just a guess." I looked over Sylvie's head at my brother. "Does she need to go by ambulance?"

He finished writing something on his clipboard and looked at me. "That would be up to her, but no. I think she'd be all right to head on in and get checked out."

I glanced at her to see what she wanted to do, and she smiled at Lee. "Duke can take me."

"Sounds good." Lee clicked his pen. "Guess I'll see if there are any other idiots who need medical attention."

"Matty's gonna need to get checked out for a concussion," I offered.

Lee straightened, a curious look on his face as he glanced toward our little cousin just as I turned and punched Matty in the jaw, knocking him out cold.

TWENTY-NINE

SYLVIE

Two hours later, I was itching for everyone to stop looking at me with pitying eyes. Duke had taken me to the hospital but wouldn't give me two inches of breathing room. MJ had followed and was running interference in the hallway, as my overprotective brothers would not stop calling.

The pressure pot in Outtatowner was whistling a shrill cry that *something* was about to explode.

I sneaked a glance at the father of my child, whose leg was bouncing as he stared at the faded linoleum floor. Maybe it was more like *someone*. Duke looked as though he was about to go nuclear.

We were only waiting for my discharge papers after a thorough checkup and being reassured that the baby was fine. The second hand tick of the clock was deafening as we waited.

"Do you think you could get me some water?" At the creak in my voice, Duke shot to his feet and looked me over from head to toe. I stifled a tiny eye roll—*I am fine*—then pasted on a small smile. Without a word, Duke stormed out of the ER room.

MJ poked her head around the doorway. "All clear?"

"I sent him on an errand." I scooted over to allow my little sister to share the small bed with me.

She lay beside me, resting her head on my shoulder. "He's like a hot, moody warden." Her body racked with an exaggerated, playful shiver.

"He's always been moody," I reminded her.

"He's worse with you."

A tiny ball of warmth bloomed in my chest. She wasn't wrong. Duke was grumpy and probably a bit overbearing, but coming from him, it wasn't stifling. It mostly made me feel loved.

Not that he loves me.

Fresh tears pricked like tiny knives behind my eyelids. I let out a slow breath.

MJ sat up to look me over. "Does it hurt again? Should I call the nurse?"

I shook my head, adjusting my bandaged arm. "It's not that. I just . . ." My hands moved over the swell of my belly. "How could I have been so dumb?" My voice was tiny. I hated myself for even admitting it aloud.

MJ snuggled closer. "You're not dumb. You're in love."

A sarcastic, congested laugh burst from my chest as I wiped my sleeve across my runny nose. "That's the dumbest part of all." Loving Duke was the ultimate King betrayal. "It just feels like too much. Everything is falling apart, and I am supposed to bring a baby into that chaos? You know there's zero chance the boys are ever going to let this go. Once Dad finds out, he'll be on a warpath."

"Dad sucks."

I laughed. It was rare MJ ever spoke her opinion about our intense, intimidating father. He adored MJ, but her admission made me wonder if his attention wasn't just added pressure—pressure that my invisibility helped me escape.

"Shit . . ." MJ frowned as she looked down at her phone. I adjusted to look at her as her fingers flew over the screen.

"What is it?"

MJ toyed with her lip. "Dad knows." Dread roiled in my stomach as I swallowed back the urge to throw up. "He's pissed about the storefront."

The storefront. Not that his pregnant daughter was injured. *Awesome.*

MJ's fingertips hammered out another text, and she lifted the phone to her ear. Her pitying eyes moved to mine. "JP."

Through the speaker I couldn't make out what my brother was saying, but the shouts on the other end were clear.

"JP, calm down. It was an accident." MJ turned her back to me, but I continued to listen. "She's fine . . . a few butterfly bandages and a thorough checkup. Yeah, the baby is good." Her hand beat a nervous rhythm against the outside of her thigh. "Don't do anything—fine. Okay, but I still think you're a bunch of idiots."

"Give me the phone." I held my good hand out as MJ turned to look at me. "Let me talk to him."

MJ glanced at her phone. "Hang on, Sylvie wants to say something."

When she got close enough, I snatched the phone from her and pressed it to my ear. "JP, what's going on?"

My older brother's smooth voice was steady on the other end. "I don't want you to worry about anything. We're just making this right."

"Making it right or getting even?" I demanded.

JP scoffed in my ear. "Same difference."

"Please don't. I'm begging you—"

"Royal, Whip, and I are just going to have a little chat." I didn't miss the malice that wove between his words.

"A chat? What does that even mean? And where's Abel?"

I waited for JP to respond, and he finally admitted with a sigh, "Abel has a record. He can't be involved."

"JP . . . please!"

"Look, we've been holding back because of the situation you're in, but that's over now. Things changed, and we have our marching orders. I'm sorry, Syl." The line went dead as my heart rattled against my ribs.

"That jerk hung up on me!" I tossed MJ's phone onto the bed and flipped the bedsheet off my legs before sitting upright. "We have to go. I need to go." Panic squeezed my throat tighter.

"You're not going anywhere." Duke stared down at me, a small Styrofoam cup clutched in his hands. "Not until the doctors give us the okay."

"I'll go." MJ's eyes communicated clearly that she would go and attempt to run interference before my brothers did something epically stupid in retaliation for the broken window. She dropped a kiss on my head. MJ gave Duke's biceps a squeeze before grabbing her coat. She was furiously texting again and I hoped it was to stop whatever my brothers were planning.

I was tired. Bone tired of not being seen. Or heard. Tired of everyone around me making decisions *in my best interest*.

Fuck. That.

I took in my huge belly and bandaged arm, helplessness washing over me. I sank into the bed as the tears rolled out of me. Duke sat next to me, and the weight of his body had me leaning into him. One muscular arm wrapped around me.

"Who was on the phone?" Duke's voice was soft, but insistent.

"My brother JP. I think something bad is going to happen." Duke tensed beside me, his feelings clearly at war with hearing me out and sending a warning to his family. "I tried to reason with him, but he totally ignored me, and then the asshole *hung up on me.*"

"I'll take care of it." MJ zipped her coat and hurried out of the emergency room.

"Fuck them." Duke's words were steeped in anger. All this time he was careful not to talk shit about my family, but the man next to me looked as though he'd snapped. "You need to stand up for yourself."

I blinked up at him and swallowed past the hurt the truth in that statement caused. "I *tried.*"

"Try harder." Duke stood, dragging his hands through his hair and down his face. As he paced the room, his frustration bubbled and grew. "You let them walk all over you and treat you like shit. How can you be okay with that?"

Defensiveness and fury slammed into place as I lifted my chin. "Excuse me?"

Duke held his hands out. "Am I wrong?"

I blinked. "Well . . . no, but it's none of your business."

He scoffed. "None of—" Duke's steps pounded on the linoleum. "None of my business? Are you fucking kidding me right now? Why can't you just stand up for yourself?"

The urge to fold in on myself was intense. I *hated* being the target for Duke's frustration, and past-me would have dipped into the shadows until the storm passed, but a small spark of defiance had been lit. That sizzling ember burned a hole through my gut and was ready to set my entire life ablaze if it had to.

I jostled myself to stand toe to toe with him. I squared my shoulders and lifted my chin to look him in the eyes.

"You can't stand it, can you?" Duke's dark brows furrowed, but I barreled on. "You're so used to saying *jump* and watching everyone happily leap into the air." I pointed to my chest. "Well, that's not me. You want me to stand up for myself? Well here I am. I am *not* just another person for you to take care of. That's not a partnership. Don't you see that?"

"What's wrong with wanting to take care of people?" Duke's voice undoubtedly spilled into the hallway, but I was beyond caring.

My skin was hot, and the baby was doing somersaults against my rib cage. "We can't live in a fantasy world forever. I won't live on the farm, tucked away where you protect me from the rumors and whispers and dirty looks. Face it, you don't treat *anyone* like an equal, least of all me."

Duke blinked as though my words were a slap across the face. The muscles in his jaw tightened as his fists flexed. "What do you want from me?"

My high-pitch scoff rang out into the small room. "I don't want anything *from* you. I want something *with* you! Why is that so hard to believe?"

Fleeting emotions flickered over his dark features as my words soaked in. His lips pressed into a thin line. I stared at his broad shoulders in disbelief as he turned his back, and left me alone in the hospital room.

THIRTY

DUKE

A QUICK TEXT to MJ and I ensured Sylvie would have a safe ride home. I didn't want MJ involved in the fight if things went south either. I hated leaving Sylvie in that small, sterile room, but her brothers were a ticking time bomb, and Sullivans were the target. I had to move fast.

You don't treat anyone like an equal, least of all me.

The truth of Sylvie's words had cut.

Deeply.

My gut reaction was to deny it, but deep down a small part of me knew she was right. Trouble was, she had no idea that I didn't think of her as an equal because I never felt I could measure up to *her*. She was so much better than I could ever be.

I'd failed her. That much I knew to be true.

My whole life had become rows of people and things I needed to take care of—Dad, my siblings, the farm. Instead of Sylvie being a part of that line, she had stood next to me and propped me up. I wasn't entirely sure of what to do with that information.

Sylvie deserved so much more than the scraps of attention her family reserved for her. It infuriated me to see them walk all over her and trample her well-meaning heart. Though I had watched a spark ignite inside her when I called her out on it. She'd also zeroed in and poked a long-standing bruise I'd tried my whole life to hide.

I considered it my duty, and an honor, really, to take care of the people I loved. But did I really disregard their feelings and forge ahead with whatever plan I deemed best?

My fingers squeezed the steering wheel until my knuckles went white. *Fuck, she was probably right about that too.*

My truck bumped along the quiet road on the way to the Kings' fortress. Animosity and adrenaline coursed through me as my scattered thoughts attempted to derail me. I wouldn't let them.

I was singularly focused on ending whatever beef our families had. At the very least, taking Sylvie and me out of the equation.

We were together. She was my woman, and if they had a problem with that, fuck 'em. They could bring their issues to me instead of constantly beating her down over the choices *we* had made.

All thoughts of reconciliation flew out the window when I rolled down the driveway and saw my little brother Lee's obnoxious black truck already askew in the drive.

The winter air slapped my cheeks, and I slammed the driver's-side door shut. My boots crunched the icy snow as I made my way toward the voices in the back. My body was tense, ready to fight. My shoulders rolled back and set, chin lifted high.

When I rounded the large estate, Kings and Sullivans were already squared off. Royal, Whip, and JP were facing Wyatt and Lee. Beckett was rolling up his shirtsleeves and staring them down. Even Abel King was there, standing in the back with his tree-trunk arms crossed over his barrel chest. Apparently his criminal record didn't stop him from jumping into the fray despite his sister's worries.

MJ stood between the line of idiots, her palms facing each side as she pleaded with her brothers.

"Step aside, Julep." Russell King glared down from his position of power on the back deck. He looked down his sharp nose at the gathering of Kings and Sullivans.

"Dad, this is childish and dangerous and—" MJ pleaded, but her father's voice sliced through the frigid air.

"I said step aside."

Resigned, MJ drooped her shoulders and strode toward me. Tears shimmered in her eyes as she walked past me. "I'm going back to get Sylvie." Her voice cracked, and I steeled my spine. Russell King was a bully and a dick. I was tired of him looking down on the Sullivans for being hard-working, salt-of-the-earth kind of men. Even more tired of seeing him push the King women around just because it made him feel like a big shot.

Shouts and obscenities stacked on top of each other, and insults were slung across an invisible line that separated my brothers and hers. I strode toward my family, and JP narrowed his eyes at me. Anger grew hot in my gut, and I shed my jacket, unfazed by the chill in the air.

I was confident the Bluebirds could quell the gossip around town, but these assholes were her brothers. Without them getting on board with a relationship between Sylvie and me, she would never find peace. She cared about them and their opinion—a fact I wished hadn't been true, but I knew in my bones it was. Sylvie would always love her lawless, reckless brothers.

"Hey!" I shouted, getting the group's attention. Whip

grunted in my direction but shut his mouth to hear what I had to say. "We aren't here to bicker like children."

"Yeah, we can end it like men." Royal smirked his shit-eating grin as his tattoos stood in stark contrast to the white snow falling around us.

I stifled an eye roll. He was always looking for trouble. I pointed at Royal. "You know this isn't about a window. We're taking care of Matty . . . and the replacement of the shop window."

Royal's jaw ticced as though he was one part surprised and another part annoyed that he couldn't hold the broken window over our heads any longer.

"It's more than a fucking window." From behind the group, Abel's deep grumble was akin to a growl. In only the soft glow of a floodlight, he was an intimidating mother-fucker, I'd give him that. He pointed right at me. "You should have kept your hands off my fucking sister. She isn't some pawn you can use to fuck us all over."

Wait . . . what?

Did he seriously think I was using Sylvie in some ploy to get back at them for years of childish pranks?

My fist clenched, wanting nothing more than to pound it into his sharp jawline. I stepped forward, ready to go, but Wyatt moved in front of me.

"Don't go there," he warned. "I doubt even a King would stoop so low. Duke's been on the fringes of this feud for as long as we've been old enough to pull our own pranks."

"She's not innocent either." JP's cunning eyes sliced over the group as one eyebrow tipped up. "Maybe she is the smart one. Trapping a Sullivan into a lifetime of servitude. Smarter than the rest of us, I'd say."

Beckett mumbled something akin to *fucking idiot*, but I

couldn't take my focus off the Kings. I seethed with anger, hating the fact I'd briefly entertained that very idea during the infancy of my friendship with her.

JP shrugged. "If not, she's a traitor to the King name." Behind him, Russell King grunted in agreement like the piece of shit he was. Pitting his own children against each other seemed to fuel his hostility.

"None of you deserve her." The words spat from my mouth as the tether to my rage frayed like a well-worn cord.

"What was that?" Royal cupped a hand by his ear and feigned ignorance.

"You don't fucking deserve to breathe the same air as her." I moved until I was chest to chest with Royal, peering into his eyes and wondering how she could ever care for these people.

"And you do?" Royal scoffed in my face as we stood toe to toe.

"Fuck no. I know I don't deserve her." His expression faltered at my admission. "But do you even realize how much this petty feud is hurting her?" I allowed my eyes to graze over the King men. "She has done *nothing* wrong, and you shun her like she means absolutely nothing to you. If you *do* find the time to acknowledge her presence, you somehow find a way to make her feel small. So no, you don't deserve her love any more than I do. You're just mad because of my last name. I worship the ground she walks on, so what the fuck is your problem?"

The frozen air was thin as our breaths puffed out in white clouds, mingling and floating above us like icy thunderclouds. I could feel the circle of men closing in on me, and I eyed them down. Lee moved forward, kicking a rock, and it bounced across the landscape, landing with a smack against JP's shin.

Fuck.

The tension snapped. Fists flew. Whip dove at Beckett, but he dropped an elbow to his back before tumbling to the snowy ground. I shoved Royal back, and he caught me in the eye with a cheap right hook. Heat and pain bloomed across my cheek.

When I dove at him, he held me at arm's length as the rest of the brothers tussled. Abel stood on the sidelines, his huge body vibrating with indecision. Russell did nothing to stop it; rather, he watched from his perch on the enclosed porch with a grin.

"Enough!" My bellow echoed in the darkness, and, *thank fuck*, everyone paused as I bent over, sucking in breaths. "We are not doing this." I held my hands up and hoped Royal wouldn't take another punk-ass shot. He lowered his hands, and I breathed an audible sigh of relief. "Why are we even doing this?" I pointed at JP. "Do you even know?" I looked at the rest of them. "Do any of us?"

JP's hands flexed at his side as Lee released the collar of his shirt with more force than necessary.

"I want to make a deal," I continued between heavy breaths. "For all intents and purposes, Sylvie and I are out of anything to do with the feud." I stood, balancing myself and painfully sucking in cold air. "I also want you to back off any inquiries into Sullivan land and the mineral rights held there." JP quirked his eyebrow, and I didn't have time to decipher the look of surprise that flickered over his features.

"What's in it for us?" Abel defiantly lifted his chin.

The porch door creaked as Russell King pushed it open and sauntered down the pristine steps. "You can have your deal if"—his voice oozed condescension like a snake oil salesman on the prowl for his next witless victim, and he held up one finger—"that baby boy of yours bears the King name."

Fresh fury tore through me. *Not a fucking chance.*

"No." Wyatt's deep rumble beat me to it as I stood in stunned, enraged silence. "It's ridiculous you would even think it was an option, old man."

Russell leaned back on his heels, clasping his hands in front of him. "Then we'll let the chips fall where they may." I wanted to wipe that smug smile off his face forever. "Sylvie will come crawling back. They always do."

With that, he turned and walked into the house without another word. Despite fresh bruises blooming on their faces, I didn't miss the uncomfortable glances the King men shared. Russell King was a monster of the highest caliber, and the choke hold he had on his children was unfathomable.

"We're leaving." Wyatt gripped my tense shoulder and guided me away. Beckett followed silently behind us. I had wanted to *end* the feud, but nothing had been accomplished. Waves of shame and defeat rolled over me. I didn't bother eyeing the brothers as they retreated into the house.

We stood beside Lee's truck as I dragged in a ragged breath. "I'm so done with this."

Beckett flexed his hand as though it was sore, and Wyatt rolled his shoulder.

Lee was visibly upset, a small cut on his lip already crusting with blood. "You tried, man. No one would blame you if you decided it isn't worth the heartache."

My eyes whipped to him. "I'm choosing her. I will *always* choose her."

Lee swallowed, his eyes wide. "I didn't mean—Jesus, man, I—"

I shook my head and swiped Wyatt's hand away from

my biceps, giving me some much-needed space to breathe. To feel my fury bubble over. "No. You both need to hear this. This relationship? The life that Sylvie and I are desperately trying to create for ourselves? It is the *only* thing I have ever taken for myself." I dragged my hand through my hair and let loose a humorless chuckle. "You have no clue, do you? No idea how many years I pined for her in deference for *your* feelings. I'm not doing it any longer."

I turned my back and climbed into my truck, closing the door with a slam. My brothers had the good sense to look stunned and ashamed as I left them in the cold darkness.

THIRTY-ONE

SYLVIE

> **DAD**
>
> Had to teach your guard dog a lesson. So that's the kind of man you're tying yourself to?

I PACED across the hardwood floors of the living room. I'd be shocked if there wasn't a groove below my feet from worrying about Duke. My emotions tumbled from praying he was okay, to being completely shocked he'd left me at the hospital so he could feed into this ridiculous and childish rivalry.

I'd finally settled into *pissed right the fuck off*.

The crunch of tires on snow had me waddling toward the couch and plopping down. I didn't want him thinking I was actually *worried*. I grabbed the magazine off the end table and thumbed through it with an aggressive flick of my wrist and a chip on my shoulder.

I didn't even look up when the door clicked closed behind him.

Flick. My eyes scanned the glossy pages without even comprehending the words. I knew it was petty to ignore his presence, but I wasn't about to be the first person to break the silence. His warm, masculine scent filled the living room, and I placed a hand on my belly after our son decided to do somersaults in greeting to his dad.

I squeezed my eyelids together. *Not now, kiddo. We're supposed to be angry.*

Duke's presence was palpable. Against my better judgment, my eyes slid to him, and I shot to my feet.

He was stoic, shoulders slumped, as he stood just inside the doorway. A defeated man stood in the shoes of my strong, resilient Duke.

My heart clenched. I sucked in a gentle breath after he lifted his head to meet my gaze.

Shock washed over me.

Bruises on his face were blooming an angry reddish purple, and one eye was dangerously close to swelling shut. A small cut in his eyebrow was actively leaking blood.

I hurried to face him and grabbed the lapels of his jacket. "Who did this to you?"

His sad, dark eyes lifted to mine, and a smirk lifted his lip. "That's supposed to be my line."

I clamped my jaw shut, fighting the surge of tears that threatened to break free. I had never seen Duke look so . . . *broken.* I was confused and hurt and angry at all of them—at the whole damn town for perpetuating a rivalry that had stopped making any sense a long, long time ago.

When my eyes trailed over his slumped shoulders and battered face, my heart softened. I gently tugged him forward. "Get over here."

Duke followed quietly as I led him to the couch and forced him to sit. Quickly, I gathered the small medical kit he kept under the kitchen sink and kneeled before him. With two fingers, I lifted his chin to examine the small cut that slashed through his eyebrow. It was superficial, but even after a few dabs of a peroxide-soaked cotton ball, I could tell it would leave a small scar.

"Which one of them?" I wanted to know exactly which of my idiotic brothers was going to be on the receiving end of the hellfire I planned to rain down on them.

"Doesn't matter." Duke's gravelly voice felt more intimate in the hushed atmosphere of his quiet living room.

"I'm going to guess Royal," I mused with a sigh. "JP typically uses his words or his money to cut people down. Whip has a hard-on for Lee, and I'm hoping Abel wasn't dumb enough to get involved. That leaves Royal and his hotheadedness."

Duke only grunted, cementing my belief that Royal was slated to get a gargantuan ass-chewing when I was finished here.

Anger mixed with frustration as I continued to clean up a solemn Duke. My breath exited my nose in a sharp sigh. "How is this the world we're bringing a *child* into?"

I gritted my teeth, willing myself not to cry because I wasn't sad. I was *furious*. The helplessness that burrowed into my chest was a knot I couldn't unfurl. I hated to see the man I loved in pain. Hated that our miracle would be born in the midst of family hatred.

So that's the kind of man you're tying yourself to?

My father had no idea the kind of man Duke Sullivan was. None of them did.

When I finished cleaning him up, I used his knee to push myself to standing. His eyes tracked me, the chocolate brown swirling with intensity. I hated seeing his perfect face marred with bruises and blood.

I stomped away, throwing the cotton balls into the trash with an unsatisfying plop. I braced myself on the counter and tried to breathe evenly as my anger simmered before fully bubbling over. "Going over there and leaving me at the hospital was a mistake."

"It wasn't." Duke's deep voice was closer, and I turned to find his feet planted in the threshold between the living room and kitchen. The soft glow from the kitchen light danced off his handsome features, and I hated that my body warmed to him so swiftly.

"I'm *pregnant*." My arms swung wide to display my very visible baby bump. "And you *left me in the hospital*!"

A muscle flexed in his jaw as his body went rigid. "The doctors were releasing you. I made sure you had a ride home. My brothers were about to make things impossibly *worse* so . . . yes, I made a decision."

Duke Sullivan, ladies and gentlemen, always fixing problems and producing results. I swear, that man should get *Do something or get out of the way* tattooed on his damn forehead.

I crossed my arms like a petulant child to keep from strangling the man I love. "So your genius decision was to choose *violence*?"

"I didn't choose any of this!" His voice boomed into the darkness, and my chin tipped up in defiance.

My eyes flared. "Exactly! Neither of us choose this. So why? *Why* would you put yourself through this? How is any of this worth it?" My voice cracked. *Damn it.* I swallowed past the lump that made it hard to breathe.

"Because of you!" His voice rattled through the kitchen. He gestured toward me. "Because *you* are worth it!"

My mouth popped open at his admission, but no words came out. In two steps, Duke was crowding my space. He cupped my face, tilting my head so I could look at him and take in the emotions roiling in his dark eyes.

"You are stubborn, woman, but you will hear me. You may have gone your whole life without people prioritizing you, but that ends with me." His eyes moved over my features as my lip quivered. "Sylvie, it's you or no one. It has *always* been you."

A hot tear streaked down my face, and I blinked it away without much success as another fell just as swiftly. My entire existence I had been fading into the background of small-town life, but this man was putting me first—not only with his words, but with every action, every day.

"Don't cry, baby. I'm trying to tell you that I love you—that I have loved you for far too long without telling you. Before we ever got pregnant, I fell in love with your smile, your humor, your heart. I used to imagine a world where Outtatowner didn't exist and I could flirt with you, sweep you off your feet, and take you for coffee. Show you off to my family. I don't care what your last name is as long as it eventually becomes Sullivan."

A sob broke free as I buried my head into his broad chest. His arms enveloped me, pulling me into his warmth. Between us, our baby went wild, dancing and kicking as if to urge, *Say it back! Daddy wants us! He loves us!*

I smiled into him and squeezed him closer. "I love you too. Please don't ever let go."

His arms grew tighter. "Never."

STARING at the opulent front door of Bug's home, I steeled my spine.

Under the guise of Aunt Bug needing help at her house, my brothers were held captive. She had them dusting high spaces, moving and rearranging furniture, and whatever else she could think of to keep them occupied before I arrived.

Behind the heavy wooden door, I could hear their grumpy, argumentative voices overlapping as they suffered through the wrath of Aunt Bug. I stifled the tiny, petty joy that brought me.

Turning the handle, I held my head high and pushed through the door. Attention swiveled my way as my brothers all paused. They had the good sense to look more humble than cocky as I crossed the threshold and removed my new winter coat.

"Hey, Syl!" Royal called out with a wave of his hand and a grin on his bruised face.

I shook my head. "Don't you 'Hey, Syl' me. I'm here to talk." I watched the humor melt from his face. "To all of you."

I crossed my arms over my chest. Slowly, my brothers set the living room furniture down and stepped toward me. I didn't miss the wave of confusion that rolled through the collective row of men standing before me. I was certain they had never experienced a steaming-mad, hormonally charged pregnant woman, especially one who knew all their secrets and was ready to detonate.

Their injuries ranged from bruises to minor cuts to scabby knuckles. I breathed in deep.

Idiots, the whole lot of them.

I didn't even know where to begin. Suddenly the overwhelming urge to fold in on myself and hide was palpable. It was so much easier being the soft, quiet King who faded into the background.

Nothing positive came from disappearing, so I set my shoulders.

"Where's the fire?" Whip laughed at his own joke, and I rolled my eyes.

"The fire"—I made air quotes as I barreled on—"is that I had sex with Duke Sullivan."

"Uh . . ." Abel's permanent scowl somehow deepened as he gestured toward my belly. "We got the memo."

Royal covered a laugh with a half-assed cough, and I glared at him.

"I had sex with Duke Sullivan because we shared a secret friendship for nearly a year, and we both developed real feelings."

They stilled at the secret I had kept for so long. I had gripped that secret so tightly, and I still wasn't able to keep it. I was ready to have the full truth out in the open. No more hiding. "I am in love with him. And he loves me." My words turned watery as my emotions swelled, but I pressed on. "I never wanted to choose between my family and him, but your petty behavior is forcing my hand."

Whip softened as tears rolled down my cheeks. "We were just looking out for you, Syl."

My eyes snapped to him, fury overtaking me. "I am a grown woman! I don't need my brothers acting like they have any say whatsoever in my life *or* my choices."

I looked at each of their faces, making eye contact with every single man-child in that room. A sick part of me was amused that they looked a little worse for wear. At least it wasn't just Duke who'd resembled a punching bag—apparently the Sullivans got a few shots in too.

Serves them all right.

"This is the line." I pointed at the ground. "If you want any kind of relationship with me or my son, you will not do this again. If you want to go around acting like children, plastic-wrapping each other's toilets or whatever else it is that you do, *fine*. But violence? Fights over things that are quite literally none of your fucking business? Absolutely not." I lifted my chin. "You will not hurt the people who will be a part of my family, and they will not hurt you. I am done with this."

I swiveled on my heels, ready to make a hasty exit when a slow clap started behind me. Stunned, I slowly turned to face my brothers. Royal stood tall, hands clapping. Only . . . he wasn't mocking me. He was *grinning*.

I narrowed my eyes at him.

"Get over here." He opened his arms and gestured for me to accept his hug. "That was the most badass proclamation, Syl. You're scary as hell. My asshole puckered."

I couldn't stop the burst of laughter that broke the tension, and I rolled my eyes at Royal before crossing the room to step into his hug. He held me in a brotherly embrace, and my words were muffled in his shirt. "I hate you."

"I love you too." He held me out as I met his gaze. "We all do." Royal looked around at my brothers, who had the good sense to look properly chastised. "I think I speak for the group when I say that we're all sorry. Things got out of hand."

Abel pushed Royal aside. "Speak for yourself." He pulled me into a hug so tightly my breath whooshed out with an *oof* sound. "I am sorry, though. I should have spoken up and stepped in to stop it."

I stared up at my surly, stoic brother. He'd gone through so much, *lost* so much that it often felt like we'd lost him, too, but he was in there. Big heart and all. I squeezed him again.

Whip sauntered up. "I'd been dying to pop Lee

Sullivan in the mouth for a while now. Can't say I'm sorry for that, but I am sorry it caused you grief."

I laughed as he hugged me. "That is the worst older-brother apology I've ever heard."

Finally I turned to JP. He stood, watching the rest of our brothers make amends and take ownership for their hand in the fight with the Sullivans. My chest tightened. JP was so much like our father—secretive and commanding, never able to just *relax*. The boy I used to stomp around in puddles with was long gone, but for a split second, I thought I saw him in there. A smile hooked at the corner of JP's mouth, and he examined the knuckle that was cracked from the fight. He raised his chin. "I'm sorry, Syl. We shouldn't have brought this to your doorstep."

I swallowed hard. That was about the extent of an apology I could ever hope for from JP King. I breathed a heavy sigh of relief.

JP cleared his throat and stepped forward as I turned. "You know . . . he tried to stop it."

I looked at him, a thousand questions fighting to break free.

"Duke," JP continued. "He was there to make peace. He stood up for you. Not just with us, but with his own brothers too."

Whip smiled and nodded. "I heard the ass-chewing he gave them too." Whip shook his head. "He was fucking scary, practically foaming at the mouth."

JP sighed. "A man like that, one that will honor his relationship above his own blood, that's someone I could grow to respect."

A smile bloomed across my face. For the first time ever, I had hope that my child with Duke could be born into a life that was, well, maybe not totally normal, but loving. Duke had stood up for me and tried to stop the fight. He was thinking of me and how it would impact our relationship.

My heart ached for him.

"One last question . . ." Royal's face was dancing with mirth. "Are you going to hate me when I tell you I *may* have orchestrated a delivery of Wyatt's favorite cookies but swapped the sugar for salt . . . ?"

"I'm out of here." On a laugh, I turned and raised my hand above my head and sailed out the front door.

THIRTY-TWO

SYLVIE

Every year in the Midwest, there was one day in March where the sun warmed and you got irrationally hopeful that spring had finally arrived. Unfortunately for all of us, and despite the fact we knew this happened every single year, winter clung to our bones for a few weeks longer. But by mid-April, the first signs of spring stuck around for more than a few days in Outtatowner.

I stood in the middle of the sidewalk with my face tipped to the warm afternoon sun and breathed in the crisp April air. I could smell the Lake Michigan water on the breeze, and I hummed to myself as I sighed. My black leggings were pulled high over my belly, and two side slits in my cozy camel-colored sweater allowed ample room for moving through the Sugar Bowl while not overheating. Despite Huck constantly hounding me to sit down, my white sneakers were comfy, and I had fully leaned into loving what pregnancy had done to my body.

Duke had loved it too.

A racy thrill danced through me as I thought of the new and creative positions Duke had dreamed up. Earlier in the morning, he'd stripped down these very leggings and taken me from behind just as I was sipping the hot tea he made me every morning. The way his rough hands glided up the back of my thighs nearly made my knees buckle. Whether it was the hormones or not, I was insatiable when it came to that man, and Duke didn't seem to mind it one bit. He couldn't keep his hands off me.

Birds were calling in the trees that lined the main thoroughfare through town, and it was our yearly reminder that soon our quiet streets would be crawling with tourists looking to escape to our cozy coastal town.

"How is it that you look so cute?" Sloane's voice cut through my daydreams of ravishing Duke when I peeked open one eye to look at her.

I grinned at my friend.

"Seriously." She rolled her eyes. "When I was as far along as you, I looked like a house. There was no glowing, only profusely sweating."

"Aren't the twins' birthdays in August?"

"Exactly. My armpits soaked through three outfits a day, and here you are looking all *coastal granny chic*."

I laughed, and Sloane wrapped me in a hug.

"Where are Ben and Tillie?"

Sloane waggled her eyebrows. "Fishing with Granddad. I'm kid-free all afternoon."

I looped my arm through hers and leaned into her as we meandered down the sidewalk. "My feet are swollen. Want to dip our toes in the water?" This time of year, the beach would be quiet and the icy water would feel glorious on my ankles.

As we walked, townies smiled and nodded in greeting. Much of the town gossip about Duke and me had faded from an outraged roar to soft murmurs. Only the occasional curmudgeon slid me an aggressive side-eye, but that was to be expected. Outtatowner had gone generations with Kings and Sullivans at odds with each other, so the current truce between our families was new territory.

I peeked into King Tattoo as we passed, and after I caught Royal's eye, he tipped his chin and raised a hand. I was surprised when he swiftly rounded the counter and pushed open the door. "Hey, Syl. Sloane. You ladies out for a walk?"

In the months since I'd lost my shit on my brothers, they'd been putting forth a little extra effort to be kind and inclusive. Nerves bunched in my chest. I still wasn't totally used to the genuine interest in me or what was going on in my life.

Is this what normal families are like? I laughed to myself, because if the Sullivans and how they were always in each other's business was any indication, this was *exactly* what normal families were like.

"I'm going to dip my toes in the lake and then get an ice-cream cone the size of my face."

"I've got work in"—Sloane checked her watch—"forty minutes, so I'm just keeping our girl company."

Royal crossed his arms. "How is working at the brewery? Is Abel treating you all right?"

Sloane's eyebrow lifted at Royal's question. "Abel isn't exactly the chatty type. I swear the man hasn't said more than six words to me. He communicates mostly in grunts and grumbles."

I laughed softly at my friend's very accurate assessment of my older brother.

Royal nodded. "Well, if he gives you any trouble, just let me know. I'll take care of it."

"Oh . . ." I looked wide eyed at my mischievous brother.

"Kind of like how someone *took care* of Lee Sullivan by rearranging all of the furniture in his living room?"

I didn't miss the twitch in Royal's cheek. "I have no knowledge of that. Talk to Whip."

He rocked back on his heels, and I narrowed my eyes at him.

"Well, I'll let you two gorgeous ladies get on with your walk." He offered a jaunty salute before disappearing back inside his shop as Sloane and I laughed.

Together we continued our walk down the sidewalk and past the marina. "Seriously, though . . . working for Abel is going okay?"

Sloane shrugged. "It's fine for now. The boss man may have a giant stick up his ass, but he is flexible with my schedule, and both times my babysitter has fallen through, he's not once complained about the kids hanging around the back while I waited for Granddad to swing by and pick them up." A sly smile deepened the dimple in her cheek. "And getting under his skin is a definite perk."

I grinned. "Good for you. Abel needs a little goading in his life."

No MATTER how many times I swept or dusted or ran a rag over the baseboards, I couldn't seem to feel like the farmhouse was clean enough. I had spent my day off fluffing pillows and washing sheets before tackling the upstairs bedrooms. I was about to start in on the nursery and demand Duke finally let me see what he was doing beyond its locked door when my hand slid over the matte-black doorknob.

"What do you think you're doing.?" I jumped and

screamed when Duke's grumbly voice startled me. I turned to see his grumpy face and his hands planted on his hips.

I didn't even bother fighting the grin that split my face. "Have I ever told you how handsome I think you are?"

Duke shook his head and pointed a finger at me. "Don't you try to get out of trouble by being sweet to me." He prowled forward, but a grin slowly spread across his bearded face, sending a jolt of heat down my spine and pooling between my legs.

God, there was already so much pressure constantly there, and I felt like one wave of his hot breath against my ear would send me straight into an orgasm.

"I was definitely not about to clean the baseboards." I blinked at him innocently and tucked the yellow rag behind my back.

"Mm-hmm. I call bullshit." He pulled me closer and laid a kiss on my neck just below my ear. "Come on, you little liar. I want to show you something."

Duke's palm caressed the inside of my elbow to my wrist before capturing my hand and leading me toward the nursery room door.

Just outside the spare bedroom door he paused. My heart danced as I looked up at him hopefully. "Is it time?"

Duke had been working on the nursery—something he said was important to him—and he wanted to surprise me. I had agreed to not peek, and the anticipation had nearly killed me. Duke slipped a slim key from his pocket and popped open the lock. Clearly he hadn't trusted me that much, but I couldn't blame him. His slight mistrust was accurate, because a time or two, I did test the handle, only to find it locked. Honestly, I didn't even fully trust myself not to look, because I was so anxious to see our baby's nursery.

Duke took a steadying breath. I had never seen the man

so nervous, and a fresh wave of love and affection rolled over me.

I placed a hand on his bearded cheek. "It's going to be perfect. Thank you for doing this."

A low grumble sounded in the back of Duke's throat as he nodded before pushing open the bedroom door.

My mouth dropped open, and my eyes went wide as I took in the nursery. The late-afternoon sun slanted through the plantation-style shutters, flooding the space with soft, ethereal light. Duke stepped inside our baby's nursery and ran his hands down his jeans. "I, um . . ." He cleared his throat. "I hope it's everything you dreamed of."

My nose burned as I struggled to find the words. Against one wall a wooden dresser that appeared handmade and solid also had a changing pad on top. A matching high-boy-style dresser stood against the far wall. A gorgeous crib was in front of the most stunning mural I had ever seen. It was moody and slightly masculine while being light and airy. Absolute perfection.

"Annie painted the mural."

"How did you, when did she . . ."

"Her flexible schedule helped. I mostly snuck her in while you were working at the Sugar Bowl."

Every detail, from the gliding chair and matching footrest to the oversize yarn blanket draped across it, was as if it were plucked from my imagination. "Okay, Duke . . . how did you—"

My fingertips came to my lips as I continued to take in the absolute perfection of the nursery.

Duke stuffed his hands into the front pocket of his jeans and shrugged. "I found your Pinterest page."

My eyes searched his as a soft blush stained his cheeks.

"I wanted this to be a space where you felt safe, where

our baby and you—all of us—could spend time together. Where he knows, no matter what, he is loved for exactly who he is."

Tears tumbled over my lashes and streaked down my cheeks as I launched myself at Duke. This man, this beautiful, gorgeous, brooding, hulking beast of a man had the kindest, sweetest heart I had ever known. He kept that heart so guarded, but I was the lucky one. He had shown it to me.

"Thank you. It's absolutely perfect."

His hand ran up my spine and pulled me closer despite the belly that separated us. "Well, don't let it ruin your makeup, because I'm taking you out tonight." He glanced at his watch. "And we don't have time for you to fuss over your face again." He ran one knuckle down my cheek to wipe away the tears. "Besides, you know I think you're gorgeous just as you are."

I sniffed and smiled up at him, swallowing down the knot of emotions in my throat. "I'll be ready in two minutes, I promise." I gave him one last squeeze before resting my head on his shoulder and taking in our baby's nursery one more time before hurrying to get ready for our date.

Two minutes was actually twenty minutes, but Duke didn't give me too much grief about it. There would always be something about the Grudge that just felt like a warm hug. Maybe it was the way old country music crooned out of the jukebox or the way your fingers could glide over the bumps and ridges of the timeworn oak bar top. Despite its outdated, dim lighting and neon beer signs, it was cute. Cozy even.

I am definitely nesting if I think the Grudge is cute and cozy.

As it always did since starting a relationship with Duke, walking into the Grudge also came with its own share of anxiety. Mostly we had claimed our spot in the middle of the bar mixed with tourists who didn't know about the feud that defined our very town.

Shoulders back and chin held high, I laced my fingers with Duke's and walked toward an open table near the center of the room. His hand gently tugged mine, and when I looked at him, he gave me a subtle shake of his head before guiding me toward the east side of the bar. I followed with tentative steps. He was willingly taking up residence in enemy territory.

I sat down and looked at him with wide eyes. "Are you sure?"

He plucked a plastic menu off the table—"Never been so sure about anything in my life"—and shot me a wink.

I didn't know if he was talking about his choice in seats or me, but I didn't care. I grinned at him and settled back into my seat.

Soon a waitress scurried over, unable to hide the look of surprise as her eyes danced between us. "Hey, folks, what can I get you?"

Duke gestured toward me. "Ladies first."

Despite the blush creeping up my neck and cheeks, I quickly scanned the menu, but opted for my usual. "Smash burger, extra cheese, extra bacon. Lettuce and tomato, please."

"Hmm." Duke grunted as though he was surprised by my order, when in fact I had ordered some version of a bacon cheeseburger nearly every time we went out to eat in the past three months. I had even conned him into throwing some patties on the grill in the snow.

"I think I'll have the same." He handed the server our menus and sat back in his chair.

It was quiet for a Tuesday evening, but the tourist

season had already started amping up, with fresh faces sprinkled in among the familiar ones. His fingers tapped along to the music from the jukebox, and he seemed not at all affected by our position in the room. Duke was jovial, lighthearted even, and it helped me relax into my own seat.

A few tables over, my brother Royal was with a group of his friends, and he tipped his glass to Duke.

Duke returned the greeting with a tip of his chin, and my nose crinkled. "What was that about?"

"Don't know what you mean." Duke's hand slid across the table, seeking mine.

My brother Whip sauntered up to our high-top table, presumably off shift from the fire station. Duke stood and immediately shook my brother's hand.

"Hey, you two." Whip greeted us as though it didn't make any difference in the world that Duke was a Sullivan. "Good to see you two out tonight." Whip turned to face Duke. "Did you finally figure out that dovetailing for the drawers?"

Duke smiled at my brother. *Actually smiled.* "I did." He nodded. "They turned out great. Couldn't have done it without you."

Duke shook Whip's hand again.

"Well, all right. Good deal. I'll let you two get back to your dinner. If you need help with anything else, you just hit me up."

Duke nodded. "Will do. Thanks again."

I stood, mouth agape as I witnessed the exchange. The server deposited two tall glasses of water to our table. Duke picked one up but paused midway to his mouth. "What?" he asked.

"Are you guys, like, friends now?"

Duke shrugged and took a sip. "I don't know. Maybe? We've come to an understanding."

I blinked and considered that. "Oh. An understanding . . . okay. That's great, I guess."

"Come on. Let me take you for a spin on the dance floor before our food gets here."

"I'm eight months pregnant. It will be like dancing with a parade float."

Duke smirked. "First of all, you're the sexiest parade float I've ever seen."

I barked a laugh and wrapped my arms around his neck. "And secondly," he continued as he peppered my neck with kisses, "that means I only have a month or so to have you all to myself. Because I'm not kidding you, I'm going to spoil the shit out of that kid."

Duke's strong arms banded around me as he guided me to the dance floor. "You up for it?"

I let him lead me to the center of the floor, and we swayed to the music. Duke's hand rode low on my hip but moved ever so subtly over my side and belly as we danced. Our baby kicked in response, something I knew Duke never got enough of.

"You know, there was one more thing besides the nursery that I wanted to give you tonight."

I leaned into him. "Oh yeah?" The corner of my mouth hooked up, along with my eyebrow. Duke knew despite my grumblings I secretly loved surprises.

Storm clouds rolled across his face, settling between his eyebrows. "It's not so much a *something*. It's . . . I don't know."

His hand reached back behind his neck to capture mine and pulled it down over his chest. He pressed my palm flat, and I felt the thrum of his heartbeat through his shirt. He lowered his forehead to mine despite everyone around us. His embrace was an intimate bubble. Just the three of us.

"You've had my heart for a long time, Sylvie. Before the baby—hell, even before the beach, I was so fucking gone for you. I have loved you for a long time. It's always been you, but I was too afraid to say it. Afraid that if I said the words out loud, I'd somehow wake up from this dream, and it would all disappear. I wanted to tell you tonight over candlelight and with flowers just the two of us—but here in this moment, I feel it. I want to go with you to Savannah, and I don't want to keep that from you for a second longer. I love you. I have always loved you. You're it for me, and I can't live this life without you."

Before I could speak and tell him I loved him too—*God, how much I love him*—and that *he* was my home, Duke slanted his mouth over mine and pulled me tight. Duke poured love and passion and heartbreak and friendship into that kiss, and I soaked it up without a care in the world for who was watching or what they were thinking.

Let them watch. Let them think whatever they wanted to about a King and a Sullivan, because none of it mattered. Not anymore.

THIRTY-THREE

DUKE

After I was told the life expectancy of someone with dementia was four to eight years, I imagined I'd be putting Dad into the ground, not moving him into a new house.

But there we were.

On the edge of the property at Haven Pines sat the newly finished, semi-independent homes. They were still maintained by Haven Pines staff, but each small home was a private, detached living space for residents who qualified. A nurse would visit him daily, and there was even a button in each house that alerted staff if an emergency were to arise. In the small community, residents had opportunities like boating, knitting, pickleball, even yoga.

Fucking *yoga*.

I looked around Dad's new living room and clenched my jaw. The community was too secluded. Too distant from the main building and staff. Too far from help if Dad had any kind of emergency. I didn't like it despite my siblings going on and on about how great it was.

"Doesn't look out on the back forty acres, but it sure as hell beats being neighbors with Winnie McCallister."

I grunted a laugh. Ms. Winnie was pushing her ninety-eighth birthday and was infamous for her lack of filter. If she didn't like breakfast or the weather or how your face looked, you'd hear about it.

I shrugged. "I kind of like the old bird."

"You would," Dad scoffed. "Kindred spirits."

He shook his head and walked another lap around the small living space before shoving at the recliner. "I don't like this."

I stepped up next to him and helped him move it two feet to the left. "Better?"

"No, but I suppose it'll do."

I laughed to myself and reached behind me into the small cooler I'd brought. I handed Dad the bottle, and his eyebrow arched upward.

"To celebrate your new move." I twisted off the top and handed it to Dad.

He didn't seem to notice it was a nonalcoholic beer and sank down on the plush couch with a sigh. "Home sweet home."

I sat next to him, taking a sip of my own bottle. "It's a nice place. I'm happy for you."

"Bullshit." Dad smiled as he took a sip of his beer. "No one I know hates change more than you."

I shook my head and considered. He wasn't wrong. "Feels like this past year has been nothing but change thrown in my face."

"And was it all bad?"

My mind immediately filled with images of Sylvie's sweet face. "No, sir. It wasn't all bad."

"Good, 'cause I've got one more to throw at you."

I shifted, eyeing my father and attempting to gauge his level of clarity. According to his medical team, the clinical trial had been a resounding success. I could think of only a handful of bad episodes in the last month, and that alone felt like a miracle. We had more calm days with our dad, and for that I'd be forever grateful.

Dad sighed. "You can't come see me every day."

My face scrunched. "What? Dad, come on . . ."

He lifted his hand. "I'm serious. There's no reason for you to come lurking around every day. You can't baby me, August."

I swallowed hard at Dad's use of my real name.

"Now I want to see you, I do, but you put your entire life on hold for me. For us. There will be days when I need you." Dad tapped his temple. "You know better than I do that I'm not always all right up here, but I also don't feel like I'm drowning. I got your mother, and we—"

I frowned, an arrow piercing my chest as he spoke. "Mom's gone, Dad."

A flicker of sorrow washed over his features as if he were reliving her death all over again. I wanted to scream, to slam my fist against *anything* to help him stop reliving the shock of her death all over again.

"I know that." Dad's voice was barely above a whisper. "Just don't always like to remember it is all." He raised his chin and pinned me in place with his bright-blue eyes. "The doctors said I was safe enough to be here. I can live out my life as best as I can with the time I've got. But you have to do the same, Son."

I pressed my fingers into my eye sockets. "What are you saying, Dad? I'm not welcome here?"

Dad's laugh startled me. "Course not, you idiot. What I am saying is you don't have to run yourself ragged worrying about me. I got plenty of people in my business around here. Pretty soon you're going to have your own family to stress over."

I nodded. The weight of the stress, worrying about how I was going to manage it all, had silently become unbearable.

How did he know?

Emotion burned behind my eyelids. "She's a King, Dad."

Dad's eyes paused as my words sank in. His lips pursed. "Do you love her?"

"Loving her is like breathing." The admission tumbled out of me in a whoosh of breath, without hesitation.

Dad considered, taking a sip of his beer and looking out onto the warm wood of the living room floor. "Then I don't guess her last name makes much of a difference, does it?"

I clamped my hand on Dad's strong shoulder, unable to tell him how much his easy acceptance of my love for Sylvie truly meant. The lump in my throat wouldn't dislodge. "Thanks, Dad."

My knee bounced, and I ran a damp palm down my leg. "I'm going to give her Mom's ring. I plan to ask for her father's blessing, even though he'll tell me to go to hell." I dipped my chin in resolution. "But I'll give it to her anyway."

Dad patted my knee and squeezed. "That's a good man. You don't need his permission, but no one can say you didn't try to make it right." Dad thought for a moment. "You know your mom's father hated me, right?" My eyes narrowed, searching his face for signs of truth. "Yeah, he couldn't stand that his Juney had fallen for a Sullivan when Russell King had been knocking at her door. Her father said she'd be wasting her life on a man like me."

"Russell King?" Even the mere mention of Sylvie's

father had my nerve endings firing. "Is *that* why he hates us all so much?"

Dad shrugged. "Russell has always had hate in his heart. Nothing was ever good enough. No amount of winning was ever enough for him. He wanted her, but she wanted me, and that pissed him right off. Went a long time buying things from under me. Undermining business deals so I'd suffer, but I didn't care. If you ask me"—Dad leaned over and winked—"I got the one thing he could never buy. Your mother's heart. Held on to that precious gift with both hands for as long as I could."

A few of the pieces of the Sullivan–King mystery clicked into place. I sighed and sat back. "I guess it makes sense. He's always had a chip on his shoulder. Been bitter." I let my mind wander over the small bits of information we'd learned about the Kings and Sullivans in the last year. "Maybe Lark was right . . . this whole thing started with and has continued because of some unhinged love triangle." I shook my head in disbelief. "Wild."

"Sure, love makes men do stupid shit, but it's always helped him to have the Sinclairs in his pocket, ears open for anything he could use against us. Those twins were playing both sides, just like their daddy and his daddy before him did."

Playing both sides? Wait . . . twins? I paused. "Sinclair?" Something about that name tumbled around and scratched my brain.

"Who's that?" Dad's eyes searched my face.

I shifted to face him. "You said Sinclair—that the Kings have always had them in their pocket. What did you mean?"

Dad's eyes shifted to mine, and confusion clouded their

color. "I didn't say that." Defensiveness and fear pitched his voice higher.

My heart raced. The last thing we needed was for Dad to panic. Today was supposed to be a good day. New beginnings. I planted my hand on his forearm. "You're right. Sorry, Dad, I must have misheard you."

He blinked, and I knew we were moments from a meltdown. I hated that I'd pushed him too far, too fast, without reading the signs that I'd lost him to his own jumbled inner thoughts. "Do you want to watch a show, or should I unload a few more boxes?"

Dad scrubbed a hand on the back of his neck and sighed, though he was still simmering with agitation. "I'm pretty tired. I think I'll rest for a while."

I swallowed back the bile that rose in the back of my throat. "No problem. Let's get you situated."

I helped my dad get comfortable, and within minutes he was out cold, but there was something there in what he'd said. The only twins I knew of were Bowlegs and Bootsy and as far as I knew, they'd lived their lives on the fringes of Outtatowner for as long as I could recall.

Something wasn't settling right, and Bootsy just may have the answers we'd been looking for.

THIRTY-FOUR

SYLVIE

I HAD to practically push Duke out of the house to get him to agree to a night out with his brothers, but I was very much looking forward to a warm bath and a smutty book. The cool late-April air floated through the house, carrying with it the subtle scents of lavender and lily of the valley. On the blueberry bushes, buds were morphing into blossoms, and it surprised me just how much anticipation hung in the air.

My hand moved over my round belly. I was a week out from my due date, and impatience had settled into my bones. I couldn't wait to meet our little man. For days I had struggled with sleep and a low pressure that made functioning barely tolerable. Kate had passed along some bath salts she said Beckett swore by, and I closed my eyes to envision the warm bubbles wrapping around me as I sank lower into the water.

Ed's yippy bark startled me, and my eyes flew open. Something had alerted him, so I stood next to the large living room window for a moment and listened. A breeze shifted through the bushes, but otherwise the world outside the farmhouse fell silent.

I glanced at the clock. *Just before nine.* There was no reason for the staff who worked the farm to be milling around, but something had put Ed on edge. My hand patted behind his ears as a low growl vibrated through him.

My eyes flicked to the door, noting it was locked, but the hairs on the back of my neck stood on end. "What is it?" I whispered to Ed.

His focused eyes stayed pinned to the front door as my heart raced faster.

"Do you need to go out?"

Ed barked again. His nails tapped against the hardwood.

"Is it Duck?"

Another louder bark and he turned in a circle.

"You *are* an overprotective dad, aren't you?" I scratched behind his ears. "I'm sure Duck is just fine. He's sleeping."

Ed took a step toward the door, his body still radiating tension. I rolled my eyes. "Stubborn like your dad, I see." I grabbed Duke's lined flannel from beside the door and slipped my arms into it. His warm, masculine scent cocooned me as I unlocked the door. I pointed at Ed to prove I was serious. "Let's go check on Duck; then I'm taking that bath."

As soon as the front door opened, Ed bounded down the stairs and across the yard toward the barn with more speed than you'd expect from a three-legged dog.

"Ed! *Shit.*" Carefully I hurried behind him, wrapping the flannel around my middle and wishing I'd thought to bring a flashlight. The large barn was closed up for the night, but I followed Ed's whine in the distance. Down a row of mowed grass, his butt stuck out from between two blueberry bushes.

"Ed!" I called again in a whisper-shout. His ears smacked himself in the face as he turned to look at me but quickly refocused on whatever was in the bushes. When I got to him, he was whining. Crouching down as best as I could with a weighted beach ball attached to my front, I peered between the bushes. The low light made it difficult to see, but sure enough, Duck's stark white feathers stood out against the blueberry canes. I nudged a stubborn Ed aside to get a closer look.

Duck quacked and attempted to move, but something was tangled around his webbed foot. "Oh, you poor thing! You're all tangled up." Reaching forward, I examined his foot as Ed circled me, sniffing and whining. Awkwardly, I was able to detach whatever was wound around his foot from the base of the blueberry bush.

"Now how did you get out, Mister?" A pathetic quack was Duck's only response. He fought my embrace, more evidence that he only loved Ed or Duke because those two could mess with him all day, and he never complained. I held him in the nook of my arm and unwound what appeared to be a fishing line or nylon string of some kind. He must have gotten tangled up on his way to bed, and it got twisted among the bramble and roots of the bushes. I made a mental note to have Duke check the fencing to be sure there wasn't a hole he'd escaped from. While it was no surprise Duck was domesticated, the last thing I wanted was him wandering out and a wild animal getting to him before we could.

"Poor guy. You're all right." Duck settled against my arm and rested his beak between my biceps and breast. I looked down and sighed. "Well, you are cute, I'll give you that." I plopped a kiss on his little head. "Let's get you back to bed."

Darkness fell around me, and I increased my pace to the barn. As I walked along the broadside, I noted that there wasn't any visible hole in the fencing where Duck could have escaped from. When I turned toward the small door to the barn, I frowned.

Duke would never have left this open.

Tiny alarm bells buzzed in the back of my mind. "Come on, Ed." I called the dog closer to me and carefully set Duck inside his pen within the barn. I worked quickly, closing the barn door behind me and wanting to shut myself within the safety of our home.

Light flashed in my peripheral vision. My heart leaped to my throat. Ed's low grumble matched the cadence of my rattling nerves. At the back of the barn, a low sliver of light flashed again. Immediately my mind went to my brothers and their stupid pranks. It had been a while since they'd pulled something, and I knew they were itching to get back at the Sullivans for paying a group of local theater kids to drop to their knees and bow any time a King walked past a few weeks back. You'd think my arrogant brothers would have loved it, but the kids really committed to the bit— following them around, openly weeping when Royal walked past. One girl even stalked JP and dropped rose petals at his feet for an entire day.

I really thought we were past this childish bullshit.

I clenched my teeth and stomped in the direction of the light. Those idiots thought they were so clever, and I was about to scare the shit out of them before giving them a piece of my mind.

Serves them right for scaring me and delaying my epic bubble bath.

I had rounded the corner, ready to jump out and scare the shit out of whichever brother was sneaking around, when my scream strangled in my throat. Ed placed himself between me and the dark figure, growling and baring his teeth.

At the choking noise that came out of me, the figure whipped around to face me. My eyes went wide when I nearly collided with Bootsy. "Oh, shit!" I was panting and took a step backward. My hand flew to my chest, clutching the flannel. "Oh my god."

The whites of his eyes were glassy and shifting in the low light. I tipped my chin. "Bootsy?"

"Miss Sylvie." He cleared his throat. "Yes, hello."

I took another step in retreat. Unease rolled through me. "What are you doing here?" My mind struggled to catch up with the fact I'd just caught the town recluse lurking around the barn after dark. "Did my brothers put you up to this?"

His eyes whipped to mine. "No, ma'am. Don't mind me. I'll be off." He chuckled and shook his head. "Get confused from time to time. Thought I had an appointment with Mr. Duke." He rubbed his forehead. "Must have been mistaken."

I was about to tell him Duke wasn't here, but the alarm bells blaring between my ears stopped me. "He's just inside," I lied as I turned toward the house. "I can grab him for you."

"No! Uh . . . no, ma'am. Not necessary. Confused . . . like I said."

My heart went out to the man. It was true he'd lived his life on the fringes of town. The good people of Outtatowner had tried to take care of him and his late brother, but often-times they had remained a mystery. I risked one last try. "Do you need help?"

He scoffed when his eyes met mine. The weathered skin and deep lines were accentuated in the shadows, casting a harsh glimmer in them. "I ain't the one needin' help. You best be careful."

An icy shiver rolled down my back. *What the fuck was that supposed to mean?* My feet stumbled on the gravel as I distanced myself from Bootsy. I recalled Mabel's story and how Bootsy's family might somehow be woven into the King–Sullivan feud.

I lifted my chin. "If there's nothing you need, then it's best you leave."

After he turned his back to me and hurried across the lawn toward the main road, I sagged and exhaled in relief.

What the actual fuck was that?

Suddenly the shadows cast from the trees were ominous and frightening. I leaned down to pat Ed's head. He was still growling at Bootsy's retreating shadow. "Good boy. You did good."

I pulled Duke's shirt tighter and moved as quickly as my feet would carry me toward the house and up the porch steps. Once inside the door, I slammed the dead bolt locked. My breaths sawed in and out of me.

Indecision gnawed at me. I didn't want to ruin Duke's well-deserved night out if it was nothing more than Bootsy being a little confused. Still, the thought of being alone in the house all night held even less appeal.

I chewed my lip and settled on a less-embarrassing option three.

Pulling up my contacts, I scrolled until I selected the numbers I was looking for.

> Hi. It's Sylvie. Wondering if anyone is free since the guys are all out tonight?

LARK

Funny you should ask. We are ALL free. We
wanted to invite you out but Duke insisted
that you had a date with the bathtub. He
made us promise we wouldn't bug you so
we planned to get snacks and come
knocking anyway!

KATE

The guys are surprising Duke with a dad-
chelor party tonight so he was already
going to be mad.

> What in the world is a dad-chelor party?

ANNIE

You know, like a bachelor party but for
being a dad. They're going to get him
drunk, make him do embarrassing bar
games, and generally haze him even
though they're all secretly jealous. It was
Lee's ridiculous brainchild.

> Oh my god . . . he's going to absolutely
> hate that.

ANNIE

I know! Isn't it great?

LARK

Wyatt promised they'd go easy on him, but
I'm pretty sure it's the first time he's ever
lied to my face.

> I didn't want to call, but that bubble bath
> never happened. I had a weird encounter
> with Bootsy at the farm and it kind of
> freaked me out. I didn't want to say
> anything to Duke because you know him—
> he'd fly off the handle and insist on coming
> home.

ANNIE

Bootsy was at the house??

LARK

We're already on the way.

KATE

Girls night in, here we come!

I smiled at my phone, my nerves already easing at the prospect of not being alone. I scrolled back up and read the text thread again. Even though Duke had tried to protect my relaxing night in, they'd planned to gather snacks and spend their free evening with *me*.

I quickly picked up the yarn blanket and attempted to drape it artfully across the chair. I fluffed my hair and planned to ditch Duke's flannel, but his scent alone made me feel better, so I opted to keep it on.

True to their word, within minutes, car doors were closing, and laughter was floating up the porch steps. I opened after one loud knock, and they all filed inside, offering quick hugs as their voices overlapped one another.

Lark was last and gripped my shoulder. "Are you okay? Tell us everything."

I smiled and scoffed. "It was probably nothing, but Ed was acting all agitated, and it turns out Duck was tangled up outside. But it was weird . . . the barn door was already open."

Annie paused and lifted an eyebrow. She'd grown up with the Sullivans, so she was practically their adopted sister. "That doesn't seem likely."

I shook my head. "It's not. Duke's very careful with locking up his equipment. Then I saw a light or something . . . I figured I was about to catch one of my dumbass brothers mid-prank, so I went to check it out—"

"Girl!" Kate's eyes went wide. "Don't you listen to true crime podcasts? Never go investigate!"

I laughed. "I know. I *know*. When I realized it wasn't any of my brothers, I kind of panicked."

"How did you get rid of him?" Annie's blue eyes were wide as she worried her lip.

"I lied and said Duke was inside. Bootsy took off pretty quick after that."

"Good thinking." With snacks unloaded onto the table, they settled around the living room furniture.

Kate tucked her feet under herself as she sank into the couch. "Something similar happened when we were renovating Tootie's house. I heard voices and someone even rattled the door handle." She let an exaggerated shiver roll through her. "I didn't want to be alone for weeks."

"They never did figure out who that was, did they?" Lark opened a container of hummus and dragged a carrot through it.

Kate shook her head. "Nope. It was right after we found the speakeasy. General consensus was it was probably more nosy reporters, but I don't know . . . that never really sat right with me." Kate's wary eyes moved over me.

"What?" I asked.

Kate hesitated before continuing, "Did Duke ever tell you about what we found down there?"

"The liquor bottle, right? The one with the *King Liquor* label on it? Yes, he did, but I didn't really know anything about it besides what we'd talked about at the Bluebirds."

Annie leaned forward. "No old family stories? Tales of bootlegging and intrigue?"

A dry, humorless laugh rolled out of me. I grabbed a cookie before nibbling a bite. Shame rose and settled into my chest. The Kings weren't like the Sullivans. We didn't sit around and reminisce about old times or family stories that would make you laugh. Mostly we spent our early years surviving under Russell King's rule in our mother's absence. As an adult, I did what we could to stay off his radar.

I shrugged. "Nothing rings a bell. It certainly doesn't add up to Bootsy Sinclair creeping around the barn . . ."

Annie sat up. "What did you say?"

I frowned at her. "What? That it was weird Bootsy was at the farm?"

Her hands ran down her black leggings. "No, no, no. The other part. His last name is Sinclair?"

I looked around as the Sullivan women stared at me. "Yes? Why is that a big deal? I thought everyone knew the Sinclair twins."

"Dude . . ." Annie started flipping through her phone, and I looked at Kate and Lark.

Kate shrugged. "I had no idea what his last name was, and I've lived here my whole life."

Lark shrugged. "I remember it being really odd that there wasn't even a last name on *anything* related to Bowlegs's funeral, either, but once I got to know this town . . ." Lark shrugged. "At the time, the quirkiness kind of tracked for around here."

"Okay," Annie interrupted. "So when Kate and Beckett found the speakeasy, there was a lockbox, and this was inside." She turned her phone to me to reveal a black-and-white picture of two men and a woman in a friendly embrace, smiling at the camera.

"When I was digging into the whole King–Sullivan feud, I found out they are Philo Sullivan, James King, and Helen Sinclair." Annie handed me her phone so I could take a closer look. "The families were friends for a long, *long* time. Like Miss Mabel said, Philo and Helen eventually got married."

I grabbed her phone to take a closer look. "So what happened? How do they go from that to whatever this feud has become?"

Kate leaned in and lifted an eyebrow. "They were bootlegging together. We also found a ledger that documented deliveries. Some of the names I still recognize—families that still live in Outtatowner—who were getting regular deliveries. Then something went ass up." She thought for a moment. "But I find it very, very weirdly coincidental that Bootsy's last name is Sinclair. It has to be related, right?"

A sick feeling settled in my stomach. "Sometimes my dad gives Bootsy money." The women stared at me, urging me to continue. "Since I was little, he and Bowlegs would have these hushed, closed-door meetings with my dad, and once I was sneaking around and definitely saw an exchange of cash."

"Hush money?" Lark asked, her eyes wide as we all leaned in.

Annie looked around our circle with anticipation. "What if . . . what if Bootsy is from the same Sinclair family as Helen. Records I found said she had a brother. What if when Helen and Philo got married, they wanted to get out of the bootlegging business because it was unsafe, like Mabel had mentioned. They were starting a family or something?"

"The timeline would be about right. Birth records show the two started a family pretty quickly after marriage." Kate shook her head in disbelief. "If the bootlegging was profitable, two-thirds of the group pulling out would be very bad for business."

I scoffed. "If James King was anything like my father, that would be enough to ignite a feud."

"Could James have teamed up with Helen's mystery brother?" Lark asked.

Annie shrugged. "It's possible. Money makes people do strange and stupid things."

Lark leaned back and put her hands by her head, gesturing like her brain was exploding. "This is wild. I can't believe we figured it out!"

"We don't know for sure," Annie said, tucking her phone back into the pocket of her leggings, "but it seems to make sense."

I stared at my hands. "Generations of greed and mistrust could have easily morphed into families feuding and, over time, completely forgetting why. All because my family was powered by anger and money."

Kate reached out to me. When my eyes met hers, there wasn't pity, only kindness. "And you're healing it with love. There's beauty in that."

I sighed. "I don't know that I'm healing much of anything. Sure, things aren't quite so heated, but our families are far from friends."

Annie gave me a smile that hinted at our blossoming friendship, and my heart pinched with hopeful longing. "We're here."

That ember of warmth glowed in my chest. Annie was right, they *were* here for no other reason than to build our budding friendship.

I relaxed and smiled at them. Those women at the Bluebird Book Club were slowly becoming more than friendly faces that I wasn't allowed to talk to outside the bookstore walls. They were women who showed up for you when you needed them and who didn't hold the sins of your father against you.

They were the kind of women I strived to be. "Thank you for coming. I feel better not having to be here alone after the night I had. I've got some lemonade in the fridge. How about a shitty rom-com and more snacks?"

Lark lifted her glass with a hoot. "Cheers to snacks!"

I pushed myself to stand, and a gush of wetness poured down my leg and onto the hardwood floor.

Oh fuck . . .

THIRTY-FIVE

DUKE

KATE

Please tell me you're not too drunk. I sent
an SOS out to the guys—YOU'RE ABOUT
TO BE A DAD!

THE WORDS FLASHED across my screen, and I was mid-
laugh when I checked it. The rumble died in my chest, and
my brain failed to comprehend my sister's message. When
my head whipped up, Lee was grinning like an idiot,
Beckett was gathering our jackets, and Wyatt was pulling
out his wallet.

Lee's hand landed on my shoulder with a thud. "Party's
over. You're going to be a dad, dude!"

Wyatt sauntered up, entirely too calm for my liking.
"Lark called. Sylvie's water broke while they were having
girls' night. They're taking her to the hospital now. Annie
stayed behind to clean up and make sure Ed was put to bed,
but she'll meet us up there. Let's roll."

Wyatt walked toward the door, but my feet were
cemented in place. Beckett came up next to me. "Can't just
stand there, man. She needs you."

She needs me. Sylvie needs me.

I swallowed hard and nodded. Thank fuck I'd had only two beers, because I absolutely was not expecting to welcome our child into the world today. My brothers had planned for a drink or two at the Grudge to publicly humiliate me with *bar games*, and then we'd settle in for the night for a beachside bonfire at Beckett's beach house.

Feedback buzzed from the speaker as the band suddenly halted mid-song. "Hey, yo!" My head turned to see Lee on stage, grabbing the microphone. "My big brother Duke is about to be a dad! Lift your glasses for Duke and Sylvie!"

I shook my head as the bar erupted in a cheer. *Only in this town.*

Lee leaped off the stage and ran toward the exit. I hurried to catch up with my brothers but stopped short. "They should know. Her family."

I looked around the bar but didn't see any of them. Beckett nodded. "I'll take care of it. You go, and I will see you up there."

I reached out to shake his hand but pulled him into a hug. "Thank you."

Beckett nodded and patted my back. I rushed outside to load myself into Lee's truck. He drove like a bat out of hell while Wyatt quietly texted in the back seat. "No news yet. Lark is giving me the play-by-play, but they're taking care of your girl."

I had never been more happy that the women in my family never listened to a word I said. They were there, by her side, when Sylvie went into labor.

Lee bounced in his seat as his foot slammed on the accelerator, zipping down the dark country road. "This is so exciting!"

～

AUGUST KINGSTON SULLIVAN was born just shy of midnight.

"You're sure about the name August, huh?" I lay curled around Sylvie, watching our son sleep on her chest. Nothing and no one existed apart from the two of them.

"I think it's perfect." She gently stroked a fingertip down his little upturned nose. Exhaustion was settling in, and I inched impossibly closer. "I think the name August is a perfect way to honor the little boy that your mother had loved so much."

I was so overwhelmed with emotion, I could barely choke out a response. "I was thinking of Kingston for a middle name."

Her eyes lifted from our son. "Kingston?"

"Mm-hmm." I nuzzled into her hair. "You're a King, but so is he. He should know that he is loved. All parts of him. Just like his mama."

Sylvie exhaled a wobbly breath. "August Kingston Sullivan. It's a mouthful."

I chuckled. "I'm sure he'll get a ridiculous nickname eventually."

She laughed softly. "I guess you're right."

Baby August blinked his eyes open as he yawned, his mouth forming a tiny O. His irises were bluish gray, but I held out hope that the tiny flecks of green and gold would deepen to match his mother's.

I nuzzled closer to her. "Everyone is still waiting to hear about him, but I don't want to leave you."

"They're all here? Together?" Sylvie patted August's butt after he started to fuss.

I shrugged. "Pretty sure half the population of Outta-towner came to show their support."

Sylvie smiled down at our son. "You should go. I'll try feeding him, and then maybe a few people can meet him?"

"If that's what you want." I unfolded myself from behind her and rose from the too-small hospital bed. With my back to her, I paused. "Our timing has always been off, but there's something I need to tell you."

I turned, and Sylvie's eyes were already shimmering with unshed tears. I reached into my pocket and pulled out my mother's ring. "Sylvie King, you deserve so much more—you deserve a helicopter ride or some grand gesture that proves my love for you."

I dropped to my knees at her bedside. "But I'm here, on my knees, begging for the honor to call you my wife."

My mother's ring sparkled in the fluorescent hospital lighting. Sylvie's arms wrapped around our newborn as her tears fell. "Yes. A thousand times yes."

I scrambled to my feet and climbed back into the bed next to her, careful not to crush her or the baby. I openly cried, relief washing over me that she and August would be mine to protect. Mine to love. Forever.

I put my forehead to hers. "I choose you over anyone else, in any circumstance, for the rest of my life. You will always know what it means to be loved by a man like me. I promise."

We kissed and cried and kissed some more until August made it clear he was *not* happy waiting to eat.

Sylvie laughed as she adjusted her gown to feed our baby. I was completely enraptured by my future wife and our beautiful son. *My everything.*

I wiped the tears from my face as I stood tall. I grunted to clear my throat and attempted to gather myself.

"I'll give you a few minutes, and then we'll let the parade begin."

Sylvie smiled down at little August. "I can't wait for them to meet him."

The waiting room was packed. A quick scan revealed dueling sides of Kings and Sullivans, much like the Grudge.

Old habits die hard, I guess.

When I walked through the door, everyone stood in curious silence.

I clapped my hands together, trying—and failing miserably—to keep my emotions in check. "Healthy baby boy."

It was all I could get out before the waiting room erupted into cheers, and I was pulled into a hug by my aunt Tootie.

In a blur of handshakes, hugs, and congratulations, I was enveloped by the townsfolk of Outtatowner. My brothers took turns hugging and patting my back, offering their congratulations. Collectively, the women cried and swooned when I showed them a picture of newborn August.

"Congratulations." Royal King stood with his hand outstretched to mine. I wasn't a fool enough to think that my relationship with Sylvie would unravel generations of contempt, but it was a start.

"Thank you." I shook and nodded. Abel, Whip, and JP followed suit, cordially shaking my hand and offering a word of congrats.

Abel rocked back on his heels. "I want to apologize for my father."

I swallowed. "Yeah." I nodded. "I think it would have meant a lot to Sylvie to have him here."

"It's not just that," Abel continued. "We know you went to him for his blessing before asking Sylvie to marry you."

My jaw clenched at my anger toward their father—not

because he flat out told me he would never condone our marriage but rather that he felt his daughter *deserved* to marry a Sullivan. As though that was some kind of eternal punishment.

"Took a lot of balls for you to come to each of us after that." Royal crossed his arms and watched me with assessing eyes.

"Felt like the right thing to do," I finally admitted. Despite our past, Sylvie loved her brothers, so I had sought out each of them and let them know my intention of marrying their sister. To my surprise, each offered their congratulations and best wishes with varying degrees of surprise.

"Can we meet him?" Annie asked as she clung to Lark's arm, barely containing her excitement.

I smiled at the pair. "The nurse said only two at a time, but yeah. She's ready to have a few visitors."

The duo squealed before making their way to the nurses' station to visit Sylvie and the baby.

JP walked up to me. "Got a minute?"

Tension between us was taut as a tightrope. I had irrefutable proof he was the one who'd been looking into mineral rights on Sullivan land. "What is it?"

"I have something for you." JP reached into his suit coat pocket to pull out a slim envelope and handed it to me.

"My father uncovered this tidbit of information during one of his backdoor business dealings. For years he has been using Bootsy Sinclair to quietly gather information. Information he held close to the vest, even from me, so he could use it to his advantage. I learned he plans to let the mineral rights on your land expire and then scoop them up and leverage that against you and your family."

I opened the envelope and stared down at the paper, my

eyes scanning the information. It was all the information I would need to ensure mineral rights for Sullivan Farms were protected. "Why are you giving this to me?"

JP shrugged. "It's just business. Figured it might come in handy one day."

I harrumphed a noncommittal noise as I looked over the paperwork a second time. I didn't love the implication that I'd *owe* JP King a damned thing, but it was hard to deny he had done me a solid. JP walked away with arrogant strides, but I had a sneaking suspicion he wasn't as heartless as he'd made himself out to be.

"Duke?" I looked up at MJ as she walked back into the waiting room. She was dressed in scrubs, and clearly her position as a fellow nurse had allowed the maternity ward staff to be flexible with the *only two visitors* rule. "She's asking for you."

I tucked the envelope into my back pocket and sucked in a breath. My entire world was waiting for me. As I walked toward her room, I smiled as I thought about my mother. *Everything could change with one decision if only we were brave enough to make it.*

My entire world was beyond that hospital door, and right there I made a promise to my mother that I would be brave enough to love Sylvie and our children—to love them out loud, without hesitation, and with every last shred of my soul.

One night had changed everything, and what a perfect night it was.

EPILOGUE

Duke

ONE YEAR Later

My eyes flicked over the stack of papers as I thumbed through them one last time. "This is everything?"

My attorney Joss's rich leather chair creaked as he leaned back and propped his hands behind his head. "It's all I've got." He shook his head and chuckled. "I have to admit, this was not how I predicted this thing would have played out."

I let out a soft grunt. *No fucking kidding.*

Joss leaned forward. "It was awfully convenient JP handed you everything his father was digging up about your land's mineral rights." His assessing eyes narrowed. "Just . . . be careful."

I swallowed and nodded. He wasn't telling me anything I didn't already know. Shortly after August was born, JP went back to his typical arrogant self, but for now—as long as I had any say in it—Sullivan Farms was protected. I would provide for Sylvie and August until my dying breath.

"I'll get everything filed on Monday." With a nod, Joss's features clicked from attorney mode to friend mode. His expression bordered on mischief and humor. "Want to grab a beer? Find some trouble?"

I scoffed. Friday nights never held much appeal, even less so now. "Nah, I can't. Got to get home to my wife."

My wife.

The words tumbled inside me and never ceased to send a ripple of excitement through my typically locked-down stoicism.

I shook Joss's hand and offered a sincere thank-you for everything he'd done for us in the last year. With the information JP had provided and piecing together bits that Lark, Annie, and the rest of the Bluebirds had dug up, a new heartbreaking history in Outtatowner came into view.

Bootsy had, in fact, been a descendant of the Sinclairs. Once that connection had been made, Annie uncovered a series of letters at the Remington County Historical Association from Helen, addressed to her brother. In it, she revealed that when she'd married Philo Sullivan, they'd wanted to get out of the bootlegging business because it was unsafe. She'd begged her brother to reconsider the offer from James to take their place.

From what we could tell, James King acted like a man betrayed, simply because his friends' departure from the illegal business was bad for his bottom line. Ultimately, he affirmed the help of Helen's brother, despite Helen's pleading. Together the two men skirted the law to successfully bootleg during Prohibition, ultimately making the Kings a prominent and wealthy family in Outtatowner. Eventually James King's greed consumed him. Slowly the Kings made enough sly business decisions, excluding the Sinclairs, relegating them to nothing more than the eyes and ears on the ground to the King empire.

The feud took a darker turn when my own father married the very woman Russell King intended to wed. His deep-seated rage couldn't handle such an affront, and Russell took it upon himself to fan the flames of the feud for *years*. Before long no one remembered the real reasons behind the Sullivan–King feud. Or maybe no one cared.

It didn't matter. Nothing and no one could stop me from loving Sylvie. I was always meant to be hers.

I stepped out of Joss's office building and into the afternoon sunlight, taking one look at where I'd parked my truck and sighing.

In its place was a giant gift-wrapped package in the exact size and shape of my truck. My jaw clenched and I bent to look beneath my truck.

They even wrapped the fucking underside.

I snapped a quick picture and sent it to Lee. His response was immediate, and I didn't bother stifling my grin.

> LEE
>
> On it.

My relationship with Sylvie was nothing short of a miracle in our small town, but that didn't mean the pranks between the Kings and Sullivans had ceased completely. Slowly we were passing the torch to the younger generation, but we always made sure the mischief lacked malice.

When I pulled down our driveway at Sullivan Farms, the crunch of tires over gravel caught Ed's attention. He bounded toward my truck with Duck waddling closely behind. Those two remained inseparable, and now I had to worry about running over two dumbasses as they barked and quaked and circled my truck.

I pushed the door open, and Ed nosed at my leg. "Yeah, yeah. I see you, buddy." I scratched behind his long ears before bending down to give Duck the affection he also demanded. I climbed out of the truck and addressed the duo. "Where's Mama?"

Ed yipped and spun in a wonky three-legged circle.

"Find Mama." Ed raced toward the farmhouse with Duck waddling behind him. As I meandered toward the porch, my heart stopped.

There she is.

On the top step, Sylvie had Gus propped on her hip, and one hand shielded her eyes from the afternoon sun.

"Hey, handsome!" A warm smile split her face, flashing pretty white teeth as she hoisted our son higher on her hip.

Gus squealed and reached for me. I took the steps two at a time just to get to them faster. My nose buried in her soft hair as I wrapped them both in my arms and inhaled the sunshine and cinnamon scents that clung to her skin.

My nose teased the thin skin along her neck, and I hummed. "I missed you two."

Sylvie's laugh vibrated her throat, and my teeth scraped against her before planting a soothing kiss. "You were gone for an hour."

I straightened, frowning down at my lovely wife. "Still missed you."

A rosy blush deepened her cheeks. I held my arms out to our son. "Come here, kid."

August launched himself at me with a babbling squeal, and I used my free arm to pull Sylvie closer. I dropped a kiss on her crown. "I have an idea."

Sylvie shifted to look at me with a curious frown.

I gently squeezed her arm. "It'll be great, I promise." I guided her toward the swinging bed we'd installed on the front porch—another Pinterest idea of hers that I was happy to build. "You, sit." Sylvie plopped onto the swing as I laid a blanket across her ankles. "Take a rest while Gus and I fix you dinner. I'll get you a glass of wine so you can read a book and relax. Then I'd like to take you somewhere." Sylvie's pert little mouth popped open to argue, but I shut her up with a kiss. "No arguing. Lark is coming by, and she and Penny are taking him to the park. It's all handled."

Even after all this time, it still seemed to surprise Sylvie how much I liked taking care of her. How I *craved* it simply because her happiness was integral to mine. I didn't think I'd ever shake the need to care for others, and it felt like nothing at all to do little things for my woman.

Sylvie picked up the paperback she kept stashed on the porch. "If you say so." Her expression grew flirtatious as she found her place marked in the book. "But I'm warning you . . . I'm getting to the dirty parts, and I'm going to want a full reenactment later."

I feigned shock and looked at our son. "Don't listen to your mama. That's for Daddy's ears only."

Sylvie's throaty laugh hummed through me as I leaned forward to whisper in her ear. I let my voice dip low and gravelly. "Baby, I'm counting on it."

SYLVIE FLOATED on the paddleboard like a weightless mermaid as her blonde hair spread through the water like oil. She was a goddess. My everything.

"Mmm . . . ," she hummed as my fingertips glided over

her smooth thighs, sending water droplets careening down her skin.

"So it was a good date?" My hands moved higher, settling at her hip.

Sylvie peeked one eye open. "It was a *perfect* date. Out here I feel so . . . relaxed."

I adjusted the paddleboard so that my hands could reach into her hair and massage her scalp. Her nipples pebbled through her bathing suit top at my touch. My mouth went dry at the appearance of those tight, hard buds, and an idea sparked.

"One last stop." Her head tilted toward me as I continued, "Let's check out our island."

When I had paddled us close to the shore, Sylvie hopped off the board and waded through the water toward the beach. She turned, and her eyes lit up with wonder as she stripped from the life jacket and deposited it on the sand. "It's exactly the same!"

I looked around as I relieved myself of my own jacket and the dry bag I'd slung over my shoulders. Not much at all had changed from the day I'd brought her to the secluded island. I glanced at Sylvie. Yet *everything* had changed.

Crowding her space, I leaned down to scoop her in my arms. Her mouth met mine in a fervor. Tongue and teeth and lips clashed as we moaned into each other. My arms tightened around her back as her legs squeezed around my waist.

"Do you remember when I brought you here? Because I remember every detail like it was yesterday." My forehead pressed to hers.

"How could I forget? A secret date with you was the biggest sin I could commit, but I couldn't help myself."

Sylvie peppered kisses across my face as I moved us closer to the tree line.

I sank to my knees, settling her back against the soft sand. "You've always been worth every sin."

Sylvie arched into me. Begging. Pleading. I knew the rhythms of her body better than I knew my own.

Our life together had been made possible by a series of improbable miracles, yet I couldn't help the overwhelming feeling of being completely grounded by her. Our pasts intertwined in a way that made me feel secure. Understood.

My palms grazed over the peaks of her breasts as she squirmed beneath me. My cock ached to stretch her open and be buried to the hilt. Nothing felt as complete as sharing myself with Sylvie. *Nothing.*

That woman was the beginning and end of everything.

Her fingertips glided down my pecs and teased the hemline of my swim trunks. "Do you remember what we talked about?" She waggled her eyebrows.

I lifted one brow. "We talk about a lot."

Her laugh sent a thousand sparks through my chest. "I think we should try. I never started my new birth control pack."

My heart thrummed, and my nostrils flared at her implication. Over the last few months we'd been toying with the idea of getting her pregnant—on purpose this time.

My palm flattened against her chest as I settled over her and drank her beauty in.

I wasn't a fool enough to think we had a whole lot of say in the matter. If our past was any indication, a baby was bound to come whenever it damn well pleased, but I knew we'd have a hell of a good time trying.

Just This Once
The Kings, Book 1

Whip King can not be the man for me.

Cocky, pierced firefighters are perfect for late-night romcoms, but in real life, they're nothing but trouble. Especially when you find out they work for your dad—***after you've already slept with them.***

Moving to my parent's small town was supposed to be the fresh start I was looking for. When a disastrous Valentine's Day leads to an unexpected encounter with a sexy stranger, and ends with the hottest night of my life, I didn't think I would ever see Whip again.

Imagine my surprise when one of my sixth grade students has a medical emergency and it's Whip who shows up, looking hot as hell, to save the day. I should be embarrassed at how we left things, but instead I'm furious he doesn't seem to remember me.

So I scrape my pride off the floor, lift my chin, and

pretend there's nothing between us. But that can only last so long. ***Stolen glances melt into forbidden touches and once we give in to temptation, we can't keep our hands off each other.***

Nothing has ever felt so right, but my guarded heart won't let me believe in happily ever after. Opening up to him may be the hardest thing I've ever done and every time we agree to one last time, we both know it's a lie.

How many times can we keep telling ourselves ***just this once*** before we realize that, when it comes to love, once is never enough?

Look for The Kings, Book 1 *Just This Once* coming soon!

THE BADGE, CHAPTER 1

Val

"Pushing those veggies around the plate isn't going to make them go away any faster," said Eric, his rumbling voice sounding behind my back.

Shooting my partner the side-eye over my shoulder, I continued to poke and prod my dinner around the sagging cardboard take-out container. It may have been well after midnight, but when you worked the midnight shift on the police force, two a.m. meant dinnertime—usually in the form of shitty takeout from Uncle Mao's Chinese Restaurant. Giving the repugnant vegetables one last scowl, I dropped the chopsticks into the container and pushed it over the edge of my desk and into the trash.

"You have the eating habits of a five-year-old," Eric teased as he approached my desk in the bullpen of the police station. The years had been kind to my partner and his salt and pepper hair and slight paunch were the only signs of his long tenure on the force.

"Well, the best thing about not actually being five is I can choose *not* to eat my vegetables. You ready to roll out?"

Eric and I had been partners in the Eleventh District of the Chicago Police Department for the past three years. Notoriously dangerous—ironically the district with the youngest and most inexperienced police officers—an assignment in the Eleventh District meant that a break for dinner lasted only fifteen or twenty minutes before we had to be back on patrol, doing whatever we could to keep innocent people alive.

Only six miles north and my job would have meant a cushy patrol learning from twenty-year veterans, but that wasn't all that appealing anyway. I loved the thrill, the challenge of solving a case and keeping my city safe.

I stood, adjusted my utility belt and vest, and slid my chair beneath the desk. I scanned my desk to ensure everything was in place before I was ready to go. "Let's do it."

I tucked myself behind the wheel of our squad car. Eric never minded that I preferred to drive—my need for control and order. Usually on quiet nights, I had to make sure his ass didn't fall asleep on the job. Eric was a lot like the older brother that teased you, but you knew always had your back. He had a decade of experience on me— but he'd also lost the hunger. The hunger to maintain justice and order amid the chaos of the city. Mostly, he looked at his job as a cop as just that—a job. To me, it was a calling.

Sensing the seriousness in my mood, Eric cleared his throat. "You should find out any day now, right?"

I tightened my grip on the steering wheel and willed my breath to steady. "I'm hoping. So far it's been a waiting game."

Eric shook his head. "Man, I can't believe you're going

to leave me to kiss ass with the ATF. You tell your folks yet?"

I huffed. "Are you kidding? They're horrified enough that I carry a gun every day."

He shrugged. "The ATF may not be all it's cracked up to be."

I rolled my eyes in his direction. Applying to be a part of the elite Bureau of Alcohol, Tobacco, Firearms, and Explosives unit, more commonly referred to as the ATF, had taken over a year, and there still was no guarantee I'd be accepted to become a federal agent. Women made up less than twenty-five percent of the entire Chicago Police Department, and even fewer had aspirations to become a special agent.

As a first-generation Mexican American woman, if that was my future, I'd have to blaze the trail myself. None of those things meant anything at all to my parents, but I could show them what it meant. Make them proud.

"You're just pissed you won't have someone watching your ass while you nap," I teased.

Eric sank lower in the seat and pulled a baseball cap farther down his brow. "Well," he grunted as he got comfortable, "you're not wrong there. Don't fuck up while I'm out."

I laughed and shook my head. I'd learned in the academy that to be a female police officer, you had to develop a thick skin and handle a certain amount of ball-busting to have a chance of surviving. It didn't matter that I had proved my skills; if you weren't one of the good ol' boys, you were *other*.

I glanced out the window and up at the passing street-lights. The rain was a slow, dreary late fall precipitation that kept everyone shuttered away from the damp cold. The

twilight hours—known as *witching hours* by the most super-
stitious cops—could be so calm they almost made your skin
crawl. City streets were all but abandoned. Some houses
were so run-down with broken windows and peeling paint
it was hard to tell which ones sheltered civilians and which
hid away criminals.

Sometimes the answer was both.

Adjusting the volume of the pop music thumping out of
the car radio, I turned the squad car for another long loop
through our section of the city. Quiet chatter on the police
radio became my company while Eric dozed beside me.

Dispatch: **Squad 9522 to dispatch.**

Me: **9522. Go ahead.**

Dispatch: **We have a reported 650 in progress.
Intersection of Kilbourn and Maypole. Possible
4210.**

650, home invasion. 4210, kidnapping. Shit.

I pushed the button on my vest walkie to respond as I
hit Eric awake with the back of my hand.

Me: **Officers 842 and 1732. En route.**

The computer to my right lit up with information from
dispatch. Apparently, a neighbor had called with
complaints of shouting and glass breaking. One witness
reported seeing a white male with a gun enter the home.
After flipping on the lights and sirens, I whipped hard down
a side street and barreled toward the address on my screen.

Tension curled up my spine and gripped me at the base
of my neck. I bumped my partner again. "Wake up, E. I've
got a bad feeling about this."

Eric rubbed his eyes and swung the computer his way to
get up to speed. I chanced only a glance in his direction as
he read through the information and relayed it aloud to me.

Eric's voice got low, muttering to himself as he scanned the words again. I couldn't catch all of what he said. "Kilbourn and Maypole. I know that house. Fuck . . ."

"What?"

Eric shook his head. His lips were in a hard line, and I'd learned his body language well enough to know he was amped.

My heart hammered as I sped through the city toward the run-down residential area. Duplexes and apartment buildings encroached abandoned storefronts and were shoehorned between industrial buildings. The dilapidated, deserted buildings were nestled between streets of residential housing. Even knowing the neighborhood, it was difficult to know which were which or what alley led to a courtyard versus a dead end.

Approaching the given address, the commotion outside pointed us to exactly where we needed to go. Two additional squad cars came flying in as I parked. Eric and I exited the car, readying our weapons.

With a series of hand movements, Eric instructed me to fall behind him. The officers behind me began their search on the east side of the looming brick building. As we pushed past the gawkers already forming on the front lawn, I could see that the front door had been kicked in. The frame was splintered around the lock, and chunks of decaying wood hadn't stood a chance from a boot or a stiff shoulder.

Once inside, I swept right and left, the light on top of my service weapon illuminating the cramped space. The room was musty and damp. More than the rain outside, the wetness clung to the air, coating the walls, ripe with mildew. I pressed my tongue to the roof of my mouth to ignore the smell of mold, piss, and dirty laundry.

The only sound was my heartbeat, hammering between

my ears as my eyes scanned the rooms. Extensive training ensured my movements were efficient and my senses were keyed into my surroundings. The house appeared empty, but it didn't *feel* empty.

The clawing sense of unease prickled my skin as goose bumps coated my arms. The groan of a single loose floorboard had me whipping my weapon to the right. A shadowed figure ran across the narrow hallway, through the kitchen, and shouldered out the back door.

"Freeze!" I commanded.

"Police!" Eric bellowed at the same time.

I called into my radio. "Suspect fleeing. Dark hoodie, denim pants. Dark sneakers."

Eric burst through the back door. I scanned the room, and instead of following him out, I halted as my eyes landed on a dark, crumpled figure in the corner.

A body.

Instinct took over, and I toed the body with my foot. A pair of wide, frantic eyes stared up at me.

I crouched. "Hey, hey. It's okay. We'll get you out of here. Stay behind me." I pulled the young girl up, and she huddled behind me. Her dark hair was matted and hung in tangled clumps. I moved forward through the house, still unconvinced the place was empty.

When movement through the kitchen caught my attention, the young woman pushed past me, nearly knocking me over, and ran toward the door.

"Stop!"

As I reached for her, the girl glanced back and didn't see the closed patio door. The old glass splintered and crashed around her. She tumbled forward, landing in the shards. I rushed to her. Disoriented, the girl shoved an elbow against my hands, and I turned her over, assessing any injuries. I called into my radio for medical assistance.

Shards of glass pierced her forearm, and deep crimson was rapidly staining the front of her rumpled beige T-shirt. I pulled at the neckline to reveal a deep slash that spread beneath her collarbone and up toward her delicate neck. I pressed my hand into it to try to stop the bleeding, and she called out, crying and fighting against my help.

Pushing onto her feet, she shoved me backward, then scrambled to steady herself. She ran haphazardly into the alley, and I went after her, leaping over garbage and old patio furniture littering the back lawn. The rain came down steadily, obscuring the light mounted to my gun.

I blinked water away and tried to refocus. My body surged forward as I searched the darkness for any signs of movement. The buildings were close together, and it left little room for hiding. In the distance, I could hear the other officers fanning out in different directions, none calling out for assistance.

I took a hesitant step into a dark alley between two brick buildings. It was a long, empty path with nothing but brick doorways to the end. Moving quickly, I pushed forward between the buildings.

Don't do it.

The words whispered through my skull a millisecond too late.

As I passed one of the darkened doorways, a figure surged out, slamming me into the opposite wall. My head rapped against the brick, and white-hot pain screeched between my eyes.

I shook my head and raised my gun. "Stop!"

It was not the same man in the hoodie, but the figure kept running. I chased after him.

"I said 'Stop!'" I yelled again. I was within my rights to shoot, but I knew if I could catch him, I wouldn't have to.

My adrenaline was coursing through my veins. My legs burned as I pushed forward toward where the person had taken off. When I reached the end of the alley, opening into a small courtyard, a hand grabbed my arm and pulled me forward. Off-balance, I struggled and rammed a knee into the ground. A strong, heavy force slammed on top of me, pinning me to the pavement. I watched in horror as my gun slid just out of reach.

"You fucking cunt!" the voice growled in my ear. He yanked my ponytail backward as I gritted my teeth.

"Fuck you!" I spat in his direction.

His reaction was to push my face into the concrete. The uneven surface caused water to surge up my nose and burn into my eyes as the gravel bit at my cheekbones.

"Fuck me? How about fuck you, lady cop." His palm pushed harder and harder into my face and jaw as I struggled to get air around the water filling my mouth and nose.

All the while, I was cataloging.

His voice: noticeable Chicago Italian, scratchy.

His breath: definitely a smoker or tobacco chewer.

His weight: at least two hundred pounds, soft fatty weight, not hard muscle.

Keeping my mind on the suspect and not the fact I was nearly drowning helped focus my thoughts. I coughed and reared my head back just enough to get a gulp of fresh air. The renewed oxygen helped me push and struggle against the knee in my back.

When my knees finally gained purchase, I shoved upward as hard as I could, knocking him unsteady. It was enough to roll and attempt to crawl away. As I turned to face him, a heavy crack radiated across my jaw.

His punch to my face snapped my head back. I moved toward where I last saw my service pistol. In the dim lighting, I felt the ground for the cold bite of the metal against my palm. My fingers curled around the slick, hard barrel as I righted it in my shaking hands. In the predawn darkness, two figures were locked in a stance, both fighting to overpower the other. Another, the young woman from the house, was slumped next to me by an overturned patio table. The sickening thud of punches and grunts filled the air as rain continued to thunder around us and the men continued to fight.

I called for additional backup through the radio on my vest, and I used the brick wall, struggling to push to my feet. As I righted myself, one man reached behind his back, a movement I recognized just as the flash of metal winked from the streetlights. Footsteps thundered behind me.

Officers approaching.

I raised my weapon and pulled the weakening young girl behind me.

Calm.

Ready to defend myself and my fellow officers.

The man raised his arm. I should have shot him. I hesitated. The pop of his gun fired twice. Once to my right and again directly at me.

I didn't feel the impact of the bullet, as I'd expected. Instead, the suspect in the hoodie had rushed forward, knocking me back against the wall as his body slammed into me. We both tumbled back to the concrete.

My ears rang from the slam of the brick against my head. My limbs were leaden and my tongue felt thick. Colors and noises swirled in front of me as I tried to focus on staying conscious. I blinked away the raindrops as they pattered into my eyes.

Standard-issue boots lay lifeless in my periphery.

An officer down.

I swallowed thickly, trying to comprehend what the *fuck* had just happened. My head couldn't make sense of it all, and the overwhelming desire to slip under the heavy blanket of darkness was overwhelming.

Flashes of red and blue shone through the alleyway on the street, muddled and swirled by the puddle water that had seeped into my eyes. The body that had slammed us both into the wall, unmoving and still half covering me, sheltered me from the cold. I attempted to shift from under the weight, but he didn't budge. I inched my head up, trying to focus on the face in front of me. Blood covered his clean-shaven face in a mask, and one eye was bruised and angry, completely swollen shut. The only distinguishable part of him was a single, faded scar connecting his upper lip and nostril.

Focus on him. The sirens. The rain. Do not pass out.

I chanted to myself over and over, but the weight on my chest and the pounding in my brain were too much.

Despair crawled inside me and curled around my heart. I should not have gone down the alleyway without backup. In the cold, dark rain, I sent up a silent prayer that this man who had taken a bullet for me and the officer lying still at my side were not dead because of me.

HENDRIX HEARTTHROBS

Want to connect? Come hang out with the Hendrix Heartthrobs on Facebook to laugh & chat with Lena! Special sneak peeks, announcements, exclusive content, & general shenanigans all happen there.

Come join us!

ABOUT THE AUTHOR

Lena Hendrix is an Amazon Top 10 bestselling contemporary romance author living in the Midwest. Her love for romance stared with sneaking racy Harlequin paperbacks and now she writes her own hot-as-sin small town romance novels. Lena has a soft spot for strong alphas with marshmallow insides, heroines who clap back, and sizzling tension. Her novels pack in small town heart with a whole lotta heat.

When she's not writing or devouring new novels, you can find her hiking, camping, fishing, and sipping a spicy margarita!

Want to hang out? Find Lena on Tiktok or IG!

ALSO BY LENA HENDRIX

Chikalu Falls

Finding You

Keeping You

Protecting You

Choosing You (origin novella)

Redemption Ranch

The Badge

The Alias

The Rebel

The Target

The Sullivans

One Look

One Touch

One Chance

One Night

One Taste (charity novella, coming soon!)

The Kings

(Book 1 coming soon!)

Printed in Great Britain
by Amazon